SIR RICHARD STEELE

The Tatler

EDITED WITH AN INTRODUCTION BY
LEWIS GIBBS

DENT : LONDON
EVERYMAN'S LIBRARY
DUTTON : NEW YORK

NO. *993*

SBN: 460 00993 1

EVERYMAN, I will go with thee,

and be thy guide,

In thy most need to go by thy side

Born March 1672 in Dublin; educated at
Charterhouse, and at Christ Church and
Merton, Oxford; left Oxford in 1694 without
taking degree; enlisted in Life Guards,
eventually captain in Lord Lucas's regiment;
appointed gazetteer, 1707; married (i) Margaret
Stretch, (ii) Mary Scurlock ('Prue'); wrote
four comedies, 1701–22, and after the *Tatler*
and *Spectator* (1709 and 1711) produced other
periodicals; M.P. for Stockbridge, 1713;
expelled from House, 1714, for pamphlet,
The Crisis; patentee of Drury Lane, 1714;
knighted, M.P. for Boroughbridge, 1715, and
Wendover, 1722; commissioner for Scottish
forfeited estates, 1716; died at Carmarthen,
1st September 1729.

INTRODUCTION

Having recommended the *Tatler* to the world in the opening number, and drawn attention to the benefits to be derived from this new publication, Steele continues as follows: 'I therefore earnestly desire all persons, without distinction, to take it for the present gratis. . . .'

This method of advertising has a curiously modern ring, and suggests that Steele, evidently a shrewd man of business, ought to have made a fortune. And in fact he had many of the qualities which are generally supposed to lead to that kind of success. He was energetic, self-assured, endlessly resourceful, and unfailingly sanguine. In his time he was a trooper in the Life Guards, a captain in Lord Lucas's regiment of foot, a dramatist, a gentleman-waiter to Prince George of Denmark, gazetteer, commissioner of stamps, the founder (and largely the writer) of numerous periodicals, a member of parliament, a patentee of Drury Lane Theatre, and one of the commission for inquiring into the estates forfeited by the rebels in 1715. And if this list—which is by no means complete—fails to give an adequate idea of the variety of his activities, it may be added that he once lost money in an attempt to find the Philosopher's Stone, and in his later life was concerned with an original, but unsuccessful, project for bringing live fish to the London market.

Instead of making a fortune, however, Steele was never out of debt. His case bears a certain resemblance to that of Sheridan, and more than one stock anecdote (such as that of the dinner-party at which the numerous servants were all bailiff's men) is told of both of them with equal force and probability. There is also an engaging likeness between him and Fielding. It was noticed by Lady Mary Wortley Montagu, who knew the former well and was related to the latter. They were both perpetually in difficulties over money, she observed, 'yet each of them was so formed for happiness it is a pity he was not immortal.'

Steele brought out the *Tatler* because he wanted money, and the result was something new in literature. Not that a periodical publication was in itself a new thing, but this one had unusual qualities. In accordance with its motto it took the whole range of social activity—*quicquid agunt homines*—for its province. Women were not overlooked. Mr. Bickerstaff (Steele borrowed the name from Swift) paid a remarkable amount of attention to them in his 'lucubrations'; and what he had to say on that subject was eagerly read. 'I resolve also,' he announced shrewdly, 'to have something which may be of entertainment to the fair sex, in honour of whom I have invented the title of this paper.' The entertainment thus provided was something of a novelty then, and even to-day much of it remains curiously fresh and attractive.

Macaulay, who regarded Steele chiefly as a foil for the impeccable Addison, was obliged to admit, though grudgingly, that he was 'not ill qualified' for the task he had undertaken. He was a man of the world, a wit, and as good a scholar as he had any need to be. Whoever bought the *Tatler* could rely on being amused, edified, and improved, in return for his penny. If the idea of Steele as a moralist seems at first a little surprising, it should be remembered that eight years earlier, when he was Captain Steele, he had written *The Christian Hero*. It is true that his knowledge of the town, which he now placed at the service of his readers, had been acquired at first hand and not without some damage to his virtue; but his heart was in the right place. He was warm-blooded and generous —a cheerful, though not unrepentant, sinner—and entirely free from smugness and hypocrisy. His moralizings are to the point and rarely dull, and they can frequently be found within hailing distance of a tolerably broad jest. His comedies, three of which were written before he began the *Tatler*, show the same tendency. 'They were the first,' said Hazlitt, 'that were written expressly with a view, not to imitate the manners, but to reform the morals of the age.'

At the outset Steele thought it prudent to provide for various tastes and interests in his readers, and therefore grouped his material under five headings: Pleasure (including Gallantry and Entertainment), Poetry, Learning, Foreign and Domestic News, and whatever he found himself able 'to offer on any other subject.' However, he did not adhere rigidly to this scheme, some departments of which proved comparatively sterile. As gazetteer, for instance, he had earlier and better foreign intelligence than could be got by *Dyer's Letter* or the *Daily Courant*; but after the failure of the peace negotiations and the costly victory of Malplaquet, foreign intelligence lost much of its attraction. The domestic news likewise took an awkward turn for the Whigs before Mr. Bickerstaff laid down his pen. As time went on it was the somewhat vague final item of the list which tended to swallow up the rest; but there was always something improvised about the make-up of the *Tatler*, and this gave (as it still gives) a pleasant sense of informality and unexpectedness. It also largely accounts for the nature of the present selection, in which complete numbers are rarely reproduced. For a while Steele's touch was uncertain: indeed, in the sixth number he was reduced to the miserable expedient of summarizing part of the story of the *Iliad*—for which he had the grace to apologize in No. 7. However, it was not long before the success of the paper was assured. The separate numbers were brought out in economical style on inferior paper and in 'scurvy letter,' but the bound volumes were handsomely produced, and sold at the stiff price of a guinea apiece. The publication ran from 12 April 1709 to 2nd January 1710/11, making 271 numbers in all. It was still in the full tide of popularity when it was brought to an end.

It is impossible to think of Steele without also thinking of Addison, and this is often unfortunate for Steele's reputation. It is true, of course, that Addison's genius was of a higher order than Steele's, but the latter had valuable qualities of his own, such as a robust inventiveness, good humour, and a warm, impulsive humanity.

The difference is not unlike that between the thoroughly human, but not infallible, Mr. Bickerstaff, and the aloof and somewhat bloodless Mr. Spectator. The finest things in the *Tatler* may be Addison's, but the *Tatler* itself is Steele's creation, and so, for that matter, is the *Spectator*. It is Steele's chief title to fame that he can fairly be described as the only begetter of both of them. He owed much to Addison and acknowledged the debt with an emphatic and generous gratitude which has been remembered and quoted against him ever since. But it was Steele himself who said, and truly, that whatever Addison had given him, it was he who had given Addison to the world.

As far as the *Tatler* is concerned it is worth while to point out that Addison left London for Ireland two days before the paper appeared, and that his first contribution was printed in No. 18. Altogether he was responsible for just over forty numbers, while Steele wrote more than four times as many, besides doing the editorial work. The pair were also jointly concerned in upwards of thirty other numbers. In his preface, Steele, after mentioning contributions from Swift, acknowledges, in a well-known passage, the help received from a gentleman 'who will be nameless,' and who, of course, is Addison. Steele observes that he has no one else to thank 'for any frequent assistance'; and, in fact, the help he got from others, such as Congreve, Hughes, Harrison, Fuller, and Greenwood, was trifling.

The fact that the *Tatler* was the forerunner of the *Spectator* should not be allowed to mislead our judgment. The truth is, the former is best considered independently: it differs in many ways from its successor and has virtues peculiar to itself. The question whether it is, or is not, inferior, is beside the point. Everyone knows something about the *Spectator*. People who have never heard of the 'Case of the Petticoat' or the 'Court of Honour,' are familiar, by name, at any rate, with Sir Roger de Coverley. The *Tatler* has been comparatively and unduly neglected. It is not pure gold throughout, but, after all, this is no more than one would have to say of the collected numbers of any periodical whatever. It is in the *Tatler*, however, that Steele is at his happiest, and it is here that we find examples of Addison's ironic wit, as exquisite as anything he wrote afterwards. Moreover, Steele's idea of dividing his paper into separate sections, often results in a delightful variety of length, subject-matter, and tone.

Besides its well understood significance in the history of literature, the *Tatler* has the special interest which is bound to belong to a work dealing familiarly with the social life of a bygone age. But whatever value we attach to these things, the present volume has been prepared in the full confidence that, quite apart from any such considerations, the reader will find it richly rewarding.

LEWIS GIBBS.

NOTE

For the sake of clearness and consistency, modern usage has been followed, as far as possible, in such matters as spelling and punctuation. The extracts have been supplied with headings, and are numbered for the purpose of reference. The corresponding numbers of the original issues will be found in the table of contents.

SELECT BIBLIOGRAPHY

PLAYS (with dates of first production). *The Funeral: or Grief À-la-mode*, 1701; *The Lying Lover: or The Ladies' Friendship*, 1703; *The Tender Husband: or The Accomplish'd Fools*, 1705; *The Conscious Lovers*, 1722.

PERIODICALS. *The Tatler*, most of which was written by Steele, ran from 12th April 1709 to 2nd January 1710–11 (271 numbers). The first collected edition appeared in 4 vols., 1710–11; and the 4-vol. edition by G. A. Aitken, 1898–9. Steele contributed also to *The Spectator* (1711–12), *The Guardian* (1713), *The Englishman* (1713–14), *The Lover* (1714), *The Reader* (1714), *Town Talk* (1715–16), *The Tea Table* (1716), *The Plebeian* (1719) and *The Theatre* (1720).

POLITICAL AND MISCELLANEOUS. *The Procession. A Poem on Her Majesty's Funeral. By a Gentleman of the Army*, 1695; *The Christian Hero: An Argument Proving that No Principles but Those of Religion are Sufficient to Make a Great Man*, 1701; *The Importance of Dunkirk consider'd*, 1713; *The Crisis: With Some Seasonable Remarks on the Danger of a Popish Successor*, 1714; *A Letter to a Member of Parliament concerning the Bill for Preventing the Growth of Schism*, 1714; *Mr Steele's Apology for Himself and His Writings: Occasioned by his Expulsion from the House of Commons*, 1714. Steele's pamphlets are collected in *Tracts and Pamphlets by Sir R. Steele*, edited by Rae Blanchard, 1944.

LETTERS. *Correspondence of Richard Steele*, edited by Rae Blanchard, 1941.

BIOGRAPHY AND CRITICISM. G. A. Aitken, *The Life of Richard Steele*, 1889; W. Connely, *Sir Richard Steele*, 1934; C. Winton, *Captain Steele: The Early Career of Richard Steele*, 1964.

CONTENTS

The numbers in parentheses are those of the original issues

1. Mr. Bickerstaff issues his proposals

Though the other papers, which are published for the use of the good people of England, have certainly very wholesome effects, and are laudable in their particular kinds, they do not seem to come up to the main design of such narrations, which, I humbly presume, should be principally intended for the use of politic persons who are so public-spirited as to neglect their own affairs to look into transactions of state. Now these gentlemen for the most part being persons of strong zeal and weak intellects, it is both a charitable and necessary work to offer something whereby such worthy and well-affected members of the commonwealth may be instructed, after their reading, what to think; which shall be the end and purpose of this my paper, wherein I shall, from time to time, report and consider all matters of what kind soever that shall occur to me, and publish such my advices and reflections every Tuesday, Thursday, and Saturday in the week, for the convenience of the post. I resolve also to have something which may be of entertainment to the fair sex, in honour of whom I have invented the title of this paper. I therefore earnestly desire all persons, without distinction, to take it in for the present gratis, and hereafter at the price of one penny, forbidding all hawkers to take more for it at their peril.[1] And I desire all persons to consider that I am at a very great charge for proper materials for this work, as well as that before I resolved upon it, I had settled a correspondence in all parts of the known and knowing world. And forasmuch as this globe is not trodden upon by mere drudges of business only, but that men of spirit and genius are justly to be esteemed as considerable agents in it, we shall not, upon a dearth of news, present you with musty foreign edicts or dull proclamations, but shall divide our relation of the passages which occur in action or discourse throughout this town,

I

as well as elsewhere, under such dates of places as may prepare you for the matter you are to expect, in the following manner.

All accounts of gallantry, pleasure, and entertainment shall be under the article of White's chocolate-house; poetry, under that of Will's coffee-house; learning, under the title of the Grecian; foreign and domestic news, you will have from Saint James's coffee-house; and what else I have to offer on any other subject shall be dated from my own apartment.

I once more desire my reader to consider that as I cannot keep an ingenious man to go daily to Will's under twopence each day, merely for his charges; to White's under sixpence; nor to the Grecian, without allowing him some plain Spanish,[2] to be as able as others at the learned table; and that a good observer cannot speak with even Kidney[3] at Saint James's without clean linen; I say, these considerations will, I hope, make all persons willing to comply with my humble request (when my gratis stock is exhausted) of a penny apiece; especially since they are sure of some proper amusement, and that it is impossible for me to want means to entertain them.

2. *Clarissa and Chloe*

All hearts at present pant for two ladies only, who have for some time engrossed the dominion of the town. They are indeed both exceeding charming, but differ very much in their excellences. The beauty of Clarissa is soft, that of Chloe piercing. When you look at Clarissa, you see the most exact harmony of feature, complexion, and shape; you find in Chloe nothing extraordinary in any one of those particulars, but the whole woman irresistible. Clarissa looks languishing; Chloe killing; Clarissa never fails of gaining admiration; Chloe of moving desire. The gazers at Clarissa are at first unconcerned, as if they were observing a fine picture. They who behold Chloe, at the first glance discover transport, as if they met with their dearest friend. These different perfections are suitably represented by the last great painter Italy has sent us, Mr. Jervase.[1] Clarissa is by that skilful hand placed in a manner that looks artless, and innocent of the torments she gives; Chloe is drawn with a liveliness that shows she is conscious of, but not affected with, her perfections. Clarissa is a shepherdess, Chloe a country girl. I must own, the design of Chloe's picture shows to me great mastery in the painter; for nothing could be better imagined than the dress he has given her of a straw hat and a ribbon, to represent that sort of beauty which enters the heart with a certain familiarity and cheats it into a belief that it has received a lover as well as an object of love. The force of their different beauties is seen also in the effects it makes on their lovers. The admirers of Chloe are eternally gay and well pleased: those of Clarissa melancholy and thoughtful. And as this passion always changes the natural man into a quite different creature from what he was before, the love of Chloe makes coxcombs; that of Clarissa, madmen. There were of each kind just now in this room. Here was one that whistles, laughs, sings, and cuts capers, for love of Chloe. Another has just now writ three lines to Clarissa, then taken a turn in the garden, then came back again, then tore his fragment, then called for some chocolate, then went away without it.

3. *Theatrical intelligence*

Letters from the Haymarket [1] inform us that on Saturday night last the opera of *Pyrrhus and Demetrius* [2] was performed with great applause. This intelligence is not very acceptable to us friends of the theatre; for the stage being an entertainment of the reason and all our faculties, this way of being pleased with the suspense of them for three hours together, and being given up to the shallow satisfaction of the eyes and ears only, seems to arise rather from the degeneracy of our understanding than an improvement of our diversions. That the understanding has no part in the pleasure is evident, from what these letters very positively assert, to wit, that a great part of the performance was done in Italian; and a great critic [3] fell into fits in the gallery at seeing, not only time and place, but languages and nations confused in the most incorrigible manner. His spleen is so extremely moved on this occasion, that he is going to publish a treatise against operas, which he thinks have already inclined us to thoughts of peace, and if tolerated must infallibly dispirit us from carrying on the war. He has communicated his scheme to the whole room, and declared in what manner things of this kind were first introduced. He has upon this occasion considered the nature of sounds in general, and made a very elaborate digression upon the London cries, wherein he had shown from reason and philosophy, why oysters are cried, card-matches sung, and turnips and all other vegetables neither cried, sung, nor said, but sold, with an accent and tone neither natural to man or beast. This piece seems to be taken from the model of that excellent discourse of Mrs. Manly the schoolmistress, concerning samplers.[4]

Advices from the upper end of Piccadilly say that Mayfair is utterly abolished [5]; and we hear Mr. Pinkethman [6] has removed his ingenious company of strollers to Greenwich. But other letters from Deptford say the company is only making thither and not yet settled; but that several heathen gods and goddesses, which are to descend in machines, landed at the King's Head stairs last Saturday. Venus and Cupid went on foot from thence to Greenwich; Mars got drunk in the town, and broke his landlord's head, for which he sat in the stocks the whole evening; but Mr. Pinkethman giving security that he should do nothing this ensuing summer, he was set at liberty. The most melancholy part of all was that Diana was taken in the act of fornication with a boatman, and committed by Justice Wrathful, which has, it seems, put a stop to the diversions of the theatre of Blackheath.

But there goes down another Diana and a Patient Grizzel next tide from Billingsgate.

4. *Mr. Bickerstaff's wit declining, he makes his last will and testament*

If any gentleman or lady sends to Isaac Bickerstaff, Esq., at Mr. Morphew's, near Stationers' Hall,[1] by the penny post, the grief or joy of their soul, what they think fit of the matter shall be related in colours as much to their advantage as those in which Jervase has drawn the agreeable Chloe. But since, without such assistance, I frankly confess and am sensible that I have not a month's wit more, I think I ought, while I am in my sound health and senses, to make my will and testament; which I do in manner and form following:

'*Imprimis*, I give to the stock-jobbers about the Exchange of London, as a security for the trusts daily reposed in them, all my real estate; which I do hereby vest in the said body of worthy citizens for ever.

'*Item*, Forasmuch as it is very hard to keep land in repair without ready cash, I do, out of my personal estate, bestow the bear-skin,[2] which I have frequently lent to several societies about this town, to supply their necessities; I say, I give also the said bear-skin as an immediate fund to the said citizens for ever.

'*Item*, I do hereby appoint a certain number of the said citizens to take all the custom-house or customary oaths concerning all goods imported by the whole city, strictly directing that some select members, and not the whole number of a body corporate, should be perjured.

'*Item*, I forbid all n——s and persons of q——ty to watch bargains near and about the Exchange, to the diminution and wrong of the said stock-jobbers.'

Thus far, in as brief and intelligible a manner as any will can appear, until it is explained by the learned, I have disposed of my real and personal estate. But as I am an adept, I have by birth an equal right to give also an indefeasible title to my endowments and qualifications, which I do in the following manner:

'*Item*, I give my chastity to all virgins who have withstood their market.

'*Item*, I give my courage among all who are ashamed of their distressed friends, all sneakers in assemblies, and men who show valour in common conversation.

'*Item*, I give my wit (as rich men give to the rich) among such as think they have enough already. And in case they shall not accept of the legacy, I give it to Bentivolio,[3] to defend his Works, from time to time, as he shall think fit to publish them.

'*Item*, I bestow my learning upon the honorary members of the Royal Society.'

Now for the disposal of this body:

'As these eyes must one day cease to gaze on Teraminta, and this heart shall one day pant no more for her indignation: that is to say, since this body must be earth, I shall commit it to the dust in a manner suitable to my character. Therefore, as there are those who dispute whether there is any such real person as Isaac Bickerstaff, or not, I shall excuse all persons who appear what they really are, from coming to my funeral. But all those who are, in their way of life, *personae*, as the Latins have it, persons assumed,[4] and who appear what they really are not, are hereby invited to that solemnity.

'The body shall be carried by six watchmen, who are never seen in the day.

'*Item*, The pall shall be held up by the six most known pretenders to honesty, wealth, and power, who are not possessed of any of them. The two first, a half-lawyer, a complete justice. The two next, a chemist, a projector.[5] The third couple, a treasury-solicitor, and a small courtier.

'To make my funeral (what that solemnity, when done to common men, really is in itself) a very farce, and since all mourners are mere actors on these occasions, I shall desire those who are professedly such to attend mine.

I humbly therefore beseech Mrs. Barry to act once more, and be my widow.[6] When she swoons away at the church-porch, I appoint the merry Sir John Falstaff, and the gay Sir Harry Wildair,[7] to support her. I desire Mr. Pinkethman to follow in the habit of a cardinal, and Mr. Bullock in that of a privy counsellor.[8] To make up the rest of the appearance, I desire all the ladies from the balconies to weep with Mrs. Barry, as they hope to be wives and widows themselves. I invite all, who have nothing else to do, to accept of gloves and scarves.'

'Thus, with the great Charles V of Spain, I resign the glories of this transitory world; yet, at the same time, to show you my indifference, and that my desires are not too much fixed upon anything, I own to you I am as willing to stay as to go; therefore leave it in the choice of my gentle readers, whether I shall hear from them, or they hear no more from me.

5. A perfectly new way of writing

This evening we were entertained with *The Old Bachelor*, a comedy of deserved reputation.[1] In the character which gives name to the play, there is excellently represented the reluctance of a battered debauchee to come into the trammels of order and decency. He neither languishes nor burns, but frets for love. The gentlemen of more regular behaviour are drawn with much spirit and wit, and the drama introduced by the dialogue of the first scene with uncommon yet natural conversation. The part of Fondlewife is a lively image of the unseasonable fondness of age and impotence. But instead of such agreeable works as these, the town has for half an age been tormented with insects called easy writers, whose abilities Mr. Wycherley one day described excellently well in one word: 'That,' said he, 'among these fellows is called easy writing, which anyone may easily write.' Such jaunty scribblers are so justly laughed at for their sonnets on *Phillis* and *Chloris*, and fantastical descriptions in them, that an ingenious kinsman of mine, of the family of the Staffs, Mr. Humphrey Wagstaff by name,[2] has, to avoid their strain, run into a way perfectly new, and described things exactly as they happen. He never forms fields, or nymphs, or groves, where they are not; but makes the incidents just as they really appear. For an example of it I stole out of his manuscript the following lines: they are a description of the morning, but of the morning in town; nay, of the morning at this end of the town, where my kinsman at present lodges.

> Now hardly here and there an hackney-coach
> Appearing, show'd the ruddy morn's approach.
> Now Betty from her master's bed had flown,
> And softly stole to discompose her own.
> The slipshod 'prentice from his master's door
> Had par'd the street, and sprinkled round the floor;
> Now Moll had whirl'd her mop with dext'rous airs,
> Prepar'd to scrub the entry and the stairs.
> The youth with broomy stumps began to trace
> The kennel-edge, where wheels had worn the place.
> The small-coal-man was heard with cadence deep,
> Till drown'd in shriller notes of chimney-sweep.
> Duns at his Lordship's gates began to meet;
> And brick-dust Moll had scream'd thro' half a street:
> The turnkey now his flock returning sees,
> Duly let out a' nights to steal for fees.
> The watchful bailiffs take their silent stands;
> And schoolboys lag with satchels in their hands.

6. *Pious stratagem of Pastorella's aunt*

It is matter of much speculation among the beaux and oglers, what it is that can have made so sudden a change, as has been of late observed, in the whole behaviour of Pastorella, who never sat still a moment until she was eighteen, which she has now exceeded by two months. Her aunt, who has the care of her, has not been always so rigid as she is at this present date; but has so good a sense of the frailty of woman, and falsehood of man, that she resolved on all manner of methods to keep Pastorella, if possible, in safety, against herself and all her admirers. At the same time the good lady knew by long experience that a gay inclination curbed too rashly would but run to the greater excesses for that restraint: she therefore intended to watch her, and take some opportunity of engaging her insensibly in her own interests, without the anguish of admonition. You are to know then, that Miss, with all her flirting and ogling, had also naturally a strong curiosity in her, and was the greatest eavesdropper breathing. Parisatis (for so her prudent aunt is called) observed this humour, and retires one day to her closet, into which she knew Pastorella would peep, and listen to know how she was employed. It happened accordingly; and the young lady saw her good governante on her knees, and, after a mental behaviour, break into these words:

'As for the dear child committed to my care, let her sobriety of carriage and severity of behaviour be such as may make that noble lord who is taken with her beauty, turn his designs to such as are honourable.'

Here Parisatis heard her niece nestle closer to the keyhole. She then goes on: 'Make her the joyful mother of a numerous and wealthy offspring, and let her carriage be such as may make this noble youth expect the blessings of a happy marriage, from the singularity of her life, in this loose and censorious age.'

Miss, having heard enough, sneaks off for fear of discovery, and immediately at her glass alters the fitting of her head, then pulls up her tucker, and forms herself into the exact manner of Lindamira,[1] in a word, becomes a sincere convert to everything that is commendable in a fine young lady; and two or three such matches as her aunt feigned in her devotions are at this day in her choice.

7. *Miss Jenny Distaff takes up the pen*

My brother Isaac, having a sudden occasion to go out of town, ordered me to take upon me the dispatch of the next advices from home, with liberty to speak in my own way; not doubting the allowances which would be given to a writer of my sex. You may be sure I undertook it with much satisfaction, and I confess I am not a little pleased with the opportunity of running over all the papers in his closet, which he has left open for my use on this occasion. The first that I lay my hands on is a treatise concerning 'the empire of beauty,' and the effects it has had in all nations of the world, upon the public and private actions of men; with an appendix, which he calls 'The bachelor's scheme for governing his wife.' The first thing he makes this gentleman propose is that she shall be no woman; for she is to have an aversion to balls, to operas, to visits. She is to think his company sufficient to fill up all the hours of life with great satisfaction. She is never to believe any other man wise, learned, or valiant; or at least, but in a second degree. In the next place, he intends she shall be a cuckold; but expects that he himself must live in perfect security from that terror. He dwells a great while on instructions for her discreet behaviour, in case of his falsehood. I have not patience with these unreasonable expectations, therefore turn back to the treatise itself. Here indeed my brother deduces all the revolutions among men from the passion of love; and in his preface answers that usual observation against us, that 'there is no quarrel without a woman in it'; with a gallant assertion that 'there is nothing else worth quarrelling for.'

My brother is of a complexion truly amorous; all his thoughts and actions carry in them a tincture of that obliging inclination, and this turn has opened his eyes to see that we are not the inconsiderable creatures which unlucky pretenders to our favour would insinuate. He observes that no man begins to make any tolerable figure until he sets out with the hopes of pleasing some one of us.   No sooner he takes that in hand, but he pleases every one else by the by.

8.   Fine writing

A kinsman has sent me a letter, wherein he informs me he had lately resolved to write an heroic poem, but by business has been interrupted, and has only made one similitude, which he should be afflicted to have wholly lost; and begs of me to apply it to something, being very desirous to see it well placed in the world.   I am so willing to help the distressed that I have taken it in.   But, though his greater genius might very well distinguish his verses from mine, I have marked where his begin.[1]   His lines are a description of the sun in eclipse, which I know nothing more like than a brave man in sorrow, who bears it as he should, without imploring the pity of his friends, or being dejected with the contempt of his enemies, as in the case of Cato.

> When all the globe to Caesar's fortune bow'd,
> Cato alone his empire disallow'd;
> With inborn strength alone oppos'd mankind,
> With heav'n in view, to all below it blind:
> Regardless of his friends' applause, or moan,
> Alone triumphant, since he falls alone.
> 'Thus when the Ruler of the genial day
> Behind some dark'ning planet forms his way,
> Desponding mortals, with officious care,
> The concave drum and magic brass prepare;
> Implore him to sustain th' important fight,
> And save depending worlds from endless night:
> Fondly they hope their labour may avail
> To ease his conflict, and assist his toil.
> Whilst he, in beams of native splendour bright,
> (Tho' dark his orb appear to human sight)
> Shines to the gods with more diffusive light;
> To distant stars with equal glory burns,
> Inflames their lamps, and feeds their golden urns,
> Sure to retain his known superior tract,
> And proves the more illustrious by *defect*.'

This is a very lively image; but I must take the liberty
to say my kinsman drives the sun a little like Phaeton.
He has all the warmth of Phoebus, but will not stay for
his direction of it. Avail and toil, defect and tract, will
never do for rhymes. But however, he has the true spirit
in him; for which reason I was willing to entertain anything he pleased to send me. The subject which he
writes upon naturally raises great reflections in the soul,
and puts us in mind of the mixed condition which we
mortals are to support; which, as it varies to good or bad,
adorns or defaces our actions to the beholders: all which
glory and shame must end in what we so much repine at,
death. But doctrines on this occasion, any other than
that of living well, are the most insignificant and most
empty of all the labours of men. None but a tragedian
can die by rule, and wait until he discovers a plot, or says
a fine thing upon his exit. In real life, this is a chimaera;
and by noble spirits it will be done decently, without the
ostentation of it. We see men of all conditions and
characters go through it with equal resolution; and if we
consider the speeches of mighty philosophers, heroes, law-
givers, and great captains, they can produce no more in
a discerning spirit than rules to make a man a fop on his
deathbed. Commend me to that natural greatness of
soul, expressed by an innocent and consequently resolute
country fellow, who said in the pains of the colic: 'If
I once get this breath out of my body, you shall hang me
before you put it in again.'

9.   *Autobiography of Mr. Bickerstaff's familiar spirit, who died at the age of one month*

It was one of the most wealthy families in Great Britain
into which I was born, and it was a very great happiness
to me that it so happened, otherwise I had still, in all
probability, been living. But I shall recount to you all
the occurrences of my short and miserable existence, just

as, by examining into the traces made in my brain, they appeared to me at that time. The first thing that ever struck at my senses was a noise over my head of one shrieking; after which, methought, I took a full jump, and found myself in the hands of a sorceress, who seemed as if she had been long waking, and employed in some incantation. I was thoroughly frightened, and cried out; but she immediately seemed to go on in some magical operation, and anointed me from head to foot. What they meant, I could not imagine; for there gathered a great crowd about me, crying: 'An heir! an heir!' upon which I grew a little still, and believed this was a ceremony to be used only to great persons, and such as made them what they called 'heirs.' I lay very quiet; but the witch, for no manner of reason or provocation in the world, takes me, and binds my head as hard as possibly she could; then ties up both my legs, and makes me swallow down an horrid mixture. I thought it a harsh entrance into life, to begin with taking physic; but I was forced to it, or else must have taken down a great instrument in which she gave it me.

When I was thus dressed, I was carried to a bedside, where a fine young lady (my mother I wot) had like to have hugged me to death. From her they faced me about, and there was a thing with quite another look from the rest of the company, to whom they talked about my nose. He seemed wonderfully pleased to see me; but I knew since, my nose belonged to another family. That into which I was born is one of the most numerous amongst you; therefore crowds of relations came every day to congratulate my arrival; among others, my cousin Betty, the greatest romp in nature. She whisks me such a height over her head that I cried out for fear of falling. She pinched me, and called me squealing chit, and threw me into a girl's arms that was taken in to tend me. The girl was very proud of the womanly employment of a nurse, and took upon her to strip and dress me anew because I made a noise, to see what ailed me. She did so, and stuck a pin in every joint about me. I still cried, upon which she lays me on my face in her lap, and, to quiet me, fell a-nailing in all the pins, by clapping me on the back, and screaming a lullaby. But my pain made me exalt my voice above hers, which brought up the nurse, the witch I first saw, and my grandmother. The girl is turned downstairs, and I stripped again, as well to find what ailed me, as to satisfy my grandam's further curiosity.

This good old woman's visit was the cause of all my troubles. You are to understand that I was hitherto bred by hand, and anybody that stood next gave me pap, if I did but open my lips; insomuch that I was grown so cunning as to pretend myself asleep when I was not, to prevent my being crammed. But my grandmother began a loud lecture upon the idleness of the wives of this age, who, for fear of their shapes, forbear suckling their own offspring; and ten nurses were immediately sent for. One was whispered to have a wanton eye, and would soon spoil her milk; another was in a consumption; the third had an ill voice, and would frighten me instead of lulling me to sleep. Such exceptions were made against all but one country milch-wench, to whom I was committed, and put to the breast. This careless jade was eternally romping with the footman, and downright starved me; insomuch that I daily pined away, and should never have been relieved had it not been that, on the thirtieth day of my life, a Fellow of the Royal Society, who had writ upon cold baths,[1] came to visit me, and solemnly protested I was utterly lost for want of that method. Upon which he soused me head and ears into a pail of water, where I had the good fortune to be drowned; and so escaped being lashed into a linguist until sixteen, running after wenches until twenty-five, and being married to an ill-natured wife until sixty.

10.   Painful position of the news-writers if peace should come [1]

This day a mail arrived from Holland, by which there
are advices from Paris that the kingdom of France is in
the utmost misery and distraction. The merchants of
Lyons have been at court, to remonstrate their great
sufferings by the failure of their public credit; but have
received no other satisfaction than promises of a sudden
peace; and that their debts will be made good by funds
out of the revenue, which will not answer but in case of
the peace which is promised. In the meantime, the cries
of the common people are loud for want of bread, the
gentry have lost all spirit and zeal for their country, and
the king himself seems to languish under the anxiety of
the pressing calamities of the nation, and retires from
hearing those grievances which he hath not power to
redress. Instead of preparations for war and the defence
of their country, there is nothing to be seen but evident
marks of a general despair; processions, fastings, public
mournings and humiliations are become the sole employ-
ments of a people who were lately the most vain and gay
of any in the universe.

The Pope has written to the French king on the subject
of a peace, and His Majesty has answered in the lowliest
terms that he entirely submits his affairs to Divine Providence, and shall soon show the world that he prefers
the tranquillity of his people to the glory of his arms and
extent of his conquests.

Letters from The Hague of the twenty-fourth say that
His Excellency the Lord Townshend [2] delivered his creden-
tials on that day to the States General, as plenipotentiary
from the Queen of Great Britain; as did also Count
Zinzendorf, who bears the same character from the
Emperor.

Prince Eugene intended to set out the next day for
Brussels, and His Grace the Duke of Marlborough on the
Tuesday following. The Marquis de Torcy [3] talks daily of

going, but still continues there. The army of the Allies
is to assemble on the seventh of next month at Helchin;
though it is generally believed that the preliminaries to
a treaty are fully adjusted.[4]

The approach of the peace strikes a panic through our
armies, though that of a battle could never do it, and they
almost repent of their bravery, that made such haste to
humble themselves and the French king. The Duke of
Marlborough, though otherwise the greatest general of
the age, has plainly shown himself unacquainted with the
arts of husbanding a war. He might have grown as old
as the Duke of Alva, or Prince Waldeck in the Low
Countries, and yet have got reputation enough every year
for any reasonable man. For the command of a general
in Flanders hath been ever looked upon as a provision for
life. For my part, I cannot see how His Grace can
answer it to the world, for the great eagerness he hath
shown to send a hundred thousand of the bravest fellows
in Europe a-begging. But the private gentlemen of the
infantry will be able to shift for themselves; a brave man
can never starve in a country stocked with hen-roosts.
'There is not a yard of linen,' says my honoured pro-
genitor, Sir John Falstaff, 'in my whole company; but
as for that,' says this worthy knight, 'I am in no great
pain; we shall find shirts on every hedge.'[5]

There is another sort of gentlemen whom I am much
more concerned for, and that is the ingenious fraternity of
which I have the honour to be an unworthy member;
I mean the news-writers of Great Britain, whether 'Post-
men' or 'Postboys,' or by what other name or title soever
dignified or distinguished.[6] The case of these gentlemen
is, I think, more hard than that of the soldiers, considering
that they have taken more towns, and fought more battles.
They have been upon parties and skirmishes when our
armies have lain still, and given the general assault to
many a place when the besiegers were quiet in their
trenches. They have made us masters of several strong
towns many weeks before our generals could do it; and
completed victories when our greatest captains have been

glad to come off with a drawn battle. Where Prince Eugene has slain his thousands, Boyer [7] has slain his ten thousands. This gentleman can indeed be never enough commended for his courage and intrepidity during this whole war. He had laid about him with an inexpressible fury; and, like the offended Marius of ancient Rome, made such havoc among his countrymen as must be the work of two or three ages to repair. It must be confessed, the redoubted Mr. Buckley has shed as much blood as the former; but I cannot forbear saying (and I hope it will not look like envy) that we regard our brother Buckley [8] as a kind of Drawcansir,[9] who spares neither friend nor foe; but generally kills as many of his own side as the enemy's. It is impossible for this ingenious sort of men to subsist after a peace: everyone remembers the shifts they were driven to in the reign of King Charles II, when they could not furnish out a single paper of news, without lighting up a comet in Germany, or a fire in Moscow. There scarce appeared a letter without a paragraph on an earthquake. Prodigies were grown so familiar, that they had lost their name, as a great poet of this age has it. I remember Mr. Dyer,[10] who is justly looked upon by all fox-hunters in the nation as the greatest statesman our country has produced, was particularly famous for dealing in whales; insomuch that in five months' time (for I had the curiosity to examine his letters on that occasion) he brought three into the mouth of the River Thames, besides two porpoises and a sturgeon. The judicious and wary Mr. I. Dawks [11] hath all along been the rival of this great writer, and got himself a reputation from plagues and famines; by which, in those days, he destroyed as great multitudes as he has lately done by the sword. In every dearth of news, Grand Cairo was sure to be unpeopled.

It being therefore visible that our society will be greater sufferers by the peace than the soldiery itself, insomuch that the *Daily Courant* is in danger of being broken, my friend Dyer of being reformed, and the very best of the whole band of being reduced to half-pay; might I presume to offer anything in the behalf of my distressed brethren,

I would humbly move that an appendix of proper apartments, furnished with pen, ink, and paper, and other necessaries of life, should be added to the hospital of Chelsea, for the relief of such decayed news-writers as have served their country in the wars; and that for their exercise they should compile the annals of their brother veterans, who have been engaged in the same service, and are still obliged to do duty after the same manner.

I cannot be thought to speak this out of an eye to any private interest; for as my chief scenes of action are coffee-houses, playhouses, and my own apartment, I am in no need of camps, fortifications, and fields of battle, to support me; I do not call out for heroes and generals to my assistance. Though the officers are broken and the armies disbanded, I shall still be safe as long as there are men or women, or politicians, or lovers, or poets, or nymphs, or swains, or cits, or courtiers, in being.

11. *Esquires*

There is nothing can give a man of any consideration greater pain, than to see order and distinction laid aside amongst men, especially when the rank (of which he himself is a member) is intruded upon by such as have no pretence to that honour. The appellation of 'Esquire' is the most notoriously abused in this kind, of any class amongst men; insomuch that it is become almost the subject of derision. But I will be bold to say, this behaviour towards it proceeds from the ignorance of the people in its true origin. I shall therefore, as briefly as possible, do myself and all true esquires the justice to look into antiquity upon this subject.

In the first ages of the world, before the invention of jointures and settlements, when the noble passion of love had possession of the hearts of men, and the fair sex were not yet cultivated into the merciful disposition which they have showed in later centuries, it was natural for great and heroic spirits to retire to rivulets, woods, and caves, to lament their destiny and the cruelty of the fair persons who were deaf to all their lamentations. The hero in this distress was generally in armour, and in a readiness to fight any man he met with, especially if distinguished by any extraordinary qualifications; it being the nature of heroic love to hate all merit, lest it should come within the observation of the cruel one by whom its own perfections are neglected. A lover of this kind had always about him a person of a second value, and subordinate to him, who could hear his afflictions, carry an enchantment for his wounds, hold his helmet when he was eating (if ever he did eat), or in his absence, when he was retired to his apartment in any king's palace, tell the prince himself, or perhaps his daughter, the birth, parentage, and adventures of his valiant master.

This trusty companion was styled his esquire, and was always fit for any offices about him; was as gentle and chaste as a gentleman-usher, quick and active as an equerry, smooth and eloquent as a master of the ceremonies. A man thus qualified was the first, as the ancients affirm, who was called an esquire; and none without these accomplishments ought to assume our order. But, to the utter disgrace and confusion of the heralds, every pretender is admitted into this fraternity, even persons the most foreign to this courteous institution. I have taken an inventory of all within this city, and looked over every letter in the post office for my better information. There are of the Middle Temple, including all in the buttery-books and in the lists of the house, five thousand. In the Inner, four thousand. In the King's-Bench Walks, the whole buildings are inhabited by esquires only. In the adjacent street of Essex, from Morris's coffee-house, and the turning towards the Grecian, you cannot meet one who is not an esquire, until you take water. Every house in Norfolk and Arundel Streets is governed also by an esquire, or his lady; Soho Square, Bloomsbury Square, and all other places where the floors rise above nine feet, are so many universities where you enter yourselves, and become of our order. However, if this were the worst of the evil, it were to be supported, because they are generally men of some figure and use; though I know no pretence they have to an honour which had its rise from chivalry.

But if you travel into the counties of Great Britain, we are still more imposed upon by innovation. We are indeed derived from the field; but shall that give title to all that ride mad after foxes, that halloo when they see an hare, or venture their necks full speed after an hawk, immediately to commence esquires? No; our order is temperate, cleanly, sober, and chaste; but these rural esquires commit immodesties upon hay-cocks, wear shirts half a week, and are drunk twice a day. These men are also, to the last degree, excessive in their food. An esquire of Norfolk eats two pounds of dumpling every meal, as if obliged to it by our order. An esquire of Hampshire is as ravenous in devouring hogsflesh. One of Essex has as little mercy on calves. But I must take the liberty to protest against them, and acquaint those persons that it is not the quantity they eat but the manner of eating, that shows an esquire.

But, above all, I am most offended at small quillmen and transcribing clerks, who are all come into our order, for no reason that I know of but that they can easily flourish it at the end of their name. I will undertake that if you read the subscriptions to all the offices in the kingdom you will not find three letters directed to any but esquires. I have myself a couple of clerks, and the rogues make nothing of leaving messages upon each other's desk. One directs, 'to Degory Goosequill, Esquire'; to which the other replies by a note, 'to Nehemiah Dashwell, Esquire, with respect'; in a word, it is now *Populus Armigerorum*, a people of esquires. And I do not know but, by the late act of naturalization, foreigners will assume that title, as part of the immunity of being Englishmen. All these improprieties flow from the negligence of the Heralds' Office. Those gentlemen in particoloured habits do not so rightly as they ought understand themselves; though they are dressed cap-à-pie in hieroglyphics, they are

inwardly but ignorant men.   I asked an acquaintance of
mine, who is a man of wit, but of no fortune, and is forced
to appear as a Jack-pudding on the stage to a mountebank:
'Prithee, Jack, why is your coat of so many colours?'
He replied: 'I act a fool, and this spotted dress is to signify
that every man living has a weak place about him; for I am
knight of the shire, and represent you all.'

I wish the heralds would know as well as this man does,
in his way, that they are to act for us in the case of our
arms and appellations; we should not then be jumbled
together in so promiscuous and absurd a manner.   I design
to take this matter into further consideration, and no man
shall be received as an esquire, who cannot bring a certificate that he has conquered some lady's obdurate heart;
that he can lead up a country dance, or carry a message
between her and her lover, with address, secrecy, and
diligence.   A squire is properly born for the service of
the sex, and his credentials shall be signed by three toasts
and one prude, before his title shall be received in my
office.

12. France needs peace.   'Authentic' letter from Madame de Maintenon

An authentic letter from Madam Maintenon to Monsieur
Torcy has been stolen by a person about him, who has
communicated a copy of it to some of the dependants of
a minister of the Allies.   That epistle is writ in the most
pathetic manner imaginable, and in a style which shows
her genius that has so long engrossed the heart of this
great monarch.

SIR,

I received yours, and am sensible of the address and
capacity with which you have hitherto transacted the
great affair under your management.   You will observe
that our wants here are not to be concealed; and that it is
vanity to use artifices with the knowing men with whom

you are to deal. Let me beg you therefore, in this representation of our circumstances, to lay aside art, which
ceases to be such when it is seen, and make use of all your
skill to gain us what advantages you can from the enemy's
jealousy of each other's greatness; which is the place where
only you have room for any dexterity. If you have any
passion for your unhappy country, or any affection for
your distressed master, come home with peace. Oh
heaven! do I live to talk of Lewis the Great as the object
of pity? The king shows a great uneasiness to be informed
of all that passes; but at the same time is fearful of every
one who appears in his presence, lest he should bring an
account of some new calamity.

I know not in what terms to represent my thoughts to
you, when I speak of the king, with relation to his bodily
health. Figure to yourself that immortal man, who stood
in our public places, represented with trophies, armour,
and terrors, on his pedestal; consider the invincible, the
great, the good, the pious, the mighty, which were the
usual epithets we gave him, both in our language and
thoughts. I say, consider him whom you knew the most
glorious and greatest of monarchs, and now think you see
the same man an unhappy lazar, in the lowest circumstances
of human nature itself, without regard to the state from
whence he is fallen. I write from his bedside: he is at
present in a slumber. I have many, many things to add;
but my tears flow too fast, and my sorrow is too big for
utterance.

                                             I am, etc.

There is such a veneration due from all men to the
persons of princes that it were a sort of dishonesty to
represent further the condition which the king is in, but
it is certain that soon after the receipt of these advices
Monsieur Torcy waited upon His Grace the Duke of
Marlborough, and the Lord Townshend; and in that
conference gave up many points which he had before
said were such as he must return to France before he
could answer.

13. The case of the unhappy gentlewoman

It is not to be imagined how far prepossession will run away with people's understandings in cases wherein they are under present uneasinesses. The following narration is a sufficient testimony of the truth of this observation.

I had the honour the other day of a visit from a gentlewoman (a stranger to me) who seemed to be about thirty. Her complexion is brown; but the air of her face has an agreeableness which surpasses the beauties of the fairest women. There appeared in her look and mien a sprightly health; and her eyes had too much vivacity to become the language of complaint, which she began to enter into. She seemed sensible of it; and therefore, with downcast looks, said she: 'Mr. Bickerstaff, you see before you the unhappiest of women; and therefore, as you are esteemed by all the world both a great civilian as well as an astrologer, I must desire your advice and assistance in putting me in a method of obtaining a divorce from a marriage which I know the law will pronounce void.'

'Madam,' said I, 'your grievance is of such a nature that you must be very ingenuous in representing the causes of your complaint, or I cannot give you the satisfaction you desire.'

'Sir,' she answers, 'I believe there would be no need of half your skill in the art of divination, to guess why a woman would part from her husband.'

'It is true,' said I, 'but suspicions, or guesses at what you mean, nay certainty of it, except you plainly speak it, are no foundation for a formal suit.'

She clapped her fan before her face.

'My husband,' said she, 'is no more an husband' (here she bursts into tears) 'than one of the Italian singers.'

'Madam,' said I, 'the affliction you complain of is to be redressed by law; but, at the same time, consider what mortifications you are to go through in bringing it into open court; how will you be able to bear the impertinent whispers of the people present at the trial, the licentious reflections of the pleaders, and the interpretations that will in general be put upon your conduct by all the world? How little (will they say) could that lady command her passions! Besides, consider, that curbing our desires is the greatest glory we can arrive at in this world, and will be most rewarded in the next.'

She answered, like a prudent matron: 'Sir, if you please to remember the office of matrimony, the first cause of its institution is that of having posterity: therefore, as to the curbing desires, I am willing to undergo any abstinence from food as you please to enjoin me; but I cannot, with any quiet of mind, live in the neglect of a necessary duty, and an express commandment: "Increase and multiply."'

Observing she was learned, and knew so well the duties of life, I turned my argument rather to dehort her from this public procedure by examples than precepts. 'Do but consider, madam, what crowds of beauteous women live in nunneries, secluded for ever from the sight and conversation of men, with all the alacrity of spirit imaginable; they spend their time in heavenly raptures, in constant and frequent devotions, and at proper hours in agreeable conversations.'

'Sir,' said she hastily, 'tell not me of papists, or any of their idolatries.'

'Well then, madam, consider how many fine ladies live innocently in the eye of the world and this gay town, in the midst of temptation. There is the witty Mrs. W—— is a virgin of forty-four, Mrs. T——s is thirty-nine, Mrs. L——ce thirty-three; yet you see they laugh, and are gay, at the park, at the playhouse, at balls, and at visits; and so much at ease that all this seems hardly a self-denial.'

'Mr. Bickerstaff,' said she, with some emotion, 'you are an excellent casuist; but the last word destroyed your whole argument; if it is not self-denial, it is no virtue. I presented you with an half-guinea, in hopes not only to have my conscience eased, but my fortune told. Yet——'

'Well, madam,' said I, 'pray of what age is your husband?'

'He is,' replied my injured client, 'fifty; and I have been his wife fifteen years.'

'How happened it you never communicated your distress in all this time, to your friends and relations?'

She answered: 'He has been thus but a fortnight.'

I am the most serious man in the world to look at, and yet could not forbear laughing out. 'Why, madam, in case of infirmity which proceeds only from age, the law gives no remedy.'

'Sir,' said she, 'I find you have no more learning than Dr. Case [1]; and I am told of a young man, not five and twenty, just come from Oxford, to whom I will communicate this whole matter, and doubt not but he will appear to have seven times more useful and satisfactory knowledge than you and all your boasted family.'

14. *May-fair closed*

This evening was acted *The Recruiting Officer*, in which Estcourt's proper sense and observation is what supports the play.[1] There is not, in my humble opinion, the humour hit in Sergeant Kite; but it is admirably supplied by his action. If I have skill to judge, that man is an excellent actor; but the crowd of the audience are fitter for representations at May-fair than a Theatre Royal. Yet that fair is now broke, as well as the theatre is breaking; but it is allowed still to sell animals there.[2] Therefore, if any lady or gentleman have occasion for a tame elephant, let them inquire of Mr. Pinkethman, who has one to dispose of at a reasonable rate. The downfall of May-fair has quite sunk the price of this noble creature, as well as of many other curiosities of nature. A tiger will sell almost as cheap as an ox; and I am credibly informed, a man may purchase a cat with three legs for very near the value of one with four. I hear likewise, that there is a great desolation among the gentlemen and ladies who were the ornaments of the town, and used to shine in plumes and diadems; the heroes being most of them pressed, and the queens beating hemp.[3] Mrs. Sarabrand, so famous for her ingenious puppet-show, has set up a shop in the Exchange, where she sells her little troop under the term of jointed babies. I could not but be solicitous to know of her, how she had disposed of that rake-hell *Punch*, whose lewd life and conversation had given so much scandal, and did not a little contribute to the ruin of the fair. She told me, with a sigh, that despairing of ever reclaiming him, she would not offer to place him in a civil family, but got him in a post upon a stall in Wapping, where he may be seen from sunrising to sunsetting, with a glass in one hand, and a pipe in the other, as sentry to a brandy-shop. The great revolutions of this nature bring to my mind the distresses of the unfortunate Camilla, who has had the ill luck to break before her voice, and to disappear at a time when her beauty was in the height of its bloom. This lady entered so thoroughly into the great characters she acted, that when she had finished her part she could not think of retrenching her equipage, but would appear in her own lodgings with the same magnificence that she did upon the stage. This greatness of soul has reduced that unhappy princess to an involuntary retirement, where she now passes her time among the woods and forests, thinking on the crowns and sceptres she has lost, and often humming over in her solitude:

> I was born of royal race,
> Yet must wander in disgrace, etc.

15. *No peace after all*

Advices from Brussels of the sixth instant say His Highness Prince Eugene had received a letter from Monsieur Torcy, wherein that minister, after many expressions of great respect, acquaints him that his master had absolutely refused to sign the preliminaries to the treaty which he had, in His Majesty's behalf, consented to at The Hague. Upon the receipt of this intelligence, the face of things at that place were immediately altered, and the necessary orders were transmitted to the troops which lay most remote from thence to move toward the place of rendezvous with all expedition. The enemy seem also to prepare for the field, and have at present drawn together twenty-five thousand men in the plains of Lens. Marshal Villars is at the head of those troops; and has given the generals under his command all possible assurances that he will turn the fate of the war to the advantage of his master.

They write from The Hague of the seventh, that Monsieur Rouille had received orders from the Court of France to signify to the States-General and the ministers of the high Allies, that the king could not consent to the preliminaries of a treaty of peace, as it was offered to him by Monsieur Torcy. The great difficulty is the business of Spain,[1] on which particular his ministers seemed only to say, during the treaty, that it was not so immediately under their master's direction, as that he could engage for its being relinquished by the Duke of Anjou.[2] But now he positively answers that he cannot comply with what his minister has promised in his behalf, even in such points as are wholly in himself to act in or not. This has had no other effect than to give the alliance fresh arguments for being diffident of engagements entered into by France. The Pensioner made a report of all which this minister had declared to the deputies of the States-General, and all things turn towards a vigorous war. The Duke of Marlborough designed to leave The Hague within two days, in order to put himself at the head of the army, which is to assemble on the seventeenth instant between the Schelde and the Lys. A fleet of eighty sail, laden with corn from the Baltic, is arrived in the Texel. The States have sent circular letters to all the provinces, to notify this change of affairs, and to animate their subjects to new resolutions in defence of their country.

16. Plain words from Mr. Bickerstaff to Louis XIV

The surprising news which arrived this day, of Your
Majesty's having refused to sign the treaty your ministers
have in a manner sued for, is what gives ground to this
application to Your Majesty, from one whose name,
perhaps, is too obscure to have ever reached your terri-
tories; but one who, with all the European world, is
affected with your determinations. Therefore, as it is
mine and the common cause of mankind, I presume to
expostulate with you on this occasion. It will, I doubt
not, appear to the vulgar extravagant, that the actions of
a mighty prince should be balanced by the censure of a
private man, whose approbation or dislike are equally contemptible in their eyes, when they regard the thrones of
sovereigns. But Your Majesty has shown, through the
whole course of your reign, too great a value for liberal
arts to be insensible that true fame lies only in the hands
of learned men, by whom it is to be transmitted to futurity,
with marks of honour or reproach to the end of time.
The date of human life is too short to recompense the
cares which attend the most private condition. Therefore it is, that our souls are made as it were too big for it;
and extend themselves in the prospect of a longer existence,
in a good fame, and memory of worthy actions, after our
decease. The whole race of men have this passion in
some degree implanted in their bosoms, which is the
strongest and noblest incitation to honest attempts.

But the base use of the arts of peace, eloquence, poetry,
and all the parts of learning, have been possessed by souls
so unworthy of those faculties, that the names and appellations of things have been confounded by the labours and
writings of prostituted men, who have stamped a reputation upon such actions as are in themselves the objects
of contempt and disgrace. This is that which has misled
Your Majesty in the conduct of your reign, and made that
life which might have been the most imitable, the most to
be avoided. To this it is, that the great and excellent

qualities, of which Your Majesty is master, are lost in
their application; and Your Majesty has been carrying on
for many years the most cruel tyranny, with all the noble
methods which are used to support a just reign.   Thus
it is that it avails nothing that you are a bountiful master;
that you are so generous as to reward even the unsuccessful
with honour and riches; that no laudable action passes un-
rewarded in your kingdom; that you have searched all
nations for obscure merit: in a word, that you are in your
private character endowed with every princely quality;
when all this is subjected to unjust and ill-taught ambition,
which, to the injury of the world, is gilded by those
endowments.

However, if Your Majesty will condescend to look into
your own soul, and consider all its faculties and weaknesses
with impartiality; if you will but be convinced that life is
supported in you by the ordinary methods of food, rest,
and sleep; you will think it impossible that you could ever
be so much imposed on, as to have been wrought into a
belief that so many thousands of the same make with yourself were formed by Providence for no other end but by
the hazard of their very being to extend the conquests and
glory of an individual of their own species.   A very little
reflection will convince Your Majesty that such cannot
be the intent of the Creator; and if not, what horror must
it give Your Majesty to think of the vast devastations your
ambition has made among your fellow creatures!

While the warmth of youth, the flattery of crowds, and
a continual series of success and triumph, indulged Your
Majesty in this illusion of mind, it was less to be wondered
at that you proceeded in this mistaken pursuit of grandeur;
but when age, disappointments, public calamities, personal
distempers, and the reverse of all that makes men forget
their true being, are fallen upon you—Heaven! Is it
possible you can live without remorse?   Can the wretched
man be a tyrant?   Can grief study torments?   Can
sorrow be cruel?

Your Majesty will observe I do not bring against you
a railing accusation; but as you are a strict professor of

religion, I beseech Your Majesty to stop the effusion of
blood, by receiving the opportunity which presents itself
for the preservation of your distressed people. Be no
longer so infatuated as to hope for renown from murder
and violence; but consider that the great day will come
in which this world and all its glory shall change in a
moment; when nature shall sicken, and the earth and sea
give up the bodies committed to them, to appear before
the last tribunal. Will it then, O king, be an answer for
the lives of millions who have fallen by the sword,
'They perished for my glory'? That day will come on,
and one like it is immediately approaching: injured nations
advance towards thy habitation. Vengeance has began
its march, which is to be diverted only by the penitence
of the oppressor. Awake, O monarch, from thy lethargy!
Disdain the abuses thou hast received. Pull down the
statue which calls thee immortal. Be truly great: tear
thy purple, and put on sackcloth. I am,

Thy generous enemy,
ISAAC BICKERSTAFF.

17.   Concerning Toasts

To know what a Toast is in the country gives as much
perplexity as she herself does in town. And indeed the
learned differ very much upon the original of this word,
and the acceptation of it among the moderns. However,
it is by all agreed to have a joyous and cheerful import.
A toast in a cold morning, heightened by nutmeg, and
sweetened with sugar, has for many ages been given to
our rural dispensers of justice before they entered upon
causes, and has been of great and politic use to take off
the severity of their sentences; but has indeed been remarkable for one ill effect, that it inclines those who use it
immoderately to speak Latin, to the admiration rather than
information of an audience. This application of a toast
makes it very obvious that the word may, without a
metaphor, be understood as an apt name for a thing which

raises us in the most sovereign degree. But many of the wits of the last age will assert that the word, in its present sense, was known among them in their youth, and had its rise from an accident at the town of Bath, in the reign of King Charles II.

It happened that on a public day a celebrated beauty of those times was in the Cross Bath, and one of the crowd of her admirers took a glass of the water in which the fair one stood, and drank her health to the company. There was in the place a gay fellow half fuddled, who offered to jump in, and swore though he liked not the liquor, he would have the toast. He was opposed in his resolution; yet this whim gave foundation to the present honour which is done to the lady we mention in our liquors, who has ever since been called a Toast.

Though this institution had so trivial a beginning, it is now elevated into a formal order; and that happy virgin who is received and drunk to at their meetings has no more to do in this life but to judge and accept of the first good offer. The manner of her inauguration is much like that of the choice of a Doge in Venice. It is performed by balloting; and when she is so chosen, she reigns indisputably for that ensuing year; but must be elected anew to prolong her empire a moment beyond it. When she is regularly chosen, her name is written with a diamond on a drinking-glass. The hieroglyphic of the diamond is to show her that her value is imaginary; and that of the glass to acquaint her that her condition is frail, and depends on the hand which holds her. This wise design admonishes her neither to overrate nor depreciate her charms; as well considering and applying, that it is perfectly according to the humour and taste of the company, whether the toast is eaten or left as an offal.

The foremost of the whole rank of Toasts, and the most indisputed in their present empire, are Mrs. Gatty and Mrs. Frontlet [1]; the first an agreeable, the second an awful beauty. These ladies are perfect friends, out of a knowledge that their perfections are too different to stand in competition. He that likes Gatty can have no relish for so solemn a creature as Frontlet; and an admirer of Frontlet will call Gatty a maypole girl. Gatty for ever smiles upon you; and Frontlet disdains to see you smile. Gatty's love is a shining quick flame; Frontlet's a slow wasting fire. Gatty likes the man that diverts her; Frontlet him who adores her. Gatty always improves the soil in which she travels; Frontlet lays waste the country. Gatty does not only smile, but laughs at her lover; Frontlet not only looks serious, but frowns at him. All the men of wit (and cox-combs their followers) are professed servants of Gatty. The politicians and pretenders give solemn worship to Frontlet. Their reign will be best judged of by its duration. Frontlet will never be chosen more; and Gatty is a Toast for life.

18. Duels

A letter from a young lady, written in the most passionate terms, wherein she laments the misfortune of a gentleman, her lover, who was lately wounded in a duel, has turned my thoughts to that subject, and inclined me to examine into the causes which precipitate men into so fatal a folly. And as it has been proposed to treat of subjects of gallantry in the article from hence, and no one point in nature is more proper to be considered by the company who frequent this place than that of duels, it is worth our consideration to examine into this chimerical groundless humour, and to lay every other thought aside, until we have stripped it of all its false pretences to credit and reputation amongst men.[1]

But I must confess, when I consider what I am going about, and run over in my imagination all the endless crowd of men of honour who will be offended at such a discourse, I am undertaking, methinks, a work worthy an invulnerable hero in romance rather than a private gentleman with a single rapier. But as I am pretty well acquainted by great opportunities with the nature of man, and know of a truth that all men fight against their will, the danger vanishes, and resolution rises upon this subject. For this reason, I shall talk very freely on a custom which all men wish exploded, though no man has courage enough to resist it.

But there is one unintelligible word which I fear will extremely perplex my dissertation, and I confess to you I find very hard to explain, which is the term 'satisfaction.' An honest country gentleman had the misfortune to fall into company with two or three modern men of honour, where he happened to be very ill treated; and one of the company being conscious of his offence, sends a note to him in the morning, and tells him, he was ready to give him satisfaction. This is fine doing (says the plain fellow); last night he sent me away cursedly out of humour, and this morning he fancies it would be a satisfaction to be run through the body.

As the matter at present stands, it is not to do handsome actions denominates a man of honour, it is enough if he dares to defend ill ones. Thus you often see a common sharper in competition with a gentleman of the first rank, though all mankind is convinced that a fighting gamester is only a pickpocket with the courage of an highwayman. One cannot with any patience reflect on the unaccountable jumble of persons and things in this town and nation, which occasions very frequently that a brave man falls by a hand below that of a common hangman, and yet his executioner escapes the clutches of the hangman for doing it. . . . Most of the quarrels I have ever known have proceeded from some valiant coxcomb's persisting in the wrong, to defend some prevailing folly and preserve himself from the ingenuity of owning a mistake.

By this means it is called 'Giving a man satisfaction,' to urge your offence against him with your sword; which puts me in mind of Peter's order to the keeper in *The Tale of a Tub*: 'If you neglect to do all this, damn you and your generation for ever: and so we bid you heartily farewell.' If the contradiction in the very terms of one of our challenges were as well explained and turned into downright English, would it not run after this manner?

Sir,

Your extraordinary behaviour last night, and the liberty
you were pleased to take with me, makes me this morning
give you this, to tell you, because you are an ill-bred
puppy, I will meet you in Hyde Park an hour hence; and
because you want both breeding and humanity, I desire
you would come with a pistol in your hand, on horseback,
and endeavour to shoot me through the head, to teach
you more manners. If you fail of doing me this pleasure,
I shall say you are a rascal on every post in town. And
so, Sir, if you will not injure me more, I shall never forgive
what you have done already. Pray, Sir, do not fail of
getting everything ready, and you will infinitely oblige,

Sir,

Your most obedient,

Humble servant, etc.

19. The King of France's reply, and other matters

Versailles, June 13, 1709

Lewis the Fourteenth to Isaac Bickerstaff, Esquire.

Sir,

I have your epistle, and must take the liberty to say
that there has been a time when there were generous
spirits in Great Britain who would not have suffered my
name to be treated with the familiarity you think fit to use.
I thought liberal men would not be such time-servers as
to fall upon a man because his friends are not in power.
But having some concern for what you may transmit to
posterity concerning me, I am willing to keep terms with
you, and make a request to you, which is, that you would
give my service to the nineteenth century (if ever you or
yours reach to them), and tell them that I have settled all
matters between them and me by Monsieur Boileau.[1]
I should be glad to see you here.

It is very odd this prince should offer to invite me into his dominions, or believe I should accept the invitation. No, no, I remember too well how he served an ingenious gentleman, a friend of mine, whom he locked up in the Bastille for no reason in the world, but because he was a wit, and feared he might mention him with justice in some of his writings.[2] His way is, that all men of sense are preferred, banished, or imprisoned. He has indeed a sort of justice in him, like that of the gamesters; for if a stander-by sees one at play cheat, he has a right to come in for shares, as knowing the mysteries of the game.

This is a very wise and just maxim; and if I have not left at Mr. Morphew's, directed to me, bank-bills for two hundred pounds, on or before this day sevennight, I shall tell how Tom Cash got his estate. I expect three hundred pounds of Mr. Soilett, for concealing all the money he has lent to himself, and his landed friend bound with him, at thirty per cent at his scrivener's. Absolute princes make people pay what they please in deference to their power: I do not know why I should not do the same, out of fear or respect to my knowledge. I always preserve decorums and civilities to the fair sex: therefore, if a certain lady, who left her coach at the New-Exchange door in the Strand and whipped down Durham Yard into a boat with a young gentleman for Vauxhall; I say, if she will send me word that I may give the fan which she dropped, and I found, to my sister Jenny, there shall be no more said of it. I expect hush-money to be regularly sent for every folly or vice any one commits in this whole town; and hope I may pretend to deserve it better than a chamber-maid or a *valet de chambre*. They only whisper it to the little set of their companions; but I can tell it to all men living, or who are to live. Therefore I desire all my readers to pay their fines, or mend their lives.

20. Miss Toss

As a rake among men is the man who lives in the constant abuse of his reason, so a coquette among women is one who lives in continual misapplication of her beauty. The chief of all whom I have the honour to be acquainted with, is pretty Miss Toss. She is ever in practice of something which disfigures her and takes from her charms, though all she does tends to a contrary effect. She has naturally a very agreeable voice and utterance, which she has changed for the prettiest lisp imaginable. She sees what she has a mind to see at half a mile distance; but poring with her eyes half shut at every one she passes by, she believes much more becoming. The Cupid on her fan and she have their eyes full on each other, all the time in which they are not both in motion. Whenever her eye is turned from that dear object, you may have a glance, and your bow, if she is in humour, returned as civilly as you make it; but that must not be in the presence of a man of greater quality: for Miss Toss is so thoroughly well bred, that the chief person present has all her regards. And she who giggles at divine service, and laughs at her very mother, can compose herself at the approach of a man of a good estate.

21.   The passionate duellist to his love

MADAM,

I have so tender a regard for you, and your interests, that I will knock any man on the head whom I observe to be of my mind, and like you. Mr. Truman, the other day, looked at you in so languishing a manner that I am resolved to run him through to-morrow morning. This, I think, he deserves for his guilt in admiring you; than which I cannot have a greater reason for murdering him, except it be that you also approve him. Whoever says

he dies for you, I will make his words good, for I will
kill him. I am,

>   Madam,
>   Your most obedient,
>   Most humble servant.

22. *Jack Careless and Colonel Constant*

The suspension of the playhouse has made me have
nothing to send you from hence; but calling here this
evening, I found the party I usually sit with upon the
business of writing, and examining what was the hand-
somest style in which to address women and write letters
of gallantry. Many were the opinions which were immediately declared on this subject. Some were for a certain
softness; some for I know not what delicacy; others for
something inexpressibly tender. When it came to me, I
said there was no rule in the world to be made for writing
letters, but that of being as near what you speak face to
face as you can; which is so great a truth that I am of
opinion writing has lost more mistresses than any one
mistake in the whole legend of love. For when you write
to a lady for whom you have a solid and honourable
passion, the great idea you have of her, joined to a quick
sense of her absence, fills your mind with a sort of tenderness that gives your language too much the air of complaint, which is seldom successful. For a man may flatter
himself as he pleases, but he will find that the women
have more understanding in their own affairs than we
have, and women of spirit are not to be won by mourners.
He that can keep handsomely within rules, and support
the carriage of a companion to his mistress, is much more
likely to prevail than he who lets her see the whole relish
of his life depends upon her. If possible, therefore, divert
your mistress rather than sigh for her. The pleasant man
she will desire for her own sake; but the languishing lover
has nothing to hope from but her pity. To show the

difference, I produced two letters a lady gave me, which had been writ by two gentlemen who pretended to her, but were both killed the next day after the date, at the battle of Almanza.[1] One of them was a mercurial gay-humoured man; the other a man of a serious, but a great and gallant spirit. Poor Jack Careless! this is his letter. You see how it is folded: the air of it is so negligent, one might have read half of it, by peeping into it without breaking it open. He had no exactness.

Madam,

It is a very pleasant circumstance I am in, that while I should be thinking of the good company we are to meet within a day or two, where we shall go to loggerheads, my thoughts are running upon a fair enemy in England. I was in hopes I had left you there; but you follow the camp, though I have endeavoured to make some of our leaguer ladies drive you out of the field. All my comfort is, you are more troublesome to my colonel than myself: I permit you to visit me only now and then; but he down-right keeps you. I laugh at his honour, as far as his gravity will allow me; but I know him to be a man of too much merit to succeed with a woman. Therefore defend your heart as well as you can: I shall come home this winter irresistibly dressed, and with quite a new foreign air. And so I had like to say, I rest, but, alas! I remain,

Madam,
Your most obedient,
Most humble servant,
JOHN CARELESS.

Now for Colonel Constant's epistle; you see it is folded and directed with the utmost care.

Madam,

I do myself the honour to write to you this evening, because I believe to-morrow will be a day of battle; and something forebodes in my breast that I shall fall in it. If it proves so, I hope you will hear I have done nothing

below a man who had the love of his country quickened
by a passion for a woman of honour.   If there be anything
noble in going to a certain death; if there be any merit,
that I meet it with pleasure, by promising myself a place
in your esteem; if your applause, when I am no more, is
preferable to the most glorious life without you—I say,
madam, if any of these considerations can have weight
with you, you will give me a kind place in your memory,
which I prefer to the glory of Caesar.   I hope this will
be read, as it is writ, with tears.

The beloved lady is a woman of a sensible mind; but
she has confessed to me that after all her true and solid
value for Constant, she had much more concern for the
loss of Careless.   Those noble and serious spirits have
something equal to the adversities they meet with, and
consequently lessen the objects of pity.   Great accidents
seem not cut out so much for men of familiar characters,
which makes them more easily pitied, and soon after
beloved.   Add to this, that the sort of love which generally
succeeds is a stranger to awe and distance.   I asked
Romana, whether of the two she should have chosen, had
they survived.   She said, she knew she ought to have
taken Constant, but believed she should have chosen
Careless.

23.   *Duels and duellists further considered*

In my dissertation against the custom of single combat,
it has been objected that there is not learning, or much
reading, shown therein, which is the very life and soul of
all treatises; for which reason, being always easy to receive
admonitions and reform my errors, I thought fit to consult this learned board on the subject.   Upon proposing
some doubts, and desiring their assistance, a very hopeful
young gentleman, my relation, who is to be called to the
bar within a year and a half at the farthest, told me that

he had ever since I first mentioned duelling turned his head that way; and that he was principally moved thereto because he designed to follow the circuits in the north of England and south of Scotland, and to reside mostly at his own estate at Landbadernawz in Cardiganshire. The northern Britons and the southern Scots are a warm people, and the Welsh 'a nation of gentlemen'; so that it behoved him to understand well the science of quarrelling. The young gentleman proceeded admirably well, and gave the board an account that he had read Fitzherbert's *Grand Abridgment*,' [1] and had found that duelling is a very ancient part of the law; for when a man is sued, be it for his life or his land, the person that joins the issue, whether plaintiff or defendant, may put the trial upon the duel. Further he argued, under favour of the court, that when the issue is joined by the duel, in treason or other capital crimes, the parties accused and accuser must fight in their own proper persons. But if the dispute be for lands, you may hire a champion at Hockley in the Hole, [2] or anywhere else. This part of the law we had from the Saxons; and they had it, as also the trial by ordeal, from the Laplanders. It is indeed agreed, said he, the southern and eastern nations never knew anything of it; for though the ancient Romans would scold and call names filthily, yet there is not an example of a challenge that ever passed among them.

His quoting the eastern nations put another gentleman in mind of an account he had from a boatswain of an East Indiaman; which was, that a Chinese had tricked and bubbled [3] him, and that when he came to demand satisfaction the next morning, and like a true tar of honour called him a son of a whore, liar, dog, and other rough appellatives used by persons conversant with winds and waves, the Chinese, with great tranquillity, desired him not to come abroad fasting, nor put himself into a heat, for it would prejudice his health. Thus the east knows nothing of this gallantry.

There sat at the left of the table a person of a venerable aspect, who asserted that half the impositions which are put upon these ages have been transmitted by writers who have given too great pomp and magnificence to the exploits of the ancient Bear-garden, and made their gladiators, by fabulous tradition, greater than Gorman [4] and others of Great Britain. He informed the company that he had searched authorities for what he said, and that a learned antiquary, Humphrey Scarecrow, Esquire, of Hockley in the Hole, recorder to the Bear-garden, was then writing a discourse on the subject. It appears by the best accounts, says this gentleman, that the high names which are used among us with so great veneration were no other than stage-fighters, and worthies of the ancient Bear-garden. The renowned Hercules always carried a quarterstaff, and was from thence called Claviger.[5] A learned chronologist is about proving what wood the staff was made of, whether oak, ash, or crab-tree. The first trial of skill he ever performed was with one Cacus, a deer-stealer; the next was with Typhonus, a giant of forty feet four inches. Indeed, it was unhappily recorded that meeting at last with a sailor's wife, she made his staff of prowess serve her own use, and dwindle away to a distaff. She clapped on him an old tar-jacket of her husband, so that this great hero drooped like a scabbed sheep. Him his contemporary Theseus succeeded in the Bear-garden, which honour he held for many years. This grand duellist went to hell, and was the only one of that sort that ever came back again. As for Achilles and Hector (as the ballads of those times mention), they were pretty smart fellows; they fought at sword and buckler, but the former had much the better of it; his mother, who was an oyster-woman, having got a blacksmith of Lemnos to make her son's weapons. There is a pair of trusty Trojans in a song of Virgil that were famous for handling their gauntlets, Dares and Entellus; and indeed it does appear they fought no sham-prize. What arms the great Alexander used is uncertain; however, the historian mentions, when he attacked Thalestris, it was only at single rapier.[6] But the weapon soon failed; for it was always observed that the Amazons had a sort of enchantment about them, which made the blade of the weapon, though of never so good metal, at every home push lose its edge, and grow feeble.

The Roman Bear-garden was abundantly more magnificent than anything Greece could boast of; it flourished most under those delights of mankind, Nero and Domitian. At one time it is recorded, four hundred senators entered the list, and thought it an honour to be cudgelled and quarterstaffed. I observe the Lanistae [7] were the people chiefly employed, which makes me imagine our Bear-garden copied much after this, the butchers being the greatest men in it.

Thus far the glory and honour of the Bear-garden stood secure, until fate, that irresistible rule of sublunary things, in that universal ruin of arts and politer learning by those savage people the Goths and Vandals, destroyed and levelled it to the ground. Then fell the grandeur and bravery of the Roman state, until at last the warlike genius (but accompanied with more courtesy) revived in the Christian world under those puissant champions, Saint George, Saint Denis, and other dignified heroes. One killed his dragon, another his lion, and were all afterwards canonized for it, having red letters before them to illustrate their martial temper. The Spanish nation, it must be owned, were devoted to gallantry and chivalry above the rest of the world! What a great figure does that great name, Don Quixote, make in history! How shines that glorious star in the western world! O renowned Hero! O mirror of Knighthood!

> Thy brandish'd whinyard all the world defies,
> And kills as sure as del Tobosa's eyes.

I am forced to break off abruptly, being sent for in haste with my rule to measure the degree of an affront, before the two gentlemen (who are now in their breeches and pumps ready to engage behind Montagu House) have made a pass.

24. *Marlborough outwits Villars and lays siege to Tournai*

Last night arrived two mails from Holland, which bring letters from The Hague of the twenty-eighth instant, with advice that the enemy lay encamped behind a strong retrenchment, with the marsh of Romiers on their right and left, extending itself as far as Bethune: La Bassée is in their front, Lens in their rear, and their camp is strengthened by another line from Lens to Douai. The Duke of Marlborough caused an exact observation to be made of their ground and the works by which they were covered, which appeared so strong that it was not thought proper to attack them in their present posture. However, the duke thought fit to make a feint as if he designed it. His Grace accordingly marched from the abbey at Loos, as did Prince Eugene from Lampret, and advanced with all possible diligence towards the enemy. To favour the appearance of an intended assault, the ways were made and orders distributed in such manner that none in either camp could have thoughts of anything but charging the enemy by break of day next morning. But soon after the fall of the night of the twenty-sixth, the whole army faced towards Tournai, which place they invested early in the morning of the twenty-seventh. The Marshal Villars was so confident that we designed to attack him, that he had drawn great part of the garrison of the place, which is now invested, into the field; for which reason, it is presumed, it must submit within a small time, which the enemy cannot prevent, but by coming out of their present camp and hazarding a general engagement. These advices add that the garrison of Mons had marched out under the command of Marshal d'Arco; which, with the Bavarians, Walloons, and the troops of Cologne, have joined the grand army of the enemy.

25. *Edifying experience of Jenny Distaff*

My brother has made an excursion into the country, and the work against Saturday lies upon me. I am very glad I have got pen and ink in my hand, for I have for some time longed for his absence, to give a right idea of things, which I thought he put in a very odd light, and some of them to the disadvantage of my own sex. It is much to be lamented that it is necessary to make discourses, and publish treatises, to keep the horrid creatures, the men, within the rules of common decency. Turning over the papers of memorials or hints for the ensuing discourses, I find a letter subscribed by Mr. Truman.

SIR,

I am lately come to town, and have read your works with much pleasure: you make wit subservient to good principles and good manners. Yet because I design to buy the *Tatlers* for my daughters to read, I take the freedom to desire you for the future, to say nothing about any combat between Alexander and Thalestris.

This offence gives me occasion to express myself with the resentment I ought, on people who take liberties of speech before that sex of whom the honoured names of mother, daughter, and sister are a part. I had like to have named wife in the number; but the senseless world are so mistaken in their sentiments of pleasure, that the most amiable term in human life is become the derision of fools and scorners. My brother and I have at least fifty times quarrelled upon this topic. I ever argue that the frailties of women are to be imputed to the false ornaments which men of wit put upon our folly and coquetry. He lays all the vices of men upon women's secret approbation of libertine characters in them. I did not care to give up a point; but now he is out of the way I cannot but own I believe there is very much in what he asserted; for if you will believe your eyes, and own that the wickedest and wittiest of them all marry one day or other, it is impossible to believe that if a man thought he should be for ever incapable of being received by a woman of merit and honour, he would persist in an abandoned way, and deny himself the possibility of enjoying the happiness of well-governed desires, orderly satisfactions, and honourable methods of life. If our sex were wise, a lover should have a certificate from the last woman he served, how he was turned away, before he was received into the service of another. But at present any vagabond is welcome, provided he promises to enter into our livery. It is wonderful that we will not take a footman without credentials from his last master; and in the greatest concern of life we make no scruple of falling into a treaty with the most notorious offender in his behaviour against others. But this breach of commerce between the sexes proceeds from an unaccountable prevalence of custom, by which a woman is to the last degree reproachable for being deceived, and a man suffers no loss of credit for being a deceiver.

Since this tyrant humour has gained place, why are we represented in the writings of men in ill figures for artifice in our carriage, when we have to do with a professed impostor? When oaths, imprecations, vows, and adorations are made use of as words of course, what arts are not necessary to defend us from such as glory in the breach of them? As for my part I am resolved to hear all, and believe none of them; and therefore solemnly declare no vow shall deceive me but that of marriage. For I am turned of twenty, and being of small fortune, some wit, and (if I can believe my lovers and my glass) handsome, I have heard all that can be said towards my undoing; and shall therefore, for warning's sake, give an account of the offers that have been made me, my manner of rejecting them, and my assistances to keep my resolution.

In the sixteenth year of my life I fell into the acquaintance of a lady extremely well known in this town for the quick advancement of her husband, and the honours and distinctions which her industry has procured him, and all

who belong to her. This excellent body sat next to me
for some months at church, and took the liberty (which
she said her years and the zeal she had for my welfare gave
her claim to) to assure me that she observed some parts in
my behaviour which would lead me into errors, and give encouragement to some to entertain hopes I did not think of.
'What made you,' said she, 'look through your fan at that
lord, when your eyes should have been turned upwards,
or closed in attention upon better objects?' I blushed,
and pretended fifty odd excuses; but confounded myself
the more. She wanted nothing but to see that confusion,
and goes on: 'Nay, child, do not be troubled that I take
notice of it; my value for you made me speak it; for
though he is my kinsman, I have a nearer regard to virtue
than any other consideration.' She had hardly done
speaking, when this noble lord came up to us, and led
her to her coach.

My head ran all that day and night on the exemplary
carriage of this woman, who could be so virtuously
impertinent as to admonish one she was hardly acquainted
with. However, it struck upon the vanity of a girl that
it may possibly be, his thoughts might have been as
favourable of me, as mine were amorous of him, and (as
unlikely things as that have happened) if he would make
me his wife. She never mentioned this more to me; but
I still in all public places stole looks at this man, who easily
observed my passion for him. It is so hard a thing to
check the return of agreeable thoughts, that he became my
dream, my vision, my food, my wish, my torment.

That minister of darkness, the Lady Sempronia, perceived too well the temper I was in, and would, one day
after evening service, needs take me to the park. When
we were there, my lord passes by; I flushed into a flame.
'Mrs. Distaff,' says she, 'you may very well remember the
concern I was in upon the first notice I took of your
regard to that lord, and, forgive me, who had a tender
friendship for your mother (now in the grave), that I am
vigilant of your conduct.' She went on with much
severity, and after great solicitation prevailed on me to

go with her into the country, and there spend the ensuing summer out of the way of a man she saw I loved, and one who she perceived meditated my ruin, by frequently desiring her to introduce him to me; which she absolutely refused, except he would give his honour that he had no other design but to marry me.

To her country house a week or two after we went. There was at the farther end of her garden a kind of wilderness, in the middle of which ran a soft rivulet by an arbour of jessamine. In this place I usually passed my retired hours, and read some romantic or poetical tale until the close of the evening. It was near that time in the heat of the summer, when gentle winds, soft murmurs of water, and notes of nightingales had given my mind an indolence, which added to that repose of soul twilight and the end of a warm day naturally throws upon the spirits. It was at such an hour and in such a state of tranquillity I sat, when, to my inexpressible amazement, I saw my lord walking towards me, whom I knew not until that moment to have been in the country. I could observe in his approach the perplexity which attends a man big with design; and I had, while he was coming forward, time to reflect that I was betrayed; the sense of which gave me a resentment suitable to such a baseness.

But when he entered into the bower where I was, my heart flew towards him, and, I confess, a certain joy came into my mind, with a hope that he might then make a declaration of honour and passion. This threw my eye upon him with such tenderness as gave him power, with a broken accent, to begin: 'Madam—you will wonder—for it is certain you must have observed—though I fear you will misinterpret the motives. But by Heaven and all that is sacred! if you could——'

Here he made a full stand, and I recovered power to say: 'The consternation I am in you will not, I hope, believe—an helpless innocent maid—besides that, the place——'

He saw me in as great confusion as himself; which, attributing to the same causes, he had the audaciousness to throw himself at my feet, talk of the stillness of the evening, and then run into deifications of my person, pure flames, constant love, eternal raptures, and a thousand other phrases drawn from the images we have of heaven, which all men use for the service of hell, when run over with uncommon vehemence. After which he seized me in his arms. His design was too evident. In my utmost distress, I fell upon my knees: 'My lord, pity me on my knees—on my knees in the cause of virtue, as you were lately in that of wickedness. Can you think of destroying the labour of a whole life, the purpose of a long education, for the base service of a sudden appetite; to throw one that loves you, that doats on you, out of the company and the road of all that is virtuous and praiseworthy? Have I taken in all the instructions of piety, religion, and reason, for no other end but to be the sacrifice of lust, and abandoned to scorn? Assume yourself, my lord, and do not attempt to vitiate a temple sacred to innocence, honour, and religion. If I have injured you, stab this bosom, and let me die, but not be ruined, by the hand I love.' The ardency of my passion made me incapable of uttering more, and I saw my lover astonished and reformed by my behaviour, when rushed in Sempronia. 'Ha! faithless base man, could you then steal out of town, and lurk like a robber about my house for such brutish purposes!'

My lord was by this time recovered, and fell into a violent laughter at the turn which Sempronia designed to give her villainy. He bowed to me with the utmost respect: 'Mrs. Distaff,' said he, 'be careful hereafter of your company'; and so retired. The fiend Sempronia congratulated my deliverance with a flood of tears.

This nobleman has since frequently made his addresses to me with honour; but I have as often refused them; as well knowing that familiarity and marriage will make him, on some ill-natured occasion, call all I said in the arbour a theatrical action. Besides that, I glory in contemning a man, who had thoughts to my dishonour. If this method were the imitation of the whole sex, innocence would be the only dress of beauty; and all affectation by any other arts to please the eyes of men would be banished to the stews for ever. The conquest of passion gives ten times more happiness than we can reap from the gratification of it; and she that has got over such a one as mine, will stand among beaux and pretty fellows, with as much safety as in a summer's day among grasshoppers and butterflies.

PS. I have ten millions of things more against men, if I ever get the pen again.

26. Snuff

However low and poor the taking snuff argues a man to be in his own stock of thoughts, or means to employ his brains and his fingers; yet there is a poorer creature in the world than he, and this is a borrower of snuff; a fellow that keeps no box of his own, but is always asking others for a pinch. Such poor rogues put me always in mind of a common phrase among schoolboys when they are composing their exercise, who run to an upper scholar, and cry: 'Pray give me a little sense.' But of all things commend me to the ladies who are got into this pretty help to discourse. I have been these three years persuading Sagissa to leave it off; but she talks so much, and is so learned, that she is above contradiction. However, an accident the other day brought that about, which my eloquence never could accomplish. She had a very pretty fellow in her closet, who ran thither to avoid some company that came to visit her. She made an excuse to go in to him for some implement they were talking of. Her eager gallant snatched a kiss; but being unused to snuff, some grains from off her upper lip made him sneeze aloud, which alarmed the visitants, and has made a discovery that profound reading, very much intelligence, and a general knowledge of who and who are together, cannot fill her vacant hours so much, but that she is sometimes obliged to descend to entertainments less intellectual.

27.   Entertainment at the expense of the
Artillery-company

There is no one thing more to be lamented in our
nation than their general affectation of everything that
is foreign; nay, we carry it so far, that we are more
anxious for our own countrymen when they have crossed
the seas than when we see them in the same dangerous
condition before our eyes at home: else how is it possible,
that on the twenty-ninth of the last month, there should
have been a battle fought in our very streets of London,
and nobody at this end of the town have heard of it?
I protest, I, who make it my business to inquire after
adventures, should never have known this, had not the
following account been sent me enclosed in a letter.   This,
it seems, is the way of giving out orders in the Artillery-
company; and they prepare for a day of action with so
little concern as only to call it: 'An Exercise of Arms.'

An Exercise at Arms of the Artillery-company, to be
performed on Wednesday, June the twenty-ninth, 1709,
under the command of Sir Joseph Woolfe, Knight and
Alderman, General; Charles Hopson, Esquire, present
Sheriff, Lieutenant-General; Captain Richard Synge,
Major; Major John Shorey, Captain of Grenadiers;
Captain William Grayhurst, Captain John Butler, Cap-
tain Robert Carellis, Captains.

'The body march from the Artillery-ground [1] through
Moorgate, Coleman Street, Lothbury, Broad Street, Finch
Lane, Cornhill, Cheapside, St. Martin's, St. Anne's Lane,
halt the pikes under the wall in Noble Street, draw up
the firelocks facing the Goldsmiths' Hall, make ready and
face to the left, and fire, and so *ditto* three times.   Beat
to arms, and march round the hall, as up Lad Lane, Gutter
Lane, Honey Lane, and so wheel to the right, and make
your salute to my Lord, and so down St. Anne's Lane, up
Aldersgate Street, Barbican, and draw up in Red Cross

Street, the right at St. Paul's Alley in the rear. March off Lieutenant-General with half the body up Beech Lane: he sends a subdivision up King's Head Court, and takes post in it, and marches two divisions round into Red Lion Market, to defend that pass, and succour the division in King's Head Court; but keeps in Whitecross Street, facing Beech Lane, the rest of the body ready drawn up. Then the General marches up Beech Lane, is attacked, but forces the division in the court into the market, and enters with three divisions while he presses the Lieutenant-General's main body; and at the same time the three divisions force those of the revolters out of the market, and so all the Lieutenant-General's body retreats into Chiswell Street, and lodges two divisions in Grub Street; and as the General marches on, they fall on his flank, but soon made to give way: but having a retreating-place in Red Lion Court, but could not hold it, being put to flight through Paul's Alley, and pursued by the General's grenadiers, while he marches up and attacks their main body, but are opposed again by a party of men as lay in Black Raven Court; but they are forced also to retire soon in the utmost confusion, and at the same time, those brave divisions in Paul's Alley ply their rear with grenadoes, that with precipitation they take to the route along Bunhill Row. So the General marches into the Artillery-ground, and being drawn up, finds the revolting party to have found entrance, and makes a show as if for a battle, and both armies soon engage in form, and fire by platoons.'

Much might be said for the improvement of this system, which, for its style and invention, may instruct generals and their historians both in fighting a battle and describing it when it is over. These elegant expressions: 'Ditto— and so—— But soon—— But having—— But could not—— But are—— But they—— Finds the party to have found, etc.'—do certainly give great life and spirit to the relation.

Indeed I am extremely concerned for the Lieutenant-General, who by his overthrow and defeat is made a deplorable instance of the fortune of war and vicissitudes

of human affairs. He, alas! has lost, in Beech Lane and
Chiswell Street, all the glory he lately gained in and about
Holborn and St. Giles's. The art of subdividing first,
and dividing afterwards, is new and surprising; and according to this method, the troops are disposed in King's
Head Court and Red Lion Market. Nor is the conduct
of these leaders less conspicuous in their choice of the
ground or field of battle. Happy was it that the greatest
part of the achievements of this day was to be performed
near Grub Street, that there might not be wanting a
sufficient number of faithful historians, who, being eye-
witnesses of these wonders, should impartially transmit
them to posterity! But then it can never be enough
regretted that we are left in the dark as to the name and
title of that extraordinary hero who commanded the
divisions in Paul's Alley; especially because those divisions
are justly styled brave, and accordingly were to push the
enemy along Bunhill Row, and thereby occasion a general
battle. But Pallas appeared in the form of a shower of
rain, and prevented the slaughter and desolation which
were threatened by these extraordinary preparations.

> *Hi motus animorum atque haec certamina tanta*
> *Pulveris exigui jactu compressa quiescent.*
>
> Virg. *Georg.* IV. 86.

Yet all those dreadful deeds, this doubtful fray,
A cast of scatter'd dust will soon allay.

DRYDEN.

28. *Illustrative anecdote*

As it is a frequent mortification to me to receive letters
wherein people tell me, without a name, they know I
meant them in such and such a passage; so that very
accusation is an argument that there are such beings in
human life as fall under our description, and that our
discourse is not altogether fantastical and groundless.
But in this case I am treated as I saw a boy was the other
day, who gave out pocky bills. Every plain fellow took

it that passed by, and went on his way without further
notice; and at last came one with his nose a little abridged,
who knocks the lad down, with a 'Why, you son of a
w——e, do you think I am p——d?'

29. *Selling-up at Drury Lane*

It is now twelve of the clock at noon, and no mail come
in; therefore I am not without hopes that the town will
allow me the liberty which my brother news-writers take,
in giving them what may be for their information in
another kind, and indulge me in doing an act of friendship, by publishing the following account of goods and
moveables.

This is to give notice, that a magnificent palace, with
great variety of gardens, statues, and water-works, may
be bought cheap in Drury Lane; where there are likewise
several castles to be disposed of, very delightfully situated;
as also groves, woods, forests, fountains, and country-
seats, with very pleasant prospects on all sides of them;
being the movables of Christopher Rich, Esquire,[1] who
is breaking up housekeeping, and has many curious pieces
of furniture to dispose of, which may be seen between
the hours of six and ten in the evening.

THE INVENTORY [2]

Spirits of right Nantz brandy, for lambent flames and
apparitions.

Three bottles and a half of lightning.

One shower of snow in the whitest French paper.

Two showers of a browner sort.

A sea, consisting of a dozen large waves; the tenth
bigger than ordinary, and a little damaged.

A dozen and half of clouds, trimmed with black, and
well-conditioned.

A rainbow, a little faded.

A set of clouds after the French mode, streaked with lightning, and furbelowed.

A new moon, something decayed.

A pint of the finest Spanish wash, being all that is left of two hogsheads sent over last winter.

A coach very finely gilt, and little used, with a pair of dragons, to be sold cheap.

A setting-sun, a pennyworth.[3]

An imperial mantle, made for Cyrus the Great, and worn by Julius Caesar, Bajazet, King Henry the Eighth, and Signor Valentini.[4]

A basket-hilted sword, very convenient to carry milk in.

Roxana's night-gown.

Othello's handkerchief.

The imperial robes of Xerxes, never worn but once.

A wild boar killed by Mrs. Tofts [5] and Dioclesian.

A serpent to sting Cleopatra.

A mustard-bowl to make thunder with.

Another of a bigger sort, by Mr. Dennis's directions, little used.[6]

Six elbow-chairs, very expert in country-dances, with six flower-pots for their partners.

The whiskers of a Turkish Bassa.

The complexion of a murderer in a band-box; consisting of a large piece of burnt cork, and a coal-black peruke.

A suit of clothes for a ghost, viz. a bloody shirt, a doublet curiously pinked, and a coat with three great eyelet-holes upon the breast.

A bale of red Spanish wool.[7]

Modern plots,[8] commonly known by the name of trap-doors, ladders of ropes, vizard-masks, and tables with broad carpets over them.

Three oak cudgels, with one of crab-tree; all bought for the use of Mr. Pinkethman.

Materials for dancing; as masks, castanets, and a ladder of ten rounds.

Aurengzebe's scimitar, made by Will. Brown in Piccadilly.

A plume of feathers, never used but by Oedipus and the Earl of Essex.

There are also swords, halbeards, sheep-hooks, cardinal's hats, turbans, drums, gallipots, a gibbet, a cradle, a rack, a cart-wheel, an altar, an helmet, a back-piece, a breastplate, a bell, a tub, and a jointed baby.

These are the hard shifts we intelligencers are forced to; therefore our readers ought to excuse us, if a westerly wind blowing for a fortnight together generally fills every paper with an order of battle; when we show our martial skill in every line, and according to the space we have to fill, we range our men in squadrons and battalions, or draw out company by company, and troop by troop; ever observing that no muster is to be made but when the wind is in a cross-point, which often happens at the end of a campaign, when half the men are deserted or killed. The *Courant* is sometimes ten deep, his ranks close; the *Postboy* is generally in files, for greater exactness; and the *Postman* comes down upon you rather after the Turkish way, sword in hand, pell-mell, without form or discipline; but sure to bring men enough into the field; and wherever they are raised, never to lose a battle for want of numbers.

30. *The Hero properly celebrated*

We were upon the heroic strain this evening, and the question was: What is the true sublime? Many very good discourses happened thereupon; after which a gentleman at the table, who is, it seems, writing on that subject, assumed the argument; and though he ran through many instances of sublimity from the ancient writers, said he had hardly known an occasion wherein the true greatness of soul which animates a general in action is so well represented, with regard to the person of whom it was spoken and the time in which it was writ, as in a few lines in a modern poem. 'There is,' continued he, 'nothing so

forced and constrained as what we frequently meet with
in tragedies; to make a man under the weight of great
sorrow, or full of meditation upon what he is soon to
execute, cast about for a simile to what he himself is, or
the thing which he is going to act. But there is nothing
more proper and natural for a poet, whose business it is
to describe, and who is spectator of one in that circumstance, when his mind is working upon a great image, and
that the ideas hurry upon his imagination—I say, there is
nothing so natural, as for a poet to relieve and clear himself from the burden of thought at that time, by uttering
his conception in simile and metaphor. The highest act
of the mind of man is to possess itself with tranquillity
in imminent danger, and to have its thoughts so free as
to act at that time without perplexity. The ancient
authors have compared this sedate courage to a rock that
remains immovable amidst the rage of winds and waves;
but that is too stupid and inanimate a similitude, and could
do no credit to the hero. At other times they are all of
them wonderfully obliged to a Libyan lion, which may
give indeed very agreeable terrors to a description, but
is no compliment to the person to whom it is applied.
Eagles, tigers, and wolves, are made use of on the same
occasion, and very often with much beauty; but this is
still an honour done to the brute rather than the hero.
Mars, Pallas, Bacchus, and Hercules, have each of them
furnished very good similes in their time, and made,
doubtless, a greater impression on the mind of a heathen
than they have on that of a modern reader. But the
sublime image that I am talking of, and which I really
think as great as ever entered into the thought of man,
is in the poem called *The Campaign* [1]; where the simile
of a ministering angel sets forth the most sedate and the
most active courage, engaged in an uproar of nature, a
confusion of elements, and a scene of divine vengeance.
Add to all, that these lines compliment the general and
his queen at the same time, and have all the natural horrors
heightened by the image that was still fresh in the mind
of every reader.

'Twas then great Marlbro's mighty soul was prov'd,
That, in the shock of charging hosts unmov'd,
Amidst confusion, horror, and despair,
Examin'd all the dreadful scenes of war;
In peaceful thought the field of death survey'd,
To fainting squadrons sent the timely aid,
Inspir'd repuls'd battalions to engage,
And taught the doubtful battle where to rage.
So when an Angel, by divine command,
With rising tempests shakes a guilty land,
Such as of late o'er pale Britannia past,
Calm and serene he drives the furious blast;
And, pleas'd th' Almighty's orders to perform,
Rides in the whirlwind, and directs the storm.

'The whole poem is so exquisitely noble and poetic, that I think it an honour to our nation and language.' The gentleman concluded his critique on this work by saying that he esteemed it wholly new, and a wonderful attempt to keep up the ordinary ideas of a march of an army, just as they happened, in so warm and great a style, and yet be at once familiar and heroic. Such a performance is a chronicle as well as a poem, and will preserve the memory of our hero, when all the edifices and statues erected to his honour are blended with common dust.

31. *Tournai captured*

This morning we received by express the agreeable news of the surrender of the town of Tournai on the twenty-eighth instant. The place was assaulted by the attacks of General Schuylemberg, and that of General Lottum, at the same time. The action at both those parts of the town was very obstinate, and the Allies lost a considerable number at the beginning of the dispute; but the fight was continued with so great bravery, that the enemy, observing our men to be masters of all the posts which were necessary for a general attack, beat the *chamade*,[1] and hostages were received from the town, and others sent from the besiegers, in order to come to a formal

capitulation for the surrender of the place. We have also
this day received advice that Sir John Leake,[2] who lies
off Dunkirk, had intercepted several ships laden with corn
from the Baltic; and that the Dutch privateers had fallen
in with others, and carried them into Holland. The
French letters advise that the young son to the Duke of
Anjou [3] lived but eight days.

32. *Tragical passion*

Tragical passion was the subject of the discourse where
I last visited this evening; and a gentleman who knows
that I am at present writing a very deep tragedy, directed
his discourse in a particular manner to me. 'It is the
common fault,' said he, 'of you gentlemen who write in
the buskin style, that you give us rather the sentiments
of such who behold tragical events, than of such who
bear a part in them themselves. I would advise all who
pretend this way, to read Shakespeare with care; and they
will soon be deterred from putting forth what is usually
called tragedy. The way of common writers in this kind
is rather the description than the expression of sorrow.
There is no medium in these attempts, and you must go
to the very bottom of the heart, or it is all mere language;
and the writer of such lines is no more a poet, than a man
is a physician for knowing the names of distempers, without the causes of them. Men of sense are professed
enemies to all such empty labours; for he who pretends
to be sorrowful, and is not, is a wretch yet more contemptible than he who pretends to be merry, and is not.
Such a tragedian is only maudlin drunk.' The gentleman
went on with much warmth, but all he could say had little
effect upon me; but when I came hither, I so far observed
his counsel that I looked into Shakespeare. The tragedy
I dipped into was *Henry IV*. In the scene where Morton
is preparing to tell Northumberland of his son's death,
the old man does not give him time to speak, but says:

> The whiteness in thy cheek
> Is apter than thy tongue to tell thy errand;
> Even such a man, so faint, so spiritless,
> So dull, so dead in look, so woebegone,
> Drew Priam's curtain in the dead of night,
> And would have told him half his Troy was burnt;
> But Priam found the fire, ere he is tongue,
> And I my Percy's death, ere thou report'st it.

The image in this place is wonderfully noble and great; yet this man in all this is but rising towards his great affliction, and is still enough himself, as you see, to make a simile. But when he is certain of his son's death, he is lost to all patience, and gives up all the regards of this life; and since the last of evils is fallen upon him, he calls for it upon all the world.

> Now let not Nature's hand
> Keep the wild flood confin'd; let order die,
> And let the world no longer be a stage,
> To feed contention in a ling'ring act;
> But let one spirit of the first-born Cain
> Reign in all bosoms, that each heart being set
> On bloody courses, the rude scene may end,
> And darkness be the burier of the dead.

Reading but this one scene has convinced me that he who describes the concern of great men must have a soul as noble and as susceptible of high thoughts, as they whom he represents: I shall therefore lay by my drama for some time and turn my thoughts to cares and griefs, somewhat below that of heroes, but no less moving. A misfortune, proper for me to take notice of, has too lately happened. The disconsolate Maria has three days kept her chamber for the loss of the beauteous Fidelia, her lap-dog. Lesbia herself did not shed more tears for her sparrow. What makes her the more concerned is that we know not whether Fidelia was killed or stolen; but she was seen in the parlour window when the Train-bands went by, and never since. Whoever gives notice of her, dead or alive, shall be rewarded with a kiss of her lady.

33. *Love and Lust, with a portrait of Aspasia*

The figures which the ancient mythologists and poets put upon Love and Lust in their writings are very instructive. Love is a beauteous blind child, adorned with a quiver and a bow, which he plays with, and shoots around him, without design or direction; to intimate to us that the person beloved has no intention to give us the anxieties we meet with, but that the beauties of a worthy object are like the charms of a lovely infant; they cannot but attract your concern and fondness, though the child so regarded is as insensible of the value you put upon it as it is that it deserves your benevolence. On the other side, the sages figured Lust in the form of a satyr; of shape, part human, part bestial; to signify that the followers of it prostitute the reason of a man to pursue the appetites of a beast. This satyr is made to haunt the paths and coverts of the wood-nymphs and shepherdesses, to lurk on the banks of rivulets, and watch the purling streams, as the resorts of retired virgins; to show that lawless desire tends chiefly to prey upon innocence, and has something so unnatural in it, that it hates its own make and shuns the object it loved as soon as it has made it like itself. Love therefore is a child that complains and bewails its inability to help itself, and weeps for assistance, without an immediate reflection or knowledge of the food it wants: Lust, a watchful thief, which seizes its prey, and lays snares for its own relief; and its principal object being innocence, it never robs but it murders at the same time.

From this idea of a Cupid and a satyr, we may settle our notions of these different desires, and accordingly rank their followers. Aspasia must therefore be allowed to be the first of the beauteous order of love, whose unaffected freedom and conscious innocence give her the attendance of the Graces in her actions.[1] That awful distance which we bear toward her in all our thoughts of her, and that cheerful familiarity with which we approach her, are certain instances of her being the truest object of love of any of

her sex. In this accomplished lady, love is the constant
effect, because it is never the design. Yet, though her
mien carries much more invitation than command, to
behold her is an immediate check to loose behaviour;
and to love her is a liberal education; for, it being the
nature of all love to create an imitation of the beloved
person in the lover, a regard for Aspasia naturally produces
a decency of manners, and good conduct of life, in her
admirers. If therefore the giggling Leucippe could but
see her train of fops assembled, and Aspasia move by them,
she would be mortified at the veneration with which she is
beheld, even by Leucippe's own unthinking equipage, whose
passions have long taken leave of their understandings.

As charity is esteemed a conjunction of the good qualities
necessary to a virtuous man, so Love is the happy com-
position of all the accomplishments that make a fine
gentleman. The motive of a man's life is seen in all his
actions; and such as have the beauteous Boy for their
inspirer have a simplicity of behaviour, and a certain
evenness of desire, which burns like the lamp of life in
their bosoms; while they who are instigated by the
satyr are ever tortured by jealousies of the object of
their wishes; often desire what they scorn, and as often
consciously and knowingly embrace where they are
mutually indifferent.

34. *Delamira resigns her fan*

Long had the crowd of the gay and young stood in
suspense as to their fate in their passion to the beauteous
Delamira; but all their hopes are lately vanished, by the
declaration that she has made of her choice, to take the
happy Archibald for her companion for life. Upon her
making this known, the expense of sweet powder and
jessamine are considerably abated; and the mercers and
milliners complain of her want of public spirit in not concealing longer a secret which was so much the benefit of

trade. But so it happened; and no one was in confidence with her in carrying on this treaty but the matchless Virgulta, whose despair of ever entering the matrimonial state made her, some nights before Delamira's resolution was published to the world, address herself to her in the following manner:

'Delamira! you are now going into that state of life wherein the use of your charms is wholly to be applied to the pleasing only one man. That swimming air of your body, that jaunty bearing of your head over one shoulder, and that inexpressible beauty in your manner of playing your fan, must be lowered into a more confined behaviour, to show that you would rather shun than receive addresses for the future. Therefore, dear Delamira, give me those excellences you leave off, and acquaint me with your manner of charming; for I take the liberty of our friendship to say, that when I consider my own stature, motion, complexion, wit, or breeding, I cannot think myself any way your inferior; yet do I go through crowds without wounding a man, and all my acquaintance marry round me, while I live a virgin unasked; and, I think, unregarded.'

Delamira heard her with great attention, and, with that dexterity which is natural to her, told her that all she had above the rest of her sex and contemporary beauties was wholly owing to a fan (that was left her by her mother, and had been long in the family), which whoever had in possession, and used with skill, should command the hearts of all her beholders. 'And since,' said she smiling, 'I have no more to do with extending my conquests or triumphs, I will make you a present of this inestimable rarity.' Virgulta made her expressions of the highest gratitude for so uncommon a confidence in her, and desired she would show her what was peculiar in the management of that utensil, which rendered it of such general force while she was mistress of it. Delamira replied: 'You see, madam, Cupid is the principal figure painted on it; and the skill in playing this fan is, in your several motions of it, to let him appear as little as possible; for honourable lovers fly all endeavours to ensnare them, and your Cupid must hide his bow and arrow or he will never be sure of his game. You may observe,' continued she, 'that in all public assemblies, the sexes seem to separate themselves, and draw up to attack each other with eye-shot: that is the time when the fan, which is all the armour of a woman, is of most use in our defence; for our minds are construed by the waving of that little instrument, and our thoughts appear in composure or agitation according to the motion of it. You may observe, when Will Peregrine comes into the side-box, Miss Gatty flutters her fan as a fly does its wings round a candle; while her elder sister, who is as much in love with him as she is, is as grave as a Vestal at his entrance, and the consequence is accordingly. He watches half the play for a glance from her sister, while Gatty is overlooked and neglected. I wish you heartily as much success in the management of it as I have had. If you think fit to go on where I left off, I will give you a short account of the execution I have made with it.

'Cimon, who is the dullest of mortals, and though a wonderful great scholar, does not only pause, but seems to take a nap with his eyes open between every other sentence in his discourse—him have I made a leader in assemblies; and one blow on the shoulder as I passed by him has raised him to a downright impertinent in all conversations. The airy Will Sampler is become as lethargic by this my wand as Cimon is sprightly. Take it, good girl, and use it without mercy; for the reign of beauty never lasted full three years but it ended in marriage, or condemnation to virginity. As you fear therefore the one, and hope for the other, I expect an hourly journal of your triumphs; for I have it by certain tradition, that it was given to the first who wore it by an enchantress, with this remarkable power, that it bestows a husband in half a year on her who does not overlook her proper minute; but assigns to a long despair the woman who is well offered, and neglects that proposal. May occasion attend your charms, and your charms slip no occasion. Give me, I say, an account of the progress of your forces at our next meeting; and you shall hear what I think of my new condition.   I shall meet my future spouse this moment.   Farewell.   Live in just terror of the dreadful words: 'She was.'

35.   *Conjugal coolness: Osmyn and Elmira*

The fate and character of the inconstant Osmyn is a just excuse for the little notice taken by his widow of his departure out of this life, which was equally troublesome to Elmira, his faithful spouse, and to himself.   That life passed between them after this manner, is the reason the town has just now received a lady with all that gaiety, after having been a relict but three months, which other women hardly assume under fifteen after such a disaster. Elmira is the daughter of a rich and worthy citizen, who gave her to Osmyn with a portion which might have obtained her an alliance with our noblest houses, and fixed her in the eye of the world, where her story had not been now to be related; for her good qualities had made her the object of universal esteem among the polite part of mankind, from whom she has been banished and immured until the death of her gaoler.   It is now full fifteen years since that beauteous lady was given into the hands of the happy Osmyn, who, in the sense of all the world, received at that time a present more valuable than the possession of both the Indies.   She was then in her early bloom, with an understanding and discretion very little inferior to the most experienced matrons.   She was not beholden to the charms of her sex that her company was preferable to any Osmyn could meet with abroad; for were all she said considered without regard to her being a woman, it might stand the examination of the severest judges.   She had all the beauty of her own sex, with all the conversation-accomplishments of ours.   But Osmyn very soon grew surfeited with the charms of her person by possession, and of her mind by want of taste; for he was one of that loose sort of men, who have but one reason for setting any value upon the fair sex; who consider even brides but as new women, and consequently neglect them when they cease to be such. All the merit of Elmira could not prevent her becoming a mere wife within few months after her nuptials; and Osmyn had so little relish for her conversation that he complained of the advantages of it. 'My spouse,' said he to one of his companions, 'is so very discreet, so good, so virtuous, and I know not what, that I think her person is rather the object of esteem than of love; and there is such a thing as a merit which causes rather distance than passion.' But there being no medium in the state of matrimony, their life began to take the usual gradations to become the most irksome of all beings. They grew in the first place very complaisant; and having at heart a certain knowledge that they were indifferent to each other, apologies were made for every little circumstance which they thought betrayed their mutual coldness. This lasted but few months, when they showed a difference of opinion in every trifle; and, as a sign of certain decay of affection, the word 'perhaps' was introduced in all their discourse. 'I have a mind to go to the park,' says she; 'but perhaps, my dear, you will want the coach on some other occasion.' He would very willingly carry her to the play: 'but perhaps she had rather go to Lady Centaur's and play at ombre.' They were both persons of good discerning, and soon found that they mortally hated each other, by their manner of hiding it. Certain it is, that there are some genios [1] which are not capable of pure affection, and a man is born with talents for it as much as for poetry or any other science.

Osmyn began too late to find the imperfection of his own heart; and used all the methods in the world to correct it, and argue himself into return of desire and passion for his wife, by the contemplation of her excellent qualities, his great obligations to her, and the high value he saw all the world except himself did put upon her. But such is man's unhappy condition, that though the weakness of the heart has a prevailing power over the strength of the head, yet the strength of the head has but

small force against the weakness of the heart. Osmyn
therefore struggled in vain to revive departed desire; and
for that reason resolved to retire to one of his estates in
the country and pass away his hours of wedlock in the
noble diversions of the field; and in the fury of a disappointed lover, made an oath to leave neither stag, fox,
nor hare living, during the days of his wife. Besides that
country sports would be an amusement, he hoped also
that his spouse would be half killed by the very sense of
seeing this town no more, and would think her life ended
as soon as she left it. He communicated his design to
Elmira, who received it, as now she did all things, like a
person too unhappy to be relieved or afflicted by the
circumstance of place. This unexpected resignation made
Osmyn resolve to be as obliging to her as possible; and if
he could not prevail upon himself to be kind, he took a
resolution at least to act sincerely and communicate frankly
to her the weakness of his temper, to excuse the indifference
of his behaviour. He disposed his household in the way
to Rutland, so as he and his lady travelled only in the
coach for the conveniency of discourse.

They had not gone many miles out of town, when
Osmyn spoke to this purpose: 'My dear, I believe I look
quite as silly now I am going to tell you I do not love you
as when I first told you I did. We are now going into the
country together, with only one hope for making this life
agreeable, survivorship. Desire is not in our power; mine
is all gone for you. What shall we do to carry it with
decency to the world, and hate one another with discretion?'

The lady answered, without the least observation on the
extravagance of the speech: 'My dear, you have lived most
of your days in a court, and I have not been wholly unacquainted with that sort of life. In courts, you see good
will is spoken with great warmth, ill will covered with
great civility. Men are long in civilities to those they
hate, and short in expressions of kindness to those they
love. Therefore, my dear, let us be well-bred still; and
it is no matter, as to all who see us, whether we love or
hate. And to let you see how much you are beholden

to me for my conduct, I have both hated and despised you, my dear, this half year; and yet neither in language nor behaviour has it been visible but that I loved you tenderly. Therefore, as I know you go out of town to divert life in pursuit of beasts, and conversation with men just above them; so, my life, from this moment I shall read all the learned cooks who have ever writ; study broths, plasters, and conserves, until from a fine lady I become a notable woman. We must take our minds a note or two lower or we shall be tortured by jealousy or anger. Thus I am resolved to kill all keen passions by employing my mind on little subjects, and lessening the uneasiness of my spirit; while you, my dear, with much ale, exercise, and ill company, are so good as to endeavour to be as contemptible as it is necessary for my quiet I should think you.'

At Rutland they arrived, and lived with great, but secret, impatience for many successive years, until Osmyn thought of an happy expedient to give their affairs a new turn. One day he took Elmira aside, and spoke as follows: 'My dear, you see here the air is so temperate and serene; the rivulets, the groves, and soil, so extremely kind to nature, that we are stronger and firmer in our health since we left the town; so that there is no hope of a release in this place. But if you will be so kind as to go with me to my estate in the Hundreds of Essex, it is possible some kind damp may one day or other relieve us. If you will condescend to accept of this offer, I will add that whole estate to your jointure in this county.'

Elmira, who was all goodness, accepted the offer, removed accordingly, and has left her spouse in that place to rest with his fathers.

This is the real figure in which Elmira ought to be beheld in this town; and not thought guilty of an indecorum in not professing the sense, or bearing the habit of sorrow, for one who robbed her of all the endearments of life, and gave her only common civility instead of complacency of manners, dignity of passion, and that constant assemblage of soft desires and affections which all feel who love, but none can express.

36.   *Clerical bellowing at Saint Paul's*

MR. BICKERSTAFF,

It being mine, as well as the opinion of many others,
that your papers are extremely well fitted to reform any
irregular or indecent practice, I present the following as
one which requires your correction.   Myself, and a great
many good people who frequent the divine service at
Saint Paul's, have been a long time scandalized by the
imprudent conduct of Stentor [1] in that cathedral.   This
gentleman, you must know, is always very exact and
zealous in his devotion, which I believe nobody blames;
but then he is accustomed to roar and bellow so terribly
loud in the responses that he frightens even us of the
congregation who are daily used to him; and one of our
petty canons, a punning Cambridge scholar, calls his way
of worship a bull-offering.   His harsh untunable pipe is
no more fit than a raven's to join with the music of a choir;
yet nobody having been enough his friend, I suppose, to
inform him of it, he never fails, when present, to drown
the harmony of every hymn and anthem by an inundation
of sound beyond that of the Bridge [2] at the ebb of the tide
or the neighbouring lions in the anguish of their hunger.[3]
This is a grievance which, to my certain knowledge,
several worthy people desire to see redressed; and if by
inserting this epistle in your paper, or by representing the
matter your own way, you can convince Stentor that dis-
cord in a choir is the same sin that schism is in the church
in general, you would lay a great obligation upon us and
make some atonement for certain of your paragraphs
which have not been highly approved by us.   I am,
                    Sir,
                          Your most humble servant,
                                GEOFFREY CHANTICLEER.

St. Paul's Churchyard, Aug. 11.

It is wonderful there should be such a general lamenta-
tion, and the grievance so frequent, and yet the offender

never know anything of it. I have received the following letter from my kinsman at the Heralds' Office, near the same place.

DEAR COUSIN,

This office, which has had its share in the impartial justice of your censures, demands at present your vindication of their rights and privileges. There are certain hours when our young Heralds are exercised in the faculties of making proclamation, and other vociferations, which of right belong to us only to utter. But at the same hours, Stentor in Saint Paul's church, in spite of the coaches, carts, London cries, and all other sounds between us, exalts his throat to so high a key that the most noisy of our order is utterly unheard. If you please to observe upon this, you will ever oblige, etc.

There have been communicated to me some other ill consequences from the same cause; as, the overturning of coaches by sudden starts of the horses as they passed that way, women pregnant frightened, and heirs to families lost; which are public disasters, though arising from a good intention. But it is hoped, after this admonition, that Stentor will avoid an act of so great supererogation, as singing without a voice.

But I am diverted from prosecuting Stentor's reformation by an account that the two faithful lovers, Lisander and Coriana, are dead; for no longer ago than the first day of the last month they swore eternal fidelity to each other, and to love until death. Ever since that time Lisander has been twice a day at the chocolate-house, visits in every circle, is missing four hours in four and twenty, and will give no account of himself. These are undoubted proofs of the departure of a lover; and consequently Coriana is also dead as a mistress. I have written to Stentor to give this couple three calls at the church door, which they must hear if they are living within the Bills of Mortality; and if they do not answer at that time, they are from that moment added to the number of my defunct.

37.   *Charles XII of Sweden defeated by Peter the Great*
('Hide, blushing Glory, hide Pultowa's day')

We have repeated advices of the entire defeat of the
Swedish army near Pultowa [1] on the twenty-seventh of
June, and letters from Berlin give the following account
of the remains of the Swedish army since the battle: Prince
Menzikoff, being ordered to pursue the victory, came up
with the Swedish army, which was left to the command of
General Lewenhaupt, on the thirtieth of June on the banks
of the Borysthenes; whereupon he sent General Lewenhaupt a summons to submit himself to his present fortune.
Lewenhaupt immediately dispatched three general officers
to that prince to treat about a capitulation; but the Swedes,
though they consisted of fifteen thousand men, were in so
great want of provision and ammunition that they were
obliged to surrender themselves at discretion.   His Czarish
Majesty dispatched an express to General Goltz with an
account of these particulars, and also with instructions to
send out detachments of his cavalry to prevent the King
of Sweden's joining his army in Poland.   That prince made
his escape with a small party by swimming over the
Borysthenes; and it was thought he designed to retire into
Poland by the way of Volhynia. [2]

38.   *Borrowed from La Bruyère*

I have heard it has been advised by a Diocesan to his
inferior clergy, that, instead of broaching opinions of their
own and uttering doctrines which may lead themselves
and hearers into error, they would read some of the most
celebrated sermons, printed by others, for the instruction
of their congregations. [1]   In imitation of such preachers
at second hand, I shall transcribe from Bruyère one of the
most elegant pieces of raillery and satire which I have ever
read. [2]   He describes the French, as if speaking of a people
not yet discovered, in the air and style of a traveller.
'I have heard talk of a country where the old men are

gallant, polite, and civil: the young men, on the contrary, stubborn, wild, without either manners or civility. They are free from passion for women at that age when in other countries they begin to feel it; and prefer beasts, victuals, and ridiculous amours before them. Amongst these people, he is sober who is never drunk with anything but wine; the too frequent use of it having rendered it flat and insipid to them. They endeavour by brandy, and other strong liquors, to quicken their taste, already extinguished, and want nothing to complete their debauches but to drink *aqua fortis*. The women of that country hasten the decay of their beauty by their artifices to preserve it. They paint their cheeks, eyebrows, and shoulders, which they lay open, together with their breasts, arms, and ears, as if they were afraid to hide those places which they think will please, and never think they show enough of them. The physiognomies of the people of that country are not at all neat, but confused and embarrassed with a bundle of strange hair, which they prefer before their natural. With this they weave something to cover their heads, which descends down half-way their bodies, hides their features, and hinders you from knowing men by their faces. This nation has, besides this, their God and their King. The Grandees go every day at a certain hour to a temple they call a Church; at the upper end of that temple there stands an altar consecrated to their God where the priest celebrates some mysteries which they call holy, sacred, and tremendous. The great men make a vast circle at the foot of the altar, standing with their backs to the priests and the holy mysteries, and their faces erected towards their King, who is seen on his knees upon a throne, and to whom they seem to direct the desires of their hearts and all their devotion. However, in this custom there is to be remarked a sort of subordination; for the people appear adoring their Prince, and their Prince adoring God. The inhabitants of this region call it ——. It is from forty-eight degrees of latitude, and more than eleven hundred leagues by sea, from the Iroquois and Hurons.'

39. *Russia not unacquainted with honour and humanity*

We have undoubted intelligence of the defeat of the
King of Sweden; and that prince, who for some years had
hovered like an approaching tempest and was looked up
at by all the nations of Europe, which seemed to expect
their fate according to the course he should take, is now,
in all probability, an unhappy exile without the common
necessaries of life.[1]   His Czarish Majesty treats his prisoners
with great gallantry and distinction.   Count Rhensfeildt
has had particular marks of His Majesty's esteem, for his
merit and services to his master; but Count Piper, whom
His Majesty believes author of the most violent counsels
into which his prince entered, is disarmed, and entertained
accordingly.   That decisive battle was ended at nine in
the morning; and all the Swedish generals dined with the
Czar that very day, and received assurances that they
should find Muscovy was not unacquainted with the laws
of honour and humanity.

40. *Sharpers represented as hounds*

Aesop has gained to himself an immortal renown for
figuring the manners, desires, passions, and interests of
men, by fables of beasts and birds.   I shall, in my future
accounts of our modern heroes and wits, vulgarly called
'sharpers,' imitate the method of that delightful moralist;
and think I cannot represent those worthies more naturally
than under the shadow of a pack of dogs; for this set of
men are like them, made up of finders, lurchers, and
setters.   Some search for the prey, others pursue, others
take it; and if it be worth it, they all come in at the death,
and worry the carcass.   It would require a most exact
knowledge of the field and the harbours where the deer
lie, to recount all the revolutions in the chase. . . .   The

present race of terriers and hounds would starve were it
not for the enchanted Actaeon, who has kept the whole
pack for many successions of hunting seasons. Actaeon
has long tracts of rich soil; but had the misfortune in his
youth to fall under the power of sorcery, and has been
ever since, some parts of the year, a deer, and in some
parts a man. While he is a man, such is the force of
magic, he no sooner grows to such a bulk and fatness, but
he is again turned into a deer, and hunted until he is lean;
upon which he returns to his human shape. Many arts
have been tried, and many resolutions taken by Actaeon
himself, to follow such methods as would break the enchantment; but all have hitherto proved ineffectual. I have
therefore, by midnight watchings and much care, found
out that there is no way to save him from the jaws of his
hounds but to destroy the pack, which, by astrological
prescience, I find I am destined to perform. For which
end I have sent out my Familiar, to bring me a list of all
the places where they are harboured that I may know
where to sound my horn and bring them together, and
take an account of their haunts and their marks against
another opportunity.

41. *Infallible method of prevailing with the Fair*

There is not anything in nature so extravagant, but that
you will find one man or other that shall practise or maintain it; otherwise Harry Spondee could not have made so
long an harangue as he did here this evening, concerning
the force and efficacy of well-applied nonsense. Among
ladies, he positively averred it was the most prevailing
part of eloquence; and had so little complaisance as to
say a woman is never taken by her reason but always by
her passion. He proceeded to assert, the way to move
that was only to astonish her. 'I know,' continued he, 'a
very late instance of this; for being by accident in the room
next to Strephon, I could not help overhearing him as he

made love to a certain great lady's woman. The true method in your application to one of this second rank of understanding, is not to elevate and surprise, but rather to elevate and amaze. Strephon is a perfect master in this kind of persuasion. His way is to run over with a soft air a multitude of words, without meaning or connection; but such as do each of them apart give a pleasing idea, though they have nothing to do with each other as he assembles them. After the common phrases of salutation and making his entry into the room, I perceived he had taken the fair nymph's hand, and kissing it said: "Witness to my happiness ye groves! Be still ye rivulets! O woods, caves, fountains, trees, dales, mountains, hills, and streams! O fairest! Could you love me?"

'To which I overheard her answer, with a very pretty lisp: "O Strephon, you are a dangerous creature. Why do you talk these tender things to me? But you men of witt——"

'"Is it then possible," said the enamoured Strephon, "that she regards my sorrows? O pity, thou balmy cure to an heart overloaded! If rapture, solicitation, soft desire, and pleasing anxiety—— But still I live in the most afflicting of all circumstances, doubt—— Cannot my charmer name the place and moment?

> There all those joys insatiably to prove,
> With which rich beauty feeds the glutton, Love.

'"Forgive me, madam, it is not that my heart is weary of its chain, but——"

'This incoherent stuff was answered by a tender sigh: "Why do you put your wit to a weak woman?"

'Strephon saw he had made some progress in her heart, and pursued it by saying that he would certainly wait upon her at such an hour near Rosamond's pond [1]; and then—"The sylvan deities, and rural powers of the place, sacred and inviolable to Love; Love, the mover of all noble hearts," should hear his vows repeated by the streams and echoes.

'The assignation was accordingly made. This style he

calls the unintelligible method of speaking his mind; and I will engage, had this gallant spoken plain English she had never understood him half so readily; for we may take it for granted that he will be esteemed as a very cold lover who discovers to his mistress that he is in his senses.'

42. More girding at the Train-bands

'*Mars Triumphant; or, London's Glory:* Being the whole art of encampment, with the method of embattling armies, marching them off, posting the officers, forming hollow squares, and the various ways of paying the salute with the half-pike; as it was performed by the trained-bands of London this year, one thousand seven hundred and nine, in that nursery of Bellona, the Artillery-ground.[1] Wherein you have a new method how to form a strong line of foot, with large intervals between each platoon, very useful to prevent the breaking in of horse. A civil way of performing the military ceremony; wherein the major alights from his horse, and at the head of his company salutes the lieutenant-colonel; and the lieutenant-colonel, to return the compliment, courteously dismounts, and after the same manner salutes his major. Exactly as it was performed, with abundance of applause, on the fifth of July last. Likewise an account of a new invention, made use of in the red regiment, to quell mutineering captains; with several other things alike useful for the public. To which is added an appendix by Major Touch-hole, proving the method of discipline now used in our armies to be very defective: with an essay towards an amendment. Dedicated to the lieutenant-colonel of the first regiment.'

43. Beauty not what it was; with an excursion to the Artillery-ground

There has been lately sent me a much harder question than was ever yet put to me since I professed astrology;

to wit, how far, and to what age, women ought to make their beauty their chief concern. The regard and care of their faces and persons are as variously to be considered, as their complexions themselves differ; but if one may transgress against the careful practice of the fair sex so much as to give an opinion against it, I humbly presume that less care, better applied, would increase their empire and make it last as long as life. Whereas now, from their own example, we take our esteem of their merit from it; for it is very just that she who values herself only on her beauty should be regarded by others on no other consideration.

There is certainly a liberal and pedantic education among women, as well as men; and the merit lasts accordingly. She therefore that is bred with freedom, and in good company, considers men according to their respective characters and distinctions; while she that is locked up from such observations will consider her father's butler, not as a butler but as a man. In like manner, when men converse with women, the well-bred and intelligent are looked upon with an observation suitable to their different talents and accomplishments, without respect to their sex; while a mere woman can be observed under no consideration but that of a woman; and there can be but one reason for placing any value upon her, or losing time in her company. Wherefore I am of opinion that the rule for pleasing long is to obtain such qualifications as would make them so, were they not women.

Let the beauteous Cleomira then show us her real face, and know that every stage of life has its peculiar charms, and that there is no necessity for fifty to be fifteen. That childish colouring of her cheeks is now as ungraceful as that shape would have been when her face wore its real countenance. She has sense, and ought to know that if she will not follow nature, nature will follow her. Time then has made that person which had, when I visited her grandfather, an agreeable bloom, sprightly air, and soft utterance, now no less graceful in a lovely aspect, an awful manner, and maternal wisdom. But her heart was so set upon her first character, that she neglects and repines at her present; not that she is against a more staid conduct in others, for she recommends gravity, circumspection, and severity of countenance to her daughter. Thus, against all chronology, the girl is the sage, the mother the fine lady.

But these great evils proceed from an unaccountable wild method in the education of the better half of the world, the women. We have no such thing as a standard for good breeding. I was the other day at my Lady Wealthy's, and asked one of her daughters how she did. She answered, she never conversed with men. The same day I visited at Lady Plantwell's, and asked her daughter the same question. She answers: 'What is that to you, you old thief?' and gives me a slap on the shoulders.

I defy any man in England, except he knows the family before he enters, to be able to judge whether he shall be agreeable or not, when he comes into it. You find either some odd old woman, who is permitted to rule as long as she lives, in hopes of her death, and to interrupt all things; or some impertinent young woman who will talk sillily upon the strength of looking beautifully. I will not answer for it, but it may be that I (like all other old fellows) have a fondness for the fashions and manners which prevailed when I was young and in fashion myself. But certain it is that the taste of grace and beauty is very much lowered. The fine women they show me nowadays are at best but pretty girls to me who have seen Sacharissa, when all the world repeated the poems she inspired; and Villaria, when a youthful king was her subject. The Things you follow, and make songs on now, should be sent to knit, or sit down to bobbins or bone-lace.[1] They are indeed neat, and so are their sempstresses; they are pretty, and so are their handmaids. But that graceful motion, that awful mien, and that winning attraction, which grew upon them from the thoughts and conversations they met with in my time, are now no more seen. They tell me I am old: I am glad I am so; for I do not like your present young ladies.

Those among us who set up for anything of decorum do so mistake the matter that they offend on the other side. Five young ladies, who are of no small fame for their great severity of manners and exemplary behaviour, would lately go nowhere with their lovers but to an organ-loft in a church; where they had a cold treat and some few opera songs, to their great refreshment and edification. Whether these prudent persons had not been as much so if this had been done at a tavern, is not very hard to determine. It is such silly starts and incoherences as these, which undervalue the beauteous sex, and puzzle us in our choice of sweetness of temper and simplicity of manners, which are the only lasting charms of woman. But I must leave this important subject, at present, for some matters which press for publication; as you will observe in the following letter:

DEAR SIR,

It is natural for distant relations to claim kindred with a rising family; though at this time, zeal to my country, not interest, calls me out. The city forces being shortly to take the field, all good Protestants would be pleased that their arms and valour should shine with equal lustre. A council of war was lately held, the Honourable Colonel Mortar being president. After many debates it was unanimously resolved, That Major Blunder, a most expert officer, should be detached for Birmingham to buy arms, and to prove his firelocks on the spot, as well to prevent expense as disappointment in the day of battle. The major, being a person of consummate experience, was invested with a discretionary power. He knew from ancient story, that securing the rear, and making a glorious retreat, was the most celebrated piece of conduct. Accordingly such measures were taken to prevent surprise in the rear of his arms, that even Pallas herself, in the shape of rust, could not invade them. They were drawn into close order, firmly embodied, and arrived securely without touch-holes. Great and national actions deserve popular applause; and as praise is no expense to the public, therefore, dearest kinsman, I communicate this to you, as well to oblige this nursery of heroes, as to do justice to my native country. I am.

Your most

Affectionate kinsman,

OFFSPRING TWIG.

London, Aug. 26, Artillery-ground.

'A war-horse, belonging to one of the colonels of the Artillery, to be let or sold. He may be seen adorned with ribands, and set forth to the best advantage, the next training day.'

44. *More about the Sharpers*

This place being frequented by persons of condition, I am desired to recommend a dog-kennel to any who shall want a pack. It lies not far from Suffolk Street, and is kept by two who were formerly dragoons in the French service; but left plundering for the more orderly life of keeping dogs; besides that, according to their expectation, they find it more profitable, as well as more conducing to the safety of their skin, to follow this trade than the beat of drum. Their residence is very convenient for the dogs to whelp in and bring up a right breed to follow the scent. The most eminent of the kennel are bloodhounds, which lead the van, and are as follow:

A list of the dogs

Jowler, of a right Irish breed, called Captain.

Rockwood, of French race, with long hair, by the courtesy of England called also Captain.

Pompey, a tall hound, kennelled in a convent in France, and knows a rich soil.

These two last hunt in couple, and are followed by

Ringwood, a French black whelp of the same breed, a fine open-mouthed dog; and an old sick hound, always in kennel, but of the true blood, with a good nose, French breed.

There is also an Italian greyhound, with good legs, and knows perfectly the ground from Ghent to Paris.

Ten setting-dogs, right English.

Four mongrels, of the same nation;

And twenty whelps, fit for any game.

It were to be wished that the curs were disposed of, for it is a very great nuisance to have them tolerated in cities. That of London takes care, that the common hunt, assisted by the serjeants and bailiffs, expel them wherever they are found within the walls; though it is said some private families keep them, to the destruction of their neighbours. But it is desired that all who know of any of these curs, or have been bit by them, would send me their marks, and the houses where they are harboured; and I do not doubt but I shall alarm the people so well as to have them used like mad dogs wherever they appear. In the meantime, I advise all such as entertain this kind of vermin, that if they give me timely notice that their dogs are dismissed, I shall let them go unregarded; otherwise am obliged to admonish my fellow subjects in this behalf, and instruct them how to avoid being worried when they are going about their lawful professions and callings. There was lately a young gentleman bit to the bone; who has now indeed recovered his health, but is as lean as a skeleton. It grieved my heart to see a gentleman's son run among the hounds; but he is, they tell me, as fleet and as dangerous as the best of the pack.

45. *The Battle of Malplaquet* [1]

It will be necessary for understanding the greatness of the action, and the several motions made in the time of the engagement, that you have in your mind an idea of the place. The two armies on the eleventh instant were both drawn up before the woods of Dour, Blaugies, Sart, and Jansart; the army of the Prince of Savoy on the right before that of Blaugies; the forces of Great Britain in the centre on his left; those of the High Allies, before the wood Sart, as well as a large interval of plain ground, and Jansart, on the left of the whole. The enemy were entrenched in the paths of the woods, and drawn up behind two entrenchments over against them, opposite to the armies of the Duke of Marlborough and Prince Eugene. There were also lines entrenched in the plains over against the army of the States. This was the posture of the French and Confederate forces when the signal was given, and the whole line moved on to the charge.

The Dutch army, commanded by the Prince of Hesse, attacked with the most undaunted bravery, and after a very obstinate resistance forced the first entrenchment of the enemy in the plain between Sart and Jansart; but were repulsed in their attack on the second with great slaughter on both sides. The Duke of Marlborough, while this was transacting on the left, had with very much difficulty marched through Sart and beaten the enemy from the several entrenchments they had thrown up in it. As soon as the duke had marched into the plain, he observed the main body of the enemy drawn up and entrenched in the front of his army. This situation of the enemy, in the ordinary course of war, is usually thought an advantage hardly to be surmounted; and might appear impracticable to any but that army which had just overcome greater difficulties. The duke commanded the troops to form, but to forbear charging until further order. In the meantime he visited the left of our line, where the troops of the States had been engaged. The slaughter on this side had been very great, and the Dutch incapable of making further progress except they were suddenly reinforced. The right of our line was attacked soon after their coming upon the plain; but they drove back the enemy with such bravery that the victory began to incline to the Allies by the precipitate retreat of the French to their works, from whence they were immediately beaten. The duke, upon observing this advantage on the right, commanded the Earl of Orkney to march with a sufficient number of battalions to force the enemy from their entrenchments on the plain between the woods of Sart and Jansart; which being performed, the horse of the Allies marched into the plains, covered by their own foot, and forming themselves in good order, the cavalry of the enemy attempted no more but to cover the foot in their retreat. The Allies made so good use of the beginning of the victory that all their troops moved on with fresh resolution, until they saw the enemy fly before them towards Condé and Maubeuge; after whom proper detachments were sent, who made a terrible slaughter in the pursuit.

In this action it is said Prince Eugene was wounded, as also the Duke of Aremberg, and Lieutenant-General Webb. The Count of Oxenstiern, Colonel Lalo, and Sir Thomas Pendergrass were killed.

This wonderful success, obtained under all the difficulties that could be opposed in the way of an army, must be acknowledged as owing to the genius, courage, and conduct of the Duke of Marlborough, a consummate hero; who has lived not only beyond the time in which Caesar said he was arrived at a satiety of life and glory, but also been so long the subject of panegyric, that it is as hard to say anything new in his praise as to add to the merit which requires such eulogiums.

46. Coffee-house comment on the battle

I came hither this evening, and expected nothing else but mutual congratulations in the company on the late victory; but found our room, which one would have hoped to have seen full of good humour and alacrity upon so glorious an occasion, full of sour animals, inquiring into the action, in doubt of what had happened and fearful of the success of their countrymen. It is natural to believe easily what we wish heartily; and a certain rule, that they are not friends to a glad occasion who speak all they can against the truth of it; who end their argument against our happiness that they wish it otherwise. When I came into the room a gentleman was declaiming: 'If,' says he, 'we have so great and complete a victory, why have we not the names of the prisoners? Why is not an exact relation of the conduct of our generals laid before the world? Why do we not know where or whom to applaud? If we are victorious, why do we not give an account of our captives and our slain?'[1] But we are to be satisfied with general notices we are conquerors, and to believe it so. Sure this is approving the despotic way of treating the world, which we pretend to fight against, if we sit down satisfied with such contradictory accounts, which have the words of triumph, but do not bear the spirit of it.'

I whispered Mr. Greenhat[2]: 'Pray, what can that dissatisfied man be?'

'He is,' answered he, 'a character you have not yet perhaps observed. You have heard of battle-painters, have mentioned a battle-poet; but this is a battle-critic. He is a fellow that lives in a government so gentle, that though it sees him an enemy, suffers his malice because they know his impotence. He is to examine the weight of an advantage before the company will allow it.'

Greenhat was going on in his explanation when Sir George England thought fit to take up the discourse in the following manner: 'Gentlemen, the action you are in so great doubt to approve of is greater than ever has been performed in any age, and the value of it I observe from your dissatisfaction; for battle-critics are like all others. You are the more offended, the more you ought to be, and are convinced you ought to be, pleased. Had this engagement happened in the time of the old Romans, and such things been acted in their service, there would not be a foot of the wood which was pierced but had been consecrated to some deity, or made memorable by the death of him who expired in it for the sake of his country. It had been said on some monument at the entrance: "Here the Duke of Argyle[3] drew his sword, and said, 'March!' Here Webb,[4] after having an accomplished fame for gallantry, exposed himself like a common soldier.

Here Rivett, who was wounded at the beginning of the day and carried off as dead, returned to the field and received his death." Medals had been struck for our General's behaviour when he first came into the plain. Here was the fury of the action, and here the hero stood as fearless as if invulnerable. Such certainly had been the cares of that state for their own honour, and in gratitude to their heroic subjects. But the wood entrenched, the plain made more impassable than the wood, and all the difficulties opposed to the most gallant army and most intrepid leaders that ever the sun shone upon, are treated by the talk of some in this room as objections to the merit of our General and our army. But,' continued he, 'I leave all the examination of this matter, and a proper discourse on our sense of public actions, to my friend Mr. Bickerstaff; who may let beaux and gamesters rest, until he has examined into the reasons of men's being malcontents, in the only nation that suffers professed enemies to breathe in open air.'

47. *Eloquence and action, with particular reference to the Clergy of Great Britain*

The subject of the discourse this evening was eloquence and graceful action. Lysander, who is something particular in his way of thinking and speaking, told us a man could not be eloquent without action; for the deportment of the body, the turn of the eye, and an apt sound to every word that is uttered must all conspire to make an accomplished speaker. Action in one that speaks in public is the same thing as a good mien in ordinary life. Thus, as a certain insensibility in the countenance recommends a sentence of humour and jest, so it must be a very lively consciousness that gives grace to great sentiments. The jest is to be a thing unexpected; therefore your undesigning manner is a beauty in expressions of mirth; but when you are to talk on a set subject, the more you are moved yourself, the more you will move others.

But of all the people on the earth there are none who puzzle me so much as the clergy of Great Britain, who are, I believe, the most learned body of men now in the world; and yet this art of speaking, with the proper ornaments of voice and gesture, is wholly neglected among them; and I will engage, were a deaf man to behold the greater part of them preach, he would rather think they were reading the contents only of some discourse they intended to make, than actually in the body of an oration, even when they are upon matters of such a nature as one would believe it were impossible to think of without emotion.

I own there are exceptions to this general observation, and that the dean we heard the other day together is an orator.[1] He has so much regard to his congregation that he commits to his memory what he is to say to them; and has so soft and graceful a behaviour that it must attract your attention. His person, it is to be confessed, is no small recommendation; but he is to be highly commended for not losing that advantage; and adding to the propriety of speech, which might pass the criticism of Longinus, an action which would have been approved by Demosthenes. He has a peculiar force in his way, and has many of his audience who could not be intelligent hearers of his discourse, were there not explanation as well as grace in his action. This art of his is used with the most exact and honest skill. He never attempts your passions until he has convinced your reason. All the objections which he can form are laid open and dispersed before he uses the least vehemence in his sermon; but when he thinks he has your head, he very soon wins your heart; and never pretends to show the beauty of holiness until he hath convinced you of the truth of it.

Would every one of our clergymen be thus careful to recommend truth and virtue in their proper figures, and show so much concern for them as to give them all the additional force they were able, it is not possible that nonsense should have so many hearers as you find it has in dissenting congregations, for no reason in the world but because it is spoken extempore; for ordinary minds are wholly governed by their eyes and ears, and there is no way to come at their hearts but by power over their imaginations.

There is my friend and merry companion Daniel.[2] He knows a great deal better than he speaks, and can form a proper discourse as well as any orthodox neighbour. But he knows very well that to bawl out: 'My beloved!' and the words 'Grace! Regeneration! Sanctification! A new light! The day! The day! Ay, my beloved, the day, or rather, the night! The night is coming! And judgment will come, when we least think of it!' And so forth. He knows to be vehement is the only way to come at his audience. Daniel, when he sees my friend Greenhat come in, can give a good hint, and cry out: 'This is only for the saints! the regenerated!' By this force of action, though mixed with all the incoherence and ribaldry imaginable, Daniel can laugh at his diocesan, and grow fat by voluntary subscription, while the parson of the parish goes to law for half his dues. Daniel will tell you: 'It is not the shepherd, but the sheep with the bell, which the flock follows.'

Another thing, very wonderful this learned body should omit, is learning to read; which is a most necessary part of eloquence in one who is to serve at the altar; for there is no man but must be sensible that the lazy tone and inarticulate sound of our common readers, depreciates the most proper form of words that were ever extant in any nation or language, to speak their own wants, or His power from whom we ask relief.

There cannot be a greater instance of the power of action than in little parson Dapper, who is the common relief to all the lazy pulpits in town. This smart youth has a very good memory, a quick eye, and a clean handkerchief. Thus equipped, he opens his text, shuts his book fairly, shows he has no notes in his Bible, opens both palms, and shows all is fair there too. Thus, with a decisive air, my young man goes on without hesitation; and though from the beginning to the end of his pretty discourse he has not used one proper gesture, yet at the conclusion the churchwarden pulls his gloves from off his hands: 'Pray, who is this extraordinary young man?' Thus the force of action is such that it is more prevalent, even when improper, than all the reason and argument in the world without it.

This gentleman concluded his discourse by saying: 'I do not doubt but if our preachers would learn to speak, and our readers to read, within six months' time we should not have a dissenter within a mile of a church in Great Britain.'

48. *Wealth and Gentility*

I have a letter from a young fellow who complains to me that he was bred a mercer, and is now just out of his time; but unfortunately (for he has no manner of education suitable to his present estate) an uncle has left him one thousand pounds per annum. The young man is sensible that he is so spruce that he fears he shall never be genteel as long as he lives; but applies himself to me to know what method to take to help his air and be a fine gentleman.

He says that several of those ladies who were formerly his customers visit his mother on purpose to fall in his way, and fears he shall be obliged to marry against his will: 'For,' says he, 'if any one of them should ask me, I shall not be able to deny her. I am,' says he further, 'utterly at a loss to deal with them; for though I was the most pert creature in the world when I was foreman, and could hand a woman of the first quality to her coach as well as her own gentleman usher, I am now quite out of my way, and speechless in their company. They commend my modesty to my face. No one scruples to say I should certainly make the best husband in the world, a man of my sober education. Mrs. Would-be watches all opportunities to be alone with me. Therefore, good Mr. Bickerstaff, here are my writings enclosed; if you can find any flaw in my title, so as it may go to the next heir, who goes to St. James's coffee-house, and

White's, and could enjoy it, I should be extremely well pleased with two thousand pounds to set up my trade, and live in a way I know I should become, rather than be laughed at all my life among too good company. If you could send for my cousin, and persuade him to take the estate on these terms, and let nobody know it, you would extremely oblige me.'

Upon first sight, I thought this a very whimsical proposal; however, upon more mature consideration, I could not but admire the young gentleman's prudence and good sense; for there is nothing so irksome as living in a way a man knows he does not become. I consulted Mr. Obadiah Greenhat on this occasion, and he is so well pleased with the man that he has half a mind to take the estate himself; but upon second thoughts he proposed this expedient: 'I should be very willing,' said he, 'to keep the estate where it is, if we could make the young man any way easy; therefore I humbly propose he should take to drinking for one half-year, and make a sloven of him, and from thence begin his education anew. For it is a maxim that one who is ill taught is in a worse condition than he who is wholly ignorant; therefore a spruce mercer is further off the air of a fine gentleman than a downright clown. To make our patient anything better, we must unmake him what he is.' I indeed proposed to flux [1] him, but Greenhat answered, that if he recovered, he would be as prim and feat [2] as ever he was. Therefore he would have it his way, and our friend is to drink until he is carbuncled and tun-bellied; after which we will send him down to smoke and be buried with his ancestors in Derbyshire. I am indeed desirous he should have his life in the estate, because he has such a just sense of himself and his abilities as to know that it is an unhappiness to him to be a man of fortune.

This youth seems to understand that a gentleman's life is that of all others the hardest to pass through with propriety of behaviour; for though he has a support without art or labour, yet his manner of enjoying that circumstance is a thing to be considered; and you see among

men, who are honoured with the common appellation of
gentlemen, so many contradictions to that character that
it is the utmost ill fortune to bear it; for which reason I
am obliged to change the circumstances of several about
this town.   Harry Lacker is so very exact in his dress that
I shall give his estate to his younger brother, and make
him a dancing-master.   Nokes Lightfoot is so nimble, and
values himself so much upon it, that I have thoughts of
making him huntsman to a pack of beagles, and give his
land to somebody that will stay upon it.

Now I am upon the topic of becoming what we enjoy,
I forbid all persons who are not of the first quality, or
who do not bear some important office that requires so
much distinction, to go to Hyde Park with six horses; for
I cannot but esteem it the highest insolence.   Therefore
hereafter no man shall do it merely because he is able,
without any other pretension.   But, what may serve all
purposes quite as well, it shall be allowed all such who
think riches the chief distinction to appear in the Ring [3]
with two horses only, and a rent-roll hanging out of each
side of their coach.   This is a thought of Mr. Greenhat's, who designs very soon to publish a sumptuary
discourse upon the subject of equipage, wherein he will
give us rules on that subject, and assign the proper duties
and qualifications of masters and servants, as well as that
of husbands and wives; with a treatise of economy without
doors, or the complete art of appearing in the world.
This will be very useful to all who are suddenly rich, or
are ashamed of being poor.

49.   More news of Malplaquet

We have received letters from the Duke of Marlborough's
camp, which bring us further particulars of the great and
glorious victory obtained over the enemy on the eleventh
instant.   The number of the wounded and prisoners is
much greater than was expected from our first account.

The day was doubtful until after twelve of the clock; but the enemy made little resistance after their first line on the left began to give way. An exact narration of the whole affair is expected next post. The French have had two days allowed them to bury their dead, and carry off their wounded men, upon parole. Those regiments of Great Britain which suffered most are ordered into garrison, and fresh troops commanded to march into the field. The States have also directed troops to march out of the towns, to relieve those who lost so many men in attacking the second entrenchment of the French in the plain between Sart and Jansart.

50. The mending of manners. Mr. Bickerstaff's Tables of Fame

No man can conceive, until he comes to try it, how great a pain it is to be a public-spirited person. I am sure I am unable to express to the world what great anxiety I have suffered, to see of how little benefit my lucubrations have been to my fellow subjects. Men will go on in their own way, in spite of all my labour. I gave Mr. Didapper a private reprimand for wearing red-heeled shoes, and at the same time was so indulgent as to connive at him for fourteen days, because I would give him the wearing of them out; but after all this, I am informed he appeared yesterday with a new pair of the same sort. I have no better success with Mr. What-d'ye-call, as to his buttons; Stentor still roars, and box and dice rattle as loud as they did before I writ against them. Partridge walks about at noonday,[1] and Aesculapius thinks of adding a new lace to his livery. However, I must still go on in laying these enormities before men's eyes, and let them answer for going on in their practice.

My province is much larger than at first sight men would imagine, and I shall lose no part of my jurisdiction, which extends not only to futurity, but also is retrospect

to things past; and the behaviour of persons, who have
long ago acted their parts, is as much liable to my examination as that of my own contemporaries.

In order to put the whole race of mankind in their
proper distinctions, according to the opinion their cohabit-
ants conceived of them, I have with very much care, and
depth of meditation, thought fit to erect a chamber of
Fame, and established certain rules, which are to be
observed in admitting members into this illustrious
society.

In this chamber of Fame there are to be three tables,
but of different lengths; the first is to contain exactly
twelve persons; the second, twenty; and the third, an
hundred. This is reckoned to be the full number of those
who have any competent share of Fame. At the first of
these tables are to be placed in their order the twelve most
famous persons in the world; not with regard to the
things they are famous for, but according to the degree
of their fame, whether in valour, wit, or learning. Thus,
if a scholar be more famous than a soldier, he is to sit
above him. Neither must any preference be given to
virtue, if the person be not equally famous.

When the first table is filled the next in renown must
be seated at the second, and so on in like manner to the
number of twenty; as also in the same order at the third,
which is to hold an hundred. At these tables, no regard
is to be had to seniority: for if Julius Caesar shall be
judged more famous than Romulus and Scipio, he must
have the precedence. No person who has not been dead
an hundred years must be offered to a place at any of these
tables; and because this is altogether a lay society, and
that sacred persons move upon greater motives than that
of fame, no persons celebrated in Holy Writ, or any
ecclesiastical men whatsoever, are to be introduced here.

At the lower end of the room is to be a side-table for
persons of great fame, but dubious existence; such as
Hercules, Theseus, Aeneas, Achilles, Hector, and others.
But because it is apprehended that there may be great
contention about precedence, the proposer humbly desires

* D 993

the opinion of the learned towards his assistance in placing every person according to his rank, that none may have just occasion of offence.

The merits of the cause shall be judged by plurality of voices.

For the more impartial execution of this important affair, it is desired that no man will offer his favourite hero, scholar, or poet; and that the learned will be pleased to send to Mr. Bickerstaff, at Mr. Morphew's near Stationers' Hall, their several lists for the first table only, and in the order they would have them placed; after which the proposer will compare the several lists, and make another for the public, wherein every name shall be ranked according to the voices it has had. . . . In the meantime, while I wait for these lists, I am employed in keeping people in a right way, to avoid the contrary to fame and applause, to wit, blame and derision. For this end, I work upon that useful project of the penny post, by the benefit of which it is proposed that a charitable society be established; from which society there shall go every day circular letters to all parts within the bills of mortality, to tell people of their faults in a friendly and private manner whereby they may know what the world thinks of them, before it is declared to the world that they are thus faulty. This method cannot fail of universal good consequences; for it is further added that they who will not be reformed by it must be contented to see the several letters printed, which were not regarded by them, that when they will not take private reprehension they may be tried further by a public one. I am very sorry I am obliged to print the following epistles of that kind to some persons, and the more because they are of the fair sex. This went on Friday last to a very fine lady.

MADAM,

I am highly sensible that there is nothing of so tender a nature as the reputation and conduct of ladies; and that when there is the least stain got into their fame, it is hardly ever to be washed out. When I have said this, you will believe I am extremely concerned to hear at every visit I make that your manner of wearing your hair is a mere affectation of beauty, as well as that your neglect of powder has been a common evil to your sex. It is to you an advantage to show that abundance of fine tresses; but I beseech you to consider that the force of your beauty, and the imitation of you, costs Eleonora great sums of money to her tire-woman for false locks, besides what is allowed to her maid for keeping the secret that she is grey. I must take leave to add to this admonition that you are not to reign above four months and odd days longer. Therefore I must desire you to raise and friz your hair a little, for it is downright insolence to be thus handsome without art; and you will forgive me for entreating you to do now out of compassion what you must soon do out of necessity. I am, madam,

Your most obedient, and most humble servant.

This person dresses just as she did before I writ; as does also the lady to whom I addressed the following billet the same day:

MADAM,

Let me beg of you to take off the patches at the lower end of your left cheek, and I will allow two more under your left eye, which will contribute more to the symmetry of your face; except you would please to remove the ten black atoms on your ladyship's chin, and wear one large patch instead of them. If so, you may properly enough retain the three patches above-mentioned. I am, etc.

This, I thought, had all the civility and reason in the world in it; but whether my letters are intercepted, or whatever it is, the lady patches as she used to do. It is to be observed by all the charitable society, as an instruction in their epistles, that they tell people of nothing but what is in their power to mend. I shall give another instance of this way of writing: Two sisters in Essex Street are eternally gaping out of the window, as if they

knew not the value of time, or would call in companions.
Upon which I writ the following line:

DEAR CREATURES,
On the receipt of this, shut your casements.

But I went by yesterday, and found them still at the
window. What can a man do in the case, but go on and
wrap himself up in his own integrity, with satisfaction
only in this melancholy truth, that virtue is its own reward;
and that if no one is the better for his admonitions,
yet he is himself the more virtuous in that he gave those
advices?

51.   The cause of tears

SIR,
Having lately read your discourse ... wherein you
observe that there are some who fall into laughter out of
a certain benevolence in their temper, and not out of the
ordinary motive, viz. contempt, and triumph over the
imperfections of others; I have conceived a good idea of
your knowledge of mankind. And, as you have a tragi-
comic genius, I beg the favour of you to give us your
thoughts of a quite different effect, which also is caused
by other motives than what are commonly taken notice
of. What I would have you treat of is the cause of shedding
tears. I desire you would discuss it a little, with observations upon the various occasions which provoke us to
that expression of our concern, etc.

To obey this complaisant gentleman, I know no way
so short as examining the various touches of my own
bosom, on several occurrences in a long life to the evening
of which I am arrived, after as many various incidents as
anybody has met with.[1] I have often reflected that there
is a great similitude in the motions of the heart in mirth
and in sorrow; and I think the usual occasion of the
latter, as well as the former, is something which is sudden
and unexpected. The mind has not a sufficient time to

recollect its force, and immediately gushes into tears before we can utter ourselves by speech or complaint. The most notorious causes of these drops from our eyes are pity, sorrow, joy, and reconciliation.

The fair sex, who are made of man and not of earth, have a more delicate humanity than we have; and pity is the most common cause of their tears. For as we are inwardly composed of an aptitude to every circumstance of life, and everything that befalls any one person might have happened to any other of human race; self-love, and a sense of the pain we ourselves should suffer in the circumstances of any whom we pity, is the cause of that compassion. Such a reflection in the breast of a woman immediately inclines her to tears; but in a man it makes him think how such a one ought to act on that occasion, suitably to the dignity of his nature. Thus a woman is ever moved for those whom she hears lament, and a man for those whom he observes to suffer in silence. It is a man's own behaviour in the circumstances he is under which procures him the esteem of others, and not merely the affliction itself which demands our pity; for we never give a man that passion which he falls into for himself. He that commends himself never purchases our applause; nor he who bewails himself, our pity.

Going through an alley the other day, I observed a noisy impudent beggar bawl out that he was wounded in a merchantman, that he had lost his poor limbs; and showed a leg clouted up. All that passed by made what haste they could out of his sight and hearing; but a poor fellow at the end of the passage, with a rusty coat, a melancholy air, and soft voice, desired them to look upon a man not used to beg. The latter received the charity of almost everyone that went by. The strings of the heart, which are to be touched to give us compassion, are not so played on but by the finest hand. We see in tragical representations it is not the pomp of language, nor the magnificence of dress, in which the passion is wrought that touches sensible spirits; but something of a plain and simple nature which breaks in upon our souls by that sympathy which is given us for our mutual goodwill and service. . . . I remember, when I was young enough to follow the sports of the field, I have more than once rode off at the death of a deer when I have seen the animal, in an affliction which appeared human, without the least noise, let fall tears when he was reduced to extremity; and I have thought of the sorrow I saw him in, when his haunch came to the table. But our tears are not given only to objects of pity, but the mind has recourse to that relief in all occasions which give us much emotion. Thus, to be apt to shed tears is a sign of a great as well as little spirit. I have heard say, the present Pope never passes through the people, who always kneel in crowds and ask his benediction, but the tears are seen to flow from his eyes. This must proceed from an imagination that he is the father of all those people; and that he is touched with so extensive a benevolence that it breaks out into a passion of tears. You see friends, who have been long absent, transported in the same manner. A thousand little images crowd upon them at their meeting, as all the joys and griefs they have known during their separation; and in one hurry of thought, they conceive how they should have participated in those occasions; and weep because their minds are too full to wait the slow expression of words.

52. Notices

'There is lately broke loose from the London pack a very tall dangerous biter. He is now at the Bath, and it is feared will make a damnable havoc amongst the game. His manner of biting is new, and he is called the Top. He secures one die betwixt his two fingers; the other is fixed by the help of a famous wax, invented by an apothecary, since a gamester; a little of which he puts upon his forefinger, and that holds the die in the box at his devotion. Great sums have been lately won by these ways; but it is hoped that this hint of his manner of cheating will open the eyes of many who are every day imposed upon.

'There is now in the press, and will be suddenly published, a book entitled, *An Appendix to the Contempt of the
Clergy* [1]; wherein will be set forth at large that all our
dissensions are owing to the laziness of persons in the
sacred ministry, and that none of the present schisms
could have crept into the flock but by the negligence of
the pastors.   There is a digression in this treatise, proving
that the pretences made by the priesthood, from time to
time, that the church was in danger, is only a trick to make
the laity passionate for that of which they themselves
have been negligent.   The whole concludes with an ex-
hortation to the clergy to the study of eloquence, and
practice of piety, as the only method to support the
highest of all honours, that of a priest who lives and acts
according to his character.'

53.   Mr. Kidney on the late glorious victory.
Editorial remarks

There is no manner of news; but people now spend
their time in coffee-houses in reflections upon the particulars of the late glorious day, and collecting the several
parts of the action, as they are produced in letters from
private hands, or notices given to us by accounts in
public papers. A pleasant gentleman, alluding to the
great fences through which we pierced, said this evening,
the French thought themselves on the right side of the
hedge, but it proved otherwise. Mr. Kidney, who has
long conversed with, and filled tea for, the most consummate politicians, was pleased to give me an account
of this piece of ribaldry; and desired me on that occasion
to write a whole paper on the subject of valour, and
explain how that quality, which must be possessed by whole
armies, is so highly preferable in one man rather than
another; and how the same actions are but mere acts of
duty in some, and instances of the most heroic virtue in
others. He advises me not to fail, in this discourse, to

mention the gallantry of the Prince of Nassau in this last engagement; who, when a battalion made a halt in the face of the enemy, snatched the colours out of the hands of the ensign, and planted them just before the line of the enemy, calling to that battalion to take care of their colours, if they had no regard to him. Mr. Kidney has my promise to obey him in this particular on the first occasion that offers.

'Mr. Bickerstaff is now compiling exact accounts of the pay of the militia, and the commission-officers under the respective lieutenancies of Great Britain; in the first place, of those of London and Westminster; and in regard that there are no common soldiers, but all housekeepers or representatives of housekeepers in these bodies, the sums raised by the officers shall be looked into; and their fellow soldiers, or rather fellow travellers from one part of the town to the other, not defrauded of the ten pounds allowed for the subsistence of the troops.'

'Whereas not very long since, at a tavern between Fleet Bridge and Charing Cross, some certain polite gentlemen thought fit to perform the bacchanalian exercises of devotion by dancing without clothes on, after the manner of the Pre-Adamites [1]: This is to certify those persons, that there is no manner of wit or humour in the said practice; and that the beadles of the parish are to be at their next meeting, where it is to be examined whether they are arrived at want of feeling, as well as want of shame.'

'Whereas a chapel-clerk was lately taken in a garret on a flock bed with two of the fair sex, who are usually employed in sifting cinders; this is to let him know that if he persists in being a scandal both to laity and clergy, as being as it were both and neither, the names of the nymphs who were with him shall be printed; therefore he is desired, as he tenders the reputation of his ladies, to repent.'

'Mr. Bickerstaff has received information that an eminent and noble preacher in the chief congregation of Great Britain, for fear of being thought guilty of Presbyterian fervency and extempory prayer, lately read his, before sermon; but the same advices acknowledging that he made the congregation large amends by the shortness of his discourse, it is thought fit to make no further observation upon it.'

54. *Voice and gesture—their misuse in the pulpit*

The following letter, in prosecution of what I have lately asserted, has urged that matter so much better than I had that I insert it as I received it. These testimonials are customary with us learned men, and sometimes are suspected to be written by the author; but I fear no one will suspect me of this.

London, Sept. 15, 1709.

Sir,

Having read your lucubrations of the tenth instant, I cannot but entirely agree with you in your notion of the scarcity of men who can either read or speak. For my part, I have lived these thirty years in the world, and yet have observed but very few who could do either in any tolerable manner; among which few, you must understand that I reckon myself. How far eloquence, set off with the proper ornaments of voice and gesture, will prevail over the passions, and how cold and unaffecting the best oration in the world would be without them, there are two remarkable instances in the case of Ligarius, and that of Milo. Caesar had condemned Ligarius. He came indeed to hear what might be said; but thinking himself his own master, resolved not to be biased by anything Cicero could say in his behalf. But in this he was mistaken; for when the orator began to speak the hero is moved, he is vanquished, and at length the criminal absolved. ... If there be a deficiency in the speaker, there will not be a sufficient attention and regard paid to the thing spoken. But, Mr. Bickerstaff, you know that as too little action is cold, so too much is fulsome. Some indeed may think themselves accomplished speakers, for no other reason than because they can be loud and noisy; for surely Stentor must have some design in his vociferations. But, dear Mr. Bickerstaff, convince them, that as harsh and irregular sound is not harmony, so neither is banging a cushion, oratory; and therefore, in my humble opinion, a certain divine of the first order, whom I allow otherwise to be a great man, would do well to leave this off; for I think his sermons would be more persuasive if he gave his auditory less disturbance. Though I cannot say that this action would be wholly improper to a profane oration; yet, I think, in a religious assembly it gives a man too warlike, or perhaps too theatrical a figure, to be suitable to a Christian congregation. I am,

Sir,

Your humble servant, etc.

55. Sharpers again

To Isaac Bickerstaff, Esquire

September 15.

Sir,

The account you gave lately of a certain dog kennel in or near Suffolk Street, was not so punctual as to the list of the dogs, as might have been expected from a person of Mr. Bickerstaff's intelligence; for if you will dispatch Pacolet [1] thither some evening, it is ten to one but he finds, besides those you mentioned:

Towzer, a large French mongrel, that was not long ago in a tattered condition, but has now got new hair; is not fleet, but, when he grapples, bites even to the marrow.

Spring, a little French greyhound, that lately made a false trip to Tunbridge.

Sly, an old battered foxhound, that began the game in France.

Lightfoot, a fine-skinned Flanders dog, that belonged to a pack at Ghent; but having lost flesh, is gone to Paris for the benefit of the air.

With several others that in time may be worth notice.

Your Familiar will see also how anxious the keepers are about the prey, and indeed not without very good reason, for they have their share of everything; nay, not so much as a poor rabbit can be run down, but these carnivorous curs swallow a quarter of it. Some mechanics in the neighbourhood that have entered into this civil society, and who furnish part of the carrion and oatmeal for the dogs, have the skin; and the bones are picked clean by a little French shock [2] that belongs to the family, etc. I am,

Sir,

Your humble servant, etc.

I had almost forgot to tell you that *Ringwood* bites at Hampstead with false teeth.[3]

56.   Mr. Bickerstaff threatened and rebuked

I have long been, against my inclination, employed in satire, and that in prosecution of such persons who are below the dignity of the true spirit of it; such who, I fear, are not to be reclaimed by making them only ridiculous. The sharpers shall therefore have a month's time to themselves free from the observation of this paper; but I must not make a truce without letting them know that at the same time I am preparing for a more vigorous war. For a friend of mine has promised me he will employ his time in compiling such a tract before the session of the ensuing parliament, as shall lay gaming home to the bosoms of all who love their country or their families; and he doubts not but it will create an Act that shall make these rogues as scandalous as those less mischievous ones on the high road.

I have received private intimations to take care of my walks, and remember there are such things as stabs and blows.[1] But as there never was anything in this design which ought to displease a man of honour, or which was not designed to offend the rascals, I shall give myself very little concern for finding what I expected, that they would be highly provoked at these lucubrations. But though I utterly despise the pack, I must confess I am at a stand at the receipt of the following letter, which seems to be written by a man of sense and worth, who has mistaken some passage that I am sure was not levelled at him. This gentleman's complaints give me compunction, when I neglect the threats of the rascals. I cannot be in jest with the rogues any longer, since they pretend to threaten. I do not know whether I shall allow them the favour of transportation.

Sept. 13.

MR. BICKERSTAFF,

Observing you are not content with lashing the many vices of the age without illustrating each with particular characters, it is thought nothing would more contribute to the impression you design by such, than always having regard to truth. In your *Tatler* of this day I observe you allow that nothing is so tender as a lady's reputation; that a stain once got in their fame is hardly ever to be washed out. This you grant, even when you give yourself leave to trifle. If so, what caution is necessary in handling the reputation of a man, whose well-being in this life perhaps entirely depends on preserving it from any wound, which, once there received, too often become fatal and incurable! Suppose some villainous hand, through personal prejudice, transmits materials for this purpose, which you publish to the world, and afterwards become fully convinced you were imposed on; as by this time you may be of a character you have sent into the world; I say, supposing this, I would be glad to know what reparation you think ought to be made the person so injured, admitting you stood in his place. It has always been held that a generous education is the surest mark of a generous mind. The former is indeed perspicuous in all your papers; and I am persuaded, though you affect often to show the latter, yet you would not keep any measures, even of Christianity, with those who should handle you in the manner you do others. The application of all this is from your having very lately glanced at a man, under a character which, were he conscious to deserve, he would be the first to rid the world of himself; and would be more justifiable in it to all sorts of men than you in your committing such a violence on his reputation, which perhaps you may be convinced of in another manner than you deserve from him.

A man of your capacity, Mr. Bickerstaff, should have more noble views, and pursue the true spirit of satire; but I will conclude, lest I grow out of temper, and will only beg you, for your own preservation, to remember the proverb of the pitcher.

I am yours,

A. J.

The proverb of the pitcher I have no regard to; but it would be an insensibility not to be pardoned, if a man could be untouched at so warm an accusation, and that laid with so much seeming temper. All I can say to it is, that if the writer, by the same method whereby he conveyed this letter, shall give me an instance wherein I have injured any good man, or pointed at anything which is not the true object of raillery, I shall acknowledge the offence in as open a manner as the press can do it, and lay down this paper for ever.

57. Unsatisfactory conduct of a vicar

ESQUIRE BICKERSTAFF,

Finding your advice and censure to have a good effect, I desire your admonition to our vicar and schoolmaster, who, in his preaching to his auditors, stretches his jaws so wide, that instead of instructing youth, it rather frightens them. Likewise in reading prayers, he has such a careless loll, that people are justly offended at his irreverent posture; besides the extraordinary charge they are put to in sending their children to dance, to bring them off of those ill

gestures.   Another evil faculty he has, in making the
bowling-green his daily residence, instead of his church,
where his curate reads prayers every day.   If the weather
is fair, his time is spent in visiting; if cold or wet, in bed,
or at least at home, though within a hundred yards of the
church.   These, out of many such irregular practices, I
write for his reclamation.   But two or three things more
before I conclude; to wit, that generally when his curate
preaches in the afternoon, he sleeps sitting in the desk on
a hassock.   With all this he is so extremely proud that
he will go but once to the sick, except they return his
visit.

58.   A Quaker's letter

The boy says, one in a black hat left the following letter:

                                        19th of the seventh month.
FRIEND,

Being of that part of Christians whom men call Quakers,
and being a seeker of the right way, I was persuaded
yesterday to hear one of your most noted teachers; the
matter he treated was necessity of well living grounded upon
a future state.   I was attentive; but the man did not appear
in earnest.   He read his discourse, notwithstanding thy
rebukes, so heavily, and with so little air of being convinced himself, that I thought he would have slept, as I
observed many of his hearers did.   I came home unedified,
and troubled in mind.   I dipt into the Lamentations, and
from thence turning to the 34th chapter of Ezekiel,
I found these words: 'Woe be to the shepherds of Israel
that do feed themselves! should not the shepherds feed
the flocks?   Ye eat the fat, and ye clothe you with the
wool, ye kill them that are fed; but ye feed not the flock.
The diseased have ye not strengthened; neither have ye
healed that which was sick; neither have ye bound up that
which was broken; neither have ye brought again that

which was driven away; neither have ye sought that which was lost; but with force and with cruelty have ye ruled them,' etc. Now, I pray thee, friend, as thou art a man skilled in many things, tell me who is meant by the diseased, the sick, the broken, the driven away, and the lost; and whether the prophecy in this chapter be accomplished, or yet to come to pass. And thou wilt oblige thy friend, though unknown.

This matter is too sacred for this paper; but I cannot see what injury it would do to any clergyman to have it in his eye, and believe all that are taken from him by his want of industry are to be demanded of him. I dare say Favonius [1] has very few of these losses. Favonius, in the midst of a thousand impertinent assailants of the divine truths, is an undisturbed defender of them. He protects all under his care by the clearness of his understanding and the example of his life. He visits dying men with the air of a man who hopes for his own dissolution, and enforces in others a contempt of this life by his own expectation of the next. His voice and behaviour are the lively images of a composed and well-governed zeal. None can leave him for the frivolous jargon uttered by the ordinary teachers among the dissenters, but such who cannot distinguish vociferation from eloquence, and argument from railing. He is so great a judge of mankind, and touches our passions with so superior a command, that he who deserts his congregation must be a stranger to the dictates of nature, as well as those of grace.

59. Concerning the Table of Fame

I have now before me several recommendations for places at my Table of Fame: three of them are of an extraordinary nature, in which I find I am misunderstood, and shall therefore beg leave to produce them. They are from a quaker, a courtier, and a citizen.

ISAAC,

Thy lucubrations, as thou lovest to call them, have been perused by several of our friends, who have taken offence; forasmuch as thou excludest out of the brotherhood all persons who are praiseworthy for religion, we are afraid that thou wilt fill thy Table with none but heathens, and cannot hope to spy a brother there; for there are none of us who can be placed among murdering heroes, or ungodly wits; since we do not assail our enemies with the arm of flesh, nor our gainsayers with the vanity of human wisdom. If therefore thou wilt demean thyself on this occasion with a right judgment, according to the gifts that are in thee, we desire thou wilt place James Nayler at the upper end of thy Table.[1]

EZEKIEL STIFFRUMP.

In answer to my good friend Ezekiel, I must stand to it that I cannot break my rule for the sake of James Nayler; not knowing whether Alexander the Great, who is a choleric hero, would not resent his sitting at the upper end of the table with his hat on.

But to my Courtier:

SIR,

I am surprised that you lose your time in complimenting the dead when you may make your court to the living. Let me only tell you in the ear, Alexander and Caesar, as generous as they were formerly, have not now a groat to dispose of. Fill your Table with good company; I know a person of quality that shall give you one hundred pounds for a place at it. Be secret, and be rich.

Yours,
You know my hand.

This gentleman seems to have the true spirit, without the formality, of an under-courtier; therefore I shall be plain with him, and let him leave the name of his courtier and one hundred pounds in Morphew's hands. If I can take it, I will.

My citizen writes the following:

MR. ISAAC BICKERSTAFF,

SIR,

Your *Tatler*, the thirteenth of September, I am now reading, and in your list of famous men, desire you not to forget Alderman Whittington, who began the world with a cat, and died worth three hundred and fifty thousand pounds sterling, which he left to an only daughter three years after his Mayoralty. If you want my further particulars of *ditto* Alderman, daughter, or cat, let me know, and *per* first will advise the needful. Which concludes,

Your loving friend,

LEMUEL LEGER.

60. *Notice to Correspondents*

I cannot forbear advertising my correspondents that I think myself treated by some of them after too familiar a manner, and in phrases that neither become them to give, nor me to take. I shall therefore desire for the future, that if anyone returns me an answer to a letter, he will not tell me he has received the favour of my letter; but if he does not think fit to say he has received the honour of it, that he tell me in plain English, he has received my letter of such a date. I must likewise insist that he would conclude with 'I am with great respect,' or plainly, 'I am,' without further addition; and not insult me by an assurance of his being with great truth and esteem my humble servant. There is likewise another mark of superiority which I cannot bear, and therefore must inform my correspondents that I discard all faithful humble servants, and am resolved to read no letters that are not subscribed 'Your most obedient,' or 'most humble servant,' or both. These may appear niceties to vulgar minds, but they are such as men of honour and distinction must have regard to. And I very well remember a famous duel in France, where four were killed of one side, and three of the other, occasioned by a gentleman's subscribing himself a most affectionate friend.

61. *Marriage of Jenny Distaff*

My sister Jenny's lover, the honest Tranquillus, for that shall be his name, has been impatient with me to dispatch the necessary directions for his marriage; that while I am taken up with imaginary schemes, as he calls them, he might not burn with real desire and the torture of expectation. When I had reprimanded him for the ardour wherein he expressed himself, which I thought had not enough of that veneration with which the marriage-bed is to be ascended, I told him, the day of his nuptials should be on the Saturday following, which was the eighth instant. On the seventh in the evening, poor Jenny came into my chamber, and having her heart full of the great change of life from a virgin condition to that of a wife, she long sat silent. I saw she expected me to entertain her on this important subject, which was too delicate a circumstance for herself to touch upon; whereupon I relieved her modesty in the following manner: 'Sister,' said I, 'you are now going from me; and be contented that you leave the company of a talkative old man for that of a sober young one. But take this along with you, that there is no mean in the state you are entering into, but you are to be exquisitely happy or miserable, and your fortune in this way of life will be wholly of your own making. In all the marriages I have ever seen, most of which have been unhappy ones, the great cause of evil has proceeded from slight occasions; and I take it to be the first maxim in a married condition, that you are to be above trifles. When two persons have so good an opinion of each other as to come together for life, they will not differ in matters of importance, because they think of each other with respect in regard to all things of consideration that may affect them, and are prepared for mutual assistance and relief in such occurrences; but for less occasions, they have formed no resolutions, but leave their minds unprepared.

'This, dear Jenny, is the reason that the quarrel between Sir Harry Willit and his lady, which began about her squirrel, is irreconcilable.   Sir Harry was reading a grave author; she runs into his study, and in a playing humour, claps the squirrel upon the folio.   He threw the animal in a rage on the floor; she snatches it up again, calls Sir Harry a sour pedant, without good nature or good manners.   This cast him into such a rage that he threw down the table before him, kicked the book round the room; then recollected himself: "Lord, madam," said he, "why did you run into such expressions?   I was," said he, "in the highest delight with that author, when you clapped your squirrel upon my book," and smiling, added upon recollection: "I have a great respect for your favourite, and pray let us all be friends."

'My lady was so far from accepting this apology that she immediately conceived a resolution to keep him under for ever; and, with a serious air, replied: "There is no regard to be had to what a man says, who can fall into so indecent a rage and such an abject submission in the same moment, for which I absolutely despise you."   Upon which she rushed out of the room.   Sir Harry stayed some minutes behind, to think and command himself; after which he followed her into her bedchamber, where she was prostrate upon the bed, tearing her hair, and naming twenty coxcombs who would have used her otherwise.   This provoked him to so high a degree that he forbore nothing but beating her; and all the servants in the family were at their several stations listening, whilst the best man and woman, the best master and mistress, defamed each other in a way that is not to be repeated even at Billingsgate.   You know this ended in an immediate separation.   She longs to return home, but knows not how to do it; he invites her home every day, and lies with every woman he can get.   Her husband requires no submission of her; but she thinks her very return will argue she is to blame, which she is resolved to be for ever, rather than acknowledge it.

'Thus, dear Jenny, my great advice to you is, be guarded against giving or receiving little provocations. Great matters of offence I have no reason to fear either from you or your husband.' After this, we turned our discourse into a more gay style, and parted; but before we did so, I made her resign her snuff-box for ever, and half drown herself with washing away the stench of the musty.[1]

But the wedding morning arrived, and our family being very numerous, there was no avoiding the inconvenience of making the ceremony and festival more public than the modern way of celebrating them makes me approve of. The bride next morning came out of her chamber, dressed with all the art and care that Mrs. Toilet the tire-woman could bestow on her. She was on her wedding-day three and twenty. Her person is far from what we call a regular beauty; but a certain sweetness in her countenance, an ease in her shape and motion, with an unaffected modesty in her looks, had attractions beyond what symmetry and exactness can inspire without the addition of these endowments. When her lover entered the room, her features flushed with shame and joy; and the ingenuous manner, so full of passion and of awe, with which Tranquillus approached to salute her, gave me good omens of his future behaviour towards her. The wedding was wholly under my care. After the ceremony at church, I was resolved to entertain the company with a dinner suitable to the occasion, and pitched upon the 'Apollo,' at the Old Devil at Temple Bar,[2] as a place sacred to mirth, tempered with discretion, where Ben Jonson and his sons used to make their liberal meetings. Here the chief of the *Staffian* race appeared; and as soon as the company were come into that ample room, Lepidus Wagstaff began to make me compliments for choosing that place, and fell into a discourse upon the subject of pleasure and entertainment, drawn from the rules of Ben's Club, which are in gold letters over the chimney. Lepidus has a way very uncommon, and speaks on subjects on which any man else

would certainly offend, with great dexterity. He gives
us a large account of the public meetings of all the well-
turned minds who had passed through this life in ages
past, and closed his pleasing narrative with a discourse
on marriage, and a repetition of the following verses out
of Milton: [3]

> Hail, wedded Love! mysterious law! true source
> Of human offspring, sole propriety
> In paradise, of all things common else.
> By thee adult'rous lust was driven from men
> Among the bestial herds to range; by thee,
> Founded in reason, loyal, just, and pure,
> Relations dear, and all the charities
> Of father, son, and brother, first were known. . . .
> Perpetual fountain of domestic sweets,
> Whose bed is undefil'd, and chaste pronounc'd,
> Present or past, as saints or patriarchs us'd.
> Here Love his golden shafts employs; here lights
> His constant lamp, and waves his purple wings:
> Reigns here and revels; not in the bought smile
> Of harlots, loveless, joyless, unendear'd,
> Casual fruition; nor in court amours,
> Mix'd dance, or wanton mask, or midnight ball,
> Or serenate, which the starv'd lover sings
> To his proud fair, best quitted with disdain.

In these verses, all the images that can come into a
young woman's head on such an occasion are raised; but
that in so chaste and elegant a manner that the bride
thanked him for his agreeable talk, and we sat down to
dinner.

Among the rest of the company there was got in a
fellow you call a 'wag.' This ingenious person is the
usual life of all feasts and merriments, by speaking absurdities, and putting everybody of breeding and modesty
out of countenance. As soon as we sat down he drank
to the bride's diversion that night; and then made twenty
double meanings on the word 'thing.' We are the best-
bred family, for one so numerous, in this kingdom; and
indeed we should all of us have been as much out of
countenance as the bride, but that we were relieved by an
honest rough relation of ours at the lower end of the

table, who is a lieutenant of marines. The soldier and sailor had good plain sense, and saw what was wrong as well as another; he had a way of looking at his plate, and speaking aloud in an inward manner; and whenever the wag mentioned the word 'thing,' or the words, 'that same,' the lieutenant in that voice cried, 'Knock him down.' The merry man wondering, angry, and looking round, was the diversion of the table. When he offered to recover, and say, 'To the bride's best thoughts,' 'Knock him down,' says the lieutenant, and so on. This silly humour diverted, and saved us from the fulsome entertainment of an ill-bred coxcomb; and the bride drank the lieutenant's health. We returned to my lodging, and Tranquillus led his wife to her apartment, without the ceremony of throwing the stocking, which generally costs two or three maidenheads, without any ceremony at all.

62.   *Flattering letter from a fair admirer*

Mr. BICKERSTAFF,

I had formerly a very good opinion of myself; but it is now withdrawn, and I have placed it upon you, Mr. Bickerstaff, for whom I am not ashamed to declare, I have a very great passion and tenderness. It is not for your face, for that I never saw; your shape and height I am equally a stranger to; but your understanding charms me, and I am lost if you do not dissemble a little love for me. I am not without hopes, because I am not like the tawdry gay things that are fit only to make bone-lace. I am neither childish-young, nor bedlam-old, but, the world says, a good agreeable woman.

Speak peace to a troubled heart, troubled only for you; and in your next paper let me find your thoughts of me.

Do not think of finding out who I am, for notwithstanding your interest in daemons,[1] they cannot help you either to my name, or a sight of my face; therefore do not let them deceive you.

I can bear no discourse, if you are not the subject; and believe me, I know more of love than you do of astronomy.[2]

Pray say some civil things in return to my generosity, and you shall have my very best pen employed to thank you, and I will confirm it. I am

Your admirer,

MARIA.

There is something wonderfully pleasing in the favour of women; and this letter has put me in so good an humour that nothing could displease me since I received it. My boy breaks glasses and pipes, and instead of giving him a knock on the pate, as my way is, for I hate scolding at servants, I only say: 'Ah, Jack! thou hast a head, and so has a pin,' or some such merry expression. But alas! how am I mortified when he is putting on my fourth pair of stockings on these poor spindles of mine! 'The fair one understands love better than I astronomy!' I am sure, without the help of that art, this poor meagre trunk of mine is a very ill habitation for love. She is pleased to speak civilly of my sense, but *Ingenium male habitat* is an invincible difficulty in cases of this nature. I had always, indeed, from a passion to please the eyes of the fair, a great pleasure in dress. Add to this that I have writ songs since I was sixty, and have lived with all the circumspection of an old beau, as I am. But my friend Horace has very well said: 'Every year takes something from us'[3]; and instructed me to form my pursuits and desires according to the stage of my life. Therefore I have no more to value myself upon than that I can converse with young people without peevishness, or wishing myself a moment younger. For which reason, when I am amongst them, I rather moderate than interrupt their diversions. But though I have this complacency, I must not pretend to write to a lady civil things, as Maria desires. Time was, when I could have told her I had received a letter from her fair hands, and, that if this paper trembled as she read it, it then best expressed its author, or some other gay conceit. Though I never saw her, I could have told her that good sense and good humour smiled in her eyes; that constancy and good-nature dwelt in her heart; that beauty and good breeding appeared in all her actions. When I was five-and-twenty, upon sight of one syllable, even wrong spelt, by a lady I never saw, I could tell her that her height was that which was fit for inviting our approach, and commanding our respect; that a smile sat on her lips, which prefaced her expressions before she uttered them; and her aspect prevented her speech. All she could say, though she had an infinite deal of wit, was but a repetition of what was expressed by her form. Her form! which struck her beholders with ideas more moving and forcible than ever were inspired by music, painting, or eloquence. At this rate I panted in those days; but, ah! sixty-three! I am very sorry I can only return the agreeable Maria a passion expressed rather from the head than the heart.

DEAR MADAM,

You have already seen the best of me, and I so passionately love you that I desire we may never meet. If you will examine your heart, you will find that you join the man with the philosopher; and if you have that kind of opinion of my sense as you pretend, I question not but you add to it complexion, air, and shape. But, dear Molly, a man in his grand climacteric is of no sex. Be a good girl, and conduct yourself with honour and virtue when you love one younger than myself. I am, with the greatest tenderness,

Your innocent lover,

I. B.

63. *Attendance of ladies at trials for rape*

I have received a letter subscribed A. B. wherein it has been represented to me as an enormity that there are more than ordinary crowds of women at the Old Bailey when a rape is to be tried; but by Mr. A. B.'s favour I cannot tell who are so much concerned in that part of the law as the sex he mentions, they being the only persons liable to such insults. Nor indeed do I think it more unreasonable that they should be inquisitive on such occasions than men of honour, when one is tried for killing another in a duel. It is very natural to inquire how the fatal pass was made that we may the better defend ourselves when we come to be attacked. Several eminent ladies appeared lately at the court of justice on such an occasion, and with great patience and attention stayed the whole trials of two persons for the abovesaid crime. The law to me indeed seems a little defective in this point; and it is a very great hardship that this crime, which is committed by men only, should have men only on their jury. I humbly therefore propose that on future trials of this sort, half of the twelve may be women; and those such whose faces are well known to have taken notes, or may be supposed to remember what happened in former trials in the same place. There is the learned Androgyne that would make a good forewoman of the panel, who, by long attendance, understands as much law and anatomy as is necessary in this case. Until this is taken care of, I am humbly of opinion it would be much more expedient that the fair were wholly absent. For to what end can it be that they should be present at such examinations, when they can only be perplexed with a fellow-feeling for the injured, without any power to avenge their sufferings? It is an unnecessary pain which the fair ones give themselves on these occasions. I have known a young woman shriek out at some parts of the evidence; and have frequently observed that when the proof grew particular and strong, there has been such a universal flutter of fans that one would think the whole female audience were falling into fits. Nor indeed can I see how men themselves can be wholly unmoved at such tragical relations.

In short, I must tell my female readers, and they may take an old man's word for it, that there is nothing in woman so graceful and becoming as modesty. It adds charms to their beauty, and gives a new softness to their sex. Without it, simplicity and innocence appear rude;

reading and good sense, masculine; wit and humour, lascivious. This is so necessary a qualification for pleasing that the loose part of womankind, whose study it is to ensnare men's hearts, never fail to support the appearance of what they know is so essential to that end. And I have heard it reported by the young fellows in my time, as a maxim of the celebrated Madam Bennet,[1] that a young wench, though never so beautiful, was not worth her board when she was past her blushing.

64. *Sound advice to Jenny in an early domestic discord*

My brother Tranquillus, who is a man of business, came to me this morning into my study, and after very many civil expressions in return for what good offices I had done him, told me he desired to carry his wife my sister that very morning to his own house. I readily told him I would wait upon him, without asking why he was so impatient to rob us of his good company. He went out of my chamber, and I thought seemed to have a little heaviness upon him, which gave me some disquiet. Soon after my sister came to me with a very matron-like air, and most sedate satisfaction in her looks, which spoke her very much at ease, but the traces of her countenance seemed to discover that she had been lately in a passion, and that air of content to flow from a certain triumph upon some advantage obtained. She no sooner sat down by me, but I perceived she was one of those ladies who begin to be managers within the time of their being brides.

Without letting her speak, which I saw she had a mighty inclination to do, I said: 'Here has been your husband, who tells me he has a mind to go home this very morning, and I have consented to it.'

'It is well,' said she, 'for you must know——'

'Nay, Jenny,' said I, 'I beg your pardon, for it is you must know. You are to understand that now is the time to fix or alienate your husband's heart for ever; and I fear you have been a little indiscreet in your expressions or behaviour towards him, even here in my house.'

'There has,' says she, 'been some words; but I will be judged by you if he was not in the wrong. Nay, I need not be judged by anybody, for he gave it up himself, and said not a word when he saw me grow passionate, but: "Madam, you are perfectly in the right of it." As you shall judge——'

'Nay, madam,' said I, 'I am judge already, and tell you that you are perfectly in the wrong of it; for if it was a matter of importance, I know he has better sense than you; if a trifle, you know what I told you on your wedding-day, that you were to be above little provocations.' She knows very well I can be sour upon occasion, therefore gave me leave to go on.

'Sister,' said I, 'I will not enter into the dispute between you, which I find his prudence put an end to before it came to extremity, but charge you to have a care of the first quarrel, as you tender your happiness; for then it is, that the mind will reflect harshly upon every circumstance that has ever passed between you. If such an accident is ever to happen, which I hope never will, be sure to keep to the circumstance before you; make no allusions to what is past, or conclusions referring to what is to come. Do not show an hoard of matter for dissension in your breast; but if it is necessary, lay before him the thing as you understand it, candidly, without being ashamed of acknowledging an error, or proud of being in the right. If a young couple be not careful in this point, they will get into an habit of wrangling; and when to displease is thought of no consequence, to please is always of as little moment. There is a play, Jenny, I have formerly been at when I was a student: we got into a dark corner with a porringer of brandy, and threw raisins into it; then set it on fire. My chamber-fellow and I diverted ourselves with the sport of venturing our fingers for the raisins; and the wantonness of the thing was to see each other look like a demon, as we burnt ourselves, and snatched out the

fruit.   This fantastical mirth was called Snapdragon.   You
may go into many a family where you see the man and wife
at this sport.   Every word at their table alludes to some
passage between themselves; and you see by the paleness
and emotion in their countenances that it is for your sake,
and not their own, that they forbear playing out the whole
game in burning each other's fingers.   In this case the
whole purpose of life is inverted, and the ambition turns
upon a certain contention, who shall contradict best, and
not upon an inclination to excel in kindness and good
offices.   Therefore, dear Jenny, remember me, and avoid
Snapdragon.'

'I thank you, brother,' said she, 'but you do not know
how he loves me; I find I can do anything with him.'

'If you can so, why should you desire to do anything
but please him?   But I have a word or two more before
you go out of the room; for I see you do not like the
subject I am upon.   Let nothing provoke you to fall upon
an imperfection he cannot help; for if he has a resenting
spirit he will think your aversion as immovable as the
imperfection with which you upbraid him.   But above
all, dear Jenny, be careful of one thing, and you will be
something more than woman; that is, a levity you are
almost all guilty of, which is, to take a pleasure in your
power to give pain.   It is even in a mistress an argument
of meanness of spirit, but in a wife it is injustice and
ingratitude.   When a sensible man once observes this in
a woman, he must have a very great or very little spirit
to overlook it.   A woman ought therefore to consider
very often how few men there are who will regard a
meditated offence as a weakness of temper.'

I was going on in my confabulation when Tranquillus
entered.   She cast all her eyes upon him with much shame
and confusion, mixed with great complacency and love,
and went up to him.   He took her in his arms, and looked
so many soft things at one glance that I could see he was
glad I had been talking to her, sorry she had been troubled,
and angry at himself that he could not disguise the concern he was in an hour before.   After which he says to

me, with an air awkward enough, but methought not un-becoming: 'I have altered my mind, brother; we will live upon you a day or two longer.' I replied: 'That is what I have been persuading Jenny to ask of you, but she is resolved never to contradict your inclination, and refused me.'

We were going on in that way which one hardly knows how to express; as when two people mean the same thing in a nice case, but come at it by talking as distantly from it as they can; when very opportunely came in upon us an honest inconsiderable fellow, Tim Dapper, a gentleman well known to us both. . . . His company left us all in good humour, and we were not such fools as to let it sink, before we confirmed it by great cheerfulness and openness in our carriage the whole evening.

65. *Sergeant Hall's epistolary style*

To Sergeant Cabe, in the Coldstream regiment of foot-guards, at the Red Lettice in the Butcher Row, near Temple Bar.

From the camp before Mons, Sept. 26.

COMRADE,

I received yours, and am glad yourself and your wife are in good health, with all the rest of my friends. Our battalion suffered more than I could wish in the action. But who can withstand fate? Poor Richard Stevenson had his fate with a great many more. He was killed dead before we entered the trenches. We had above two hundred of our battalion killed and wounded. We lost ten sergeants, six are as followeth: Jennings, Castles, Roach, Sherring, Meyrick, and my son Smith.[1] The rest are not your acquaintance. I have received a very bad shot in my head myself, but am in hopes, and please God, I shall recover. I continue in the field, and lie at my colonel's quarters. Arthur is very well; but I can give you no account of Elms; he was in the hospital before I

came into the field. I will not pretend to give you an
account of the battle, knowing you have a better in the
prints. Pray give my service to Mrs. Cook and her
daughter, to Mr. Stoffet and his wife, and to Mr. Lyver,
and Thomas Hogsdon, and to Mr. Ragdell, and to all my
friends and acquaintance in general who do ask after me.
My love to Mrs. Stevenson. I am sorry for the sending
such ill news. Her husband was gathering a little money
together to send to his wife, and put it into my hands.
I have seven shillings and threepence, which I shall take
care to send her; wishing your wife a safe delivery, and
both of you all happiness, rest

Your assured friend,

and comrade,

JOHN HALL.

We had but an indifferent breakfast; but the Monseers
never had such a dinner in all their lives.

My kind love to my comrade Hinton, and Mrs. Morgan,
and to John Brown and his wife. I sent two shillings,
and Stevenson sixpence, to drink with you at Mr. Cook's;
but I have heard nothing from him. It was by Mr. Edgar.

Corporal Hartwell desires to be remembered to you, and
desires you to inquire of Edgar what is become of his wife
Peg; and when you write, to send word in your letter what
trade she drives.

We have here very bad weather, which I doubt will be
an hindrance to the siege; but I am in hopes we shall be
masters of the town in a little time, and then I believe we
shall go to garrison.

I saw the critics prepared to nibble at my letter; therefore examined it myself, partly in their way, and partly
my own. This is, said I, truly a letter, and an honest
representation of that cheerful heart which accompanies
the poor soldier in his warfare. Is not there in this all
the topic of submitting to our destiny as well discussed, as
if a greater man had been placed, like Brutus, in his tent
at midnight, reflecting on all the occurrences of past life,

and saying fine things on Being itself? What Sergeant Hall knows of the matter is, that he wishes there had not been so many killed; and he had himself a very bad shot in the head, and should recover if it pleased God. But be that as it will, he takes care, like a man of honour, as he certainly is, to let the widow Stevenson know that he had seven and threepence for her, and that if he lives he is sure he shall go into garrison at last. I doubt not but all the good company at the Red Lettice drank his health with as much real esteem as we do of any of our friends. All that I am concerned for is that Mrs. Peggy Hartwell may be offended at showing this letter, because her conduct in Mr. Hartwell's absence is a little inquired into. But I could not sink that circumstance, because you critics would have lost one of the parts, which I doubt not but you have much to say upon: Whether the familiar way is well hit in this style or not? As for myself, I take a very particular satisfaction in seeing any letter that is fit only for those to read who are concerned in it, but especially on such a subject.

If we consider the heap of an army, utterly out of all prospect of rising and preferment, as they certainly are, and such great things executed by them, it is hard to account for the motive of their gallantry. But to me, who was a cadet at the battle of Coldstream in Scotland, when Monk charged at the head of the regiment, now called Coldstream from the victory of that day; [2] I remember it as well as if it were yesterday, I stood on the left of old West, who I believe is now at Chelsea—I say, to me who know very well this part of mankind, I take the gallantry of private soldiers to proceed from the same, if not from a nobler impulse than that of gentlemen and officers. They have the same taste of being acceptable to their friends, and go through the difficulties of that profession by the same irresistible charm of fellowship and the communication of joys and sorrows, which quickens the relish of pleasure and abates the anguish of pain. Add to this that they have the same regard to fame, though they do not expect so great a share as men above them

hope for; but I will engage Sergeant Hall would die ten
thousand deaths, rather than a word should be spoken at
the Red Lettice, or any part of the Butcher Row, in prejudice to his courage or honesty. If you will have my
opinion then of the sergeant's letter, I pronounce the
style to be mixed, but truly epistolary; the sentiment
relating to his own wound is in the sublime; the post-
script of Peg Hartwell, in the gay; and the whole, the
picture of the bravest sort of man, that is to say, a man
of great courage and small hopes.

66. *Extraordinary behaviour of the gentleman next door*

I was this morning awakened by a sudden shake of the
house; and as soon as I had got a little out of my consternation I felt another, which was followed by two or
three repetitions of the same convulsion. I got up as fast
as possible, girt on my rapier, and snatched up my hat,
when my landlady came up to me and told me that the
gentlewoman of the next house begged me to step thither,
for that a lodger she had taken in was run mad and she
desired my advice, as indeed everybody in the whole lane
does upon important occasions. I am not, like some
artists,[1] saucy because I can be beneficial, but went immediately. Our neighbour told us she had the day before
let her second floor to a very genteel youngish man, who
told her he kept extraordinary good hours, and was
generally at home most part of the morning and evening
at study; but that this morning he had for an hour together
made this extravagant noise which we then heard. I went
upstairs with my hand upon the hilt of my rapier and
approached this new lodger's door. I looked in at the
keyhole, and there I saw a well-made man look with great
attention on a book, and on a sudden jump into the air
so high that his head almost touched the ceiling. He came
down safe on his right foot and again flew up, alighting

on his left; then looked again at his book, and holding out his right leg, put it into such a quivering motion that I thought he would have shaken it off. He used the left after the same manner, when on a sudden, to my great surprise, he stooped himself incredibly low, and turned gently on his toes. After this circular motion, he continued bent in that humble posture for some time, looking on his book. After this, he recovered himself with a sudden spring and flew round the room in all the violence and disorder imaginable, until he made a full pause for want of breath.

In this interim my woman asked what I thought. I whispered that I thought this learned person an enthusiast, who possibly had his first education in the Peripatetic way, which was a sect of philosophers who always studied when walking. But observing him much out of breath, I thought it the best time to master him if he were disordered, and knocked at his door. I was surprised to find him open it, and say with great civility and good mien that he hoped he had not disturbed us. I believed him in a lucid interval, and desired he would please to let me see his book. He did so, smiling. I could not make anything of it, and therefore asked in what language it was writ. He said it was one he studied with great application; but it was his profession to teach it, and could not communicate his knowledge without a consideration. I answered that I hoped he would hereafter keep his thoughts to himself, for this meditation this morning had cost me three coffee-dishes and a clean pipe.[2] He seemed concerned at that, and told me he was a dancing-master, and had been reading a dance or two before he went out, which had been written by one who taught at an academy in France. He observed me at a stand, and went on to inform me that now articulate motions, as well as sounds, were expressed by proper characters; and that there is nothing so common as to communicate a dance by a letter. I beseeched him hereafter to meditate in a ground-room, for that otherwise it would be impossible for an artist of any other kind to live near him; and that I was sure several of his thoughts this morning would have shaken my spectacles off my nose had I been myself at study.

I then took my leave of this virtuoso, and returned to my chamber, meditating on the various occupations of rational creatures.

67.   *Reprehensible practice of gagging*

I was very well pleased this evening to hear a gentleman express a very becoming indignation against a practice which I myself have been very much offended at. 'There is nothing,' said he, 'more ridiculous, than for an actor to insert words of his own in the part he is to act, so that it is impossible to see the poet for the player. You will have Pinkethman and Bullock helping out Beaumont and Fletcher. It puts me in mind,' continued he, 'of a collection of antique statues which I once saw in a gentleman's possession, who employed a neighbouring stonecutter to add noses, ears, arms, or legs to the maimed works of Phidias or Praxiteles. You may be sure this addition disfigured the statues much more than time had. I remember Venus, that, by the nose he had given her, looked like Mother Shipton; and a Mercury, with a pair of legs that seemed very much swelled with the dropsy.'

I thought the gentleman's observations very proper, and he told me I had improved his thought in mentioning on this occasion those wise commentators who had filled up the hemistichs of Virgil; particularly that notable poet who, to make the *Aeneid* more perfect, carried on the story to Lavinia's wedding. If the proper officer will not condescend to take notice of these absurdities, I shall myself, as a Censor of the people, animadvert upon such proceedings.

68. Visit from the fair admirer

I was very much surprised this evening with a visit from one of the top Toasts of the town, who came privately in a chair, and bolted into my room while I was reading a chapter of Agrippa upon the occult sciences[1]; but as she entered with all the air and bloom that nature ever bestowed on woman, I threw down the conjurer, and met the charmer. I had no sooner placed her at my right hand by the fire, but she opened to me the reason of her visit. 'Mr. Bickerstaff,' said the fine creature, 'I have been your correspondent some time, though I never saw you before; I have writ by the name of Maria. You have told me you were too far gone in life to think of love; therefore I am answered as to the passion I spoke of, and,' continued she smiling, 'I will not stay until you grow young again, as you men never fail to do in your dotage; but am come to consult you about disposing of myself to another. My person you see; my fortune is very considerable; but I am at present under much perplexity how to act in a great conjuncture. I have two lovers, Crassus and Lorio: Crassus is prodigiously rich, but has no one distinguishing quality; though at the same time he is not remarkable on the defective side. Lorio has travelled, is well bred, pleasant in discourse, discreet in his conduct, agreeable in his person; and with all this, he has a competency of fortune without superfluity. When I consider Lorio, my mind is filled with an idea of the great satisfactions of a pleasant conversation. When I think of Crassus, my equipage, numerous servants, gay liveries, and various dresses, are opposed to the charms of his rival. In a word, when I cast my eyes upon Lorio I forget and despise fortune; when I behold Crassus I think only of pleasing my vanity, and enjoying an uncontrolled expense in all the pleasure of life, except love.' She paused here.

'Madam,' said I, 'I am confident you have not stated your case with sincerity, and that there is some secret pang which you have concealed from me. For I see by your aspect the generosity of your mind; and that open ingenuous air lets me know that you have too great a sense of the generous passion of love to prefer the ostentation of life in the arms of Crassus to the entertainments and conveniencies of it in the company of your beloved Lorio; for so he is indeed, madam; you speak his name with a different accent from the rest of your discourse. The idea his image raises in you gives new life to your features, and new grace to your speech. Nay, blush not, madam, there is no dishonour in loving a man of merit; I assure you, I am grieved at this dallying with yourself when you put another in competition with him for no other reason but superior wealth.'

'To tell you, then,' said she, 'the bottom of my heart, there is Clotilda lies by, and plants herself in the way of Crassus, and I am confident will snap him if I refuse him. I cannot bear to think that she will shine above me: when our coaches meet, to see her chariot hung behind with four footmen, and mine with but two; hers, powdered, gay, and saucy, kept only for show; mine, a couple of careful rogues that are good for something, I own I cannot bear that Clotilda should be in all the pride and wantonness of wealth, and I only in the ease and affluence of it.'

Here I interrupted: 'Well, madam, now I see your whole affliction; you could be happy, but that you fear another would be happier. Or rather, you could be solidly happy, but that another is to be happy in appearance. This is an evil which you must get over, or never know happiness. We will put the case, madam, that you married Crassus, and she Lorio.'

She answered: 'Speak not of it. I could tear her eyes out at the mention of it.'

'Well then, I pronounce Lorio to be the man; but I must tell you, that what we call settling in the world is, in a kind, leaving it; and you must at once resolve to keep your thoughts of happiness within the reach of your fortune, and not measure it by comparison with others.

'But indeed, madam, when I behold that beauteous form of yours, and consider the generality of your sex as to their disposal of themselves in marriage, or their parents doing it for them without their own approbation, I cannot but look upon all such matches as the most impudent prostitutions. Do but observe, when you are at a play, the familiar wenches that sit laughing among the men. These appear detestable to you in the boxes. Each of them would give up her person for a guinea; and some of you would take the worst there for life for twenty thousand. If so, how do you differ but in price? As to the circumstance of marriage, I take that to be hardly an alteration of the case; for wedlock is but a more solemn prostitution, where there is not a union of minds. You would hardly believe it, but there have been designs even upon me.

'A neighbour in this very lane, who knows I have, by leading a very wary life, laid up a little money, had a great mind to marry me to his daughter. I was frequently invited to their table: the girl was always very pleasant and agreeable. After dinner, Miss Molly would be sure to fill my pipe for me, and put more sugar than ordinary into my coffee; for she was sure I was good-natured. If I chanced to hem, the mother would applaud my vigour; and has often said on that occasion: "I wonder, Mr. Bickerstaff, you do not marry: I am sure you would have children." Things went so far that my mistress presented me with a wrought night-cap and a laced band of her own working. I began to think of it in earnest; but one day, having an occasion to ride to Islington, as two or three people were lifting me upon my pad, I spied her at a convenient distance laughing at her lover, with a parcel of romps of her acquaintance. One of them, who I suppose had the same design upon me, told me she said: "Do you see how briskly my old gentleman mounts?" This made me cut off my amour, and to reflect with myself that no married life could be so unhappy as where the wife proposes no other advantage from her husband than that of making herself fine, and keeping her out of the dirt.'

My fair client burst out a-laughing at the account I gave her of my escape, and went away seemingly convinced of the reasonableness of my discourse to her.

69. *Mr. Bickerstaff prepares to defend himself*

I had several hints and advertisements from unknown hands that some, who are enemies to my labours, design to demand the fashionable way of satisfaction for the disturbance my lucubrations have given them. I confess, as things now stand, I do not know how to deny such inviters, and am preparing myself accordingly: I have bought pumps and foils, and am every morning practising in my chamber. My neighbour, the dancing-master, has demanded of me why I take this liberty, since I would not allow it him. But I answered his was an act of an indifferent nature, and mine of necessity. My late treatises against duels have so far disobliged the fraternity of the noble science of defence, that I can get none of them to show me so much as one pass. I am therefore obliged to learn my book; and have accordingly several volumes wherein all the postures are exactly delineated. I must confess I am shy of letting people see me at this exercise, because of my flannel waistcoat, and my spectacles, which I am forced to fix on, the better to observe the posture of the enemy.

I have upon my chamber walls, drawn at full length, the figures of all sorts of men, from eight feet to three feet two inches. Within this height, I take it that all the fighting men of Great Britain are comprehended. But as I push, I make allowances for my being of a lank and spare body, and have chalked out in every figure my own dimensions; for I scorn to rob any man of his life by taking advantage of his breadth. Therefore I press purely in a line down from his nose, and take no more of him to assault than he has of me. For to speak impartially, if a lean fellow wounds a fat one in any part to the right or

left, whether it be in 'Cart' or in 'Terse,'[1] beyond the
dimensions of the said lean fellow's own breadth, I take it
to be murder, and such a murder as is below a gentleman
to commit.   As I am spare, I am also very tall, and behave
myself with relation to that advantage with the same
punctilio; and I am ready to stoop or stand, according to
the stature of my adversary.   I must confess I have had
great success this morning, and have hit every figure round
the room in a mortal part, without receiving the least
hurt, except a little scratch by falling on my face in pushing
at one at the lower end of my chamber; but I recovered
so quick and jumped so nimbly into my guard that if he
had been alive he could not have hurt me.   It is confessed
I have writ against duels with some warmth; but in all my
discourses I have not ever said that I knew how a gentleman could avoid a duel if he were provoked to it; and
since that custom is now become a law, I know nothing
but the legislative power, with new animadversions upon
it, can put us in a capacity of denying challenges, though
we were afterwards hanged for it.   But no more of this
at present.   As things stand, I shall put up no more
affronts; and I shall be so far from taking ill words that
I will not take ill looks.   I therefore warn all hot young
fellows not to look hereafter more terrible than their
neighbours; for if they stare at me with their hats cocked
higher than other people, I will not bear it.   Nay, I give
warning to all people in general to look kindly at me; for
I will bear no frowns, even from ladies; and if any woman
pretends to look scornfully at me, I shall demand satisfaction of the next of kin of the masculine gender.

70.   *Arrangements for burying those morally dead*

I have already taken great pains to inspire notions of
honour and virtue into the people of this kingdom, and
used all gentle methods imaginable to bring those who
are dead in idleness, folly, and pleasure, into life by applying

themselves to learning, wisdom, and industry. But since
fair means are ineffectual, I must proceed to extremities,
and shall give my good friends, the company of upholders,[1] full power to bury all such dead as they meet
with, who are within my former descriptions of deceased
persons. In the meantime the following remonstrance of
that corporation I take to be very just.

From our office near the Haymarket, Nov. 23.

WORTHY SIR,
    Upon reading your *Tatler* on Saturday last, by which
we received the agreeable news of so many deaths, we
immediately ordered in a considerable quantity of blacks;
and our servants have wrought night and day ever since,
to furnish out the necessaries for these deceased. But
so it is, Sir, that of this vast number of dead bodies
that go putrefying up and down the streets, not one of
them has come to us to be buried. Though we should be
loth to be any hindrance to our good friends the physicians,
yet we cannot but take notice what infection Her Majesty's
subjects are liable to from the horrible stench of so many
corpses. Sir, we will not detain you; our case in short is
this: here are we embarked in this undertaking for the
public good. Now if people should be suffered to go on
unburied at this rate, there is an end of the usefullest
manufactures and handicrafts of the kingdom; for where
will be your sextons, coffin-makers, and plumbers? What
will become of your embalmers, epitaph-mongers, and
chief mourners? We are loth to drive this matter any
further, though we tremble at the consequences of it; for
if it shall be left to every dead man's discretion not to be
buried until he sees his time, no man can say where that
will end; but thus much we will take upon us to affirm,
that such a toleration will be intolerable.
    What would make us easy in this matter is no more but
that your worship would be pleased to issue out your
orders to *ditto* dead to repair forthwith to our office, in
order to their interment; where constant attendance shall

be given to treat with all persons according to their quality, and the poor to be buried for nothing. And for the convenience of such persons as are willing enough to be dead, but that they are afraid their friends and relations should know it, we have a back door into Warwick Street, from whence they may be interred with all secrecy imaginable, and without loss of time or hindrance of business. But in case of obstinacy, for we would gladly make a thorough riddance, we desire a further power from your worship, to take up such deceased as shall not have complied with your first orders, wherever we meet them. And if after that there shall be complaints of any persons so offending, let them lie at our doors. We are,

Your worship's until death,
THE MASTER AND COMPANY
OF UPHOLDERS.

PS. We are ready to give in our printed proposals at large; and if your worship approves of our undertaking, we desire the following advertisement may be inserted in your next paper:

Whereas a commission of interment has been awarded against Doctor John Partridge, Philomath,[2] professor of Physic and Astrology; and whereas the said Partridge hath not surrendered himself, nor shown cause to the contrary; these are to certify that the company of upholders will proceed to bury him from Cordwainers' Hall, on Tuesday the twenty-ninth instant, where any six of his surviving friends, who still believe him to be alive, are desired to come prepared to hold up the pall.

Note: we shall light away at six in the evening, there being to be a sermon.

71. *Sufferings of authors from piratical printers*

The progress of my intended account of what happened when justice visited mortals is at present interrupted by the observation and sense of an injustice against which there is no remedy, even in a kingdom more happy in the care taken of the liberty and property of the subject than any other nation upon earth. This iniquity is committed by a most impregnable set of mortals, men who are rogues within the law; and in the very commission of what they are guilty of, professedly own that they forbear no injury but from the terror of being punished for it. These miscreants are a set of wretches we authors call pirates, who print any book, poem, or sermon, as soon as it appears in the world, in a smaller volume; and sell it, as all other thieves do stolen goods, at a cheaper rate. I was in my rage calling them rascals, plunderers, robbers, highwaymen. But they acknowledge all that, and are pleased with those, as well as any other titles; nay, will print them themselves to turn the penny.

I am extremely at a loss how to act against such open enemies, who have not shame enough to be touched with our reproaches, and are as well defended against what we can say as what we can do. Railing therefore we must turn into complaint, which I cannot forbear making when I consider that all the labours of my long life may be disappointed by the first man that pleases to rob me. I had flattered myself that my stock of learning was worth a hundred and fifty pounds per annum, which would very handsomely maintain me and my little family, who are so happy, or so wise, as to want only necessaries. Before men had come up to this barefaced impudence, it was an estate to have a competency of understanding.

An ingenious droll, who is since dead (and indeed it is well for him he is so, for he must have starved had he lived to this day), used to give me an account of his good husbandry in the management of his learning. He was a general dealer, and had his amusements as well comical as serious. The merry rogue said, when he wanted a dinner, he writ a paragraph of Table Talk, and his bookseller upon sight paid the reckoning. He was a very good judge of what would please the people, and could aptly hit both the genius of his readers and the season of the year in his writings. His brain, which was his estate, had as regular and different produce as other men's land. From the beginning of November until the opening of the campaign,[1] he writ pamphlets and letters to members of parliament, or friends in the country. But sometimes he would relieve his ordinary readers with a murder, and lived comfortably a week or two upon 'strange and lamentable accidents.' A little before the armies took the field, his way was to open your attention with a prodigy; and a monster, well writ, was two guineas the lowest price. This prepared his readers for 'his great and bloody news' from Flanders in June and July. Poor Tom! he is gone. But I observed, he always looked well after a battle, and was apparently fatter in a fighting year. Had this honest careless fellow lived until now, famine had stared him in the face and interrupted his merriment; as it must be a solid affliction to all those whose pen is their portion.

72. *Mr. Bickerstaff deals firmly with fopperies*

There is nothing gives a man a greater satisfaction than the sense of having dispatched a great deal of business, especially when it turns to the public emolument. I have much pleasure of this kind upon my spirits at present, occasioned by the fatigue of affairs which I went through last Saturday. It is some time since I set apart that day for examining the pretensions of several who had applied to me for canes, perspective-glasses,[1] snuff-boxes, orange-flower-waters, and the like ornaments of life. In order to adjust this matter, I had before directed Charles Lillie, of Beaufort Buildings,[2] to prepare a great bundle of blank licences in the following words:

You are hereby required to permit the bearer of this cane to pass and repass through the streets and suburbs of London, or any place within ten miles of it, without let or molestation; provided that he does not walk with it under his arm, brandish it in the air, or hang it on a button: in which case it shall be forfeited; and I hereby declare it forfeited to anyone who shall think it safe to take it from him.

ISAAC BICKERSTAFF.

The same form, differing only in the provisos, will serve for a perspective, snuff-box, or perfumed handkerchief. I had placed myself in my elbow-chair at the upper end of my great parlour, having ordered Charles Lillie to take his place upon a joint-stool, with a writing-desk before him. John Morphew also took his station at the door; I having, for his good and faithful services, appointed him my chamber-keeper upon court days. He let me know that there were a great number attending without; upon which I ordered him to give notice that I did not intend to sit upon snuff-boxes that day; but that those who appeared for canes might enter. The first presented me with the following petition, which I ordered Mr. Lillie to read.

To ISAAC BICKERSTAFF, ESQUIRE, Censor of Great Britain.

The humble petition of Simon Trippit,
Showeth,

That your petitioner having been bred up to a cane from his youth, it is now become as necessary to him as any other of his limbs.

That a great part of his behaviour depending upon it, he should be reduced to the utmost necessities if he should lose the use of it.

That the knocking of it upon his shoe, leaning one leg upon it, or whistling with it on his mouth, are such great reliefs to him in conversation that he does not know how to be good company without it.

That he is at present engaged in an amour, and must despair of success if it be taken from him.

Your petitioner therefore hopes that, the premises tenderly considered, your worship will not deprive him of so useful and so necessary a support.

And your petitioner shall ever, etc.

Upon the hearing of his case, I was touched with some compassion, and the more so, when upon observing him nearer, I found he was a prig. I bid him produce his cane in court, which he had left at the door. He did so and I finding it to be very curiously clouded,[3] with a transparent amber head, and a blue riband to hang upon his wrist, I immediately ordered my clerk Lillie to lay it up, and deliver out to him a plain joint, headed with walnut; and then, in order to wean him from it by degrees, permitted him to wear it three days in a week, and to abate proportionally until he found himself able to go alone.

The second who appeared came limping into the court, and setting forth in his petition many pretences for the use of a cane, I caused them to be examined one by one; but finding him in different stories, and confronting him with several witnesses who had seen him walk upright, I ordered Mr. Lillie to take in his cane, and rejected his petition as frivolous.

A third made his entry with great difficulty, leaning upon a slight stick, and in danger of falling every step he took. I saw the weakness of his hams; and hearing that he had married a young wife about a fortnight before, I bid him leave his cane and gave him a new pair of crutches, with which he went off in great vigour and alacrity. This gentleman was succeeded by another, who seemed very much pleased while his petition was reading, in which he had represented that he was extremely afflicted with the gout, and set his foot upon the ground with the caution and dignity which accompany that distemper. I suspected him for an impostor, and having ordered him to be searched, I committed him into the hands of Doctor Thomas Smith in King Street, my own corn-cutter, who attended in an outward room, and wrought so speedy a cure upon him that I thought fit to send him also away without his cane.

While I was thus dispensing justice, I heard a noise in my outward room; and inquiring what was the occasion of it, my door-keeper told me that they had taken up one in the very fact as he was passing by my door. They immediately brought in a lively fresh-coloured young man, who made great resistance with hand and foot, but did not offer to make use of his cane, which hung upon his fifth button. Upon examination I found him to be an Oxford scholar, who was just entered at the Temple. He at first disputed the jurisdiction of the court; but being driven out of his little law and logic, he told me very pertly that he looked upon such a perpendicular creature as man to make a very imperfect figure without a cane in his hand. It is well known, says he, we ought, according to the natural situation of our bodies, to walk upon our hands and feet; and that the wisdom of the ancients had described man to be an animal of four legs in the morning, two at noon, and three at night; by which they intimated that a cane might very properly become part of us in some period of life. Upon which I asked him whether he wore it at his breast to have in readiness when that period should arrive. My young lawyer immediately told me he had a property in it, and a right to hang it where he pleased, and to make use of it as he thought fit, provided that he did not break the peace with it. And further said that he never took it off his button unless it were to lift it up at a coachman, hold it over the head of a drawer, point out the circumstances of a story, or for other services of the like nature, that are all within the laws of the land. I did not care for discouraging a young man, who, I saw, would come to good; and because his heart was set upon his new purchase, I only ordered him to wear it about his neck, instead of hanging it upon his button, and so dismissed him.

There were several appeared in court whose pretensions I found to be very good, and therefore gave them their licences upon paying their fees; as many others had their licences renewed, who required more time for recovery of their lameness than I had before allowed them.

Having dispatched this set of my petitioners, there came in a well-dressed man, with a glass tube in one hand and his petition in the other. Upon his entering the room he threw back the right side of his wig, put forward his right leg, and advancing the glass to his right eye, aimed it directly at me. In the meanwhile, to make my observations also, I put on my spectacles; in which posture we surveyed each other for some time. Upon the removal of our glasses, I desired him to read his petition, which he did very promptly and easily; though at the same time it set forth that he could see nothing distinctly, and was within very few degrees of being utterly blind; concluding with a prayer that he might be permitted to strengthen and extend his sight by a glass. In answer to this I told him he might sometimes extend it to his own destruction. 'As you are now,' said I, 'you are out of the reach of beauty; the shafts of the finest eyes lose their force before they can come at you; you cannot distinguish a Toast from an orange-wench; you can see a whole circle of beauty without any interruption from an impertinent face to discompose you. In short, what are snares for others——' My petitioner would hear no more, but told me very seriously, 'Mr. Bickerstaff, you quite mistake your man; it is the joy, the pleasure, the employment of my life, to frequent public assemblies and gaze upon the fair.' In a word, I found his use of a glass was occasioned by no other infirmity but his vanity, and was not so much designed to make him see, as to make him be seen and distinguished by others. I therefore refused him a licence for a perspective, but allowed him a pair of spectacles, with full permission to use them in any public assembly as he should think fit. He was followed by so very few of this order of men that I have reason to hope this sort of cheats are almost at an end.

The orange-flower men appeared next with petitions, perfumed so strongly with musk that I was almost overcome with the scent; and for my own sake was obliged forthwith to license their handkerchiefs, especially when I found they had sweetened them at Charles Lillie's, and that some of their persons would not be altogether inoffensive without them. John Morphew, whom I have made the general of my dead men, acquainted me that the petitioners were all of that order, and could produce certificates to prove it, if I required it. I was so well pleased with this way of their embalming themselves, that I commanded the abovesaid Morphew to give it in orders to his whole army, that everyone who did not surrender himself up to be disposed of by the upholders should use the same method to keep himself sweet during his present state of putrefaction.

I finished my session with great content of mind, reflecting upon the good I had done; for however slightly men may regard these particularities and little follies in dress and behaviour, they lead to greater evils. The bearing to be laughed at for such singularities teaches us insensibly an impertinent fortitude, and enables us to bear public censure for things which more substantially deserve it. By this means they open a gate to folly, and oftentimes render a man so ridiculous as to discredit his virtues and capacities, and unqualify them from doing any good in the world. Besides, the giving in to uncommon habits of this nature is a want of that humble deference which is due to mankind, and, what is worst of all, the certain indication of some secret flaw in the mind of the person that commits them. When I was a young man, I remember a gentleman of great integrity and worth was very remarkable for wearing a broad belt, and a hanger instead of a fashionable sword, though in all other points a very well-bred man. I suspected him at first sight to have something wrong in him, but was not able for a long while to discover any collateral proofs of it. I watched him narrowly for six and thirty years, when at last, to the surprise of everybody but myself, who had long expected to see the folly break out, he married his own cook-maid.

73. Domestic happiness of Jenny and her husband

My brother Tranquillus being gone out of town for some days, my sister Jenny sent me word she would come and dine with me, and therefore desired me to have no other company. I took care accordingly, and was not a little pleased to see her enter the room with a decent and matron-like behaviour, which I thought very much became her. I saw she had a great deal to say to me, and easily discovered in her eyes, and the air of her countenance, that she had abundance of satisfaction in her heart, which she longed to communicate. However, I was resolved to let her break into her discourse her own way, and reduced her to a thousand little devices and intimations to bring me to the mention of her husband. But finding I was resolved not to name him, she began of her own accord: 'My husband,' said she, 'gives his humble service to you.' To which I only answered: 'I hope he is well'; and without waiting for a reply, fell into other subjects.

She at last was out of all patience, and said, with a smile and manner that I thought had more beauty and spirit than I had ever observed before in her: 'I did not think, brother, you had been so ill-natured. You have seen, ever since I came in, that I had a mind to talk of my husband, and you will not be so kind as to give me an occasion.'

'I did not know,' said I, 'but it might be a disagreeable subject to you. You do not take me for so old-fashioned a fellow as to think of entertaining a young lady with the discourse of her husband. I know nothing is more acceptable than to speak of one who is to be so; but to speak of one who is so! Indeed, Jenny, I am a better bred man than you think me.'

She showed a little dislike at my raillery; and by her bridling up, I perceived she expected to be treated hereafter not as Jenny Distaff, but Mrs. Tranquillus. I was very well pleased with this change in her humour; and upon talking with her on several subjects, I could not but fancy that I saw a great deal of her husband's way and manner in her remarks, her phrases, the tone of her voice, and the very air of her countenance. This gave me an unspeakable satisfaction, not only because I had found her an husband from whom she could learn many things that were laudable, but also because I looked upon her imitation

of him as an infallible sign that she entirely loved him.
This is an observation that I never knew fail, though I do
not remember that any other has made it. The natural
shyness of her sex hindered her from telling me the greatness of her own passion; but I easily collected it from the
representation she gave me of his. 'I have everything,'
says she, 'in Tranquillus that I can wish for; and enjoy
in him what indeed you have told me were to be met with
in a good husband, the fondness of a lover, the tenderness
of a parent, and the intimacy of a friend.'

It transported me to see her eyes swimming in tears of
affection when she spoke. 'And is there not, dear sister,'
said I, 'more pleasure in the possession of such a man
than in all the little impertinences of balls, assemblies, and
equipage, which it cost me much pains to make you con-
temn?'

She answered, smiling: 'Tranquillus has made me a
sincere convert in a few weeks, though I am afraid you
could not have done it in your whole life. To tell you
truly, I have only one fear hanging upon me, which is apt to
give me trouble in the midst of all my satisfactions: I am
afraid, you must know, that I shall not always make the
same amiable appearance in his eye that I do at present.
You know, brother Bickerstaff, that you have the reputation of a conjurer; and if you have any one secret in your
art to make your sister always beautiful, I should be
happier than if I were mistress of all the worlds you have
shown me in a starry night.'

'Jenny,' said I, 'without having recourse to magic, I
shall give you one plain rule that will not fail of making
you always amiable to a man who has so great a passion
for you, and is of so equal and reasonable a temper as
Tranquillus. Endeavour to please, and you must please;
be always in the same disposition as you are when you ask
for this secret, and you may take my word, you will never
want it. An inviolable fidelity, good humour, and complacency of temper, outlive all the charms of a fine face,
and make the decays of it invisible.'

74. *Story of Will Rosin*

Will Rosin, the fiddler of Wapping, who is a man as much made for happiness and a quiet life as any one breathing, has been lately entangled in so many intricate and unreasonable distresses as would have made him, had he been a man of too nice honour, the most wretched of all mortals. I came to the knowledge of his affairs by mere accident. Several of the narrow end of our lane having made an appointment to visit some friends beyond Saint Katherine's, where there was to be a merry meeting, they would needs take with them the old gentleman, as they are pleased to call me. I, who value my company by their goodwill, which naturally has the same effect as good breeding, was not too stately, or too wise, to accept of the invitation. Our design was to be spectators of a sea-ball; to which I readily consented, provided I might be *incognito*, being naturally pleased with the survey of human life in all its degrees and circumstances. In order to this merriment, Will Rosin, who is the Corelli of the Wapping side, as Tom Scrape is the Bononcini of Red-riffe,[1] was immediately sent for; but to our utter disappointment, poor Will was under an arrest, and desired the assistance of all his kind masters and mistresses, or he must go to gaol. The whole company received his message with great humanity, and very generously threw in their halfpence apiece in a great dish, which purchased his redemption out of the hands of the bailiffs. During the negotiation for his enlargement, I had an opportunity of acquainting myself with his history.

Mr. William Rosin, of the parish of Saint Katherine, is somewhat stricken in years, and married to a young widow who has very much the ascendant over him, this degenerate age being so perverted in all things, that even in the state of matrimony, the young pretend to govern their elders. The musician is extremely fond of her, but is often obliged to lay by his fiddle to hear louder notes of hers, when she is pleased to be angry with him; for you are to know,

Will is not of consequence enough to enjoy her conversation but when she chides him, or makes use of him to carry on her amours. For she is a woman of stratagem; and even in that part of the world where one would expect but very little gallantry, by the force of natural genius she can be sullen, sick, out of humour, splenetic, want new clothes, and more money, as well as if she had been bred in Cheapside or Cornhill. She was lately under a secret discontent upon account of a lover she was like to lose by his marriage; for her gallant, Mr. Ezekiel Boniface, had been twice asked in the church, in order to be joined in matrimony with Mrs. Winifred Dimple, spinster, of the same parish. Hereupon Mrs. Rosin was far gone in that distemper which well-governed husbands know by the description of: 'I am I know not how'; and Will soon understood that it was his part to inquire into the occasion of her melancholy, or suffer as the cause of it himself.

After much importunity, all he could get out of her was that she was the most unhappy and the most wicked of all women, and had no friend in the world to tell her grief to. Upon this Will doubled his importunities; but she said that she should break her poor heart if he did not take a solemn oath upon a book that he would not be angry; and that he would expose the person who had wronged her to all the world, for the ease of her mind, which was no way else to be quieted. The fiddler was so melted that he immediately kissed her, and afterwards the book. When his oath was taken she begun to lament herself, and revealed to him that, miserable woman as she was, she had been false to his bed. Will was glad to hear it was no worse; but before he could reply: 'Nay,' said she, 'I will make you all the atonement I can, and take shame upon me by proclaiming it to all the world, which is the only thing that can remove my present terrors of mind.'

This was indeed too true, for her design was to prevent Mr. Boniface's marriage, which was all she apprehended. Will was thoroughly angry, and begun to curse and swear, the ordinary expressions of passion in persons of his condition. Upon which his wife: 'Ah, William! how well you mind the oath you have taken, and the distress of your poor wife, who can keep nothing from you; I hope you will not be such a perjured wretch as to forswear yourself.' The fiddler answered that his oath obliged him only not be angry at what was past; 'but I find you intend to make me laughed at all over Wapping.'

'No, no,' replied Mrs. Rosin, 'I see well enough what you would be at, you poor-spirited cuckold! You are afraid to expose Boniface who has abused your poor wife, and would fain persuade me still to suffer the stings of conscience; but I assure you, sirrah, I will not go to the devil for you.' Poor Will was not made for contention, and beseeching her to be pacified, desired she would consult the good of her soul her own way, for he would not say her nay in anything.

Mrs. Rosin was so very loud and public in her invectives against Boniface that the parents of his mistress forbad the banns, and his match was prevented; which was the whole design of this deep stratagem. The father of Boniface brought his action of defamation, arrested the fiddler, and recovered damages. This was the distress from which he was relieved by the company; and the good husband's air, history, and jollity upon his enlargement, gave occasion to very much mirth; especially when Will, finding he had friends to stand by him, proclaimed himself a cuckold by way of insult over the family of the Bonifaces. Here is a man of tranquillity without reading Seneca! What work had such an incident made among persons of distinction! The brothers and kindred of each side must have been drawn out, and hereditary hatred entailed on the families as long as their very names remained in the world. Who would believe that Herod, Othello, and Will Rosin were of the same species? [2]

75. *The morally dead: cases of Mr. Groggram and Florinda*

Whereas Mr. Jeffery Groggram has surrendered himself by his letter bearing date December 7, and has sent an acknowledgment that he is dead, praying an order to the company of upholders for interment at such a reasonable rate as may not impoverish his heirs: the said Groggram having been dead ever since he was born, and added nothing to his small patrimony, Mr. Bickerstaff has taken the premises into consideration; and being sensible of the ingenuous and singular behaviour of this petitioner, pronounces the said Jeffery Groggram a live man, and will not suffer that he should bury himself out of modesty; but requires him to remain among the living, as an example to those obstinate dead men, who will neither labour for life nor go to their grave.

N.B. Mr. Groggram is the first person that has come in upon Mr. Bickerstaff's dead warrant.

Florinda demands by her letter of this day to be allowed to pass for a living woman, having danced the Derbyshire Hornpipe in the presence of several friends on Saturday last.
Granted; provided she can bring proof that she can make a pudding on the twenty-fourth instant.

76. *Literature and the dignity of man*

It is not to be imagined how great an effect well-disposed lights, with proper forms and orders in assemblies, have upon some tempers. I am sure I feel it in so extraordinary a manner that I cannot in a day or two get out of my imagination any very beautiful or disagreeable impression which I receive on such occasions. For this reason I frequently look in at the playhouse, in order to enlarge my thoughts and warm my mind with some new ideas that may be serviceable to me in my lucubrations.

In this disposition I entered the theatre the other day, and placed myself in a corner of it, very convenient for seeing, without being myself observed. I found the audience hushed in a very deep attention, and did not question but some noble tragedy was just then in its crisis, or that an incident was to be unravelled which would determine the fate of an hero. While I was in this suspense, expecting every moment to see my old friend Mr. Betterton[1] appear in all the majesty of distress, to my unspeakable amazement there came up a monster with a face between his feet; and as I was looking on he raised himself on one leg in such a perpendicular posture that the other grew in a direct line above his head. It afterwards twisted itself into the motions and wreathings of several different animals, and after great variety of shapes and transformations went off the stage in the figure of an human creature. The admiration, the applause, the satisfaction of the audience during this strange entertainment is not to be expressed. I was very much out of countenance for my dear countrymen, and looked about with some apprehension for fear any foreigner should be present. Is it possible, thought I, that human nature can rejoice in its disgrace, and take pleasure in seeing its own figure turned to ridicule, and distorted into forms that raise horror and aversion? There is something disingenuous and immoral in the being able to bear such a sight. Men of elegant and noble minds are shocked at the seeing characters of persons who deserve esteem for their virtue, knowledge, or services to their country, placed in wrong lights, and by misrepresentation made the subject of buffoonery. Such a nice abhorrence is not indeed to be found among the vulgar; but methinks it is wonderful that those who have nothing but the outward figure to distinguish them as men should delight in seeing it abused, vilified, and disgraced.

I must confess there is nothing that more pleases me, in all that I read in books or see among mankind, than such passages as represent human nature in its proper dignity. As man is a creature made up of different extremes, he has something in him very great and very mean. A skilful artist may draw an excellent picture of him in either of these views. The finest authors of antiquity have taken him on the more advantageous side. They cultivate the natural grandeur of the soul, raise in her a generous ambition, feed her with hopes of immortality and perfection, and do all they can to widen the partition between the virtuous and the vicious, by making the difference betwixt them as great as between gods and brutes. In short, it is impossible to read a page in Plato, Tully, and a thousand other ancient moralists, without being a greater and a better man for it. On the contrary, I could never read any of our modish French authors, or those of our own country who are the imitators and admirers of that trifling nation, without being for some time out of humour with myself and at everything about me. Their business is to depreciate human nature and consider it under its worst appearances. They give mean interpretations and base motives to the worthiest actions; they resolve virtue and vice into constitution. In short, they endeavour to make no distinction between man and man, or between the species of men and that of brutes. As an instance of this kind of authors, among many others, let any one examine the celebrated Rochefoucauld, who is the great philosopher for administering of consolation to the idle, the envious, and worthless part of mankind.

I remember a young gentleman of moderate understanding but great vivacity, who by dipping into many authors of this nature, had got a little smattering of knowledge, just enough to make an atheist or a free-thinker, but not a philosopher or a man of sense. With these accomplishments he went to visit his father in the country, who was a plain, rough, honest man, and wise, though not learned. The son, who took all opportunities to show his learning, began to establish a new religion in the family, and to enlarge the narrowness of their country notions; in which he succeeded so well that he had seduced the butler by his table-talk, and staggered his eldest sister. The old gentleman began to be alarmed at the schisms that arose among his children, but did not yet believe his son's doctrine to be so pernicious as it really was, until one day talking of his setting-dog, the son said, he did not question but Trey was as immortal as any one of the family; and in the heat of the argument told his father that for his own part, he expected to die like a dog. Upon which the old man, starting up in a very great passion, cried out: 'Then, sirrah, you shall live like one'; and taking his cane in his hand, cudgelled him out of his system. This had so good an effect upon him that he took up from that day, fell to reading good books, and is now a bencher in the Middle Temple.

I do not mention this cudgelling part of the story with a design to engage the secular arm in matters of this nature; but certainly, if it ever exerts itself in affairs of opinion and speculation it ought to do it on such shallow and despicable pretenders to knowledge who endeavour to give man dark and uncomfortable prospects of his being, and destroy those principles which are the support, happiness, and glory of all public societies, as well as private persons.

I think it is one of Pythagoras's golden sayings; that a man should take care above all things to have a due respect to himself. And it is certain that this licentious sort of authors, who are for depreciating mankind, endeavour to disappoint and undo what the most refined spirits have been labouring to advance since the beginning of the world. The very design of dress, good breeding, outward ornaments, and ceremony, were to lift up human nature, and set it off to an advantage. Architecture, painting, and statuary were invented with the same design; as indeed every art and science contributes to the embellishment of life, and to the wearing off and throwing into shades the mean and low parts of our nature. Poetry carries on this great end more than all the rest, as may be seen in the following passage, taken out of Sir Francis Bacon's *Advancement of Learning*, which gives a truer and better account of this art than all the volumes that were ever written upon it:

'Poetry, especially heroical, seems to be raised altogether from a noble foundation, which makes much for the dignity of man's nature. For seeing this sensible world is in dignity inferior to the soul of man, poesy seems to endow human nature with that which history denies; and to give satisfaction to the mind, with at least the shadow of things, where the substance cannot be had. For if the matter be thoroughly considered, a strong argument may be drawn from poesy, that a more stately greatness of things, a more perfect order, and a more beautiful variety delights the soul of man than any way can be found in nature since the fall. Wherefore seeing the acts and events, which are the subjects of true history, are not of that amplitude as to content the mind of man; poesy is ready at hand to feign acts more heroical. Because true history reports the successes of business not proportionable to the merit of virtues and vices, poesy corrects it, and presents events and fortunes according to desert, and according to the law of Providence. Because true history, through the frequent satiety and similitude of things, works a distaste and misprision in the mind of man; poesy cheereth and refresheth the soul, chanting things rare and various, and full of vicissitudes. So as poesy serveth and conferreth to delectation, magnanimity, and morality; therefore it may seem deservedly to have some participation of divineness, because it doth raise the mind and exalt the spirit with high raptures, by proportioning the shows of things to the desires of the mind, and not submitting the mind to things as reason and history do. And by these allurements and congruities, whereby it cherisheth the soul of man, joined also with consort of music, whereby it may more sweetly insinuate itself; it hath won such access that it hath been in estimation even in rude times and barbarous nations, when other learning stood excluded.'

But there is nothing which favours and falls in with

this natural greatness and dignity of human nature so much as religion, which does not only promise the entire refinement of the mind, but the glorifying of the body and the immortality of both.

77. *Refractory conduct of certain dead persons*

Having received from the society of upholders sundry complaints of the obstinate and refractory behaviour of several dead persons, who have been guilty of very great outrages and disorders, and by that means elapsed the proper time of their interment; and having on the other hand received many appeals from the aforesaid dead persons, wherein they desire to be heard before such their interment; I have set apart Wednesday, the twenty-first instant, as an extraordinary court-day for the hearing both parties. If, therefore, anyone can allege why they or any of their acquaintance should or should not be buried, I desire they may be ready with their witnesses at that time, or that they will for ever after hold their tongues.

N.B. This is the last hearing on this subject.

78. *Cases of the aforesaid dead persons heard by Mr. Bickerstaff*

As soon as I had placed myself in my chair of judicature, I ordered my clerk, Mr. Lillie, to read to the assembly, who were gathered together according to notice, a certain declaration, by way of charge, to open the purpose of my session, which tended only to this explanation, that as other courts were often called to demand the execution of persons dead in law, so this was held to give the last orders relating to those who are dead in reason. The solicitor of the new company of upholders near the Haymarket appeared in behalf of that useful society, and brought in an accusation of a young woman, who herself stood at the bar before me. Mr. Lillie read her indictment, which was in substance: That whereas Mrs. Rebecca Pindust, of the parish of Saint Martin in the Fields, had by the use of one instrument called a looking-glass, and by the further use of certain attire, made either of cambric, muslin, or other linen wares, upon her head, attained to such an evil art and magical force in the motion of her eyes and turn of her countenance, that she, the said Rebecca, had put to death several young men of the said parish; and that the said young men had acknowledged in certain papers, commonly called love-letters, which were produced in court, gilded on the edges, and sealed with a particular wax, with certain amorous and enchanting words wrought upon the said seals, that they died for the said Rebecca: and whereas the said Rebecca persisted in the said evil practice; this way of life the said society construed to be, according to former edicts, a state of death, and demanded an order for the interment of the said Rebecca.

I looked upon the maid with great humanity, and desired her to make answer to what was said against her. She said it was indeed true that she had practised all the arts and means she could to dispose of herself happily in marriage, but thought she did not come under the censure expressed in my writings for the same; and humbly hoped I would not condemn her for the ignorance of her accusers, who, according to their own words, had rather represented her killing than dead. She further alleged that the expressions mentioned in the papers written to her were become mere words, and that she had been always ready to marry any of those who said they died for her; but that they made their escape as soon as they found themselves pitied or believed. She ended her discourse by desiring I would for the future settle the meaning of the words, 'I die,' in letters of love.

Mrs. Pindust behaved herself with such an air of innocence that she easily gained credit and was acquitted. Upon which occasion I gave it as a standing rule that any person, who in any letter, billet, or discourse should tell a woman he died for her, should, if she pleased, be obliged to live with her, or be immediately interred upon such their own confession, without bail or mainprize.

It happened that the very next who was brought before me was one of her admirers, who was indicted upon that very head. A letter which he acknowledged to be his own hand was read, in which were the following words: 'Cruel creature, I die for you.' It was observable that he took snuff all the time his accusation was reading. I asked him how he came to use these words if he were not a dead man. He told me he was in love with the lady, and did not know any other way of telling her so; and that all his acquaintance took the same method. Though I was moved with compassion towards him by reason of the weakness of his parts, yet for example's sake I was forced to answer: 'Your sentence shall be a warning to all the rest of your companions not to tell lies for want of wit.' Upon this he began to beat his snuff-box with a very saucy air; and opening it again: 'Faith, Isaac,' said he, 'thou art a very unaccountable old fellow. Prithee, who gave thee power of life and death? What a pox hast thou to do with ladies and lovers? I suppose thou wouldst have a man be in company with his mistress and say nothing to her. Dost thou call breaking a jest, telling a lie? Ha! is that thy wisdom, old stiffrump, ha?' He was going on with this insipid commonplace mirth, sometimes opening his box, sometimes shutting it, then viewing the picture on the lid, and then the workmanship of the hinge, when in the midst of his eloquence I ordered his box to be taken from him; upon which he was immediately struck speechless, and carried off stone dead.

The next who appeared was a hale old fellow of sixty. He was brought in by his relations, who desired leave to bury him. Upon requiring a distinct account of the prisoner, a credible witness deposed that he always rose at ten of the clock, played with his cat until twelve, smoked tobacco until one, was at dinner until two, then took another pipe, played at backgammon until six, talked of one Madam Frances, an old mistress of his, until eight, repeated the same account at the tavern until ten, then returned home, took the other pipe, and then to bed.

I asked him what he had to say for himself. 'As to what,' said he, 'they mention concerning Madam Frances——' I did not care for hearing a Canterbury tale, and therefore thought myself seasonably interrupted by a young gentleman, who appeared in the behalf of the old man, and prayed an arrest of judgment; for that he, the said young man, held certain lands by his the said old man's life. Upon this, the solicitor of the upholders took an occasion to demand him also, and thereupon produced several evidences that witnessed to his life and conversation. It appeared that each of them divided their hours in matters of equal moment and importance to themselves and to the public. They rose at the same hour. While the old man was playing with his cat, the young one was looking out of his window; while the old man was smoking his pipe, the young man was rubbing his teeth; while one was at dinner the other was dressing; while one was at backgammon the other was at dinner; while the old fellow was talking of Madam Frances, the young one was either at play, or toasting women whom he never conversed with. The only difference was that the young man had never been good for anything; the old man, a man of worth before he knew Madam Frances. Upon the whole, I ordered them to be both interred together, with inscriptions proper to their characters, signifying that the old man died in the year 1689, and was buried in the year 1709. And over the young one it was said that he departed this world in the twenty-fifth year of his death.

The next class of criminals were authors in prose and verse. Those of them who had produced any stillborn work were immediately dismissed to their burial, and were followed by others who, notwithstanding some sprightly issue in their lifetime, had given proofs of their death by some posthumous children that bore no resemblance to their elder brethren. As for those who were the fathers of a mixed progeny, provided always they could prove the last to be a live child, they escaped with life, but not with-out loss of limbs; for in this case I was satisfied with amputation of the parts which were mortified.

These were followed by a great crowd of superannuated benchers of the Inns of Court, senior fellows of colleges, and defunct statesmen; all whom I ordered to be deci-mated indifferently, allowing the rest a reprieve for one year, with a promise of a free pardon in case of resuscitation.

There were still great multitudes to be examined, but finding it very late, I adjourned the court; not without the secret pleasure that I had done my duty, and furnished out an handsome execution.

79. *A morally deceased gentleman's effects. Burning question of the new-fashioned petticoat*

Whereas the gentleman that behaved himself in a very disobedient and obstinate manner at his late trial in Sheer Lane [1] on the twentieth instant, and was carried off dead upon taking away of his snuff-box, remains still unburied; the company of upholders, not knowing otherwise how they should be paid, have taken his goods in execution to defray the charge of his funeral. His said effects are to be exposed to sale by auction, at their office in the Hay-market, on the fourth of January next, and are as follows:

A very rich tweezer-case, containing twelve instruments for the use of each hour in the day.

Four pounds of scented snuff, with three gilt snuff-boxes; one of them with an invisible hinge, and a looking-glass in the lid.

Two more of ivory, with the portraitures on their lids of two ladies of the town; the originals to be seen every night in the side-boxes of the playhouse.

A sword with a steel diamond hilt, never drawn but once at Mayfair.

Six clean packs of cards, a quart of orange-flower-water,

a pair of French scissors, a toothpick case, and an eyebrow brush.

A large glass case containing the linen and clothes of the deceased; among which are two embroidered suits, a pocket perspective, a dozen pair of red-heeled shoes, three pair of red silk stockings, and an amber-headed cane.

The strong box of the deceased, wherein were found five *billet-doux*, a Bath shilling,[2] a crooked sixpence, a silk garter, a lock of hair, and three broken fans.

A press for books, containing on the upper shelf:
Three bottles of diet-drink.
Two boxes of pills.
A syringe, and other mathematical instruments.
On the second shelf are several miscellaneous works, as:
Lampoons.
Plays.
Tailors' bills.
And an almanac for the year seventeen hundred.
On the third shelf:
A bundle of letters unopened, endorsed, in the hand of the deceased: 'Letters from the old gentleman.'
Lessons for the flute.
Toland's *Christianity not Mysterious*,[3] and a paper filled with patterns of several fashionable stuffs.
On the lowest shelf:
One shoe.
A pair of snuffers.
A French grammar.
A mourning hatband; and half a bottle of usquebaugh.[4]

There will be added to these goods, to make a complete auction, a collection of gold snuff-boxes and clouded canes, which are to continue in fashion for three months after the sale.

The whole are to be set up and priced by Charles Bubbleboy, who is to open the auction with a speech.

I find I am so very unhappy, that while I am busy in correcting the folly and vice of one sex, several exorbitances break out in the other. I have not thoroughly examined their new-fashioned petticoats, but shall set aside one day in the next week for that purpose.   The following petition on this subject was presented to me this morning.

The humble petition of William Jingle, Coach-maker and Chair-maker of the liberty of Westminster.

To Isaac Bickerstaff, Esquire, Censor of
Great Britain:

Showeth,

'That upon the late invention of Mrs. Catherine Cross-stitch, mantua-maker, the petticoats of ladies were too wide for entering into any coach or chair which was in use before the said invention.

'That for the service of the said ladies, your petitioner has built a round chair, in the form of a lantern, six yards and an half in circumference, with a stool in the centre of it; the said vehicle being so contrived as to receive the passenger by opening in two in the middle, and closing mathematically when she is seated.

'That your petitioner has also invented a coach for the reception of one lady only, who is to be let in at the top.

'That the said coach has been tried by a lady's-woman in one of these full petticoats, who was let down from a balcony, and drawn up again by pulleys, to the great satisfaction of her lady and all who beheld her.

'Your petitioner therefore most humbly prays that for the encouragement of ingenuity and useful inventions, he may be heard before you pass sentence upon the petticoats aforesaid.

'And your Petitioner, etc.'

I have likewise received a female petition, signed by several thousands, praying that I would not any longer defer giving judgment in the case of the petticoat, many of them having put off the making new clothes, until such time as they know what verdict will pass upon it.   I do therefore hereby certify to all whom it may concern, that I do design to set apart Tuesday next for the final determination of that matter, having already ordered a jury of matrons to be impanelled, for the clearing up of any difficult points that may arise in the trial.

80.   From a well-wisher

SAGE SIR,
   You cannot but know there are many scribblers, and others, who revile you and your writings.   It is wondered that you do not exert yourself, and crush them at once. I am, Sir,
         With great respect,
               Your most humble admirer and disciple.

In answer to this I shall act like my predecessor Aesop, and give him a fable instead of a reply.

It happened one day as a stout and honest mastiff, that guarded the village where he lived against thieves and robbers, was very gravely walking with one of his puppies by his side, all the little dogs in the street gathered about him and barked at him.   The little puppy was so offended at this affront done to his sire, that he asked him why he would not fall upon them, and tear them to pieces.   To which the sire answered, with a great composure of mind: 'If there were no curs, I should be no mastiff.'

81.   The case of the Petticoat

The court being prepared for proceeding on the cause of the petticoat,[1] I gave orders to bring in a criminal who was taken up as she went out of the puppet-show about three nights ago, and was now standing in the street with a great concourse of people about her.   Word was brought me that she had endeavoured twice or thrice to come in but could not do it by reason of her petticoat, which was

too large for the entrance of my house, though I had
ordered both the folding doors to be thrown open for its
reception.   Upon this, I desired the jury of matrons, who
stood at my right hand, to inform themselves of her condition, and know whether there were any private reasons
why she might not make her appearance separate from her
petticoat.   This was managed with great discretion, and
had such an effect that upon the return of the verdict from
the bench of matrons, I issued out an order forthwith,
that the criminal should be stripped of her encumbrances
until she became little enough to enter my house.   I had
before given directions for an engine of several legs, that
could contract or open itself like the top of an umbrella,
in order to place the petticoat upon it, by which means
I might take a leisurely survey of it, as it should appear in
its proper dimensions.   This was all done accordingly;
and forthwith, upon the closing of the engine, the petticoat was brought into court.   I then directed the machine
to be set upon the table and dilated in such a manner as
to show the garment in its utmost circumference; but my
great hall was too narrow for the experiment, for before it
was half unfolded, it described so immoderate a circle
that the lower part of it brushed upon my face as I sat in
my chair of judicature.   I then inquired for the person
that belonged to the petticoat; and, to my great surprise,
was directed to a very beautiful young damsel, with so
pretty a face and shape that I bid her come out of the
crowd, and seated her upon a little crock at my left hand.
'My pretty maid,' said I, 'do you own yourself to have been
the inhabitant of the garment before us?'   The girl I found
had good sense, and told me with a smile, that notwithstanding it was her own petticoat, she should be very glad
to see an example made of it; and that she wore it for no
other reason but that she had a mind to look as big and
burly as other persons of her quality; that she had kept
out of it as long as she could, and until she began to appear
little in the eyes of all her acquaintance; that if she laid it
aside people would think she was not made like other
women.   I always give great allowances to the fair sex

upon account of the fashion, and therefore was not displeased with the defence of my pretty criminal. I then
ordered the vest which stood before us to be drawn up
by a pulley to the top of my great hall, and afterwards to
be spread open by the engine it was placed upon, in such
a manner that it formed a very splendid and ample canopy
over our heads, and covered the whole court of judicature
with a kind of silken rotunda, in its form not unlike the
cupola of Saint Paul's. I entered upon the whole cause
with great satisfaction as I sat under the shadow of it.

The counsel for the petticoat were now called in, and
ordered to produce what they had to say against the
popular cry which was raised against it. They answered
the objections with great strength and solidity of argument,
and expatiated in very florid harangues, which they did
not fail to set off and furbelow, if I may be allowed the
metaphor, with many periodical sentences and turns of
oratory. The chief arguments for their client were taken,
first, from the great benefit that might arise to our woollen
manufactory from this invention, which was calculated as
follows: The common petticoat has not above four yards
in the circumference, whereas this over our heads had
more in the semi-diameter; so that by allowing it twenty-
four yards in the circumference, the five millions of woollen
petticoats, which, according to Sir William Petty,[2] supposing what ought to be supposed in a well-governed
state, that all petticoats are made of that stuff, would
amount to thirty millions of those of the ancient mode.
A prodigious improvement of the woollen trade! and what
could not fail to sink the power of France in a few years.

To introduce the second argument, they begged leave
to read a petition of the rope-makers, wherein it was
represented that the demand for cords, and the price of
them, were much risen since this fashion came up. At
this, all the company who were present lifted up their
eyes into the vault; and I must confess, we did discover
many traces of cordage, which were interwoven in the
stiffening of the drapery.

A third argument was founded upon a petition of the

Greenland trade, which likewise represented the great consumption of whalebone which would be occasioned by the present fashion, and the benefit which would thereby accrue to that branch of the British trade.

To conclude, they gently touched upon the weight and unwieldiness of the garment, which they insinuated might be of great use to preserve the honour of families.

These arguments would have wrought very much upon me, as I then told the company in a long and elaborate discourse, had I not considered the great and additional expense which such fashions would bring upon fathers and husbands; and therefore by no means to be thought of until some years after a peace. I further urged that it would be a prejudice to the ladies themselves, who could never expect to have any money in the pocket if they laid out so much on the petticoat. To this I added the great temptation it might give to virgins, of acting in security like married women, and by that means give a check to matrimony, an institution always encouraged by wise societies.

At the same time, in answer to the several petitions produced on that side, I showed one subscribed by the women of several persons of quality, humbly setting forth that since the introduction of this mode, their respective ladies had, instead of bestowing on them their cast gowns, cut them into shreds, and mixed them with the cordage and buckram, to complete the stiffening of their under-petticoats. For which, and sundry other reasons, I pronounced the petticoat a forfeiture. But to show that I did not make that judgment for the sake of filthy lucre, I ordered it to be folded up, and sent it as a present to a widow gentlewoman, who has five daughters; desiring she would make each of them a petticoat out of it, and send me back the remainder, which I design to cut into stomachers, caps, facings of my waistcoat-sleeves, and other garnitures suitable to my age and quality.

I would not be understood that, while I discard this monstrous invention, I am an enemy to the proper ornaments of the fair sex. On the contrary, as the hand of nature has poured on them such a profusion of charms and graces, and sent them into the world more amiable and finished than the rest of her works; so I would have them bestow upon themselves all the additional beauties that art can supply them with, provided it does not interfere with, disguise, or pervert those of nature.

I consider woman as a beautiful romantic animal, that may be adorned with furs and feathers, pearls and diamonds, ores and silks. The lynx shall cast its skin at her feet to make her a tippet; the peacock, parrot, and swan shall pay contributions to her muff; the sea shall be searched for shells, and the rocks for gems; and every part of nature furnish out its share towards the embellishment of a creature that is the most consummate work of it. All this I shall indulge them in; but as for the petticoat I have been speaking of, I neither can nor will allow it.

82. Salutary effects of the 'Tatler'

SIR,   December 31.

I have perused your *Tatler* of this day, and have wept over it with great pleasure. I wish you would be more frequent in your family pieces, for as I consider you under the notion of a great designer, I think these are not your least valuable performances. I . . . think you have employed yourself more in grotesque figures than in beauties, for which reason I would rather see you work upon history pieces than on single portraits. Your several draughts of dead men appear to me as pictures of still life, and have done great good in the place where I live. The Esquire of a neighbouring village, who had been a long time in the number of nonentities, is entirely recovered by them. For these several years past, there was not an hare in the country that could be at rest for him; and I think the greatest exploit he ever boasted of was that when he was High Sheriff of the county, he hunted a fox so far that he could not follow him any further by the laws of the land. All the hours he spent at home were in swelling himself with *October*,[1] and rehearsing the wonders he did in the field. Upon reading your papers, he has sold his dogs, shook off his dead companions, looked into his estate, got the multiplication table by heart, paid his tithes, and intends to take upon him the office of churchwarden next year. I wish the same success with your other patients, and am, etc.

83. *The humble petition of Penelope Prim*

SHOWETH,

That your petitioner was bred a clear-starcher and sempstress, and for many years worked to the Exchange, and to several aldermen's wives, lawyers' clerks, and merchants' apprentices.

That through the scarcity caused by regrators [1] of bread corn, of which starch is made, and the gentry's immoderate frequenting the operas, the ladies, to save charges, have their heads washed at home, and the beaux put out their linen to common laundresses; so that your petitioner has little or no work at her trade: for want of which she is reduced to such necessity that she and her seven fatherless children must inevitably perish, unless relieved by your worship.

That your petitioner is informed, that in contempt of your judgment pronounced on Tuesday the third instant against the new-fashioned petticoat, or old-fashioned fardingal, the ladies design to go on in that dress. And since it is presumed your worship will not suppress them by force, your petitioner humbly desires you would order that ruffs may be added to the dress; and that she may be heard by her counsel, who has assured your petitioner he has such cogent reasons to offer to your court, that ruffs and fardingals are inseparable, that he questions not but two-thirds of the greatest beauties about town will have cambric collars on their necks before the end of Easter term next. He further says that the design of our great-grandmothers in this petticoat was to appear much bigger than the life; for which reason they had false shoulder-blades, like wings, and the ruff above-mentioned, to make their upper and lower parts of their bodies appear proportionable; whereas the figure of a woman in the present dress, bears, as he calls it, the figure of a cone, which, as he advises, is the same with that of an extinguisher, with a little knob at the upper end, and widening downward, until it ends in a basis of a most enormous circumference.

Your petitioner therefore most humbly prays that you would restore the ruff to the fardingal, which in their nature ought to be as inseparable as the two Hungarian twins.

And your petitioner shall ever pray.

I have examined into the allegations of this petition, and find, by several ancient pictures of my own predecessors, particularly that of Dame Deborah Bickerstaff, my great-grandmother, that the ruff and fardingal are made use of as absolutely necessary to preserve the symmetry of the figure; and Mrs. Pyramid Bickerstaff, her second sister, is recorded in our family book, with some observations to her disadvantage, as the first female of our house that discovered, to any besides her nurse and her husband, an inch below her chin, or above her instep. This convinces me of the reasonableness of Mrs. Prim's demand; and therefore I shall not allow the reviving of any one part of the ancient mode, except the whole is complied with. Mrs. Prim is therefore hereby empowered to carry home ruffs to such as she shall see in the above-mentioned petticoats, and require payment on demand.

84.   Mr. Bickerstaff's expectations from the new lottery

I went on Saturday last to make a visit in the city; and as I passed through Cheapside, I saw crowds of people turning down towards the Bank, and struggling who should first get their money into the new-erected lottery. It gave me a great notion of the credit of our present government and administration to find people press as eagerly to pay money as they would to receive it; and at the same time a due respect for that body of men who have found out so pleasing an expedient for carrying on the common cause that they have turned a tax into a diversion. The cheerfulness of spirit, and the hopes of success which this project has occasioned in this great city, lightens the burden of the war, and puts me in mind of some games which they say were invented by wise men, who were lovers of their country, to make their fellow citizens undergo the tediousness and fatigues of a long siege. I think there is a kind of homage due to fortune, if I may call it so, and that I should be wanting to myself if I did not lay in my pretences to her favour, and pay my compliments to her by recommending a ticket to her disposal. For this reason, upon my return to my lodgings, I sold off a couple of globes and a telescope, which, with the cash I had by me, raised the sum that was requisite for that purpose. I find by my calculations that it is but an hundred and fifty thousand to one against my being worth a thousand pounds per annum for thirty-two years; and if any Plumb [1] in the city will lay me an hundred and fifty thousand pounds to twenty shillings, which is an even bet, that I am not this fortunate man, I will take the wager, and shall look upon him as a man of singular courage and fair dealing; having giving orders to Mr. Morphew to subscribe such a policy in my behalf, if any person accepts of the offer. I must confess I have had such private intimations from the twinkling of a certain star in some of my astronomical observations, that I should be unwilling to take fifty pounds a year for my chance, unless it were to oblige a particular friend. My chief business at present is to prepare my mind for this change of fortune. For as Seneca, who was a greater moralist, and a much richer man than I shall be with this addition to my present income, says, *Munera ista fortunae putatis ?*

Insidiae sunt. 'What we look upon as gifts and presents of fortune, are traps and snares which she lays for the unwary.' [2]

85. *Base conduct of composers of wines*

There is in this city a certain fraternity of chemical operators who work underground in holes, caverns, and dark retirements, to conceal their mysteries from the eyes and observations of mankind.　These subterraneous philosophers are daily employed in the transmutation of liquors, and, by the power of magical drugs and incantations, raising under the streets of London the choicest products of the hills and valleys of France.　They can squeeze Bordeaux out of the sloe, and draw champagne from an apple.　Virgil, in that remarkable prophecy,

> *Incultisque rubens pendebit sentibus uva,*
>
> VIRG. EC. IV. 29.

　　The rip'ning grape shall hang on every thorn,

seems to have hinted at this art, which can turn a plantation of northern hedges into a vineyard.　These adepts are known among one another by the name of 'wine-brewers,' and, I am afraid, do great injury, not only to Her Majesty's customs, but to the bodies of many of her good subjects.

Having received sundry complaints against these invisible workmen, I ordered the proper officer of my court to ferret them out of their respective caves, and bring them before me, which was yesterday executed accordingly.

The person who appeared against them was a merchant who had by him a great magazine of wines that he had laid in before the war: but these gentlemen, as he said, had so vitiated the nation's palate, that no man could believe his to be French, because it did not taste like what they sold for such.　As a man never pleads better than where his own personal interest is concerned, he exhibited

to the court, with great eloquence, that this new corporation of druggists had inflamed the bills of mortality, and
puzzled the college of physicians with diseases for which
they neither knew a name nor cure. He accused some of
giving all their customers colics and megrims; and mentioned one who had boasted he had a tun of claret by him
that in a fortnight's time should give the gout to a dozen
of the healthfullest men in the city, provided that their
constitutions were prepared for it by wealth and idleness.
He then enlarged, with a great show of reason, upon the
prejudice which these mixtures and compositions had done
to the brains of the English nation; as is too visible, said
he, from many late pamphlets, speeches, and sermons, as
well as from the ordinary conversations of the youth of
this age. He then quoted an ingenious person who would
undertake to know by a man's writings the wine he most
delighted in; and on that occasion named a certain satirist,
whom he had discovered to be the author of a lampoon,
by the manifest taste of the sloe, which showed itself in
it by much roughness and little spirit.

In the last place, he ascribed to the unnatural tumults
and fermentations which these mixtures raise in our blood,
the divisions, heats, and animosities that reign among
us; and, in particular, asserted most of the modern
enthusiasms and agitations to be nothing else but the
effects of adulterated Port.

The counsel for the brewers had a face so extremely
inflamed and illuminated with carbuncles, that I did not
wonder to see him an advocate for these sophistications.
His rhetoric was likewise such as I should have expected
from the common draught, which I found he often drank
to a great excess. Indeed, I was so surprised at his figure
and parts, that I ordered him to give me a taste of his
usual liquor; which I had no sooner drunk, but I found a
pimple rising in my forehead; and felt such a sensible
decay in my understanding that I would not proceed in
the trial until the fume of it was entirely dissipated.

This notable advocate had little to say in the defence
of his clients, but that they were under a necessity of

making claret, if they would keep open their doors; it being the nature of mankind to love everything that is prohibited. He further pretended to reason that it might be as profitable to the nation to make French wine as French hats; and concluded with the great advantage that this practice had already brought to part of the kingdom. Upon which he informed the court that the lands in Herefordshire were raised two years' purchase since the beginning of the war.

When I had sent out my summons to these people, I gave, at the same time, orders to each of them to bring the several ingredients he made use of in distinct phials, which they had done accordingly, and ranged them into two rows on each side of the court. The workmen were drawn up in ranks behind them. The merchant informed me that in one row of phials were the several colours they dealt in, and in the other, the tastes. He then showed me, on the right hand, one who went by the name of Tom Tintoret, who, as he told me, was the greatest master in his colouring of any vintner in London. To give me a proof of his art, he took a glass of fair water, and, by the infusion of three drops out of one of his phials, converted it into a most beautiful pale Burgundy. Two more of the same kind heightened it into a perfect Languedoc. From thence it passed into a florid Hermitage; and after having gone through two or three other changes, by the addition of a single drop, ended in a very deep Pontac. This ingenious virtuoso, seeing me very much surprised at his art, told me that he had not an opportunity of showing it in perfection, having only made use of water for the ground-work of his colouring; but that if I were to see an operation upon liquors of stronger bodies, the art would appear to a much greater advantage. He added that he doubted not but it would please my curiosity to see the cider of one apple take only a vermilion, when another, with a less quantity of the same infusion, would rise into a dark purple, according to the different texture of parts in the liquor. He informed me also, that he could hit the different shades and degrees of red, as they appear in the pink

and the rose, the clove and the carnation, as he had Rhenish
or Moselle, Perry or White Port, to work in.

I was so satisfied with the ingenuity of this virtuoso,
that after having advised him to quit so dishonest a profession, I promised him, in consideration of his great
genius, to recommend him as a partner to a friend of mine,
who has heaped up great riches and is a scarlet-dyer.

The artists on my other hand were ordered, in the
second place, to make some experiments of their skill
before me. Upon which the famous Harry Sippet stepped
out and asked me what I would be pleased to drink.
At the same time he filled out three or four white liquors
in a glass and told me that it should be what I pleased
to call for; adding very learnedly that the liquor before
him was as the naked substance, or first matter of his
compound, to which he and his friend, who stood over
against him, could give what accidents or form they
pleased. Finding him so great a philosopher, I desired he
would convey into it the qualities and essence of right
Bordeaux. 'Coming, coming, Sir,' said he, with the air
of a drawer; and, after having cast his eye on the several
tastes and flavours that stood before him, he took up a
little cruet that was filled with a kind of inky juice, and
pouring some of it out into the glass of white wine,
presented it to me and told me this was the wine over
which most of the business of the last term had been
dispatched. I must confess, I looked upon that sooty
drug which he held up in his cruet as the quintessence
of English Bordeaux; and therefore desired him to give
me a glass of it by itself, which he did with great un-
willingness. My cat at that time sat by me upon the
elbow of my chair; and as I did not care for making the
experiment upon myself, I reached it to her to sip of it,
which had like to have cost her her life; for notwithstanding it flung her at first into freakish tricks, quite
contrary to her usual gravity, in less than a quarter of an
hour she fell into convulsions; and, had it not been a
creature more tenacious of life than any other, would
certainly have died under the operation.

I was so incensed by the tortures of my innocent domestic and the unworthy dealings of these men, that I told them, if each of them had as many lives as the injured creature before them, they deserved to forfeit them for the pernicious arts which they used for their profit. I therefore bid them look upon themselves as no better than as a kind of assassins and murderers within the law. However, since they had dealt so clearly with me, and laid before me their whole practice, I dismissed them for that time; with a particular request that they would not poison any of my friends and acquaintance, and take to some honest livelihood without loss of time.

For my own part, I have resolved hereafter to be very careful in my liquors; and have agreed with a friend of mine in the army, upon their next march, to secure me two hogsheads of the best stomach-wine in the cellars of Versailles, for the good of my lucubrations and the comfort of my old age.

86. *An old-fashioned Major corrects a young officer*

When I was a young man about this town, I frequented the ordinary [1] of the Black Horse in Holborn, where the person that usually presided at the table was a rough old-fashioned gentleman, who, according to the customs of those times, had been the major and preacher of a regiment. It happened one day that a noisy young officer, bred in France, was venting some newfangled notions, and speaking, in the gaiety of his humour, against the dispensations of Providence. The major, at first, only desired him to talk more respectfully of one for whom all the company had an honour; but finding him run on in his extravagance, began to reprimand him after a more serious manner. 'Young man,' said he, 'do not abuse your Benefactor whilst you are eating His bread. Consider whose air you breathe, whose presence you are in, and who it is that gave you the power of that very speech which you make use of to His dishonour.'

The young fellow, who thought to turn matters into a jest, asked him if he was going to preach, but at the same time desired him to take care what he said when he spoke to a man of honour. 'A man of honour!' says the major; 'thou art an infidel and a blasphemer, and I shall use thee as such.' In short, the quarrel ran so high that the major was desired to walk out. Upon their coming into the garden, the old fellow advised his antagonist to consider the place into which one pass might drive him; but finding him grow upon him to a degree of scurrility, as believing the advice proceeded from fear: 'Sirrah,' says he, 'if a thunderbolt does not strike thee dead before I come at thee, I shall not fail to chastise thee for thy profaneness to thy Maker, and thy sauciness to His servant.'

Upon this he drew his sword, and cried out with a loud voice: 'The sword of the Lord and of Gideon!' which so terrified his antagonist that he was immediately disarmed and thrown upon his knees. In this posture he begged his life; but the major refused to grant it before he had asked pardon for his offence in a short extemporary prayer, which the old gentleman dictated to him upon the spot, and which his proselyte repeated after him in the presence of the whole ordinary, that were now gathered about him in the garden.

87. The humble petition of Deborah Hark, Sarah Threadpaper, and Rachel Thimble, spinsters, and single women, commonly called waiting-maids, in behalf of themselves and their sisterhood.

SHOWETH,

That your worship has been pleased to order and command that no person or persons shall presume to wear quilted petticoats, on forfeiture of the said petticoats, or penalty of wearing ruffs, after the seventeenth instant now expired.

That your petitioners have, time out of mind, been entitled to wear their ladies' clothes, or to sell the same.

That the sale of the said clothes is spoiled by your worship's said prohibition.

Your petitioners therefore most humbly pray that your worship would please to allow that all gentlewomen's gentlewomen may be allowed to wear the said dress, or to repair the loss of such a perquisite in such manner as your worship shall think fit.

And your petitioners, etc.

I do allow the allegations of this petition to be just; and forbid all persons but the petitioners, or those who shall purchase from them, to wear the said garment after the date hereof.

88. *Letters from Dorothy Drumstick, Lydia, and Chloe*

Sir,

This comes from a relation of yours, though unknown to you, who, besides the tie of consanguinity, has some value for you on the account of your lucubrations, those being designed to refine our conversation, as well as cultivate our minds. I humbly beg the favour of you, in one of your *Tatlers*, after what manner you please, to correct a particular friend of mine, for an indecorum he is guilty of in discourse, of calling his acquaintance, when he speaks of them, 'Madam': as for example, my cousin Jenny Distaff, 'Madam Distaff'; which I am sure you are sensible is very unpolite, and it is what makes me often uneasy for him, though I cannot tell him of it myself, which makes me guilty of this presumption, that I depend upon your goodness to excuse; and I do assure you, the gentleman will mind your reprehension, for he is, as I am, Sir,

Your most humble servant and cousin,
DOROTHY DRUMSTICK.

I write this in a thin under-petticoat, and never did or will wear a fardingal.

I had no sooner read the just complaint of Mrs.

Drumstick, but I received an urgent one from another of the fair sex, upon faults of more pernicious consequence.

MR. BICKERSTAFF,

I beg of you to forbear giving . . . any account of our religion or manners until you have rooted out certain misdemeanours even in our churches. Among others, that of bowing, saluting, taking snuff, and other gestures. Lady Autumn made me a very low curtsy the other day from the next pew, and with the most courtly air imaginable called herself 'miserable sinner.' Her niece, soon after, in saying 'Forgive us our trespasses,' curtsied with a gloating look at my brother. He returned it, opening his snuff-box, and repeating yet a more solemn expression. I beg of you, good Mr. Censor . . . to believe this does not come from one of a morose temper, mean birth, rigid education, narrow fortune, or bigotry in opinion, or from one in whom time has worn out all taste of pleasure. I assure you it is far otherwise, for I am possessed of all the contrary advantages; and I hope wealth, good humour, and good breeding may be best employed in the service of religion and virtue; and desire you would, as soon as possible, remark upon the above-mentioned indecorums, that we may not long transgress against the latter, to preserve our reputation in the former.

Your humble servant,
LYDIA.

The last letter I shall insert is what follows. This is written by a very inquisitive lady; and, I think, such interrogative gentlewomen are to be answered no other way than by interrogation. Her billet is this:

DEAR MR. BICKERSTAFF,

Are you quite as good as you seem to be?

CHLOE.

To which I can only answer:

DEAR CHLOE,

Are you quite as ignorant as you seem to be?

I. B.

89. To all gentlemen, ladies, and others, that delight in soft lines

These are to give notice that, the proper time of the year for writing pastorals now drawing near, there is a stage-coach settled from the One Bell in the Strand to Dorchester, which sets out twice a week, and passes through Basingstoke, Sutton, Stockbridge, Salisbury, Blandford, and so to Dorchester, over the finest downs in England. At all which places, there are accommodations of spreading beeches, beds of flowers, turf seats, and purling streams, for happy swains; and thunderstruck oaks, and left-handed ravens,[1] to foretell misfortunes to those that please to be wretched, with all other necessaries for pensive passion.

And for the conveniency of such whose affairs will not permit them to leave this town, at the same place they may be furnished, during the season, with opening buds, flowering thyme, warbling birds, sporting lambkins, and fountain-water, right and good, and bottled on the spot by one sent down on purpose.

N.B. The nymphs and swains are further given to understand, that in those happy climes they are so far from being troubled with wolves that for want of even foxes, a considerable pack of hounds have been lately forced to eat sheep.[2]

90. The Complainers

Among the various sets of correspondents who apply to me for advice, and send up their cases from all parts of Great Britain, there are none who are more importunate with me, and whom I am more inclined to answer, than the 'complainers.' One of them dates his letter to me from the banks of a purling stream, where he used to ruminate in solitude upon the divine Clarissa, and where he is now looking about for a convenient leap, which he tells me he is resolved to take, unless I support him under the loss of that charming perjured woman.   Poor Lavinia presses as much for consolation on the other side, and is reduced to such an extremity of despair by the inconstancy of Philander, that she tells me she writes her letter with her pen in one hand and her garter in the other.   A gentleman of an ancient family in Norfolk is almost out of his wits upon the account of a greyhound that, after having been his inseparable companion for ten years, is at last run mad. Another, who I believe is serious, complains to me, in a very moving manner, of the loss of a wife; and another, in terms still more moving, of a purse of money that was taken from him on Bagshot Heath, and which, he tells me, would not have troubled him if he had given it to the poor.   In short, there is scarce a calamity in human life that has not produced me a letter.

It is indeed wonderful to consider how men are able to raise affliction to themselves out of everything.   Lands and houses, sheep and oxen, can convey happiness and misery into the hearts of reasonable creatures.   Nay, I have known a muff, a scarf, or a tippet become a solid blessing or misfortune.   A lap-dog has broke the hearts of thousands.   Flavia, who had buried five children and two husbands, was never able to get over the loss of her parrot.   How often has a divine creature been thrown into a fit by a neglect at a Ball or an Assembly!   Mopsa has kept her chamber ever since the last masquerade, and is in greater danger of her life upon being left out of it, than Clarinda from the violent cold she caught at it.

91. *Mr. Bickerstaff receives an acceptable present*

Upon my coming home last night, I found a very handsome present of wine left for me, as a taste 'of two hundred and sixteen hogsheads, which are put to sale at twenty pounds a hogshead, at Garraway's coffee-house in Exchange Alley, on the twenty-second instant, at three in the afternoon, and to be tasted in Major Long's vaults from the twentieth instant until the time of sale.' This having been sent me with a desire that I would give my judgment upon it, I immediately impanelled a jury of men of nice palates and strong heads, who, being all of them very scrupulous, and unwilling to proceed rashly in a matter of so great importance, refused to bring in their verdict until three in the morning; at which time the foreman pronounced, as well as he was able, 'Extra-a-ordinary French claret.' For my own part, as I love to consult my pillow in all points of moment, I slept upon it before I would give my sentence, and this morning confirmed the verdict.

Having mentioned this tribute of wine, I must give notice to my correspondents for the future, who shall apply to me on this occasion, that as I shall decide nothing unadvisedly in matters of this nature, I cannot pretend to give judgment of a right good liquor without examining at least three dozen bottles of it. I must, at the same time, do myself the justice to let the world know that I have resisted great temptations in this kind; as it is well known to a butcher in Clare Market who endeavoured to corrupt me with a dozen and a half of marrow-bones. I had likewise a bribe sent me by a fishmonger, consisting of a collar of brawn, and a joll of salmon [1]; but not finding them excellent in their kinds, I had the integrity to eat them both up, without speaking one word of them. However, for the future, I shall have an eye to the diet of this great city, and will recommend the best and most wholesome food to them if I receive these proper and respectful notices from the sellers, that it may not be said hereafter that my readers were better taught than fed.

92. *Concerning the nuptial state*

I have received the following letter upon the subject of my last paper. The writer of it tells me I there spoke of marriage as one that knows it only by speculation, and for that reason he sends me his sense of it, as drawn from experience.

MR. BICKERSTAFF,

I have received your paper of this day, and think you have done the nuptial state a great deal of justice . . . but give me leave to tell you that it is impossible for you, that are a bachelor, to have so just a notion of this way of life as to touch the affections of your readers in a particular wherein every man's own heart suggests more than the nicest observer can form to himself without experience. I, therefore, who am an old married man, have sat down to give you an account of the matter from my own knowledge, and the observations which I have made upon the conduct of others in that most agreeable or wretched condition.

It is very commonly observed that the most smart pangs which we meet with are in the beginning of wedlock, which proceed from ignorance of each other's humour, and want of prudence to make allowances for a change from the most careful respect to the most unbounded familiarity. Hence it arises that trifles are commonly occasions of the greatest anxiety; for contradiction being a thing wholly unusual between a new-married couple, the smallest instance of it is taken for the highest injury; and it very seldom happens that the man is slow enough in assuming the character of a husband, or the woman quick enough in condescending to that of a wife. It immediately follows that they think they have all the time of their courtship been talking in masks to each other, and therefore begin to act like disappointed people. Philander finds Delia ill-natured and impertinent; and Delia, Philander surly and inconstant.

I have known a fond couple quarrel in the very honeymoon about cutting up a tart. Nay, I could name two, who, after having had seven children, fell out and parted beds upon the boiling of a leg of mutton. My very next neighbours have not spoke to one another these three days, because they differed in their opinions whether the clock should stand by the window or over the chimney. It may seem strange to you, who are not a married man, when I tell you how the least trifle can strike a woman dumb for a week together. But if you ever enter into this state, you will find that the soft sex as often express their anger by an obstinate silence as by an ungovernable clamour.

Those indeed who begin this course of life without jars at their setting out, arrive within few months at a pitch of benevolence and affection, of which the most perfect friendship is but a faint resemblance. As in the unfortunate marriage, the most minute and indifferent things are objects of the sharpest resentment; so in an happy one, they are occasions of the most exquisite satisfaction. For what does not oblige in one we love? What does not offend in one we dislike? For these reasons I take it for a rule, that in marriage, the chief business is to acquire a prepossession in favour of each other. They should consider one another's words and actions with a secret indulgence. There should be always an inward fondness pleading for each other, such as may add new beauties to everything that is excellent, give charms to what is indifferent, and cover everything that is defective. For want of this kind propensity and bias of mind, the married pair often take things ill of each other, which no one else would take notice of in either of them.

93. *Unhappy consequences of women's love of finery*

When artists would expose their diamonds to an advantage, they usually set them to show in little cases of black velvet. By this means the jewels appear in their true and genuine lustre, while there is no colour that can infect their brightness, or give a false cast to the water. When I was at the Opera the other night, the assembly of ladies in mourning made me consider them in the same kind of view. A dress wherein there is so little variety shows the face in all its natural charms, and makes one differ from another only as it is more or less beautiful. Painters are ever careful of offending against a rule which is so essential in all just representations. The chief figure must have the strongest point of light, and not be injured by any gay colourings that may draw away the attention to any less considerable part of the picture. The present fashion obliges everybody to be dressed with propriety, and makes the ladies' faces the principal objects of sight. Every beautiful person shines out in all the excellence with which nature has adorned her; gaudy ribands and glaring colours being now out of use, the sex has no opportunity given them to disfigure themselves, which they seldom fail to do whenever it lies in their power. When a woman comes to her glass, she does not employ her time in making herself look more advantageously what she really is; but endeavours to be as much another creature as she possibly can. Whether this happens because they stay so long and attend their work so diligently that they forget the faces and persons which they first sat down with, or whatever it is, they seldom rise from the toilet the same women they appeared when they began to dress. What jewel can the charming Cleora place in her ears that can please her beholders so much as her eyes? The cluster of diamonds upon the breast can add no beauty to the fair chest of ivory which supports it. It may indeed tempt a man to steal a woman, but never to love her. Let Thalestris change herself into a motley, particoloured animal. The pearl necklace, the flowered stomacher, the artificial nose-gay, and shaded furbelow, may be of use to attract the eye of the beholder, and turn it from the imperfections of her features and shape. But if ladies will take my word for it, and as they dress to please men they ought to consult our fancy rather than their own in this particular, I can assure them there is nothing touches our imagination so much as a beautiful woman in a plain dress. There might be more agreeable ornaments found in our own manufacture than any that rise out of the looms of Persia.

This, I know, is a very harsh doctrine to womankind, who are carried away with everything that is showy, and with what delights the eye, more than any one species of living creatures whatsoever. Were the minds of the sex

laid open, we should find the chief idea in one to be a
tippet, in another a muff, in a third a fan, and in a fourth a
fardingal. The memory of an old visiting lady is so filled
up with gloves, silks, and ribands that I can look upon
it as nothing else but a toy-shop. A matron of my
acquaintance, complaining of her daughter's vanity, was
observing that she had all of a sudden held up her head
higher than ordinary, and taken an air that showed a secret
satisfaction in herself, mixed with a scorn of others. 'I did
not know,' says my friend, 'what to make of the carriage of
this fantastical girl, until I was informed by her eldest
sister that she had a pair of striped garters on.' This odd
turn of mind often makes the sex unhappy, and disposes
them to be struck with everything that makes a show,
however trifling and superficial.

Many a lady has fetched a sigh at the toss of a wig, and
been ruined by the tapping of a snuff-box. It is impossible
to describe all the execution that was done by the shoulder-
knot while that fashion prevailed, or to reckon up all the
virgins that have fallen a sacrifice to a pair of fringed
gloves. A sincere heart has not made half so many conquests as an open waistcoat; and I should be glad to see
an able head make so good a figure in a woman's company
as a pair of red heels. A Grecian hero,[1] when he was
asked whether he could play upon the lute, thought he had
made a very good reply when he answered: 'No; but I
can make a great city of a little one.' Notwithstanding
his boasted wisdom, I appeal to the heart of any Toast in
town, whether she would not think the lutenist preferable
to the statesman. I do not speak this out of any aversion
that I have to the sex. On the contrary, I have always
had a tenderness for them; but I must confess it troubles
me very much to see the generality of them place their
affections on improper objects, and give up all the pleasures
of life for gewgaws and trifles.

Mrs. Margery Bickerstaff, my great-aunt, had a thousand
pounds to her portion, which our family was desirous of
keeping among themselves, and therefore used all possible
means to turn off her thoughts from marriage. The

method they took was, in any time of danger, to throw a new gown or petticoat in her way. When she was about twenty-five years of age, she fell in love with a man of an agreeable temper and equal fortune, and would certainly have married him, had not my grandfather, Sir Jacob, dressed her up in a suit of flowered satin; upon which she set so immoderate a value upon herself that the lover was contemned and discarded. In the fortieth year of her age she was again smitten; but very luckily transferred her passion to a tippet, which was presented to her by another relation who was in the plot. This, with a white sarsenet hood, kept her safe in the family until fifty. About sixty, which generally produces a kind of latter spring in amorous constitutions, my aunt Margery had again a colt's tooth in her head [2]; and would certainly have eloped from the mansion-house, had not her brother Simon, who was a wise man and a scholar, advised to dress her in cherry-coloured ribands, which was the only expedient that could have been found out by the wit of man to preserve the thousand pounds in our family, part of which I enjoy at this time.

94. *Married happiness, illustrated from Cicero's letters*

The wits of this island, for above fifty years past, instead of correcting the vices of the age, have done all they could to inflame them. Marriage has been one of the common topics of ridicule that every stage scribbler hath found his account in; for whenever there is an occasion for a clap, an impertinent jest upon matrimony is sure to raise it. This hath been attended with very pernicious consequences. Many a country esquire, upon his setting up for a man of the town, has gone home in the gaiety of his heart and beat his wife. A kind husband hath been looked upon as a clown, and a good wife as a domestic animal unfit for the company or conversation of the *beau monde*. In short, separate beds, silent tables, and solitary homes have been introduced by your men of wit and pleasure of the age.

As I shall always make it my business to stem the torrents of prejudice and vice, I shall take particular care to put an honest father of a family in countenance, and endeavour to remove all the evils out of that state of life, which is either the most happy or most miserable that a man can be placed in. In order to this, let us, if you please, consider the wits and well-bred persons of former times. I have shown in another paper that Pliny, who was a man of the greatest genius, as well as of the first quality of his age, did not think it below him to be a kind husband, and to treat his wife as a friend, companion, and counsellor. I shall give the like instance of another, who in all respects was a much greater man than Pliny, and hath writ a whole book of letters to his wife. They are not so full of 'turns' as those translated out of the former author, who writes very much like a modern; but are full of that beautiful simplicity which is altogether natural, and is the distinguishing character of the best ancient writers. The author I am speaking of is Cicero; who, in the following passages which I have taken out of his letters, shows that he did not think it inconsistent with the politeness of his manners, or the greatness of his wisdom, to stand upon record in his domestic character.

These letters were written in a time when he was banished from his country, by a faction that then prevailed at Rome.[1]

CICERO TO TERENTIA

I

I learn from the letters of my friends, as well as from common report, that you give incredible proofs of virtue and fortitude, and that you are indefatigable in all kinds of good offices. How unhappy a man am I, that a woman of your virtue, constancy, honour, and good nature should fall into so great distresses upon my account; and that my dear Tulliola should be so much afflicted for the sake of a father with whom she had once so much reason to be pleased! How can I mention little Cicero, whose first knowledge of things began with the sense of his own misery? If all this had happened by the decrees of fate, as you would kindly persuade me, I could have borne it. But, alas! it is all befallen me by my own indiscretion, who thought I was beloved by those that envied me, and did not join with them who sought my friendship. At present, since my friends bid me hope, I shall take care of my health, that I may enjoy the benefit of your affectionate services. Plancius hopes we may some time or other come together into Italy. If I ever live to see that day; if I ever return to your dear embraces; in short, if I ever again recover you and myself, I shall think our conjugal piety very well rewarded. As for what you write to me about selling your estate, consider, my dear Terentia, consider, alas! what would be the event of it. If our present fortune continues to oppress us, what will become of our poor boy? My tears flow so fast that I am not able to write any further; and I would not willingly make you weep with me. Let us take care not to undo the child that is already undone. If we can leave him anything, a little virtue will keep him from want, and a little fortune raise him in the world. Mind your health, and let me know frequently what you are doing. Remember me to Tulliola and Cicero.

II

Do not fancy that I write longer letters to anyone than to yourself, unless when I chance to receive a longer letter from another, which I am indispensably obliged to answer in every particular. The truth of it is, I have no subject for a letter at present; and as my affairs now stand, there is nothing more painful to me than writing. As for you, and our dear Tulliola, I cannot write to you without abundance of tears; for I see both of you miserable, whom I always wished to be happy, and whom I ought to have made so. I must acknowledge you have done everything for me with the utmost fortitude and the utmost affection;

nor indeed is it more than I expected from you; though at the same time it is a great aggravation of my ill fortune that the afflictions I suffer can be relieved only by those which you undergo for my sake. For honest Valerius has written me a letter which I could not read without weeping very bitterly, wherein he gives me an account of the public procession which you have made for me at Rome. Alas! my dearest life, must then Terentia, the darling of my soul, whose favour and recommendation have been so often sought by others—must my Terentia droop under the weight of sorrow, appear in the habit of a mourner, pour out floods of tears, and all this for my sake—for my sake who have undone my family by consulting the safety of others? As for what you write about selling your house, I am very much afflicted that what is laid out upon my account may any way reduce you to misery and want. If we can bring about our design, we may indeed recover everything; but if fortune persists in persecuting us, how can I think of your sacrificing for the poor remainder of your possessions? No, my dearest life, let me beg you to let those bear my expenses who are able, and perhaps willing to do it; and if you would show your love to me, do not injure your health, which is already too much impaired. You present yourself before my eyes day and night; I see you labouring amidst innumerable difficulties; I am afraid lest you should sink under them; but I find in you all the qualifications that are necessary to support you. Be sure therefore to cherish your health, that you may compass the end of your hopes and your endeavours. Farewell, my Terentia, my heart's desire, farewell!

III

Aristocritus hath delivered to me three of your letters, which I have almost defaced with my tears. Oh! my Terentia, I am consumed with grief, and feel the weight of your sufferings more than of my own. I am more miserable than you are, notwithstanding you are very much so; and that for this reason, because though our calamity is common, it is my fault that brought it upon us. I ought to have died rather than have been driven out of the city: I am therefore overwhelmed not only with grief, but with shame. I am ashamed that I did not do my utmost for the best of wives, and the dearest of children. You are ever present before my eyes in your mourning, your affliction, and your sickness. Amidst all which there scarce appears to me the least glimmering of hope. However, as long as you hope, I will not despair. I will do what you advise me. I have returned my thanks to those friends whom you mentioned, and have let them know that you have acquainted me with their good offices. I am sensible of Piso's extraordinary zeal and endeavours to serve me. Oh, would the gods grant that you and I might live together in the enjoyment of such a son-in-law,[2] and of our dear children! As for what you write of your coming to me if I desire it, I would rather you should be where you are, because I know you are my principal agent at Rome. If you succeed, I shall come to you: if not—— But I need say no more. Be careful of your health; and be assured that nothing is, or ever was, so dear to me as yourself. Farewell, my Terentia! I fancy that I see you, and therefore cannot command my weakness so far as to refrain from tears.

IV

I do not write to you as often as I might, because, notwithstanding I am afflicted at all times, I am quite overcome with sorrow whilst I am writing to you, or reading any letters that I receive from you. If these evils are not to be removed, I must desire to see you, my dearest life, as soon as possible, and to die in your embraces; since neither the gods, whom you always religiously worshipped, nor the men, whose good I always promoted, have rewarded us according to our deserts. What a distressed wretch am I! Should I ask a weak woman, oppressed with cares and sickness, to come and live with me; or shall I not ask her? Can I live without you? But I find I must.   If there be any hopes of my return, help it forward, and promote it as much as you are able.   But if all that is over, as I fear it is, find out some way or other of coming to me.   This you may be sure of, that I shall not look upon myself as quite undone whilst you are with me.   But what will become of Tulliola?   You must look to that; I must confess I am entirely at a loss about her.   Whatever happens, we must take care of the reputation and marriage of that dear unfortunate girl.   As for Cicero, he shall live in my bosom, and in my arms.   I cannot write any further, my sorrows will not let me.   Support yourself, my dear Terentia, as well as you are able.   We have lived and flourished together amidst the greatest honours.   It is not our crimes, but our virtues, that have distressed us.   Take more than ordinary care of your health; I am more afflicted with your sorrows than my own.   Farewell, my Terentia, thou dearest, faithfullest, and best of wives!

Methinks it is a pleasure to see this great man in his family, who makes so different a figure in the Forum, or Senate of Rome.   Everyone admires the orator and the consul, but for my part, I esteem the husband and the father.   His private character, with all the little weaknesses of humanity, is as amiable as the figure he makes in public is awful and majestic.   But at the same time that I love to surprise so great an author in his private walks, and to survey him in his most familiar lights, I think it would be barbarous to form to ourselves any idea of mean-spiritedness from those natural openings of his heart and disburdening of his thoughts to a wife.   He has written several other letters to the same person, but none with so great passion as these of which I have given the foregoing extracts.

It would be ill nature not to acquaint the English reader that his wife was successful in her solicitations for this great man; and saw her husband return to the honours of which he had been deprived, with all the pomp and acclamation that usually attended the greatest triumph.

95. Mr. Bickerstaff as the Censor of Great Britain

From my own apartment, April 21.

In my younger years I used many endeavours to get a place at court, and indeed continued my pursuits until I arrived at my grand climacteric.[1] But at length, altogether despairing of success, whether it were for want of capacity, friends, or due application, I at last resolved to erect a new office, and for my encouragement to place myself in it. For this reason, I took upon me the title and dignity of 'Censor of Great Britain,' reserving to myself all such perquisites, profits, and emoluments, as should arise out of the discharge of the said office. These in truth have not been inconsiderable; for, besides those weekly contributions which I receive from John Morphew, and those annual subscriptions which I propose to myself from the most elegant part of this great island, I daily live in a very comfortable affluence of wine, stale beer, Hungary water, beef, books, and marrow-bones, which I receive from many well-disposed citizens; not to mention the forfeitures which accrue to me from the several offenders that appear before me on court days.

Having now enjoyed this office for the space of a twelve-month, I shall do what all good officers ought to do, take a survey of my behaviour, and consider carefully whether I have discharged my duty and acted up to the character with which I am invested. For my direction in this particular, I have made a narrow search into the nature of the old Roman censors, whom I always must regard, not only as my predecessors, but as my patterns in this great employment; and have several times asked my own heart with great impartiality, whether Cato will not bear a more venerable figure among posterity than Bickerstaff.

I find the duty of the Roman censor was twofold. The first part of it consisted in making frequent reviews of the people, in casting up their numbers, ranging them under their several tribes, disposing them into proper classes, and subdividing them into their respective centuries.

In compliance with this part of the office, I have taken many curious surveys of this great city. I have collected into particular bodies the Dappers and the Smarts, the natural and affected Rakes, the Pretty Fellows and the Very Pretty Fellows. I have likewise drawn out in several distinct parties your Pedants and Men of Fire, your Gamesters and Politicians. I have separated Cits from Citizens, Free-thinkers from Philosophers, Wits from Snuff-takers, and Duellists from Men of Honour. I have likewise made a calculation of Esquires; not only considering the several distinct swarms of them that are settled in the different parts of this town, but also that more rugged species that inhabit the fields and woods, and are often found in pot-houses, and upon hay-cocks.

I shall pass the soft sex over in silence, having not yet reduced them into any tolerable order; as likewise the softer tribe of lovers, which will cost me a great deal of time, before I shall be able to cast them into their several centuries and subdivisions.

The second part of the Roman censor's office was to look into the manners of the people; and to check any growing luxury, whether in diet, dress, or building. This duty likewise I have endeavoured to discharge, by those wholesome precepts which I have given my countrymen in regard to beef and mutton, and the severe censures which I have passed upon ragouts and fricassees. There is not, as I am informed, a pair of red heels to be seen within ten miles of London; which I may likewise ascribe, without vanity, to the becoming zeal which I expressed in that particular. I must own, my success with the petticoat is not so great; but as I have not yet done with it, I hope I shall in a little time put an effectual stop to that growing evil. As for the article of building, I intend hereafter to enlarge upon it; having lately observed several warehouses, nay, private shops, that stand upon Corinthian pillars; and whole rows of tin pots showing themselves, in order to their sale, through a sash window.

I have likewise followed the example of the Roman censors in punishing offences according to the quality of the offender. It was usual for them to expel a senator who had been guilty of great immoralities out of the senate-house, by omitting his name when they called over the list of his brethren. In the same manner, to remove effectually several worthless men who stand possessed of great honours, I have made frequent drafts of dead men out of the vicious part of the nobility, and given them up to the new society of upholders, with the necessary orders for their interment. . . . When my great predecessor, Cato the elder, stood for the censorship of Rome, there were several other competitors who offered themselves; and to get an interest amongst the people, gave them great promises of the mild and gentle treatment which they would use towards them in that office. Cato on the contrary told them he presented himself as a candidate because he knew the age was sunk in immorality and corruption; and that if they would give him their votes, he would promise them to make use of such a strictness and severity of discipline as should recover them out of it. The Roman historians, upon this occasion, very much celebrated the public-spiritedness of that people, who chose Cato for their censor, notwithstanding his method of recommending himself. I may in some measure extol my own country-men upon the same account; who, without any respect to party, or any application from myself, have made such generous subscriptions for the Censor of Great Britain, as will give a magnificence to my old age, and which I esteem more than I would any post in Europe of an hundred times the value. I shall only add, that upon looking into my catalogue of subscribers, which I intend to print alpha-betically in the front of my lucubrations, I find the names of the greatest beauties and wits in the whole island of Great Britain; which I only mention for the benefit of any of them who have not yet subscribed, it being my design to close the subscription in a very short time.[1]

96. Mr. Softly's Sonnet [1]

I yesterday came hither about two hours before the company generally make their appearance, with a design to read over all the newspapers; but upon my sitting down, I was accosted by Ned Softly, who saw me from a corner in the other end of the room, where I found he had been writing something. 'Mr. Bickerstaff,' says he, 'I observe by a late paper of yours that you and I are just of a humour; for you must know, of all impertinences, there is nothing which I so much hate as news. I never read a gazette in my life, and never trouble my head about our armies, whether they win or lose, or in what part of the world they lie encamped.' Without giving me time to reply, he drew a paper of verses out of his pocket, telling me that he had something which would entertain me more agreeably and that he would desire my judgment upon every line, for that we had time enough before us until the company came in.

Ned Softly is a very pretty poet, and a great admirer of easy lines. Waller is his favourite, and as that admirable writer has the best and worst verses of any among our great English poets, Ned Softly has got all the bad ones without book; which he repeats upon occasion, to show his reading and garnish his conversation. Ned is indeed a true English reader, incapable of relishing the great and masterly strokes of this art, but wonderfully pleased with the little Gothic ornaments of epigrammatical conceits, turns, points, and quibbles which are so frequent in the most admired of our English poets, and practised by those who want genius and strength to represent, after the manner of the ancients, simplicity in its natural beauty and perfection.

Finding myself unavoidably engaged in such a conversation, I was resolved to turn my pain into a pleasure, and to divert myself as well as I could with so very odd a fellow. 'You must understand,' says Ned, 'that the sonnet I am going to read to you was written upon a lady who

showed me some verses of her own making, and is, perhaps, the best poet of our age. But you shall hear it.'
Upon which he began to read as follows:

'To Mira, on her incomparable poems.

I

'When dress'd in laurel wreaths you shine,
    And tune your soft melodious notes,
You seem a sister of the Nine,
    Or Phoebus' self in petticoats.

II

'I fancy, when your song you sing
    (Your song you sing with so much art),
Your pen was pluck'd from Cupid's wing;
    For, ah! it wounds me like his dart.'

'Why,' says I, 'this is a little nosegay of conceits, a very
lump of salt. Every verse hath something in it that piques;
and then the dart in the last line is certainly as pretty a
sting in the tail of an epigram, for so I think you critics
call it, as ever entered into the thought of a poet.'

'Dear Mr. Bickerstaff,' says he, shaking me by the hand,
'everybody knows you to be a judge of these things; and
to tell you truly, I read over Roscommon's translation of
Horace's *Art of Poetry* [2] three several times, before I sat
down to write the sonnet which I have shown you. But
you shall hear it again, and pray observe every line of it;
for not one of them shall pass without your approbation.

'When dress'd in laurel wreaths you shine,

'That is,' says he, 'when you have your garland on;
when you are writing verses.' To which I replied: 'I
know your meaning: a metaphor?' 'The same,' said he,
and went on:

'And tune your soft melodious notes,

'Pray observe the gliding of that verse; there is scarce
a consonant in it; I took care to make it run upon liquids.
Give me your opinion of it.' 'Truly,' said I, 'I think it

as good as the former.' 'I am very glad to hear you say so,' says he; 'but mind the next:

'You seem a sister of the Nine,

'That is,' says he, 'you seem a sister of the Muses; for, if you look into ancient authors, you will find it was their opinion that there were nine of them.' 'I remember it very well,' said I. 'But pray proceed.'

'Or Phoebus' self in petticoats.

'Phoebus,' says he, 'was the god of poetry. These little instances, Mr. Bickerstaff, show a gentleman's reading. Then to take off from the air of learning, which Phoebus and the Muses have given to this first stanza, you may observe how it falls all of a sudden into the familiar "in petticoats"!

'Or Phoebus' self in petticoats.'

'Let us now,' says I, 'enter upon the second stanza; I find the first line is still a continuation of the metaphor.

'I fancy, when your song you sing,——'

'It is very right,' says he; 'but pray observe the turn of words in those two lines. I was a whole hour in adjusting of them, and have still a doubt upon me whether in the second line it should be "Your song you sing"; or, "You sing your song." You shall hear them both:

'I fancy, when your song you sing,
    (Your song you sing with so much art)

or,

'I fancy, when your song you sing,
    (You sing your song with so much art).'

'Truly,' said I, 'the turn is so natural either way that you have made me almost giddy with it.' 'Dear sir,' said he, grasping me by the hand, 'you have a great deal of patience; but pray what do you think of the next verse?

'Your pen was pluck'd from Cupid's wing;'

'Think!' says I; 'I think you have made Cupid look like a little goose.' 'That was my meaning,' says he.

'I think the ridicule is well enough hit off.   But we come now to the last, which sums up the whole matter.

'For, Ah! it wounds me like his dart.

'Pray how do you like that "Ah"?   Doth it not make a pretty figure in that place?   "Ah!"——   It looks as if I felt the dart and cried out at being pricked with it.

'For, Ah! it wounds me like his dart.

'My friend Dick Easy,' continued he, 'assured me, he would rather have written that "Ah!" than to have been the author of the *Aeneid*. He indeed objected, that I made Mira's pen like a quill in one of the lines, and like a dart in the other.   But as to that——' 'Oh! as to that,' says I, 'it is but supposing Cupid to be like a porcupine, and his quills and darts will be the same thing.'   He was going to embrace me for the hint, but half a dozen critics coming into the room, whose faces he did not like, he conveyed the sonnet into his pocket and whispered me in the ear he would show it me again as soon as his man had written it over fair.

97.   *Mr. Bickerstaff and his correspondents*

There is no particular in which my correspondents of all ages, conditions, sexes, and complexions universally agree, except only in their thirst after scandal.   It is impossible to conceive how many have recommended their neighbours to me upon this account, or how unmercifully I have been abused by several unknown hands, for not publishing the secret histories of cuckoldom that I have received from almost every street in town.

It would indeed be very dangerous for me to read over the many praises and eulogiums which come post to me from all the corners of the nation, were they not mixed with many checks, reprimands, scurrilities, and reproaches, which several of my good-natured countrymen cannot forbear sending me, though it often costs them twopence

or a groat before they can convey them to my hands; so
that sometimes when I am put into the best humour in the
world after having read a panegyric upon my performances,
and looked upon myself as a benefactor to the British
nation, the next letter, perhaps, I open, begins with: 'You
old doting scoundrel! Are not you a sad dog? Sirrah,
you deserve to have your nose slit'; and the like ingenious
conceits. These little mortifications are necessary to suppress that pride and vanity which naturally arise in the
mind of a received author, and enable me to bear the
reputation which my courteous readers bestow upon me,
without becoming a coxcomb by it. It was for the same
reason that when a Roman general entered the city in the
pomp of a triumph, the commonwealth allowed of several
little drawbacks to his reputation by conniving at such of
the rabble as repeated libels and lampoons upon him within
his hearing; and by that means engaged his thoughts upon
his weakness and imperfections, as well as on the merits
that advanced him to so great honours. The conqueror,
however, was not the less esteemed for being a man in
some particulars, because he appeared as a god in others.

There is another circumstance in which my countrymen have dealt very perversely with me, and that is, in
searching not only into my own life, but also into the
lives of my ancestors. If there has been a blot in my
family for these ten generations, it hath been discovered
by some or other of my correspondents. In short, I find
the ancient family of the Bickerstaffs has suffered very
much through the malice and prejudice of my enemies.
Some of them twit me in the teeth with the conduct of
my aunt Margery. Nay, there are some who have been
so disingenuous as to throw Maud the milkmaid into my
dish, notwithstanding I myself was the first who discovered
that alliance. I reap, however, many benefits from the
malice of these enemies, as they let me see my own faults
and give me a view of myself in the worst light; as they
hinder me from being blown up by flattery and self-conceit;
as they make me keep a watchful eye over my own actions,
and at the same time make me cautious how I talk of

others, and particularly of my friends and relations, or value myself upon the antiquity of my family.

But the most formidable part of my correspondents are those whose letters are filled with threats and menaces. I have been treated so often after this manner that not thinking it sufficient to fence well, in which I am now arrived at the utmost perfection, and carry pistols about me which I have always tucked within my girdle, I several months since made my will, settled my estate, and took leave of my friends, looking upon myself as no better than a dead man. Nay, I went so far as to write a long letter to the most intimate acquaintance I have in the world, under the character of a departed person, giving him an account of what brought me to that untimely end, and of the fortitude with which I met it. This letter being too long for the present paper, I intend to print it by itself very suddenly; and at the same time I must confess I took my hint of it from the behaviour of an old soldier in the civil wars, who was corporal of a company in a regiment of foot, about the same time that I myself was a cadet in the King's army.

This gentleman was taken by the enemy, and the two parties were upon such terms at that time, that we did not treat each other as prisoners of war, but as traitors and rebels. The poor corporal, being condemned to die, wrote a letter to his wife when under sentence of execution. He writ on the Thursday, and was to be executed on the Friday. But considering that the letter would not come to his wife's hands until Saturday, the day after execution, and being at that time more scrupulous than ordinary in speaking exact truth, he formed his letter rather according to the posture of his affairs when she should read it, than as they stood when he sent it; though it must be confessed there is a certain perplexity in the style of it, which the reader will easily pardon, considering his circumstances.

DEAR WIFE,

Hoping you are in good health, as I am at this present writing; this is to let you know that yesterday, between the hours of eleven and twelve, I was hanged, drawn, and quartered. I died very penitently, and everybody thought my case very hard. Remember me kindly to my poor fatherless children.

Yours, until death,

W. B.

It so happened that this honest fellow was relieved by a party of his friends and had the satisfaction to see all the rebels hanged who had been his enemies. I must not omit a circumstance which exposed him to raillery his whole life after. Before the arrival of the next post, that would have set all things clear, his wife was married to a second husband, who lived in the peaceable possession of her; and the corporal, who was a man of plain understanding, did not care to stir in the matter, as knowing that she had the news of his death under his own hand, which she might have produced upon occasion.

98. *Mr. Clayton's new musical entertainment*

I was looking out of the parlour window this morning, and receiving the honours which Margery, the milkmaid to our lane, was doing me, by dancing before my door with the plate of half her customers on her head, when Mr. Clayton, the author of *Arsinoë*,[1] made me a visit, and desired me to insert the following advertisement in my ensuing paper.

'The pastoral Masque, composed by Mr. Clayton, author of *Arsinoë*, will be performed on Wednesday, the third instant, in the great room at York Buildings. Tickets are to be had at White's chocolate-house, St. James's coffee-house in St. James's Street, and Young Man's coffee-house.

'Note, the tickets delivered out for the twenty-seventh of April, will be taken then.'

When I granted his request, I made one to him, which was that the performers should put their instruments in tune before the audience came in; for that I thought the resentment of the eastern prince, who, according to the old story, took tuning for playing, to be very just and natural. He was so civil as not only to promise that favour, but also to assure me that he would order the heels of the performers to be muffled in cotton, that the artists in so polite an age as ours may not intermix with their harmony a custom which so nearly resembles the stamping dances of the West Indians or Hottentots.

ADVERTISEMENT

Whereas the several churchwardens of most of the parishes within the bills of mortality have in an earnest manner applied themselves by way of petition, and have also made a presentment, of the vain and loose deportment during divine service of persons of too great figure in all their said parishes for their reproof; and whereas it is therein set forth that by salutations given each other, hints, shrugs, ogles, playing of fans, fooling with canes at their mouths, and other wanton gesticulations, their whole congregation appears rather a theatrical audience than an house of devotion; it is hereby ordered that all canes, cravats, bosom-laces, muffs, fans, snuff-boxes, and all other instruments made use of to give persons unbecoming airs, shall be immediately forfeited and sold; and of the sum arising from the sale thereof, a ninth part shall be paid to the poor, and the rest to the overseers.

99. *Funeral of Thomas Betterton, the actor*

Having received notice that the famous actor Mr. Betterton [1] was to be interred this evening in the cloisters near Westminster Abbey, I was resolved to walk thither and see the last office done to a man whom I had always very much admired, and from whose action I had received more strong impressions of what is great and noble in human nature, than from the arguments of the most solid philosophers, or the descriptions of the most charming poets I had ever read. As the rude and untaught multitude are no way wrought upon more effectually than by seeing public punishments and executions; so men of letters and education feel their humanity most forcibly exercised when they attend the obsequies of men who had arrived at any perfection in liberal accomplishments. Theatrical action is to be esteemed as such, except it be objected that we cannot call that an art which cannot be attained by art. Voice, stature, motion, and other gifts must be very bountifully bestowed by nature, or labour and industry will but push the unhappy endeavourer in that way the further off his wishes.

Such an actor as Mr. Betterton ought to be recorded with the same respect as Roscius among the Romans. The greatest orator has thought fit to quote his judgment and celebrate his life. Roscius was the example to all that would form themselves into proper and winning behaviour. His action was so well adapted to the sentiments he expressed that the youth of Rome thought they wanted only to be virtuous to be as graceful in their appearance as Roscius. The imagination took a lively impression of what was great and good; and they, who never thought of setting up for the art of imitation, became themselves inimitable characters.

There is no human invention so aptly calculated for the forming a free-born people as that of a theatre. Tully reports that the celebrated player of whom I am speaking used frequently to say: 'The perfection of an actor is only to become what he is doing.' Young men who are too inattentive to receive lectures are irresistibly taken with performances. Hence it is that I extremely lament the little relish the gentry of this nation have at present for the just and noble representations in some of our tragedies. The operas which are of late introduced can leave no trace behind them that can be of service beyond the present moment. To sing and to dance are accomplishments very few have any thoughts of practising; but to speak justly, and move gracefully, is what every man thinks he does perform, or wishes he did.

I have hardly a notion that any performer of antiquity could surpass the action of Mr. Betterton in any of the occasions in which he has appeared on our stage. The wonderful agony which he appeared in when he examined the circumstance of the handkerchief in *Othello*; the mixture of love that intruded upon his mind upon the innocent answers Desdemona makes, betrayed in his gesture such a variety and vicissitude of passions as would admonish a man to be afraid of his own heart, and perfectly convince him that it is to stab it, to admit that worst of daggers, jealousy. Whoever reads in his closet this admirable scene will find that he cannot, except he has as warm an imagination as Shakespeare himself, find any but dry, incoherent, and broken sentences. But a reader that has seen Betterton act it observes there could not be a word added; that longer speeches had been unnatural, nay, impossible, in Othello's circumstances. The charming passage in the same tragedy, where he tells the manner of winning the affection of his mistress, was urged with so moving and graceful an energy that while I walked in the cloisters, I thought of him with the same concern as if I waited for the remains of a person who had in real life done all that I had seen him represent. The gloom of the place, and faint lights before the ceremony appeared, contributed to the melancholy disposition I was in, and I began to be extremely afflicted that Brutus and Cassius had any difference; that Hotspur's gallantry was so unfortunate; and that the mirth and good humour of Falstaff could not exempt him from the grave. Nay, this occasion, in me who look upon the distinctions amongst men to be merely scenical, raised reflections upon the emptiness of all human perfection and greatness in general; and I could not but regret that the sacred heads which lie buried in the neighbourhood of this little portion of earth in which my poor old friend is deposited, are returned to dust as well as he, and that there is no difference in the

grave between the imaginary and the real monarch.   This
made me say of human life itself, with Macbeth [2]:

> To-morrow, to-morrow, and to-morrow,
> Creeps in a stealing pace from day to day,
> To the last moment of recorded time!
> And all our yesterdays have lighted fools
> To the eternal night!   Out, out, short candle!
> Life's but a walking shadow, a poor player
> That struts and frets his hour upon the stage,
> And then is heard no more.

The mention I have here made of Mr. Betterton, for
whom I had, as long as I have known anything, a very
great esteem and gratitude for the pleasure he gave me,
can do him no good; but it may possibly be of service to
the unhappy woman he has left behind him, to have it
known that this great tragedian was never in a scene half
so moving as the circumstances of his affairs created at his
departure.   His wife, after a cohabitation of forty years in
the strictest amity, has long pined away with a sense of
his decay, as well in his person as his little fortune; and,
in proportion to that, she has herself decayed both in
her health and reason.   Her husband's death, added to
her age and infirmities, would certainly have determined her
life, but that the greatness of her distress has been her
relief, by a present deprivation of her senses.   This
absence of reason is her best defence against age, sorrow,
poverty, and sickness.   I dwell upon this account so
distinctly, in obedience to a certain great spirit, who hides
her name, and has by letter applied to me to recommend
to her some object of compassion from whom she may
be concealed.

This, I think, is a proper occasion for exerting such
heroic generosity; and as there is an ingenuous shame in
those who have known better fortune, to be reduced to
receive obligations, as well as a becoming pain in the
truly generous to receive thanks; in this case both those
delicacies are preserved; for the person obliged is as incapable of knowing her benefactress, as her benefactress
is unwilling to be known by her.

100. First Sorrow

The first sense of sorrow I ever knew was upon the death of my father, at which time I was not quite five years of age; but was rather amazed at what all the house meant, than possessed with a real understanding why nobody was willing to play with me. I remember I went into the room where his body lay, and my mother sat weeping alone by it. I had my battledore in my hand, and fell a-beating the coffin and calling Papa; for, I know not how, I had some slight idea that he was locked up there. My mother catched me in her arms, and, transported beyond all patience of the silent grief she was before in, she almost smothered me in her embraces; and told me in a flood of tears, papa could not hear me, and would play with me no more, for they were going to put him underground, whence he could never come to us again. She was a very beautiful woman, of a noble spirit, and there was a dignity in her grief amidst all the wildness of her transport; which, methought, struck me with an instinct of sorrow, that, before I was sensible of what it was to grieve, seized my very soul, and has made pity the weakness of my heart ever since.

101. Pleasures of the Playhouse

The town grows so very empty that the greater number of my gay characters are fled out of my sight into the country. My beaux are now shepherds, and my belles wood-nymphs. They are lolling over rivulets, and covered with shades, while we who remain in town hurry through the dust about impertinences, without knowing the happiness of leisure and retirement. To add to this calamity, even the actors are going to desert us for a season, and we shall not shortly have so much as a landscape or a forest scene to refresh ourselves with in the midst of our fatigues.

This may not, perhaps, be so sensible a loss to any other as to me; for I confess it is one of my greatest delights to sit unobserved and unknown in the gallery, and entertain myself either with what is personated on the stage, or observe what appearances present themselves in the audience. If there were no other good consequences in a playhouse, than that so many persons of different ranks and conditions are placed there in their most pleasing aspects, that prospect only would be very far from being below the pleasures of a wise man. There is not one person you can see, in whom, if you look with an inclination to be pleased, you may not behold something worthy or agreeable. Our thoughts are in our features; and the visage of those in whom love, rage, anger, jealousy, or envy have their frequent mansions, carries the traces of those passions wherever the amorous, the choleric, the jealous, or the envious are pleased to make their appearance. However, the assembly at a play is usually made up of such as have a sense of some elegance in pleasure; by which means the audience is generally composed of those who have gentle affections, or at least of such as, at that time, are in the best humour you can ever find them. This has insensibly a good effect upon our spirits; and the musical airs which are played to us put the whole company into a participation of the same pleasure, and by consequence, for that time equal in humour, in fortune, and in quality. Thus far we gain only by coming into an audience; but if we find, added to this, the beauties of proper action, the force of eloquence, and the gaiety of well-placed lights and scenes, it is being happy, and seeing others happy, for two hours; a duration of bliss not at all to be slighted by so short-lived a creature as man.

102. *Notice to readers*

'Whereas Mr. Bickerstaff has lately received a letter out of Ireland, dated June the ninth, importing that he is grown very dull, for the postage of which Mr. Morphew charges one shilling; and another without date of place or time, for which he, the said Morphew, charges twopence; it is desired that for the future his courteous and uncourteous readers will go a little further in expressing their good and ill will, and pay for the carriage of their letters; otherwise the intended pleasure or pain, which is designed for Mr. Bickerstaff will be wholly disappointed.'

103. Pernicious consequences of reading the 'Tatler'

ESQUIRE BICKERSTAFF,
   I do not know by what chance one of your *Tatlers* is got into my family, and has almost turned the brains of my eldest daughter Winifred; who has been so undutiful as to fall in love of her own head, and tells me a foolish heathen story that she has read in your paper, to persuade me to give my consent.   I am too wise to let children have their own wills in a business like marriage.   It is a matter in which neither I myself, nor any of my kindred, were ever humoured.   My wife and I never pretended to love one another like your Sylvias and Philanders; and yet, if you saw our fireside, you would be satisfied we are not always a-squabbling.   For my part, I think that where man and woman come together by their own good liking, there is so much fondling and fooling that it hinders young people from minding their business.   I must therefore desire you to change your note. . . .   Our great-grandmothers were all bid to marry first, and love would come afterwards; and I do not see why their daughters should follow their own inventions.   I am resolved Winifred shall not.

                                        Yours, etc.

   This letter is a natural picture of ordinary contracts, and of the sentiments of those minds that lie under a kind of intellectual rusticity.   This trifling occasion made me run over in my imagination the many scenes I have observed of the married condition, wherein the quintessence of pleasure and pain are represented, as they accompany that state, and no other. It is certain there are many thousands like the above-mentioned yeoman and his wife, who are never highly pleased or distasted in their whole lives. But when we consider the more informed part of mankind, and look upon their behaviour, it then appears that very little of their time is indifferent, but generally spent in the most anxious vexation, or the highest satisfaction. Shakespeare has admirably represented both the aspects of this state in the most excellent tragedy of *Othello*. In the character of Desdemona, he runs through all the sentiments of a virtuous maid and a tender wife. She is captivated by his virtue, and faithful to him as well from that motive as regard to her own honour. Othello is a great and noble spirit, misled by the villainy of a false friend to suspect her innocence; and resents it accordingly. When, after the many instances of passion, the wife is told her husband is jealous, her simplicity makes her incapable of believing it, and say, after such circumstances as would drive another woman into distraction:

> I think the sun where he was born
> Drew all such humours from him.[1]

This opinion of him is so just, that his noble and tender heart beats itself to pieces before he can affront her with the mention of his jealousy; and he owns this suspicion has blotted out all the sense of glory and happiness which before it was possessed with, when he laments himself in the warm allusions of a mind accustomed to entertainments so very different from the pangs of jealousy and revenge. How moving is his sorrow, when he cries out as follows:

> I had been happy, if the gen'ral camp,
> Pioneers and all, had tasted her sweet body,
> So I had nothing known. O, now, for ever
> Farewell the tranquil mind! farewell content!
> Farewell the plumed troop, and the big wars
> That make ambition virtue! O, farewell!

Farewell the neighing steed and the shrill trump,
The spirit-stirring drum, th' ear-piercing fife,
The royal banner, and all quality,
Pride, pomp, and circumstance of glorious war!
And, O you mortal engines, whose rude throats
Th' immortal Jove's dread clamours counterfeit,
Farewell! Othello's occupation's gone.[2]

I believe I may venture to say there is not in any other part of Shakespeare's works more strong and lively pictures of nature than in this. I shall therefore steal incognito to see it, out of curiosity to observe how Wilks and Cibber [3] touch those places where Betterton and Sandford [4] so very highly excelled.

104. *A coach journey and reflections occasioned by it*

Some years since I was engaged with a coachful of friends to take a journey as far as the Land's End. We were very well pleased with one another the first day, everyone endeavouring to recommend himself by his good humour and complaisance to the rest of the company. This good correspondence did not last long; one of our party was soured the very first evening by a plate of butter which had not been melted to his mind, and which spoiled his temper to such a degree that he continued upon the fret to the end of our journey. A second fell off from his good humour the next morning, for no other reason that I could imagine, but because I chanced to step into the coach before him and place myself on the shady side. This, however, was but my own private guess; for he did not mention a word of it, nor indeed of anything else, for three days following. The rest of our company held out very near half the way, when on a sudden Mr. Sprightly fell asleep, and instead of endeavouring to divert and oblige us, as he had hitherto done, carried himself with an unconcerned, careless, drowsy behaviour until we came to our last stage. There were three of us who still held up our heads and did all we could to make our journey agreeable; but, to my shame be it spoken, about three miles on this side Exeter, I was taken with an unaccountable fit of sullenness, that hung upon me for above threescore miles; whether it were for want of respect, or from an accidental tread upon my foot, or from a foolish maid's calling me 'the old gentleman,' I cannot tell. In short, there was but one who kept his good humour to the Land's End.

There was another coach that went along with us, in which I likewise observed that there were many secret jealousies, heart-burnings, and animosities. For when we joined companies at night, I could not but take notice that the passengers neglected their own company and studied how to make themselves esteemed by us, who were altogether strangers to them; until at length they grew so well acquainted with us that they liked us as little as they did one another. When I reflect upon this journey, I often fancy it to be a picture of human life, in respect to the several friendships, contracts, and alliances that are made and dissolved in the several periods of it. The most delightful and most lasting engagements are generally those which pass between man and woman; and yet upon what trifles are they weakened, or entirely broken! Sometimes the parties fly asunder even in the midst of courtship, and sometimes grow cool in the very honey-month. Some separate before the first child, and some after the fifth; others continue good until thirty, others until forty; while some few, whose souls are of an happier make, and better fitted to one another, travel on together to the end of their journey in a continual intercourse of kind offices and mutual endearments.

105. *Odds and ends*

My almanac is to be published on the twenty-second, and from that instant all lovers, in raptures or epistles, are of justice in town and country, where clerks are the counsellors to their masters.

But as I cannot expect that the Censor of Great Britain should publish a letter wherein he is censured with too much reason himself; yet I hope you will be the better for it, and think upon the themes I have mentioned, which must certainly be of greater service to the world, yourself, and Mr. Morphew, than to let us know whether you are a Whig or a Tory.   I am still

Your admirer and servant,
Cato Junior.

This gentleman and I differ about the words 'staggering' and 'better part'; but instead of answering to the particulars of this epistle, I shall only acquaint my correspondent that . . . I have given positive orders to Don Saltero of Chelsea the tooth-drawer,[2] and Doctor Thomas Smith the corn-cutter of King Street, Westminster, who have the modesty to confine their pretensions to manual operations, to bring me in, with all convenient speed, complete lists of all who are but of equal learning with themselves, and yet administer physic beyond the feet and gums.   These advices I shall reserve for my future leisure; but have now taken a resolution to dedicate the remaining part of this instant July to the service of the fair sex, and have almost finished a scheme for settling the whole remainder of that sex who are unmarried, and above the age of twenty-five.

In order to this good and public service, I shall consider the passion of love in its full extent, as it is attended both with joys and inquietudes; and lay down, for the conduct of my lovers, such rules as shall banish the cares and heighten the pleasures which flow from that amiable spring of life and happiness.   There is no less than an absolute necessity that some provision be made to take off the dead stock of women in city, town, and country.   Let there happen but the least disorder in the streets, and in an instant you see the inequality of the numbers of males and females.   Besides that the feminine crowd on such occasions is more numerous in the open way, you may observe

to forbear the comparison of their mistresses' eyes to stars, I having made use of that simile in my dedication for the last time it shall ever pass, and on the properest occasion that it was ever employed.   All ladies are hereby desired to take notice that they never receive that simile in payment for any similes they shall bestow for the future.

.   .   .   .   .

On Saturday night last a gentlewoman's husband strayed from the playhouse in the Haymarket.   If the lady who was seen to take him up will restore him, she shall be asked no questions; he being of no use but to the owner.

.   .   .   .   .

Whereas Philander signified to Clarinda by letter bearing date Thursday twelve o'clock, that he had lost his heart by a shot from her eyes, and desired she would condescend to meet him the same day at eight in the evening at Rosamond's pond; faithfully protesting, that in case she would not do him that honour, she might see the body of the said Philander the next day floating on the said lake of love, and that he desired only three sighs upon view of his said body; it is desired, if he has not made away with himself accordingly, that he would forthwith show himself to the coroner of the city of Westminster; or Clarinda, being an old offender, will be found guilty of wilful murder.

.   .   .   .   .

Whereas several have industriously spread abroad that I am in partnership with Charles Lillie, the perfumer, at the corner of Beaufort Buildings; I must say with my friend Partridge, that they are knaves who reported it. However, since the said Charles has promised that all his customers shall be mine, I must desire all mine to be his; and dare answer for him, that if you ask in my name for snuff, Hungary, or orange water, you shall have the best the town affords at the cheapest rate.

.   .   .   .   .

A stage-coach sets out exactly at six from Nando's

coffee-house to Mr. Tiptoe's dancing-school, and returns at eleven every evening, for one shilling and fourpence.

N.B. Dancing shoes, not exceeding four inches height in the heel, and periwigs, not exceeding three feet in length, are carried in the coachbox gratis.

.   .   .   .   .

A certain author brought a poem to Mr. Cowley for his perusal and judgment of the performance, which he demanded at the next visit with a poetaster's assurance; and Mr. Cowley, with his usual modesty, desired that he would be pleased to look a little to the grammar of it. 'To the grammar of it! What do you mean, Sir? Would you send me to school again?'

'Why, Mr. ——, would it do you any harm?'

.   .   .   .   .

St. Clement's, Oct. 5.

MR. BICKERSTAFF,

I observe, as the season begins to grow cold, so does people's devotion; insomuch that instead of filling the churches, that united zeal might keep one warm there, one is left to freeze in almost bare walls by those who in hot weather are troublesome the contrary way. This, Sir, needs a regulation that none but you can give to it, by causing those who absent themselves on account of weather only this wintertime, to pay the apothecaries' bills occasioned by coughs, catarrhs, and other distempers contracted by sitting in empty seats. Therefore to you I apply myself for redress, having got such a cold on Sunday was sevennight, that has brought me almost to your worship's age from sixty, within less than a fortnight. I am

Your worship's in all obedience,
W. E.

106. *Remonstrance from Cato junior. Benevolent project of Mr. Bickerstaff*

SIR,

I am afraid there is something in the suspicions of some people, that you begin to be short of matter for your lucubrations. Though several of them now and then did appear somewhat dull and insipid to me, I was always charitably inclined to believe the fault lay in myself, and that I wanted the true key to decipher your mysteries; and remember your advertisement upon this account. But since I have seen you fall into an unpardonable error, yea, with a relapse; I mean, since I have seen you turn politician in the present unhappy dissensions, I have begun to stagger, and could not choose but lessen the great value I had for the Censor of our isle. How is it possible that a man, whom interest did naturally lead to a constant impartiality in these matters, and who hath wit enough to judge that his opinion was not like to make many proselytes—how is it possible, I say, that a little passion (for I have still too good an opinion of you to think you was bribed by the staggering party) could blind you so far as to offend the very better half of the nation, and to lessen off so much the number of your friends? Mr. Morphew will not have cause to thank you unless you give over and endeavour to regain what you have lost. There are still a great many themes you have left untouched, such as the ill management of matters relating to law and physic; the setting down rules for knowing the quacks in both professions. What a large field is there left in discovering the abuses of the college,[1] who had a charter and privileges granted them to hinder the creeping in and prevailing of quacks and pretenders; and yet grant licences to barbers, and write letters of recommendation in the country towns, out of the reach of their practice, in favour of mere boys; valuing the health and lives of their countrymen no farther than they get money by them. You have said very little or nothing about the dispensation

them also to the very garrets huddled together, four at least at a casement. Add to this, that by an exact calculation of all that have come to town by stage-coach or wagon for this twelvemonth last, three times in four the treated persons have been males. This over-stock of beauty, for which there are so few bidders, calls for an immediate supply of lovers and husbands; and I am the studious knight-errant who have suffered long nocturnal contemplations to find out methods for the relief of all British females who at present seem to be devoted to involuntary virginity.

107. *Lottery for the relief of the fair sex*

July 14.

Mr. Bickerstaff,

This comes to you from one of those virgins of twenty-five years old and upwards, that you, like a patron of the distressed, promised to provide for; who makes it her humble request that no occasional stories or subjects may, as they have for three or four of your last days, prevent your publishing the scheme you have communicated to Amanda; for every day and hour is of the greatest consequence to damsels of so advanced an age. Be quick then, if you intend to do any service for

Your admirer,

Diana Forecast.

In this important affair I have not neglected the proposals of others. Among them is the following sketch of a lottery for persons. The author of it has proposed very ample encouragement, not only to myself, but also to Charles Lillie and John Morphew. If the matter bears, I shall not be unjust to his merit. I only desire to enlarge his plan; for which purpose I lay it before the town, as well for the improvement as the encouragement of it.

The amicable contribution for raising the fortunes of ten young ladies.

'*Imprimis.* It is proposed to raise one hundred thousand crowns by way of lots, which will advance for each lady two thousand five hundred pounds; which sum, together with one of the ladies, the gentleman that shall be so happy as to draw a prize, provided they both like, will be entitled to, under such restrictions hereafter mentioned. And in case they do not like, then either party that refuses shall be entitled to one thousand pounds only, and the remainder to him or her that shall be willing to marry, the man being first to declare his mind. But it is provided that if both parties shall consent to have one another, the gentleman shall, before he receives the money thus raised, settle one thousand pounds of the same in substantial hands; who shall be as trustees for the said lady, and shall have the whole and sole disposal of it for her use only.

'*Note*, each party shall have three months' time to consider, after an interview had, which shall be within ten days after the lots are drawn.

'*Note* also, the name and place of abode of the prize shall be placed on a proper ticket.

'*Item*, they shall be ladies that have had a liberal education, between fifteen and twenty-three; all genteel, witty, and of unblamable characters.

'The money to be raised shall be kept in an iron box; and when there shall be two thousand subscriptions, which amounts to five hundred pounds, it shall be taken out and put into the goldsmith's hand,[1] and the note made payable to the proper lady, or her assigns, with a clause therein to hinder her from receiving it until the fortunate person that draws her shall first sign the note, and so on until the whole sum is subscribed for. And as soon as one hundred thousand subscriptions are completed, and two hundred crowns more to pay the charges, the lottery shall be drawn at a proper place, to be appointed a fortnight before the drawing.

'*Note*, Mr. Bickerstaff objects to the marriageable years here mentioned; and is of opinion they should not commence until after twenty-three. But he appeals to the learned, both of Warwick Lane and Bishopsgate Street,[2] on this subject.'

108. Woman—destroying fiend or guardian angel

In the commerce of lovers, the man makes the address, assails, and betrays; and yet stands in the same degree of acceptance as he was in before he committed that treachery. The woman, for no other crime but believing one who she thought loved her, is treated with shyness and indifference at the best, and commonly with reproach and scorn. He that is past the power of beauty may talk of this matter with the same unconcern as of any other subject; therefore I shall take upon me to consider the sex, as they live within rules, and as they transgress them. The ordinary class of the good or the ill have very little influence upon the actions of others; but the eminent, in either kind, are those who lead the world below. The ill are employed in communicating scandal, infamy, and disease, like furies; the good distribute benevolence, friendship, and health, like angels. The ill are damped with pain and anguish at the sight of all that is laudable, lovely, or happy. The virtuous are touched with commiseration towards the guilty, the disagreeable, and the wretched. There are those who betray the innocent of their own sex, and solicit the lewd of ours. There are those who have abandoned the very memory, not only of innocence, but shame. There are those who never forgave, nor could ever bear being forgiven. There are those also who visit the beds of the sick, lull the cares of the sorrowful, and double the joys of the joyful. Such is the destroying fiend, such the guardian angel, woman.

109. *Letter and notices*

MR. BICKERSTAFF,

You, that are a philosopher, know very well the make of the mind of women, and can best instruct me in the conduct of an affair which highly concerns me. I never can admit my lover to speak to me of love; yet think him impertinent when he offers to talk of anything else. What shall I do with a man that always believes me? It is a strange thing, this distance in men of sense! Why do not they always urge their fate? If we are sincere in our severity, you lose nothing by attempting. If we are hypocrites, you certainly succeed.

· · · · ·

From the *Trumpet* in Sheer Lane [1]

Ordered, that for the improvement of the pleasures of society, a member of this house, one of the most wakeful of the soporific assembly beyond Smithfield Bars, and one of the order of story-tellers in Holborn, may meet and exchange stale matter, and report the same to their principals.

N.B. No man is to tell above one story in the same evening; but has liberty to tell the same the night following.

· · · · ·

Mr. Bickerstaff desires his love-correspondents to vary the names they shall assume in their future letters, for that he is overstocked with Philanders.

110. *The vanity of ambition*

This afternoon I went to visit a gentleman of my acquaintance at Mile End; and passing through Stepney churchyard, I could not forbear entertaining myself with the inscriptions on the tombs and graves. Among others, I observed one with this notable memorial:

'Here lies the Body of T. B.'

This fantastical desire of being remembered only by the two first letters of a name, led me into the contemplation of the vanity and imperfect attainments of ambition in general. When I run back in my imagination all the men whom I have ever known and conversed with in my whole life, there are but very few who have not used their faculties in the pursuit of what it is impossible to acquire; or left the possession of what they might have been, at their setting out, masters, to search for it where it was out of their reach.[1] In this thought it was not possible to forget the instance of Pyrrhus, who proposing to himself in discourse with a philosopher, one, and another, and another conquest, was asked what he would do after all that. 'Then,' says the king, 'we will make merry.'

He was well answered: 'What hinders your doing that in the condition you are already?'

The restless desire of exerting themselves above the common level of mankind is not to be resisted in some tempers; and minds of this make may be observed in every condition of life. Where such men do not make to themselves, or meet with, employment, the soil of their constitution runs into tares and weeds. An old friend of mine, who lost a major's post forty years ago, and quitted, has ever since studied maps, encampments, retreats, and countermarches; with no other design but to feed his spleen and ill humour, and furnish himself with matter for arguing against all the successful actions of others. He that, at his first setting out in the world, was the gayest man in our regiment; ventured his life with alacrity, and enjoyed it with satisfaction; encouraged men below him, and was courted by men above him, has been ever since the most froward creature breathing. His warm complexion spends itself now only in a general spirit of contradiction; for which he watches all occasions, and is in his conversation still upon sentry, treats all men like enemies, with every other impertinence of a speculative warrior.

He that observes in himself this natural inquietude should take all imaginable care to put his mind in some method of gratification, or he will soon find himself grow into the condition of this disappointed major. Instead of courting proper occasions to rise above others, he will be ever studious of pulling others down to him; it being the common refuge of disappointed ambition, to ease themselves by detraction. It would be no great argument against ambition that there are such mortal things in the disappointment of it; but it certainly is a forcible exception, that there can be no solid happiness in the success of it. If we value popular praise, it is in the power of the meanest of the people to disturb us by calumny. If the fame of being happy, we cannot look into a village but we see crowds in actual possession of what we seek only the appearance. To this may be added that there is I know not what malignity in the minds of ordinary men, to oppose you in what they see you fond of; and it is a certain exception against a man's receiving applause, that he visibly courts it. However, this is not only the passion of great and undertaking spirits; but you see it in the lives of such as, one would believe, were far enough removed from the ways of ambition. The rural esquires of this nation even eat and drink out of vanity. A vainglorious fox-hunter shall entertain half a county for the ostentation of his beef and beer, without the least affection for any of the crowd about him. He feeds them because he thinks it a superiority over them that he does so; and they devour him, because they know he treats them out of insolence. This indeed is ambition in grotesque; but may figure to us the condition of politer men, whose only pursuit is glory. When the superior acts out of a principle of vanity, the dependant will be sure to allow it him, because he knows it destructive of the very applause which is courted by the man who favours him, and consequently makes him nearer himself.

111. *The widow Flavia and her daughter*

To follow nature is the only agreeable course, which is what I would fain inculcate to those jarring companions,

Flavia and Lucia. They are mother and daughter. Flavia, who is the mamma, has all the charms and desires of youth still about her, and is not much turned of thirty; Lucia is blooming and amorous, and but a little above fifteen. The mother looks very much younger than she is, the girl very much older. If it were possible to fix the girl to her sick bed, and preserve the portion, the use of which the mother partakes, the good widow Flavia would certainly do it. But for fear of Lucia's escape, the mother is forced to be constantly attended with a rival, that explains her age and draws off the eyes of her admirers. The jest is, they can never be together in strangers' company but Lucy is eternally reprimanded for something very particular in her behaviour; for which she has the malice to say, she hopes she shall always obey her parents. She carried her passion and jealousy to that height the other day, that coming suddenly into the room, and surprising Colonel Lofty speaking rapture on one knee to her mother, she clapped down by him, and asked her blessing.

112. *Doubtful case of the forlorn virgin*

MR. BICKERSTAFF,

I have lived a pure and undefiled virgin these twenty-seven years, and I assure you it is with great grief and sorrow of heart I tell you that I become weary and impatient of the derision of the gigglers of our sex; who call me old maid, and tell me I shall lead apes.[1] If you are truly a patron of the distressed, and an adept in astrology, you will advise whether I shall, or ought to, be prevailed upon by the impertinences of my own sex, to give way to the importunities of yours. I assure you I am surrounded with both, though at present a forlorn.

I am, etc.

I must defer my answer to this lady out of a point of chronology. She says she has been twenty-seven years a maid; but I fear, according to a common error, she dates her virginity from her birth, which is a very erroneous method; for a woman of twenty is no more to be thought chaste so many years, than a man of that age can be said to have been so long valiant. We must not allow people the favour of a virtue until they have been under the temptation to the contrary. A woman is not a maid until her birthday, as we call it, of her fifteenth year. My plaintiff is therefore desired to inform me whether she is at present in her twenty-eighth or forty-third year, and she shall be dispatched accordingly.

113. The masked rider

August 15, 1710.

MR. BICKERSTAFF,

Taking the air the other day on horseback in the green lane that leads to Southgate, I discovered coming towards me a person well mounted, in a mask; and I accordingly expected, as any one would, to have been robbed. But when we came up with each other, the Spark, to my greater surprise, very peaceably gave me the way; which made me take courage enough to ask him if he masqueraded, or how? He made me no answer, but still continued incognito. This was certainly an ass in a lion's skin; a harmless bull-beggar, who delights to fright innocent people and set them a-galloping. I bethought myself of putting as good a jest upon him, and had turned my horse with a design to pursue him to London and get him apprehended on suspicion of being a highwayman. But when I reflected that it was the proper office of the magistrate to punish only knaves, and that we had a Censor of Great Britain for people of another denomination, I immediately determined to prosecute him in your court only. This unjustifiable frolic I take to be neither wit nor humour, therefore hope you will do me, and as many others as were that day frighted, justice. I am,

Sir,

Your friend and servant,

J. L.

Sir,

The gentleman begs your pardon, and frighted you out of fear of frighting you; for he is just come out of the smallpox.

. . . . .

Mr. Bickerstaff,

Your distinction concerning the time of commencing virgins is allowed to be just. I write you my thanks for it, in the twenty-eighth year of life, and twelfth of my virginity. But I am to ask you another question: 'May a woman be said to live any more years a maid than she continues to be courted?'

I am, etc.

114. The humble petition of the Company of Linendrapers, residing within the liberty of Westminster

Showeth,

That there has of late prevailed among the ladies so great an affectation of nakedness, that they have not only left the bosom wholly bare, but lowered their stays some inches below the former mode.

That in particular, Mrs. Arabella Overdo has not the least appearance of linen; and our best customers show but little above the small of their backs.

That by this means your petitioners are in danger of losing the advantage of covering a ninth part of every woman of quality in Great Britain.

Your petitioners humbly offer the premises to your indulgence's consideration, and shall ever, etc.

115. The Partridge joke continued

Advertisement

Whereas an ignorant upstart in astrology has publicly endeavoured to persuade the world that he is the late John Partridge who died the twenty-eighth of March

1708, these are to certify all whom it may concern, that the true John Partridge was not only dead at that time, but continues so to this present day.

Beware of counterfeits, for such are abroad.

116. Scolds—with an illustration from the Garden of Eden

As I was passing by a neighbour's house this morning, I overheard the wife of the family speaking things to her husband which gave me much disturbance and put me in mind of a character which I wonder I have so long omitted, and that is an outrageous species of the fair sex which is distinguished by the term scolds. The generality of women are by nature loquacious; therefore mere volubility of speech is not to be imputed to them, but should be considered with pleasure when it is used to express such passions as tend to sweeten or adorn conversation. But when through rage females are vehement in their eloquence, nothing in the world has so ill an effect upon the features; for by the force of it I have seen the most amiable become the most deformed; and she that appeared one of the Graces, immediately turned into one of the Furies. I humbly conceive the great cause of this evil may proceed from a false notion the ladies have of what we call a modest woman. They have too narrow a conception of this lovely character, and believe they have not at all forfeited their pretensions to it, provided they have no imputations on their chastity. But alas! the young fellows know they pick out better women in the side-boxes,[1] than many of those who pass upon the world and themselves for modest.

Modesty never rages, never murmurs, never pouts; when it is ill treated, it pines, it beseeches, it languishes. The neighbour I mention is one of your common modest women, that is to say, those who are ordinarily reckoned such. Her husband knows every pain in life with her but jealousy.   Now because she is clear in this particular, the man cannot say his soul is his own but she cries: 'No modest woman is respected nowadays.'   What adds to the comedy in this case is that it is very ordinary with this sort of women to talk in the language of distress: they will complain of the forlorn wretchedness of their condition, and then the poor helpless creatures shall throw the next thing they can lay their hands on at the person who offends them.   Our neighbour was only saying to his wife she went a little too fine, when she immediately pulled his periwig off, and stamping it under her feet, wrung her hands and said: 'Never modest woman was so used.'   These ladies of irresistible modesty are those who make virtue unamiable; not that they can be said to be virtuous, but as they live without scandal; and being under the common denomination of being such, men fear to meet their faults in those who are as agreeable as they are innocent.

I take the bully among men, and the scold among women, to draw the foundation of their actions from the same defect in the mind.   A bully thinks honour consists wholly in being brave; and therefore has regard to no one rule of life, if he preserves himself from the accusation of cowardice.   The froward woman knows chastity to be the first merit in a woman; and therefore since no one can call her one ugly name, she calls all mankind all the rest.

These ladies, where their companions are so imprudent as to take their speeches for any other than exercises of their own lungs and their husbands' patience, gain by the force of being resisted, and flame with open fury, which is no way to be opposed but by being neglected; though at the same time human frailty makes it very hard to relish the philosophy of contemning even frivolous reproach. There is a very pretty instance of this infirmity in the man of the best sense that ever was, no less a person than Adam himself.   According to Milton's description of the first couple, as soon as they had fallen and the turbulent passions of anger, hatred, and jealousy first entered their breast, Adam grew moody, and talked to his wife, as you may find it in the three hundred and fifty-ninth page and ninth book of *Paradise Lost*, in the octavo edition, which out of heroics, and put into domestic style, would run thus:

'Madam, if my advices had been of any authority with you when that strange desire of gadding possessed you this morning, we had still been happy; but your cursed vanity and opinion of your own conduct, which is certainly very wavering when it seeks occasions of being proved, has ruined both yourself and me, who trusted you.'

Eve had no fan in her hand to ruffle, or tucker to pull down; but with a reproachful air she answered:

'Sir, do you impute that to my desire of gadding, which might have happened to yourself, with all your wisdom and gravity? The Serpent spoke so excellently, and with so good a grace, that—— Besides, what harm had I ever done him, that he should design me any? Was I to have been always at your side, I might as well have continu:d there, and been but your rib still. But if I was so weak a creature as you thought me, why did you not interpose your sage authority more absolutely? You denied me going as faintly as you say I resisted the Serpent. Had not you been too easy, neither you nor I had now transgressed.'

Adam replied: 'Why, Eve, hast thou the impudence to upbraid me as the cause of thy transgression for my indulgence to thee? Thus will it ever be with him who trusts too much to woman; at the same time that she refuses to be governed, if she suffers by her obstinacy she will accuse the man that shall leave her to herself.'

> Thus they in mutual accusation spent
> The fruitless hours, but neither self-condemning;
> And of their vain contest appear'd no end.

This, to the modern, will appear but a very faint piece of conjugal enmity; but you are to consider that they were but just begun to be angry, and they wanted new words for expressing their new passions. But by her accusing him of letting her go, and telling him how good a speaker and how fine a gentleman the devil was, we must reckon, allowing for the improvements of time, that she gave him the same provocation as if she had called him cuckold. The passionate and familiar terms with which the same case repeated daily for so many thousand years has furnished the present generation, were not then in use; but the foundation of debate has ever been the same, a contention about their merit and wisdom. Our general mother was a beauty; and hearing there was another now in the world, could not forbear, as Adam tells her, showing herself, though to the devil, by whom the same vanity made her liable to be betrayed.

I cannot, with all the help of science and astrology, find any other remedy for this evil but what was the medicine in this first quarrel; which was, as appears in the next book, that they were convinced of their being both weak, but the one weaker than the other.

If it were possible that the beauteous could but rage a little before a glass, and see their pretty countenances grow wild, it is not to be doubted but it would have a very good effect; but that would require temper. For Lady Firebrand, upon observing her features swell when her maid vexed her the other day, stamped her dressing-glass under her feet. In this case, when one of this temper is moved, she is like a witch in an operation, and makes all things turn round with her. The very fabric is in a vertigo when she begins to charm. In an instant, whatever was the occasion that moved her blood, she has such intolerable servants, Betty is so awkward, Tom cannot carry a message, and her husband has so little respect for her, that she, poor woman, is weary of this life, and was born to be unhappy.

Desunt multa.

ADVERTISEMENT

The season now coming on in which the town will

begin to fill, Mr. Bickerstaff gives notice that from the first of October next he will be much wittier than he has hitherto been.

117. Requests from two readers

'I suppose you know we women are not too apt to forgive; for which reason, before you concern yourself any further with our sex, I would advise you to answer what is said against you by those of your own. I enclose to you business enough until you are ready for your promise of being witty. You must not expect to say what you please without admitting others to take the same liberty. Marry come up! You a Censor? Pray read over all these pamphlets, and these notes upon your lucubrations; by that time you shall hear further. It is, I suppose, from such as you that people learn to be censorious, for which I and all our sex have an utter aversion; when once people come to take the liberty to wound reputations——'

This is the main body of the letter; but she bids me turn over, and there I find:

'MR. BICKERSTAFF,
'If you will draw Mrs. Cicely Trippet according to the enclosed description, I will forgive you all.'

. . . . .

To ISAAC BICKERSTAFF, ESQUIRE.
The humble Petition of Joshua Fairlove of Stepney,

SHOWETH,
That your petitioner is a general lover who for some months last past has made it his whole business to frequent the by-paths and roads near his dwelling, for no other purpose but to hand such of the fair sex as are obliged to pass through them.

That he has been at great expense for clean gloves to
offer his hand with.

That towards the evening he approaches near London,
and employs himself as a convoy towards home.

> Your petitioner therefore most humbly prays
> that for such his humble services, he may be
> allowed the title of an Esquire.

Mr. Morphew has orders to carry the proper instruments;
and the petitioner is to be hereafter writ to upon gilt
paper, by the title of Joshua Fairlove, Esquire.

118. The Church Thermometer

The Church Thermometer, which I am now to treat of,
is supposed to have been invented in the reign of Henry
the Eighth, about the time when that religious prince put
some to death for owning the Pope's supremacy, and others
for denying transubstantiation. I do not find, however,
any great use made of this instrument until it fell into the
hands of a learned and vigilant priest or minister, for he
frequently wrote himself both one and the other, who was
sometime vicar of Bray. This gentleman lived in his
vicarage to a good old age, and, after having seen several
successions of his neighbouring clergy either burned or
banished, departed this life with the satisfaction of having
never deserted his flock, and died vicar of Bray. As this
glass was first designed to calculate the different degrees of
heat in religion, as it raged in popery, or as it cooled and
grew temperate in the Reformation; it was marked at
several distances, after the manner our ordinary thermometer is to this day, viz. 'Extreme Hot, Sultry Hot, Very
Hot, Hot, Warm, Temperate, Cold, Just Freezing, Frost,
Hard Frost, Great Frost, Extreme Cold.'

It is well known that Toricellius,[1] the inventor of the
common weather-glass, made the experiment in a long
tube which held thirty-two feet of water; and that a more

modern virtuoso finding such a machine altogether un-
wieldy and useless, and considering that thirty-two inches
of quicksilver weighed as much as so many feet of water in
a tube of the same circumference, invented that sizable
instrument which is now in use. After this manner, that
I might adapt the thermometer I am now speaking of to
the present constitution of our Church, as divided into
High and Low, I have made some necessary variations
both in the tube and the fluid it contains. In the first
place, I ordered a tube to be cast in a planetary hour, and
took care to seal it hermetically when the sun was in conjunction with Saturn. I then took the proper precautions
about the fluid, which is a compound of two very different
liquors; one of them a spirit drawn out of a strong heady
wine; the other a particular sort of rock-water, colder than
ice and clearer than crystal. The spirit is of a red fiery
colour, and so very apt to ferment that unless it be mingled
with a proportion of the water, or pent up very close, it
will burst the vessel that holds it, and fly up in fume and
smoke. The water, on the contrary, is of such a subtle
piercing cold, that unless it be mingled with a proportion
of the spirits, it will sink almost through everything that
it is put into; and seems to be of the same nature as
the water mentioned by Quintus Curtius,[2] which, says
the historian, could be contained in nothing but in the
hoof, or, as the Oxford manuscript has it, in the skull
of an ass. The thermometer is marked according to the
following figure; which I set down at length, not only
to give my reader a clear idea of it, but also to fill up my
paper.

> Ignorance.
> Persecution.
> Wrath.
> Zeal.
> CHURCH.
> Moderation.
> Lukewarmness.
> Infidelity.
> Ignorance.

The reader will observe that the Church is placed in the middle point of the glass, between Zeal and Moderation; the situation in which she always flourishes, and in which every good Englishman wishes her who is a friend to the constitution of his country. However, when it mounts to Zeal, it is not amiss; and, when it sinks to Moderation, is still in a most admirable temper. The worst of it is, that when once it begins to rise it has still an inclination to ascend; insomuch that it is apt to climb up from Zeal to Wrath, and from Wrath to Persecution, which always ends in Ignorance, and very often proceeds from it. In the same manner, it frequently takes its progress through the lower half of the glass; and when it has a tendency to fall, will gradually descend from Moderation to Luke-warmness, and from Lukewarmness to Infidelity, which very often terminates in Ignorance, and always proceeds from it.

It is a common observation that the ordinary thermometer will be affected by the breathing of people who are in the room where it stands; and indeed it is almost incredible to conceive how the glass I am now describing will fall by the breath of a multitude crying 'Popery'; or on the contrary, how it will rise when the same multitude, as it sometimes happens, cry out in the same breath: 'The Church is in danger.'

As soon as I had finished this my glass, and adjusted it to the above-mentioned scale of religion, that I might make proper experiments with it, I carried it under my cloak to several coffee-houses and other places of resort about this great city. At Saint James's coffee-house the liquor stood at moderation; but at Will's, to my great surprise, it subsided to the very lowest mark on the glass. At the Grecian it mounted but just one point higher; at the Rainbow it still ascended two degrees; Child's fetched it up to Zeal, and other adjacent coffee-houses to Wrath.

It fell in the lower half of the glass as I went further into the city, until at length it settled at Moderation, where it continued all the time I stayed about the Exchange, as also while I passed by the Bank. And here I cannot but

take notice that through the whole course of my remarks
I never observed my glass to rise at the same time that the
stocks did.

To complete the experiment, I prevailed upon a friend
of mine, who works under me in the occult sciences, to
make a progress with my glass through the whole island
of Great Britain; and after his return, to present me with
a register of his observations. I guessed beforehand at
the temper of several places he passed through, by the
characters they have had time out of mind. Thus that
facetious divine, Doctor Fuller,[3] speaking of the town of
Banbury near a hundred years ago, tells us it was a place
famous for cakes and zeal, which I find by my glass is true
to this day as to the latter part of this description; though
I must confess, it is not in the same reputation for cakes
that it was in the time of that learned author; and thus of
other places. In short, I have now by me digested in an
alphabetical order all the counties, corporations, and
boroughs in Great Britain, with their respective tempers,
as they stand related to my thermometer. But this I shall
keep to myself, because I would by no means do anything
that may seem to influence any ensuing elections.[4]

The point of doctrine which I would propagate by this
my invention, is the same which was long ago advanced
by that able teacher Horace, out of whom I have taken my
text for this discourse[1]: we should be careful not to over-
shoot ourselves in the pursuits even of virtue. Whether
zeal or moderation be the point we aim at, let us keep
fire out of the one, and frost out of the other. But alas!
the world is too wise to want such a precaution. The
terms High-church and Low-church, as commonly used,
do not so much denote a principle, as they distinguish a
party. They are like words of battle, that have nothing
to do with their original signification; but are only given
out to keep a body of men together, and to let them know
friends from enemies.

I must confess I have considered, with some little attention, the influence which the opinions of these great
national sects have upon their practice; and do look upon

it as one of the unaccountable things of our times, that multitudes of honest gentlemen, who entirely agree in their lives, should take it in their heads to differ in their religion.

119. Scolds—an ingenious physician's remedy

GOOD MR. BICKERSTAFF,

I am convinced by a late paper of yours that a passionate woman, who among the common people goes under the name of a scold, is one of the most insupportable creatures in the world. But alas! Sir, what can we do? I have made a thousand vows and resolutions every morning, to guard myself against this frailty; but have generally broken them before dinner, and could never in my life hold out until the second course was set upon the table. What most troubles me is that my husband is as patient and good-natured as your own worship, or any man living, can be. Pray give me some directions, for I would observe the strictest and severest rules you can think of to cure myself of this distemper, which is apt to fall into my tongue every moment. I am,

Sir,
Your most humble servant, etc.

In answer to this most unfortunate lady, I must acquaint her that there is now in town an ingenious physician of my acquaintance, who undertakes to cure all the vices and defects of the mind by inward medicines or outward applications. I shall give the world an account of his patients and his cures in other papers, when I shall be more at leisure to treat upon this subject. I shall only here inform my correspondent, that for the benefit of such ladies as are troubled with virulent tongues, he has pre-pared a cold bath, over which there is fastened, at the end of a long pole, a very convenient chair, curiously gilt and carved. When the patient is seated in this chair, the doctor lifts up the pole, and gives her two or three total immersions in the cold bath, until such time as she has quite lost the use of speech. This operation so effectually chills the tongue and refrigerates the blood, that a woman, who at her entrance into the chair is extremely passionate and sonorous, will come out as silent and gentle as a lamb. The doctor told me he would not practise this experiment upon women of fashion, had not he seen it made upon those of meaner condition with very good effect.

120. Reflections on Serenades

Whereas, by letters from Nottingham, we have advice that the young ladies of that place complain for want of sleep, by reason of certain riotous lovers, who for this last summer have very much infested the streets of that eminent city with violins and bass-viols, between the hours of twelve and four in the morning, to the great disturbance of many of Her Majesty's peaceable subjects; and whereas I have been importuned to publish some edict against those midnight alarms, which, under the name of serenades, do greatly annoy many well-disposed persons, not only in the place above-mentioned, but also in most of the polite towns of this island:

I have taken that matter into my serious consideration, and do find that this custom is by no means to be indulged in this country and climate.

It is indeed very unaccountable that most of our British youth should take such great delight in these nocturnal expeditions. Your robust true-born Briton, that has not yet felt the force of flames and darts, has a natural inclination to break windows; while those whose natural ruggedness has been soothed and softened by gentle passions, have as strong a propensity to languish under them, especially if they have a fiddler behind them to utter their complaints. For, as the custom prevails at present, there is scarce a young man of any fashion in a corporation who does not make love with the town music. The Waits often help him through his courtship; and my friend Mr. Banister [1] has told me he was proffered five hundred pounds by a young fellow, to play but one winter under the window of a lady that was a great fortune, but more cruel than ordinary. One would think they hoped to conquer their mistresses' hearts as people tame hawks and eagles, by keeping them awake, or breaking their sleep when they are fallen into it.

I have endeavoured to search into the original of this impertinent way of making love, which, according to some authors, is of great antiquity. If we may believe Monsieur Dacier [2] and other critics, Horace's tenth Ode of the third book was originally a serenade. And if I was disposed to show my learning, I could produce a line of him in another place, which seems to have been the burden of an old heathen serenade:

> . . . *audis minus, & minus jam :*
> '*Me tuo longas pereunte noctes,*
> *Lydia, dormis ?*'
>
> Hor. *Od.* ix.xv. 8.

> Now less and less assail thine ear
> These plaints: 'Ah! sleepest thou, my dear,
> While I, whole nights, thy true love here
> Am dying?'
>
> Francis.

But notwithstanding the opinions of many learned men upon this subject, I rather agree with them who look upon this custom, as now practised, to have been introduced by castrated musicians, who found out this way of applying themselves to their mistresses at these hours, when men of hoarser voices express their passions in a more vulgar method. It must be confessed that your Italian eunuchs do practise this manner of courtship to this day.

But whoever were the persons that first thought of the serenade, the authors of all countries are unanimous in ascribing the invention to Italy.

There are two circumstances which qualified that country above all other for this midnight music.

The first I shall mention was the softness of their climate.

This gave the lover opportunities of being abroad in the air, or of lying upon the earth whole hours together, without fear of damps or dews; but as for our tramontane lovers,[3] when they begin their midnight complaint with:

My lodging is on the cold ground,

we are not to understand them in the rigour of the letter; since it would be impossible for a British swain to condole himself long in that situation, without really dying for his mistress. A man might as well serenade in Greenland as in our region. Milton seems to have had in his thoughts the absurdity of these northern serenades, in the censure which he passes upon them [4]:

. . . or midnight ball,
Or serenade, which the starv'd lover sings
To his proud fair, best quitted with disdain.

The truth of it is, I have often pitied, in a winter night, a vocal musician, and have attributed many of his trills and quavers to the coldness of the weather.

The second circumstance which inclined the Italians to this custom, was that musical genius which is so universal among them. Nothing is more frequent in that country, than to hear a cobbler working to an opera tune. You can scarce see a porter that has not one nail much longer than the rest, which you will find, upon inquiry, is cherished for some instument. In short, there is not a labourer, or handicraft man, that in the cool of the evening does not relieve himself with solos and sonatas.

The Italian soothes his mistress with a plaintive voice, and bewails himself in such melting music that the whole neighbourhood sympathizes with him in his sorrow.

Qualis populea maerens Philomela sub umbra . . .
Flet noctem, ramoque sedens miserabile carmen
Integrat, & maestis late loca questibus implet.
VIRG. Georg. IV. 511.

Thus Philomel beneath the poplar shade
With plaintive murmurs warbles thro' the glade . . .
Her notes harmonious tedious nights prolong,
And Echo multiplies the mournful song.
R. WYNNE.

On the contrary, our honest countrymen have so little an inclination to music that they seldom begin to sing until they are drunk; which also is usually the time when they are most disposed to serenade.

121. Concerning advertisements

It is my custom, in a dearth of news, to entertain myself with those collections of advertisements that appear at the end of all our public prints. These I consider as accounts of news from the little world, in the same manner that the foregoing parts of the paper are from the great. If in one we hear that a sovereign prince is fled from his capital city, in the other we hear of a tradesman who hath shut up his shop, and run away. If in one we find the victory of a general, in the other we see the desertion of a private soldier. I must confess I have a certain weakness in my temper that is often very much affected by these little domestic occurrences, and have frequently been caught with tears in my eyes over a melancholy advertisement.

But to consider this subject in its most ridiculous lights, advertisements are of great use to the vulgar; first of all, as they are instruments of ambition. A man that is by no means big enough for the *Gazette* may easily creep into the advertisements; by which means we often see an apothecary in the same paper of news with a pleni-potentiary, or a running-footman with an ambassador. An advertisement from Piccadilly goes down to posterity with an article from Madrid, and John Bartlett of Good-man's Fields is celebrated in the same paper with the Emperor of Germany. Thus the fable tells us that the wren mounted as high as the eagle, by getting upon his back.

A second use which this sort of writings hath been turned to of late years has been the management of controversy; insomuch that above half the advertisements one meets with nowadays are purely polemical. The inventors of

'Strops for razors' have written against one another this
way for several years, and that with great bitterness; as the
whole argument pro and con in the case of the morning-
gown is still carried on after the same manner. I need
not mention the several proprietors of Dr. Anderson's
pills; nor take notice of the many satirical works of this
nature so frequently published by Dr. Clark, who has had
the confidence to advertise upon that learned knight, my
very worthy friend, Sir William Read.[1] But I shall not
interpose in their quarrel; Sir William can give him his
own in advertisements that, in the judgment of the
impartial, are as well penned as the Doctor's.

The third and last use of these writings is to inform the
world where they may be furnished with almost everything that is necessary for life. If a man has pains in his
head, colics in his bowels, or spots in his clothes, he may
here meet with proper cures and remedies. If a man
would recover a wife or a horse that is stolen or strayed;
if he wants new sermons, electuaries, ass's milk, or anything else, either for his body or his mind, this is the place
to look for them in.

The great art in writing advertisements is the finding
out a proper method to catch the reader's eye, without
which a good thing may pass over unobserved, or be lost
among commissions of bankrupts. Asterisks and hands
were formerly of great use for this purpose. Of late
years the 'N.B.' has been much in fashion, as also
little cuts and figures, the invention of which we must
ascribe to the author of spring-trusses. I must not here
omit the blind Italian character, which, being scarce
legible, always fixes and detains the eye, and gives the
curious reader something like the satisfaction of prying
into a secret.

But the great skill in an advertiser is chiefly seen in the
style which he makes use of. He is to mention 'the
universal esteem, or general reputation,' of things that
were never heard of. If he is a physician or astrologer,
he must change his lodgings frequently; and, though he
never saw anybody in them besides his own family, give

public notice of it 'for the information of the Nobility and Gentry.' Since I am thus usefully employed in writing criticisms on the works of these diminutive authors, I must not pass over in silence an advertisement which has lately made its appearance and is written altogether in a Ciceronian manner. It was sent to me with five shillings, to be inserted among my advertisements; but as it is a pattern of good writing in this way, I shall give it a place in the body of my paper.

'The highest compounded spirit of lavender, the most glorious, if the expression may be used, enlivening scent and flavour that can possibly be, which so raptures the spirits, delights the gust, and gives such airs to the countenance, as are not to be imagined but by those that have tried it. The meanest sort of the thing is admired by most gentlemen and ladies; but this far more, as by far it exceeds it, to the gaining among all a more than common esteem. It is sold, in neat flint bottles fit for the pocket, only at the Golden Key in Wharton's Court near Holborn Bars, for three shillings and sixpence, with directions.'

At the same time that I recommend the several flowers in which this spirit of lavender is wrapped up, if the expression may be used, I cannot excuse my fellow labourers for admitting into their papers several uncleanly advertisements, not at all proper to appear in the works of polite writers. Among these I must reckon the 'Carminative Wind-expelling Pills.' If the doctor had called them only his Carminative Pills, he had been as cleanly as one could have wished; but the second word entirely destroys the decency of the first. There are other absurdities of this nature so very gross that I dare not mention them; and shall therefore dismiss this subject with a public admonition to Michael Parrot, that he do not presume any more to mention a certain worm he knows of,[2] which, by the way, has grown seven feet in my memory; for if I am not much mistaken, it is the same that was but nine feet long about six months ago.

By the remarks I have here made, it plainly appears that
a collection of advertisements is a kind of miscellany; the
writers of which, contrary to all authors, except men of
quality, give money to the booksellers who publish their
copies. The genius of the bookseller is chiefly shown
in his method of ranging and digesting these little tracts.
The last paper I took up in my hand places them in the
following order:

> The true Spanish blacking for shoes, etc.
> The beautifying cream for the face, etc.
> Pease and plasters, etc.
> Nectar and Ambrosia, etc.
> Four freehold tenements of fifteen pounds *per annum*, etc.
> The present state of England, etc.
> Annotations upon the *Tatler*, etc.

122. Curious history of Doctor Young

It is one of the designs of this paper to transmit to
posterity an account of everything that is monstrous in
my own times. For this reason, I shall here publish to
the world the life of a person who was neither man nor
woman; as written by one of my ingenious correspondents,
who seems to have imitated Plutarch in that multifarious
erudition, and those occasional dissertations, which he has
wrought into the body of his history. The life I am
putting out is that of Margery, alias John Young, commonly known by the name of Doctor Young; who, as the
town very well knows, was a woman that practised physic
in a man's clothes, and, after having had two wives and
several children, died about a month since.

'Sir,
    '. . . I do not find anything remarkable in the life I am
about to write, until the year 1695; at which time the
Doctor, being about twenty-three years old, was brought

to bed of a bastard child.   The scandal of such a misfortune gave so great an uneasiness to pretty Mrs. Peggy,
for that was the name by which the Doctor was then called,
that she left her family and followed her lover to London,
with a fixed resolution some way or other to recover her
lost reputation.   But instead of changing her life, which
one would have expected from so good a disposition of
mind, she took it in her head to change her sex.   This was
soon done by the help of a sword and a pair of breeches.
I have reason to believe that her first design was to turn
man-midwife, having herself had some experience in those
affairs; but thinking this too narrow a foundation for her
future fortune, she at length bought her a gold-buttoned
coat, and set up for a physician.   Thus we see the same
fatal miscarriage in her youth made Mrs. Young a doctor,
that formerly made one of the same sex a Pope.

'The Doctor succeeded very well in his business at first;
but very often met with accidents that disquieted him.
As he wanted that deep magisterial voice which gives
authority to a prescription, and is absolutely necessary for
the right pronouncing of these words: 'Take these pills,'
he unfortunately got the nickname of the Squeaking
Doctor.   If this circumstance alarmed the Doctor, there
was another which gave him no small disquiet, and very
much diminished his gains.   In short, he found himself
run down, as a superficial prating quack, in all families
that had at the head of them a cautious father or a jealous
husband.   These would often complain among one another, that they did not like such a smock-faced physician;
though in truth, had they known how justly he deserved
that name, they would rather have favoured his practice
than have apprehended anything from it.

'Such were the motives that determined Mrs. Young
to change her condition, and take in marriage a virtuous
young woman, who lived with her in good reputation,
and made her the father of a very pretty girl.   But this
part of her happiness was soon after destroyed by a
distemper which was too hard for our physician, and
carried off his first wife.   The Doctor had not been a

widow long before he married his second lady, with whom also he lived in very good understanding. It so happened that the Doctor was with child at the same time that his lady was; but the little ones coming both together, they passed for twins. The Doctor having entirely established the reputation of his manhood, especially by the birth of the boy of whom he had been lately delivered, and who very much resembled him, grew into good business, and was particularly famous for the cure of venereal distempers; but would have had much more practice among his own sex, had not some of them been so unreasonable as to demand certain proofs of their cure, which the Doctor was not able to give them. The florid blooming look, which gave the Doctor some uneasiness at first, instead of betraying his person, only recommended his physic. Upon this occasion I cannot forbear mentioning what I thought a very agreeable surprise in one of Molière's plays, where a young woman applies herself to a sick person in the habit of a quack, and speaks to her patient, who was something scandalized at the youth of his physician, to the following purpose: "I began to practise in the reign of Francis the First, and am now in the hundred and fiftieth year of my age; but, by the virtue of my medicaments, have maintained myself in the same beauty and freshness I had at fifteen." For this reason, Hippocrates lays it down as a rule that a student in physic should have a sound constitution and a healthy look; which indeed seem as necessary qualifications of a physician, as a good life and virtuous behaviour for a divine. But to return to our subject. About two years ago, the Doctor was very much afflicted with the vapours, which grew upon him to such a degree that about six weeks since they made an end of him. His death discovered the disguise he had acted under, and brought him back again to his former sex. It is said that at his burial the pall was held up by six women of some fashion. The Doctor left behind him a widow and two fatherless children, if they may be called so, besides the little boy before-mentioned; in relation to whom we may say of the

Doctor, as the good old ballad about the Children in the Wood says of the unnatural uncle, that he was father and mother both in one. These are all the circumstances that I could learn of Doctor Young's life, which might have given occasion to many obscene fictions. But as I know those would never have gained a place in your paper, I have not troubled you with any impertinence of that nature, having stuck to the truth very scrupulously, as I always do when I subscribe myself,

> 'Sir,
> 'Yours, etc.'

123. Letters

A man of business, who makes a public entertainment, may sometimes leave his guests, and beg them to divert themselves as well as they can until his return. I shall here make use of the same privilege, being engaged in matters of some importance relating to the family of the Bickerstaffs, and must desire my readers to entertain one another until I can have leisure to attend them. I have therefore furnished out this paper, as I have done some few others, with letters of my ingenious correspondents, which I have reason to believe will please the public as much as my own more elaborate lucubrations.

Lincoln, Sept. 9.

SIR,
I have long been of the number of your admirers, and take this opportunity of telling you so. I know not why a man so famed for astrological observations may not also be a good casuist; upon which presumption it is I ask your advice in an affair that at present puzzles quite that slender stock of divinity I am master of. I have now been some time in holy orders, and fellow of a certain college in one of the universities; but, weary of that unactive life, I resolve to be doing good in my generation. A worthy gentleman has lately offered me a fat rectory; but

means, I perceive, his kinswoman should have the benefit of the clergy. I am a novice in the world, and confess it startles me how the body of Mrs. Abigail can be annexed to the cure of souls. Sir, would you give us in one of your *Tatlers*, the original and progress of smock-simony, and show us that where the laws are silent, men's consciences ought to be so too, you could not more oblige our fraternity of young divines, and among the rest,

Your humble servant,
HIGH-CHURCH.

I am very proud of having a gentleman of this name for my admirer, and may, some time or other, write such a treatise as he mentions. In the meantime, I do not see why our clergy, who are very frequently men of good families, should be reproached if any of them chance to espouse a handmaid with a rectory *in commendam*, since the best of our peers have often joined themselves to the daughters of very ordinary tradesmen, upon the same valuable considerations.

·　　·　　·　　·

MR. BICKERSTAFF,

I am going to set up for a scrivener, and have thought of a project which may turn both to your account and mine. It came into my head upon reading that learned and useful paper of yours concerning advertisements. You must understand, I have made myself master in the whole art of advertising, both as to the style and the letter. Now if you and I could so manage it that nobody should write advertisements besides myself, or print them anywhere but in your paper, we might both of us get estates in a little time. For this end I would likewise propose that you should enlarge the design of advertisements; and have sent you two or three samples of my work in this kind, which I have made for particular friends, and intend to open shop with. The first is for a gentleman who would willingly marry if he could find a wife to his liking; the second is for a poor whig, who is lately turned out of his post [1]; and the third for a person of a contrary party, who is willing to get into one.

Whereas A. B. next door to the Pestle and Mortar, being about thirty years old, of a spare make, with dark-coloured hair, bright eye, and a long nose, has occasion for a good-humoured, tall, fair young woman, of about three thousand pounds fortune; these are to give notice, that if any such young woman has a mind to dispose of herself in marriage to such a person as the above-mentioned, she may be provided with a husband, a coach and horses, and proportionable settlement.

C. D. designing to quit his place, has great quantities of paper, parchment, ink, wax, and wafers to dispose of, which will be sold at very reasonable rates.

E. F. a person of good behaviour, six feet high, of a black complexion and sound principles, wants an employ. He is an excellent penman and accountant, and speaks French.

124.   *Corruption of our English tongue*

The following letter has laid before me many great and manifest evils in the world of letters which I had over-looked; but they open to me a very busy scene, and it will require no small care and application to amend errors which are become so universal.   The affectation of polite-ness is exposed in this epistle with a great deal of wit and discernment; so that whatever discourses I may fall into hereafter upon the subjects the writer treats of, I shall at present lay the matter before the world, without the least alteration from the words of my correspondent.[1]

TO ISAAC BICKERSTAFF, ESQUIRE.

SIR,

There are some abuses among us of great consequence, the reformation of which is properly your province; though, as far as I have been conversant in your papers, you have not yet considered them.   These are, the deplorable

ignorance that for some years hath reigned among our
English writers, the great depravity of our taste, and
the continual corruption of our style. I say nothing here
of those who handle particular sciences, divinity, law,
physic, and the like; I mean the traders in history and
politics, and the *belles lettres*; together with those by whom
books are not translated, but, as the common expressions
are, 'done out of' French, Latin, or other language, and
'made English.' I cannot but observe to you, that until
of late years a Grub Street book was always bound in
sheepskin, with suitable print and paper, the price never
above a shilling, and taken off wholly by common tradesmen or country pedlars; but now they appear in all sizes
and shapes, and in all places. They are handed about
from lapfuls in every coffee-house to persons of quality;
are shown in Westminster Hall and the Court of Requests.
You may see them gilt, and in royal paper of five or six
hundred pages, and rated accordingly. I would engage to
furnish you with a catalogue of English books published
within the compass of seven years past, which at the first
hand would cost you a hundred pounds, wherein you shall
not be able to find ten lines together of common grammar
or common sense.

These two evils, ignorance and want of taste, have
produced a third; I mean the continual corruption of our
English tongue, which, without some timely remedy, will
suffer more by the false refinements of twenty years past,
than it hath been improved in the foregoing hundred.
And this is what I design chiefly to enlarge upon, leaving
the former evils to your animadversion.

But instead of giving you a list of the last refinements
crept into our language, I here send you the copy of a
letter I received, some time ago, from a most accomplished
person in this way of writing; upon which I shall make
some remarks. It is in these terms:

'SIR,
   'I *cou'd n't* get the things you sent for all *about Town*——
I *thôt* to *ha* come down myself, and then *I'd h' brot 'um*; but

I *ha'nt don't*, and I believe I *can't do't*, that's *Pozz*—— Tom
begins to *gi'mself* airs, because *he's* going with the *Plenipo's*
—— 'Tis said the French King will *bamboozl us agen*,
which causes many speculations. The *Jacks* and others of
that *Kidney* are very *uppish*, and *alert upon't*, as you may see
by their *Phizz's*——Will Hazard has got the *hipps*, having
lost *to the Tune of* five *hundr'd* pound, *tho'* he understands
play very well, *no Body better*. He has promis't me upon
rep, to leave off play; but you know 'tis a weakness *he's*
too apt to *give into, tho'* he has as much wit as any man,
no Body more. He has lain *incog* ever since—— The *mob's*
very quiet with us now—— I believe you *thôt* I *banter'd* you
in my last, like a *country put* [2]—— I *shan't* leave town this
month, *etc.*'

This letter is in every point an admirable pattern of the
present polite way of writing; nor is it of less authority for
being an epistle. You may gather every flower in it,
with a thousand more of equal sweetness, from the books,
pamphlets, and single papers offered us every day in the
coffee-houses. And these are the beauties introduced to
supply the want of wit, sense, humour, and learning,
which formerly were looked upon as qualifications for a
writer. If a man of wit, who died forty years ago, were
to rise from the grave on purpose, how would he be able
to read this letter? And after he had got through that
difficulty, how would he be able to understand it? The
first thing that strikes your eye is the breaks at the end of
almost every sentence; of which I know not the use, only
that it is a refinement, and very frequently practised.
Then you will observe the abbreviations and elisions, by
which consonants of most obdurate sound are joined
together, without one softening vowel to intervene; and
all this only to make one syllable of two, directly contrary
to the example of the Greeks and Romans, altogether of
the Gothic strain, and a natural tendency towards relapsing
into barbarity, which delights in monosyllables, and
uniting of mute consonants, as it is observable in all the
northern languages. And this is still more visible in the

next refinement, which consists in pronouncing the first syllable in a word that has many, and dismissing the rest, such as 'phizz, hipps, mob, pozz, rep,' and many more, when we are already overloaded with monosyllables, which are the disgrace of our language. Thus we cram one syllable, and cut off the rest, as the owl fattened her mice after she had bit off their legs to prevent them from running away; and if ours be the same reason for maiming our words, it will certainly answer the end; for I am sure no other nation will desire to borrow them. Some words are hitherto but fairly split, and therefore only in their way to perfection, as Incog, and Plenipo. But in a short time, it is to be hoped, they will be further docked to Inc. and Plen. This reflection has made me of late years very impatient for a peace, which I believe would save the lives of many brave words, as well as men. The war has introduced abundance of polysyllables, which will never be able to live many more campaigns, 'speculations, operations, preliminaries, ambassadors, palisadoes, communication, circumvallation, battalions,' as numerous as they are, if they attack us too frequently in our coffee-houses, we shall certainly put them to flight, and cut off the rear.

The third refinement, observable in the letter I send you, consists in the choice of certain words invented by some pretty fellows, such as 'banter, bamboozle, country put, and kidney,' as it is there applied; some of which are now struggling for the vogue, and others are in possession of it. I have done my utmost for some years past, to stop the progress of 'mob' and 'banter,' but have been plainly borne down by numbers, and betrayed by those who promised to assist me.

In the last place, you are to take notice of certain choice phrases scattered through the letter, some of them tolerable enough, until they were worn to rags by servile imitators. You might easily find them though they were not in a different print, and therefore I need not disturb them.

These are the false refinements in our style which you ought to correct; first, by argument and fair means, but if those fail, I think you are to make use of your authority as Censor, and by an annual *Index Expurgatorius* expunge all words and phrases that are offensive to good sense and condemn those barbarous mutilations of vowels and syllables. In this last point the usual pretence is that they spell as they speak: a noble standard for language! to depend upon the caprice of every coxcomb, who, because words are the clothing of our thoughts, cuts them out and shapes them as he pleases, and changes them oftener than his dress. I believe all reasonable people would be content that such refiners were more sparing in their words and liberal in their syllables; and upon this head I should be glad you would bestow some advice upon several young readers in our churches, who, coming up from the university full fraught with admiration of our town politeness, will needs correct the style of their prayer-books. In reading the absolution, they are very careful to say 'Pardons and Absolves'; but in the prayer for the Royal Family, it must be *endue'um*, *enrich'um*, *prosper'um*, and *bring'um*. Then in their sermons they use all the modern terms of art, 'sham, banter, mob, bubble, bully, cutting, shuffling, and palming'; all which, and many more of the like stamp, as I have heard them often in the pulpit from such young sophisters, so I have read them in some of 'those sermons that have made most noise of late.' The design, it seems, is to avoid the dreadful imputation of pedantry; to show us that they know the town, understand men and manners, and have not been poring upon old unfashionable books in the university.

I should be glad to see you the instrument of introducing into our style that simplicity which is the best and truest ornament of most things in life, which the politer ages always aimed at in their building and dress, *simplex munditiis*, as well as their productions of wit. It is manifest that all new affected modes of speech, whether borrowed from the court, the town, or the theatre, are the first perishing parts in any language; and, as I could prove by many hundred instances, have been so in ours. The writings of Hooker,[3] who was a country clergyman, and of Parsons the Jesuit,[4] both in the reign of Queen Elizabeth, are in a style that, with very few allowances, would not offend any present reader, and are much more clear and intelligible than those of Sir Harry Wotton, Sir Robert Naunton, Osborn, Daniel the historian, and several others who writ later[5]; but being men of the court, and affecting the phrases then in fashion, they are often either not to be understood, or appear perfectly ridiculous.

What remedies are to be applied to these evils I have not room to consider, having, I fear, already taken up most of your paper. Besides, I think it is our office only to represent abuses, and yours to redress them. I am with great respect,

Sir,

Your, etc.

125. Bitter words about the Royal Society

There is no study more becoming a rational creature, than that of natural philosophy; but as several of our modern virtuosos manage it, their speculations do not so much tend to open and enlarge the mind as to contract and fix it upon trifles.

This in England is in a great measure owing to the worthy elections that are so frequently made in our Royal Society. They seem to be in a confederacy against men of polite genius, noble thought, and diffusive learning; and choose into their assemblies such as have no pretence to wisdom, but want of wit; or to natural knowledge, but ignorance of everything else. I have made observations in this matter so long that when I meet with a young fellow that is an humble admirer of these sciences, but more dull than the rest of the company, I conclude him to be a Fellow of the Royal Society.[1]

126. Ithuriel's Spear

Coming home last night before my usual hour, I took a book into my hand in order to divert myself with it until bed-time. Milton chanced to be my author, whose admirable poem of *Paradise Lost* serves at once to fill the mind with pleasing ideas and with good thoughts, and was therefore the most proper book for my purpose. I was amusing myself with that beautiful passage in which the poet represents Eve sleeping by Adam's side, with the devil sitting at her ear and inspiring evil thoughts, under the shape of a toad. Ithuriel, one of the guardian angels of the place, taking his nightly rounds, saw the great enemy of mankind hid in this loathsome animal, which he touched with his spear. This spear being of a celestial temper, had such a secret virtue in it, that whatever it was applied to immediately flung off all disguise, and appeared in its natural figure. I am afraid the reader will not pardon me if I content myself with explaining the passage in prose without giving it in the author's own inimitable words.[1]

> On he led his radiant files,
> Dazzling the moon: these to the bower direct,
> In search of whom they sought. Him there they found,
> Squat like a toad, close at the ear of Eve;
> Essaying by his devilish art to reach
> The organs of her fancy, and with them forge
> Illusions as he lists, phantasms and dreams;
> Or if, inspiring venom, he might taint
> The animal spirits (that from pure blood arise
> Like gentle breaths from rivers pure), thence raise
> At least distemper'd, discontented thoughts,
> Vain hopes, vain aims, inordinate desires,
> Blown up with high conceits engendring pride.
> Him, thus intent, Ithuriel with his spear
> Touch'd lightly; for no falsehood can endure
> Touch of celestial temper, but returns
> Of force to his own likeness. Up he starts
> Discover'd and surpris'd. As when a spark
> Lights on a heap of nitrous powder, laid
> Fit for the tun, some magazine to store
> Against a rumour'd war, the smutty grain,
> With sudden blaze diffus'd, inflames the air;
> So started up in his own shape the fiend.

I could not forbear thinking how happy a man would

be in the possession of this spear; or what an advantage it would be to a minister of state, were he master of such a white staff. It would help him to discover his friends from his enemies, men of abilities from pretenders. It would hinder him from being imposed upon by appearances and professions; and might be made use of as a kind of state test, which no artifice could elude.

These thoughts made very lively impressions on my imagination, which were improved, instead of being defaced, by sleep, and produced in me the following dream: I was no sooner fallen asleep, but methought the angel Ithuriel appeared to me, and, with a smile that still added to his celestial beauty, made me a present of the spear which he held in his hand, and disappeared. To make trials of it, I went into a place of public resort.

The first person that passed by me was a lady that had a particular shyness in the cast of her eye, and a more than ordinary reservedness in all the parts of her behaviour. She seemed to look upon man as an obscene creature, with a certain scorn and fear of him. In the height of her airs I touched her gently with my wand, when, to my unspeakable surprise, she fell upon her back, and kicked up her heels in such a manner as made me blush in my sleep. As I was hasting away from this undisguised prude, I saw a lady in earnest discourse with another, and overheard her say, with some vehemence: 'Never tell me of him, for I am resolved to die a virgin!'

I had a curiosity to try her; but as soon as I laid my wand upon her head, she immediately fell in labour. My eyes were diverted from her by a man and his wife, who walked near me hand in hand after a very loving manner. I gave each of them a gentle tap, and the next instant saw the woman in breeches, and the man with a fan in his hand.

It would be tedious to describe the long series of metamorphoses that I entertained myself with in my night's adventure, of Whigs disguised in Tories, and Tories in Whigs; men in red coats that denounced terror in their countenances, trembling at the touch of my spear; others in black with peace in their mouths, but swords in their hands. I could tell stories of noblemen changed into usurers, and magistrates into beadles; of free-thinkers into penitents, and reformers into whoremasters. I must not, however, omit the mention of a grave citizen who passed by me with an huge clasped Bible under his arm and a band of a most immoderate breadth; but upon a touch on the shoulder, he let drop his book and fell a-picking my pocket.

127. *Verses on a City shower—by an eminent hand*

Storms at sea are so frequently described by the ancient poets and copied by the moderns, that whenever I find the winds begin to rise in a new heroic poem, I generally skip a leaf or two until I come into fair weather. Virgil's tempest is a masterpiece in this kind, and is indeed so naturally drawn that one who has made a voyage can scarce read it without being seasick.[1]

Land showers are no less frequent among the poets than the former, but I remember none of them which have not fallen in the country; for which reason they are generally filled with the lowings of oxen and the bleatings of sheep, and very often embellished with a rainbow.

Virgil's land shower is likewise the best in its kind. It is indeed a shower of consequence, and contributes to the main design of the poem, by cutting off a tedious ceremonial and bringing matters to a speedy conclusion between two potentates of different sexes.[2] My ingenious kinsman, Mr. Humphrey Wagstaff,[3] who treats of every subject after a manner that no author has done, and better than any other can do, has sent me the description of a city shower. I do not question but the reader remembers my cousin's description of the morning as it breaks in town, which is printed in the ninth *Tatler*, and is another exquisite piece of this local poetry.

Careful observers may foretell the hour,
By sure prognostics, when to dread a shower;
While rain depends, the pensive cat gives o'er
Her frolics, and pursues her tail no more.
Returning home at night, you'll find the sink [4]
Strike your offended sense with double stink.
If you be wise, then go not far to dine,
You'll spend in coach hire more than save in wine.
A coming show'r your shooting corns presage,
Old aches throb, your hollow tooth will rage.
Saunt'ring in coffee-house is Dulman seen;
He damns the climate, and complains of spleen.

Meanwhile the south, rising with dabbled wings,
A sable cloud athwart the welkin flings,
That swill'd more liquor than it could contain,
And like a drunkard gives it up again.
Brisk Susan whips her linen from the rope,
While the first drizzling show'r is borne aslope.
Such is that sprinkling which some careless quean [5]
Flirts on you from her mop, but not so clean.
You fly, invoke the gods; then turning, stop
To rail; she singing, still whirls on her mop.
Not yet the dust had shunn'd the unequal strife,
But aided by the wind fought still for life;
And wafted with its foe by violent gust,
'Twas doubtful which was rain, and which was dust.
Ah! where must needy poet seek for aid,
When dust and rain at once his coat invade;
His only coat, where dust confus'd with rain
Roughen the nap, and leave a mingled stain?

Now in contiguous drops the flood comes down,
Threat'ning with deluge this devoted town.
To shops in crowds the daggled females fly,
Pretend to cheapen goods, but nothing buy.
The Templar [6] spruce, while ev'ry spout's abroach,
Stays till 'tis fair, yet seems to call a coach.
The tuck'd-up sempstress walks with hasty strides,
While streams run down her oil'd umbrella's sides.
Here various kinds, by various fortunes led,
Commence acquaintance underneath a shed.

Triumphant Tories and desponding Whigs
Forget their feuds, and join to save their wigs.
Box'd in a chair the beau impatient sits,
While spouts run clatt'ring o'er the roof by fits;
And ever and anon with frightful din
The leather sounds; he trembles from within.
So when Troy chairmen bore the wooden steed,
Pregnant with Greeks impatient to be freed,
Those bully Greeks who, as the moderns do,
Instead of paying chairmen, run them through;
Laoco'n struck the outside with his spear,
And each imprison'd hero quak'd for fear.

Now from all parts the swelling kennels [7] flow,
And bear their trophies with them as they go:
Filth of all hues and odours seem to tell
What street they sail'd from, by their sight and smell.
They, as each torrent drives, with rapid force,
From Smithfield or St. Pulchre's [8] shape their course,
And in huge confluent join'd at Snow Hill ridge,
Fall from the conduit, prone to Holborn Bridge.
Sweepings from butchers' stalls, dung, guts, and blood,
Drown'd puppies, stinking sprats, all drench'd in mud,
Dead cats and turnip tops come tumbling down the flood.

128. Quacks

Ordinary quacks and charlatans are thoroughly sensible
how necessary it is to support themselves by . . . collateral
assistances, and therefore always lay their claims to some
supernumerary accomplishments which are wholly foreign
to their profession.

About twenty years ago it was impossible to walk the
streets without having an advertisement thrust into your
hand, of a doctor 'who was arrived at the knowledge of
the green and red dragon, and had discovered the female
fern seed.' Nobody ever knew what this meant; but the
green and red dragon so amused the people that the doctor
lived very comfortably upon them. About the same time

there was pasted a very hard word upon every corner of the streets. This, to the best of my remembrance, was

TETRACHYMAGOGON,

which drew great shoals of spectators about it, who read the bill that it introduced with an unspeakable curiosity; and when they were sick would have nobody but this learned man for their physician.

I once received an advertisement of one 'who had studied thirty years by candlelight for the good of his countrymen.' He might have studied twice as long by daylight, and never have been taken notice of. But lucubrations cannot be over-valued. There are some who have gained themselves great reputation for physic by their birth, as the 'seventh son of a seventh son'; and others by not being born at all, as the 'Unborn Doctor,' who, I hear, is lately gone the way of his patients; having died worth five hundred pounds per annum, though he was not born to a halfpenny.

My ingenious friend Doctor Saffold [1] succeeded my old contemporary Doctor Lilly [2] in the studies both of physic and astrology, to which he added that of poetry, as was to be seen both upon the sign where he lived, and in the bills which he distributed. He was succeeded by Doctor Case,[3] who erased the verses of his predecessor out of the sign-post, and substituted in their stead two of his own, which were as follow:

Within this place
Lives Doctor Case.

He is said to have got more by this distich than Mr. Dryden did by all his works. There would be no end of enumerating the several imaginary perfections and unaccountable artifices by which this tribe of men ensnare the minds of the vulgar, and gain crowds of admirers. I have seen the whole front of a mountebank's stage, from one end to the other, faced with patents, certificates, medals, and great seals, by which the several Princes of Europe have testified their particular respect and esteem for the doctor. Every great man with a sounding title has

been his patient. I believe I have seen twenty mounte-
banks that have given physic to the Czar of Muscovy.
The Great Duke of Tuscany escapes no better. The
Elector of Brandenburgh was likewise a very good patient.

This great condescension of the doctor draws upon him
much goodwill from his audience; and it is ten to one
but if any of them be troubled with an aching tooth, his
ambition will prompt him to get it drawn by a person
who has had so many princes, kings, and emperors under
his hands.

I must not leave this subject without observing that as
physicians are apt to deal in poetry, apothecaries endeavour
to recommend themselves by oratory, and are therefore
without controversy the most eloquent persons in the
whole British nation. I would not willingly discourage
any of the arts, especially that of which I am an humble
professor; but I must confess, for the good of my native
country, I could wish there might be a suspension of
physic for some years, that our kingdom, which has
been so much exhausted by the wars, might have leave
to recruit itself.

As for myself, the only physic which has brought me
safe to almost the age of man, and which I prescribe to all
my friends, is abstinence. This is certainly the best physic
for prevention, and very often the most effectual against
a present distemper. In short, my recipe is: 'Take
nothing.'

129. *England or Great Britain?*

MR. BICKERSTAFF,
   I was the other day in company with a gentleman, who,
in reciting his own qualifications, concluded every period
with these words: 'The best of any man in England.'
Thus for example: 'He kept the best house of any man in
England.' 'He understood this, and that, and the other,
the best of any man in England.'

   How harsh and ungrateful soever this expression might
   * I 993

sound to one of my nation, yet the gentleman was one whom it no ways became me to interrupt; but perhaps a new term put into his by-words (as they call a sentence a man particularly affects) may cure him. I therefore took a resolution to apply to you, who, I dare say, can easily persuade this gentleman, whom I cannot believe an enemy to the Union,[1] to mend his phrase, and be hereafter the wisest of any man in Great Britain. I am,

        Sir,
        Your most humble servant,
              SCOTO-BRITANNUS.

•   •   •   •   •

ADVERTISEMENT

Whereas Mr. Humphry Trelooby, wearing his own hair, a pair of buckskin breeches, a hunting-whip, with a new pair of spurs, has complained to the Censor, that on Thursday last he was defrauded of half a crown under pretence of a duty to the sexton for seeing the cathedral of St. Paul, London; it is hereby ordered, that none hereafter require above sixpence of any country gentleman under the age of twenty-five for that liberty; and that all which shall be received above the said sum, of any person, for beholding the inside of that sacred edifice, be forthwith paid to Mr. Morphew, for the use of Mr. Bickerstaff, under pain of further censure on the abovementioned extortion.

130.   Gyges's ring

I have somewhere made mention of Gyges's ring; and intimated to my reader that it was at present in my possession, though I have not since made any use of it. The tradition concerning this ring is very romantic, and taken notice of both by Plato and Tully,[1] who each of them make an admirable use of it for the advancement of morality. This Gyges was the master-shepherd to King

Candaules. As he was wandering over the plains of Lydia, he saw a great chasm in the earth, and had the curiosity to enter it. After having descended pretty far into it, he found the statue of a horse in brass, with doors in the sides of it. Upon opening them, he found the body of a dead man, bigger than ordinary, with a ring upon his finger, which he took off, and put it upon his own. The virtues of it were much greater than he at first imagined; for, upon his going into the assembly of shepherds, he observed that he was invisible when he turned the stone of the ring within the palm of his hand, and visible when he turned it towards his company. . . . As for myself, I have with much study and application arrived at this great secret of making myself invisible, and by that means conveying myself where I please; or to speak in Rosicrucian lore, I have entered into the clifts of the earth, discovered the brazen horse, and robbed the dead giant of his ring. The tradition says further of Gyges, that by the means of this ring he gained admission into the most retired parts of the court, and made such use of those opportunities that he at length became King of Lydia. For my own part, I, who have always rather endeavoured to improve my mind than my fortune, have turned this ring to no other advantage than to get a thorough insight into the ways of men, and to make such observations upon the errors of others as may be useful to the public, whatever effect they may have upon myself.

About a week ago, not being able to sleep, I got up, and put on my magical ring; and with a thought transported myself into a chamber where I saw a light. I found it inhabited by a celebrated beauty, though she is of that species of women which we call a slattern. Her headdress and one of her shoes lay upon a chair, her petticoat in one corner of the room, and her girdle, that had a copy of verses made upon it but the day before, with her thread stockings in the middle of the floor. I was so foolishly officious that I could not forbear gathering up her clothes together, to lay them upon the chair that stood by her bedside; when, to my great surprise, after a little muttering,

she cried out: 'What do you do?   Let my petticoat alone.'
I was startled at first, but soon found that she was in a
dream; being one of those who, to use Shakespeare's
expression, are 'so loose of thought' that they utter in
their sleep everything that passes in their imagination.
I left the apartment of this female rake, and went into her
neighbour's, where there lay a male coquette. He had a
bottle of salts hanging over his head, and upon the table
by his bedside Suckling's poems, with a little heap of
black patches on it. His snuff-box was within reach on
a chair. But while I was admiring the disposition which
he made of the several parts of his dress, his slumber
seemed interrupted by a pang that was accompanied by
a sudden oath, as he turned himself over hastily in his
bed. I did not care for seeing him in his nocturnal pains,
and left the room.

I was no sooner got into another bed-chamber, but I
heard very harsh words uttered in a smooth uniform tone.
I was amazed to hear so great a volubility in reproach,
and thought it too coherent to be spoken by one asleep;
but upon looking nearer I saw the headdress of the person
who spoke, which showed her to be a female, with a man
lying by her side broad awake and as quiet as a lamb.
I could not but admire his exemplary patience, and discovered by his whole behaviour that he was then lying
under the discipline of a curtain-lecture.

I was entertained in many other places with this kind
of nocturnal eloquence, but observed that most of those
whom I found awake were kept so either by envy or by
love. Some of these were sighing, and others cursing, in
soliloquy; some hugged their pillows, and others gnashed
their teeth.

The covetous I likewise found to be a very wakeful
people. I happened to come into a room where one of
them lay sick. His physician and his wife were in close
whisper near his bedside. I overheard the doctor say to
the poor gentlewoman: 'He cannot possibly live until five
in the morning.' She received it like the mistress of a
family, prepared for all events. At the same instant came

in a servant maid, who said: 'Madam, the undertaker is below according to your order.' The words were scarce out of her mouth when the sick man cried out with a feeble voice: 'Pray, Doctor, how went bank-stock to-day at '*Change*?' This melancholy object made me too serious for diverting myself further this way; but as I was going home I saw a light in a garret, and entering into it heard a voice crying: 'And, hand, stand, band, fanned, tanned.' I concluded him by this, and the furniture of his room, to be a lunatic; but upon listening a little longer, perceived it was a poet, writing an heroic upon the ensuing peace.[2]

It was now towards morning, an hour when spirits, witches, and conjurers are obliged to retire to their own apartments; and feeling the influence of it, I was hastening home, when I saw a man had got half-way into a neighbour's house. I immediately called to him, and turning my ring appeared in my proper person. There is something magisterial in the aspect of the Bickerstaffs which made him run away in confusion.

As I took a turn or two in my own lodging, I was thinking that, old as I was, I need not go to bed alone, but that it was in my power to marry the finest lady in this kingdom if I would wed her with this ring. For what a figure would she that should have it make at a visit, with so perfect a knowledge as this would give her of all the scandal in the town! But instead of endeavouring to dispose of myself and it in matrimony, I resolved to lend it to my loving friend the author of the *Atlantis*, to furnish a new 'Secret History of Secret Memoirs.'[3]

131. Inventory of goods lately stolen from Lady Fardingale

The lady hereafter mentioned, having come to me in very great haste, and paid me much above the usual fee, as a cunning-man, to find her stolen goods, and also having approved my late discourse of advertisements, obliged me to draw up this and insert it in the body of my paper.

ADVERTISEMENT

Whereas Bridget Howd'ye, late servant to the Lady Fardingale, a short, thick, lively, hard-favoured wench, of about twenty-nine years of age, her eyes small and bleared, and nose very broad at bottom and turning up at the end, her mouth wide, and lips of an unusual thickness, two teeth out before, the rest black and uneven, the tip of her left ear being of a mouse colour, her voice loud and shrill, quick of speech, and something of a Welsh accent, withdrew herself on Wednesday last from her ladyship's dwelling-house, and, with the help of her consorts, carried off the following goods of her said lady,[1] viz: a thick wadded calico wrapper, a musk-coloured velvet mantle lined with squirrel skins, eight night-shifts, four pair of silk stockings curiously darned, six pair of laced shoes, new and old, with the heels of half two inches higher than their fellows; a quilted petticoat of the largest size, and one of canvas with whalebone hoops; three pair of stays, bolstered below the left shoulder, two pair of hips of the newest fashion, six roundabout aprons with pockets, and four striped muslin night-rails very little frayed; a silver pot for coffee or chocolate, the lid much bruised; a broad-brimmed flat silver plate for sugar with Rhenish wine, a silver ladle for plum-porridge; a silver cheese-toaster with three tongues, an ebony handle, and silvering at the end; a silver posnet to butter eggs; one caudle and two cordial-water cups, two cocoa-cups, and an ostrich's egg with rims and feet of silver; a marrow-spoon with a scoop at the other end, a silver orange strainer, eight sweetmeat spoons made with forks at the end, an agate-handle knife and fork in a sheath; a silver tongue-scraper, a silver tobacco-box with a tulip graved on the top, and a Bible bound in shagreen, with gilt leaves and clasps, never opened but once. Also a small cabinet, with six drawers inlaid with red tortoiseshell, and brass gilt ornaments at the four corners, in which were two leather forehead-cloths, three

pair of oiled dog-skin gloves, seven cakes of superfine
Spanish wool, half a dozen of Portugal dishes, and a quire
of paper from thence; two pair of brand-new plumpers,
four black-lead combs, three pair of fashionable eyebrows, two sets of ivory teeth, little the worse for wearing, and one pair of box for common use; Adam and Eve
in bugle-work, without fig-leaves, upon canvas, curiously
wrought with her ladyship's own hand; several filigrane
curiosities; a crotchet of one hundred and twenty-two
diamonds, set strong and deep in silver, with a rump-jewel
after the same fashion; bracelets of braided hair, pomander,
and seed-pearl; a large old purple velvet purse embroidered
and shutting with a spring, containing two pictures in
miniature, the features visible; a broad thick gold ring
with a hand in hand graved upon it, and within this posy:
'While life does last, I'll hold thee fast'; another set round
with small rubies and sparks, six wanting; another of
Turkey stone, cracked through the middle; an Elizabeth
and four Jacobuses, one guinea, the first of the coin, an
angel with a hole bored through, a broken half of a Spanish
piece of gold, a crown-piece with the breeches, an old
ninepence bent both ways by Lilly the almanack-maker
for luck at langteraloo, and twelve of the shells called blackamoor's tooth; one small amber box with apoplectic
balsam, and one silver gilt of a larger size for cachou and
caraway comfits, to be taken at long sermons, the lid
enamelled, representing a Cupid fishing for hearts with a
piece of gold on his hook; over his head this rhyme:
'Only with gold, you me shall hold.' In the lower drawer
was a large new gold repeating watch made by a French-
man; a gold chain, and all the proper appurtenances hung
upon steel swivels, to wit, lockets with the hair of dead
and living lovers, seals with arms, emblems and devices
cut in cornelian, agate, and onyx, with cupids, hearts,
darts, altars, flames, rocks, pickaxes, roses, thorns, and
sunflowers; as also variety of ingenious French mottoes; together with gold etuys for quills, scissors, needles, thimbles,
and a sponge dipped in Hungary water, left but the night
before by a young lady going upon a frolic *incog*. There

was also a bundle of letters, dated between the years one thousand six hundred and seventy and one thousand six hundred and eighty-two, most of them signed Philander, the rest Strephon, Amyntas, Corydon, and Adonis; together with a collection of receipts to make pastes for the hands, pomatums, lip-salves, white-pots, beautifying creams, water of talk, and frog-spawn water; decoctions for clearing the complexion, and an approved medicine to procure abortion.

Whoever can discover the aforesaid goods so that they may be had again, shall have fifty guineas for the whole, or proportionable for any part.

N.B. Her ladyship is pleased to promise ten pounds for the packet of letters over and above, or five for Philander's only, being her first love. My lady bestows those of Strephon to the finder, being so written that they may serve to any woman who reads them.

POSTSCRIPT

As I am patron of persons who have no other friend to apply to, I cannot suppress the following complaint.

SIR,

I am a blackamoor boy, and have, by my lady's order, been christened by the chaplain. The good man has gone further with me, and told me a great deal of good news; as, that I am as good as my lady herself as I am a Christian, and many other things. But for all this, the parrot, who came over with me from our country, is as much esteemed by her as I am. Besides this, the shock-dog has a collar that cost almost as much as mine.[2] I desire also to know, whether now I am a Christian I am obliged to dress like a Turk, and wear a turban. I am,

Sir,

Your most humble servant,
POMPEY.

132. Jenny answers a correspondent

Mr. Bickerstaff   Edenburgh, Octob. 23.

I presume to lay before you an affair of mine, and begs you will be very sinceir in giving me your judgment and advice in this matter, which is as follows:

A very agreeable young gentleman, who is endowed with all the good qualities that can make a man complete, has this long time maid love to me in the most passionate manner that was posable. He has left nothing unsaid to make me believe his affections real; and in his letters expressed himself so hansomly, and tenderly, that I had all the reason imaginable to believe him sincere. In short, he positively has promised me he would marry me. But I find all he said nothing; for when the question was put to him, he would not; but still would continue my humble servant, and would go on at the ould rate, repeating the assurances of his fidelity, and at the same time has none in him. He now writs to me in the same endearing stile he ust to do, would have me speak to no man but himself. His estate is in his own hand, his father being dead. My fortune at my own disposal, mine being also dead, and to the full answers his estate. Pray, Sir, be ingeinous, and tell me cordially, if you do not think I shall do myself an injury if I keep company or a corospondance any longer with this gentleman. I hope you will faver an honest North Britain, as I am, with your advice in this amour; for I am resolved just to follow your directions. Sir, you will do me a sensable pleasure, and very great honour, if you will please to insert this poor scrole, with your answer to it, in your *Tatler*. Pray fail not to give me your answer; for on it depends the happiness of,

DISCONSOLAT ALMEIRA.

Madam,

I have frequently read over your Letter, and am of opinion, that as lamentable as it is, it is the most common of any evil that attends our sex. I am very much troubled for the tenderness you express towards your lover, but rejoice at the same time that you can so far surmount your inclination for him as to resolve to dismiss him when you have my brother's opinion for it. His sense of the matter, he desired me to communicate to you. Oh Almeira! the common failing of our sex is to value the merit of our lovers rather from the grace of their address than the sincerity of their hearts. 'He has expressed himself so handsomely!' Can you say that, after you have reason to doubt his truth? It is a very melancholy thing that in this circumstance of love, which is the most important of all others in female life, we women, who are, they say, always weak, are still weakest. The true way of valuing a man is to consider his reputation among the men. For want of this necessary rule towards our conduct, when it is too late we find ourselves married to the outcast of that sex; and it is generally from being disagreeable among men that fellows endeavour to make themselves pleasing to us. The little accomplishments of coming into a room with a good air, and telling while they are with us what we cannot hear among ourselves, usually make up the whole of a woman's man's merit. But if we, when we began to reflect upon our lovers, in the first place considered what figures they make in the camp, at the bar, on the exchange, in their country, or at court, we should behold them in quite another view than at present.

Were we to behave ourselves according to this rule, we should not have the just imputation of favouring the silliest of mortals, to the great scandal of the wisest; who value our favour as it advances their pleasure, not their reputation. In a word, Madam, if you would judge aright in love, you must look upon it as in a case of friendship. Were this gentleman treating with you for anything but yourself, when you had consented to his offer, if he fell off, you would call him a cheat and an impostor. There is therefore nothing left for you to do, but to despise him, and yourself for doing it with regret.

I am,

Madam, etc.

133. *History of a shilling*

I was last night visited by a friend of mine who has an inexhaustible fund of discourse and never fails to entertain his company with a variety of thoughts and hints that are altogether new and uncommon. Whether it were in complaisance to my way of living, or his real opinion, he advanced the following paradox: that it required much greater talents to fill up and become a retired life, than a life of business. Upon this occasion he rallied very agreeably the busy men of the age, who only valued themselves for being in motion, and passing through a series of trifling and insignificant actions. In the heat of his discourse, seeing a piece of money lying on my table, 'I defy,' says he, 'any of these active persons to produce half the adventures that this twelvepenny piece has been engaged in, were it possible for him to give us an account of his life.'

My friend's talk made so odd an impression upon my mind, that soon after I was abed I fell insensibly into a most unaccountable reverie, that had neither moral nor design in it, and cannot be so properly called a dream as a delirium.

Methought the shilling that lay upon the table reared itself upon its edge, and turning the face towards me, opened its mouth, and in a soft silver sound gave me the following account of his life and adventures.

'I was born,' says he, 'on the side of a mountain, near a little village of Peru, and made a voyage to England in an ingot, under the convoy of Sir Francis Drake. I was, soon after my arrival, taken out of my Indian habit, refined, naturalized, and put into the British mode, with the face of Queen Elizabeth on one side, and the arms of the country on the other. Being thus equipped, I found in me a wonderful inclination to ramble, and visit all the parts of the new world into which I was brought. The people very much favoured my natural disposition, and shifted me so fast from hand to hand, that before I was five years old I had travelled into almost every corner of the nation. But in the beginning of my sixth year, to my unspeakable grief, I fell into the hands of a miserable old fellow who clapped me into an iron chest, where I found five hundred more of my own quality who lay under the same confinement. The only relief we had was to be taken out and counted over in the fresh air every morning and evening. After an imprisonment of several years, we heard somebody knocking at our chest and breaking it open with an hammer. This we found was the old man's heir, who, as his father lay dying, was so good as to come to our release; he separated us that very day. What was the fate of my companions I know not. As for myself, I was sent to the apothecary's shop for a pint of sack. The apothecary gave me to an herb-woman, the herb-woman to a butcher, the butcher to a brewer, and the brewer to his wife, who made a present of me to a nonconformist preacher. After this manner I made my way merrily through the world; for, as I told you before, we shillings love nothing so much as travelling. I sometimes fetched in a shoulder of mutton, sometimes a play-book, and often had the satisfaction to treat a Templar at a twelvepenny ordinary, or carry him with three friends to Westminster Hall.

'In the midst of this pleasant progress, which I made from place to place, I was arrested by a superstitious old woman, who shut me up in a greasy purse in pursuance of a foolish saying, that while she kept a Queen Elizabeth's shilling about her, she should never be without money. I continued here a close prisoner for many months until at last I was exchanged for eight and forty farthings.

'I thus rambled from pocket to pocket until the beginning of the civil wars, when, to my shame be it spoken, I was employed in raising soldiers against the King. For being of a very tempting breadth a sergeant made use of me to inveigle country fellows, and lift them into the service of the Parliament.

'As soon as he had made one man sure, his way was to oblige him to take a shilling of a more homely figure, and then practise the same trick upon another. Thus I continued doing great mischief to the crown, until my officer chancing one morning to walk abroad earlier than ordinary, sacrificed me to his pleasures, and made use of me to seduce a milkmaid. This wench bent me, and gave me to her sweetheart, applying more properly than she intended the usual form of: "To my love and from my love." This ungenerous gallant marrying her within a few days after, pawned me for a dram of brandy; and drinking me out next day, I was beaten flat with an hammer, and again set a-running.

'After many adventures, which it would be tedious to relate, I was sent to a young spendthrift, in company with the will of his deceased father. The young fellow, who I found was very extravagant, gave great demonstrations of joy at receiving the will; but opening it, he found himself disinherited, and cut off from the possession of a fair estate by virtue of my being made a present to him. This put him into such a passion that after having taken me in his hand and cursed me, he squirred [1] me away from him as far as he could fling me. I chanced to light in an unfrequented place under a dead wall, where I lay undiscovered and useless during the usurpation of Oliver Cromwell.

'About a year after the King's return, a poor cavalier that was walking there about dinner-time fortunately cast his eye upon me, and, to the great joy of us both, carried me to a cook's shop, where he dined upon me, and drank the King's health. When I came again into the world, I found that I had been happier in my retirement than I thought, having probably by that means escaped wearing a monstrous pair of breeches.[2]

'Being now of great credit and antiquity, I was rather looked upon as a medal than an ordinary coin; for which reason a gamester laid hold of me, and converted me to a counter, having got together some dozens of us for that use. We led a melancholy life in his possession, being busy at those hours wherein current coin is at rest, and partaking the fate of our master; being in a few moments valued at a crown, a pound, or a sixpence, according to the situation in which the fortune of the cards placed us. I had at length the good luck to see my master break, by which means I was again sent abroad under my primitive denomination of a shilling.

'I shall pass over many other accidents of less moment, and hasten to that fatal catastrophe when I fell into the hands of an artist, who conveyed me underground, and with an unmerciful pair of shears cut off my titles, clipped my brims, retrenched my shape, rubbed me to my inmost ring; and in short, so spoiled and pillaged me, that he did not leave me worth a groat. You may think what a confusion I was in to see myself thus curtailed and disfigured. I should have been ashamed to have shown my head, had not all my old acquaintance been reduced to the same shameful figure, excepting some few that were punched through the belly. In the midst of this general calamity, when everybody thought our misfortune irretrievable and our case desperate, we were thrown into the furnace together, and, as it often happens with cities rising out of a fire, appeared with greater beauty and lustre than we could ever boast of before. What has happened to me since this change of sex which you now see, I shall take some other opportunity to relate. In the meantime I shall only repeat two adventures as being very extraordinary and neither of them having ever happened to me above once in my life. The first was my being in a poet's pocket, who was so taken with the brightness and novelty of my appearance that it gave occasion to the finest burlesque poem in the British language, entitled from me, *The Splendid Shilling*.³ The second adventure, which I must not omit, happened to me in the year one thousand seven hundred and three, when I was given away in charity to a blind man; but indeed this was by mistake, the person who gave me having thrown heedlessly me into the hat among a pennyworth of farthings.'

134. Mr. Bickerstaff's Court of Honour

As I last year presided over a court of justice, it is my intention this year to set myself at the head of a court of honour. There is no court of this nature anywhere at present, except in France; where, according to the best of my intelligence, it consists of such only as are Marshals of that kingdom. I am likewise informed that there is not one of that honourable board at present, who has not been driven out of the field by the Duke of Marlborough; but whether this be only an accidental or a necessary qualification, I must confess I am not able to determine.

As for the court of honour of which I am here speaking, I intend to fit myself in it as president, with several men of honour on my right hand, and women of virtue on my left, as my assistants. The first place on the bench I have given to an old Tangereen captain[1] with a wooden leg. The second is a gentleman of a long twisted periwig without a curl in it, a muff with very little hair upon it, and a threadbare coat with new buttons; being a person of great worth, and second brother to a man of quality. The third is a gentleman-usher, extremely well read in romances, and grandson to one of the greatest wits in Germany, who was some time Master of the Ceremonies to the Duke of Wolfenbüttel.

As for those who sit further on my right hand, as it is usual in public courts, they are such as will fill up the number of faces upon the bench, and serve rather for ornament than use.

The chief upon my left hand are:

An old maiden lady, that preserves some of the best blood of England in her veins.

A Welsh woman of a little stature, but high spirit.

An old prude that has censured every marriage for these thirty years, and is lately wedded to a young rake.

Having thus furnished my bench, I shall establish correspondences with the Horse-guards and the veterans of Chelsea College; the former to furnish me with twelve men of honour as often as I shall have occasion for a grand jury, and the latter with as many good men and true for a petty jury.

As for the women of virtue, it will not be difficult for me to find them about midnight at crimp and basset.[2]

Having given this public notice of my court, I must further add that I intend to open it on this day seven-night, being Monday the twentieth instant; and do hereby invite all such as have suffered injuries and affronts that are not to be redressed by the common laws of this land, whether they be short bows, cold salutations, supercilious looks, unreturned smiles, distant behaviour, or forced familiarity; as also all such as have been aggrieved by any ambiguous expression, accidental jostle, or unkind repartee; likewise all such as have been defrauded of their right to the wall, tricked out of the upper end of the table, or have been suffered to place themselves, in their own wrong, on the back seat of the coach. These, and all of these, I do, as I above said, invite to bring in their several cases and complaints, in which they shall be relieved with all imaginable expedition.

I am very sensible that the office I have now taken upon me will engage me in the disquisition of many weighty points that daily perplex the youth of the British nation, and therefore I have already discussed several of them for my future use, as: how far a man may brandish his cane in telling a story without insulting his hearer; what degree of contradiction amounts to the lie; how a man shall resent another's staring and cocking a hat in his face; if asking pardon is an atonement for treading upon one's toes; whether a man may put up a box on the ear received from a stranger in the dark; or whether a man of honour may take a blow of his wife; with several other subtleties of the like nature.

For my direction in the duties of my office, I have furnished myself with a certain astrological pair of scales, which I have contrived for this purpose. In one of them I lay the injuries, in the other the reparations. The first are represented by little weights made of a metal resembling

iron, and the other of gold. These are not only lighter
than the weights made use of in avoirdupois, but also than
such as are used in troy-weight. The heaviest of those
that represent the injuries amount but to a scruple; and
decrease by so many subdivisions, that there are
several imperceptible weights which cannot be seen without the help of a very fine microscope. I might acquaint
my reader that these scales were made under the influence
of the sun when he was in Libra, and describe many
signatures on the weights both of injury and reparation;
but as this would look rather to proceed from an ostentation of my own art than any care for the public, I shall
pass it over in silence.

135.   Thoughts on drinking

The following letter, and several others to the same
purpose, accuse me of a rigour of which I am far from being
guilty, to wit, the disallowing the cheerful use of wine.

From my country house, October 25.

MR. BICKERSTAFF,
   Your discourse against drinking, in Tuesday's *Tatler*,
I like well enough in the main; but in my humble opinion
you are become too rigid, where you say to this effect:
Were there only this single consideration, that we are the
less masters of ourselves if we drink the least proportion
beyond the exigence of thirst. . . . I hope no one drinks
wine to allay this appetite. This seems to be designed for
a loftier indulgence of nature; for it were hard to suppose
that the Author of nature, who imposed upon her necessities
and pains, does not allow her proper pleasures; and we
may reckon among the latter the moderate use of the
grape. And though I am as much against excess, or
whatever approaches it, as yourself; yet I conceive one
may safely go farther than the bounds you there prescribe,
not only without forfeiting the title of being one's own
master, but also to possess it in a much greater degree,
if a man's expressing himself upon any subject with more

life and vivacity, more variety of ideas, more copiously, more fluently, and more to the purpose, argues it he thinks clearer, speaks more ready, and with greater choice of comprehensive and significant terms.

I have the good fortune now to be intimate with a gentleman remarkable for this temper, who has an inexhaustible source of wit to entertain the curious, the grave, the humorous, and the frolic. He can transform himself into different shapes, and adapt himself to every company; yet in a coffee-house, or in the ordinary course of affairs, he appears rather dull than sprightly. You can seldom get him to the tavern; but when once he is arrived to his pint, and begins to look about and like his company, you admire a thousand things in him which before lay buried. Then you discover the brightness of his mind, and the strength of his judgment, accompanied with the most graceful mirth. In a word, by this enlivening aid, he is whatever is polite, instructive, and diverting. What makes him still more agreeable is that he tells a story, serious or comical, with as much delicacy of humour as Cervantes himself. And for all this, at other times even after a long knowledge of him you shall scarce discern in this incomparable person a whit more than what might be expected from one of a common capacity. Doubtless there are men of great parts that are guilty of downright bashfulness, that, by a strange hesitation and reluctance to speak, murder the finest and most elegant thoughts, and render the most lively conceptions flat and heavy.

In this case, a certain quantity of my white or red cordial, which you will, is an easy, but an infallible remedy. It awakens the judgment, quickens the memory, ripens the understanding, disperses melancholy, cheers the heart; in a word, restores the whole man to himself and his friends, without the least pain or indisposition to the patient. To be taken only in the evening, in a reasonable quantity, before going to bed. Note: My bottles are sealed with three flower-de-luces and a bunch of grapes. Beware of counterfeits. I am,

Your most humble servant, etc.

136. Extract of the Journal of the Court of Honour, 1710

The court being sat, an oath prepared by the Censor was administered to the assistants on his right hand, who were all sworn upon their honour. The women on his left hand took the same oath upon their reputation. Twelve gentlemen of the Horse-guards were empanelled, having unanimously chosen Mr. Alexander Truncheon, who is their right-hand man in the troop, for their foreman in the jury. Mr. Truncheon immediately drew his sword, and holding it with the point towards his own body, presented it to the Censor. Mr. Bickerstaff received it; and after having surveyed the breadth of the blade and sharpness of the point with more than ordinary attention, returned it to the foreman in a very graceful manner. The rest of the jury, upon the delivery of the sword to their foreman, drew all of them together as one man, and saluted the bench with such an air as signified the most resigned submission to those who commanded them, and the greatest magnanimity to execute what they should command.

Mr. Bickerstaff, after having received the compliments on his right hand, cast his eye upon the left, where the whole female jury paid their respects by a low curtsy, and by laying their hands upon their mouths. Their forewoman was a professed Platonist that had spent much of her time in exhorting the sex to set a just value upon their persons, and to make the men know themselves.

There followed a profound silence, when at length, after some recollection, the Censor, who continued hitherto, uncovered, put on his hat with great dignity; and, after having composed the brims of it in a manner suitable to the gravity of his character, he gave the following charge, which was received with silence and attention, that being the only applause which he admits of, or is ever given in his presence.

'The nature of my office, and the solemnity of this occasion, requiring that I should open my first session with a speech, I shall cast what I have to say under two principal heads.

'Under the first, I shall endeavour to show the necessity and usefulness of this new-erected court; and under the second, I shall give a word of advice and instruction to every constituent part of it.

'As for the first, it is well observed by Phaedrus, an heathen poet [1]:

Nisi utile est quod facimus, frustra est gloria,

which is the same, ladies, as if I should say: "It would be of no reputation for me to be president of a court which is of no benefit to the public." Now the advantages that may arise to the weal-public from this institution will more plainly appear if we consider what it suffers for the want of it. Are not our streets daily filled with wild pieces of justice, and random penalties? Are not crimes undetermined, and reparations disproportioned? How often have we seen the lie punished by death, and the liar himself deciding his own cause! Nay, not only acting the judge, but the executioner. Have we not known a box on the ear more severely accounted for than manslaughter? In these extrajudicial proceedings of mankind, an unmannerly jest is frequently as capital as a premeditated murder.

'But the most pernicious circumstance in this case is that the man who suffers the injury must put himself upon the same foot of danger with him that gave it, before he can have his just revenge; so that the punishment is altogether accidental, and may fall as well upon the innocent as the guilty.

'I shall only mention a case which happens frequently among the more polite nations of the world, and which I the rather mention, because both sexes are concerned in it, and which therefore you gentlemen, and you ladies of the jury, will the rather take notice of; I mean that great and known case of cuckoldom. Supposing the person who has suffered insults in his dearer and better half; supposing, I say, this person should resent the injuries done to his tender wife, what is the reparation he may expect? Why, to be used worse than his poor lady, run through the body, and left breathless upon the bed of honour. What then, will you on my right hand say, must the man do that is affronted? Must our sides be elbowed, our shins broken? Must the wall, or perhaps our mistress, be taken from us? May a man knit his forehead into a frown, toss up his arm, or pish at what we say, and must the villain live after it? Is there no redress for injured honour? Yes, gentlemen, that is the design of the judicature we have here established.

'A court of conscience, we very well know, was first instituted for the determining of several points of property that were too little and trivial for the cognizance of higher courts of justice. In the same manner, our court of honour is appointed for the examination of several niceties and punctilios that do not pass for wrongs in the eye of our common laws. But notwithstanding no legislators of any nation have taken into consideration these little circumstances, they are such as often lead to crimes big enough for their inspection, though they come before them too late for their redress.

'Besides, I appeal to you, ladies,'

(*Here Mr. Bickerstaff turned to his left hand.*)

'if these are not the little stings and thorns in life that make it more uneasy than its most substantial evils. Confess ingenuously, did you never lose a morning's devotions because you could not offer them up from the highest place of the pew? Have you not been in pain, even at a ball, because another has been taken out to dance before you? Do you love any of your friends so much as those that are below you? Or have you any favourites that walk on your right hand? You have answered me in your looks; I ask no more.

'I come now to the second part of my discourse, which obliges me to address myself in particular to the respective members of the court, in which I shall be very brief.

'As for you gentlemen and ladies, my assistants and grand juries, I have made choice of you on my right hand, because I know you very jealous of your honour; and you on my left, because I know you very much concerned for the reputation of others; for which reason I expect great exactness and impartiality in your verdicts and judgments.

'I must in the next place address myself to you, gentlemen of the council. You all know that I have not chose you for your knowledge in the litigious parts of the law; but because you have all of you formerly fought duels, of which I have reason to think you have repented, as being now settled in the peaceable state of benchers. My advice to you is only that in your pleadings you will be short and expressive; to which end you are to banish out of your discourses all synonymous terms, and unnecessary multiplications of verbs and nouns. I do moreover forbid you the use of the words "also" and "likewise"; and must further declare that if I catch any one among you, upon any pretence whatsoever, using the particle "or," I shall instantly order him to be stripped of his gown and thrown over the bar.'

This is a true copy:

CHARLES LILLIE.

137. *Shabby treatment of the clergy*

To the Censor of Great Britain

SIR,

I am at present under very great difficulties which it is not in the power of anyone, besides yourself, to redress. Whether or no you shall think it a proper case to come before your court of honour, I cannot tell; but thus it is. I am chaplain to an honourable family, very regular at the hours of devotion, and I hope of an unblamable life; but for not offering to rise at second course, I found my patron and his lady very sullen and out of humour, though at first I did not know the reason of it. At length, when I happened to help myself to a jelly, the lady of the house, otherwise a devout woman, told me that it did not become a man of my cloth to delight in such frivolous food. But as I still continued to sit out the last course, I was yesterday informed by the butler that his lordship had no further occasion for my service. All which is humbly submitted to your consideration, by,

Sir,

Your most humble servant, etc.

The case of this gentleman deserves pity; especially if he loves sweetmeats, to which, if I may guess by his letter, he is no enemy. In the meantime, I have often wondered at the indecency of discharging the holiest man from the table as soon as the most delicious parts of the entertainment are served up, and could never conceive a reason for so absurd a custom. Is it because a liquorish palate, or a sweet tooth as they call it, is not consistent with the sanctity of his character? This is but a trifling pretence. No man of the most rigid virtue gives offence by any excesses in plum-pudding or plum-porridge, and that because they are the first parts of the dinner. Is there anything that tends to incitation in sweetmeats more than in ordinary dishes? Certainly not. Sugar-plums are a very innocent diet, and conserves of a much colder nature than your common pickles. I have sometimes thought that the ceremony of the chaplain's flying away from the dessert was typical and figurative, to mark out to the company how they ought to retire from all the luscious baits of temptation, and deny their appetites the gratifications that are most pleasing to them; or at least, to signify that we ought to stint ourselves in our most lawful satisfactions, and not make our pleasure, but our support, the end of eating. But most certainly, if such a lesson of temperance had been necessary at a table, our clergy would have recommended it to all the lay-masters of families, and not have disturbed other men's tables with such unseasonable examples of abstinence. The original therefore of this barbarous custom I take to have been merely accidental.

The chaplain retired, out of pure complaisance, to make room for the removal of the dishes, or possibly for the ranging of the dessert. This by degrees grew into a duty, until at length, as the fashion improved, the good man found himself cut off from the third part of the entertainment; and if the arrogance of the patron goes on, it is not impossible but, in the next generation, he may see himself reduced to the tithe, or tenth dish of the table; a sufficient caution not to part with any privilege we are once possessed of. It was usual for the priest in old times to feast upon the sacrifice, nay the honey-cake, while the hungry laity looked upon him with great devotion; or, as the late Lord Rochester [1] describes it, in a very lively manner,

> And while the priest did eat the people star'd.

At present the custom is inverted; the laity feast, while the priest stands by as an humble spectator. This necessarily puts the good man upon making great ravages on all the dishes that stand near him; and distinguishing himself by voraciousness of appetite, as knowing that his time is short. I would fain ask those stiff-necked patrons whether they would not take it ill of a chaplain that in his grace after meat should return thanks for the whole entertainment with an exception to the dessert. And yet I cannot but think that in such a proceeding he would but deal with them as they deserved. What would a Roman Catholic priest think, who is always helped first, and placed next the ladies, should he see a clergyman giving his company the slip at the first appearance of the tarts or sweetmeats? Would not he believe that he had the same antipathy to a candied orange, or a piece of puff-paste, as some have to a Cheshire cheese, or a breast of mutton? Yet to so ridiculous a height is this foolish custom grown, that even the Christmas pie, which in its very nature is a kind of consecrated cate, a badge of distinction, is often forbidden to the Druid of the family. Strange that a sirloin of beef, whether boiled or roasted, when entire, is exposed to his utmost depredations and incisions; but, if minced into small pieces, and tossed up with plums and sugar, changes its property, and, forsooth, is meat for his master!

In this case I know not which to censure, the patron or the chaplain, the insolence of power or the abjectness of dependence. For my own part, I have often blushed to see a gentleman, whom I knew to have much more wit and learning than myself, and who was bred up with me at the university upon the same foot of a liberal education, treated in such an ignominious manner, and sunk beneath those of his own rank, by reason of that character which ought to bring him honour. This deters men of generous minds from placing themselves in such a station of life, and by that means frequently excludes persons of quality from the improving and agreeable conversation of a learned and obsequious friend.

Mr. Oldham [2] lets us know that he was affrighted from the thought of such an employment by the scandalous sort of treatment which often accompanies it.

> Some think themselves exalted to the sky,
> If they light in some noble family:
> Diet, an horse, and thirty pounds a year,
> Besides th' advantage of his lordship's ear,
> The credit of the bus'ness, and the state,
> Are things that in a youngster's sense sound great.
> Little the unexperienced wretch does know,
> What slavery he oft must undergo;
> Who, tho' in silken scarf and cassock drest,
> Wears but a gayer livery at best.
> When dinner calls, the implement must wait
> With holy words to consecrate the meat,
> But hold it for a favour seldom known,
> If he be deign'd the honour to sit down.
> Soon as the tarts appear: Sir Crape, withdraw,
> Those dainties are not for a spiritual maw.
> Observe your distance, and be sure to stand
> Hard by the cistern with your cap in hand:
> There for diversion you may pick your teeth,
> Till the kind voider [3] comes for your relief.
> Let others, who such meannesses can brook,
> Strike countenance to ev'ry great man's look;
> I rate my freedom higher.

This author's raillery is the raillery of a friend, and does not turn the sacred order into ridicule; but is a just censure on such persons as take advantage from the necessities of a man of merit, to impose on him hardships that are by no means suitable to the dignity of his profession.

138. English, Scotch, or British?

To Isaac Bickerstaff, Esquire

Nov. 22, 1710.

Sir,

Dining yesterday with Mr. South-British and Mr. William North-Briton, two gentlemen, who, before you ordered it otherwise, were known by the names of Mr. English and Mr. William Scot, among other things the maid of the house, who in her time I believe may have been a North-British warming-pan, brought us up a dish of North-British collops. We liked our entertainment very well; only we observed the table-cloth being not so fine as we could have wished, was North-British cloth. But the worst of it was, we were disturbed all dinner-time by the noise of the children, who were playing in the paved court at North-British hoppers [1]; so we paid our North-Briton sooner than we designed, and took coach to North-Briton Yard, about which place most of us live. We had indeed gone afoot, only we were under some apprehensions lest a North-British mist should wet a South-British man to the skin.

We think this matter properly expressed, according to the accuracy of the new style, settled by you in one of your late papers. You will please to give your opinion upon it to,

Sir,

Your most humble servants,

J. S., M. P., N. R.[2]

139. A continuation of the journal of the Court of Honour held in Sheer Lane on Monday the twenty-seventh of November before Isaac Bickerstaff, Esquire, Censor of Great Britain

Elizabeth Makebate, of the parish of St. Catharine's, spinster, was indicted for surreptitiously taking away the hassock from under the Lady Grave-Airs, between the hours of four and five, on Sunday the twenty-sixth of November. The prosecutor deposed that as she stood up to make a curtsy to a person of quality in a neighbouring pew, the criminal conveyed away the hassock by stealth; insomuch that the prosecutor was obliged to sit all the while she was at church, or to say her prayers in a posture that did not become a woman of her quality. The prisoner pleaded inadvertency; and the jury were going to bring it in chance-medley, had not several witnesses been produced against the said Elizabeth Makebate, that she was an old offender and a woman of a bad reputation. It appeared in particular, that on the Sunday before she had detracted from a new petticoat of Mrs. Mary Doelittle, having said in the hearing of several credible witnesses that the said petticoat was scoured, to the great grief and detriment of the said Mary Doelittle. There were likewise many evidences produced against the criminal, that though she never failed to come to church on Sunday, she was a most notorious sabbath-breaker; and that she spent her whole time, during divine service, in disparaging other people's clothes and whispering to those who sat next her. Upon the whole, she was found guilty of the indictment, and received sentence to ask pardon of the prosecutor upon her bare knees, without either cushion or hassock under her, in the face of the court.

N.B. As soon as the sentence was executed on the criminal, which was done in open court with the utmost severity, the first lady of the bench on Mr. Bickerstaff's right hand stood up, and made a motion to the court, that whereas it was impossible for women of fashion to dress themselves before the church was half done, and whereas many confusions and inconveniences did arise thereupon, it might be lawful for them to send a footman in order to keep their places, as was usual in other polite and well-regulated assemblies. The motion was ordered to be entered in the books, and considered at a more convenient time.

Charles Cambrick, linen-draper, in the city of West-minster, was indicted for speaking obscenely to the Lady Penelope Touchwood. It appeared that the prosecutor and her woman going in a stage-coach from London to Brentford, where they were to be met by the lady's own chariot, the criminal and another of his acquaintance travelled with them in the same coach, at which time the prisoner talked bawdy for the space of three miles and a half. The prosecutor alleged that over against the Old Fox at Knightsbridge, he mentioned the word linen; that at the further end of Kensington he made use of the term smock; and that before he came to Hammersmith, he talked almost a quarter of an hour upon wedding-shifts. The prosecutor's woman confirmed what her lady had said, and added further that she had never seen her lady in so great a confusion, and in such a taking, as she was during the whole discourse of the criminal. The prisoner had little to say for himself, but that he talked only in his own trade, and meant no hurt by what he said. The jury however found him guilty, and represented by their fore-woman, that such discourses were apt to sully the imagina-tion, and that by a concatenation of ideas, the word linen implied many things that were not proper to be stirred up in the mind of a woman who was of the prosecutor's quality, and therefore gave it as their verdict that the linen-draper should lose his tongue. Mr. Bickerstaff said he thought the prosecutor's ears were as much to blame as the prisoner's tongue, and therefore gave sentence as follows: that they should both be placed over against one another in the midst of the court, there to remain for the space of one quarter of an hour, during which time the linen-draper was to be gagged, and the lady to hold her hands close upon both her ears; which was executed accordingly.

Edward Callicoat was indicted as an accomplice to Charles Cambrick, for that he the said Edward Callicoat did, by his silence and smiles, seem to approve and abet the said Charles Cambrick, in everything he said. It appeared that the prisoner was foreman of the shop to the aforesaid Charles Cambrick, and, by his post, obliged to smile at everything that the other should be pleased to say; upon which he was acquitted.

Josiah Shallow was indicted in the name of Dame Winifred, sole relict of Richard Dainty, Esquire, for having said several times in company, and in the hearing of several persons there present, that he was extremely obliged to the widow Dainty, and that he should never be able sufficiently to express his gratitude. The prosecutor urged that this might blast her reputation, and that it was in effect a boasting of favours which he had never received. The prisoner seemed to be much astonished at the construction which was put upon his words, and said that he meant nothing by them, but that the widow had befriended him in a lease, and was very kind to his younger sister. The jury finding him a little weak in his understanding, without going out of the court, brought in their verdict *Ignoramus*.

Ursula Goodenough was accused by the Lady Betty Wou'dbe, for having said that she, the Lady Betty Wou'dbe, was painted. The prisoner brought several persons of good credit to witness to her reputation, and proved by undeniable evidences that she was never at the place where the words were said to have been uttered. The Censor, observing the behaviour of the prosecutor, found reason to believe that she had indicted the prisoner for no other reason but to make her complexion be taken notice of; which indeed was very fresh and beautiful. He therefore asked the offender with a very stern voice, how she could presume to spread so groundless a report and whether she saw any colours in the Lady Wou'dbe's face that could procure credit to such a falsehood. 'Do you see,' says he, 'any lilies or roses in her cheeks, any bloom, any probability?' The prosecutor, not able to bear such language any longer, told him that he talked like a blind old fool, and that she was ashamed to have entertained any opinion of his wisdom. But she was soon put to silence, and sentenced to wear her mask for five months, and not to presume to show her face until the town should be empty.

Benjamin Buzzard, Esquire, was indicted for having told the Lady Everbloom at a public Ball, that she looked very well for a woman of her years. The prisoner not denying the fact, and persisting before the court that he looked upon it as a compliment, the jury brought him in *Non compos mentis*.

The court then adjourned to Monday the eleventh instant.

Copia vera,

CHARLES LILLIE.

140. *Further proceedings of the Court of Honour*

Timothy Treatall, gentleman, was indicted by several ladies of his sister's acquaintance for a very rude affront offered to them at an entertainment to which he had invited them on Tuesday the seventh of November last past, between the hours of eight and nine in the evening. The indictment set forth that the said Mr. Treatall, upon the serving up of the supper, desired the ladies to take their places according to their different age and seniority; for that it was the way always at his table to pay respect to years. The indictment added, that this produced an unspeakable confusion in the company; for that the ladies, who before had pressed together for a place at the upper end of the table, immediately crowded with the same disorder towards the end that was quite opposite; that Mrs. Frontley had the insolence to clap herself down at the very lowest place of the table; that the widow Partlet seated herself on the right hand of Mrs. Frontley, alleging for her excuse that no ceremony was to be used at a round table; that Mrs. Fidget and Mrs. Fescue disputed above half an hour for the same chair and that the latter would not give up the cause until it was decided by the parish register, which happened to be kept hard by. The indictment further saith that the rest of the company who sat down did it with a reserve to their right, which they were at liberty to assert on another occasion; and that Mrs. Mary Pippe, an old maid, was placed by the unanimous vote of the whole company at the upper end of the table, from whence she had the confusion to behold several mothers of families among her inferiors. The criminal alleged in his defence that what he had done was to raise mirth and avoid ceremony; and that the ladies did not complain of his rudeness until the next morning, having eaten up what he had provided for them with great readiness and alacrity. The Censor, frowning upon him, told him that he ought not to discover so much levity in matters of a serious nature; and, upon the jury's bringing him in guilty, sentenced him to treat the whole assembly of ladies over again, and to take care that he did it with the decorum which was due to persons of their quality.

Rebecca Shapely, spinster, was indicted by Mrs. Sarah Smack, for speaking many words reflecting upon her reputation, and the heels of her silk slippers, which the prisoner had maliciously suggested to be two inches higher than they really were. The prosecutor urged, as an aggravation of her guilt, that the prisoner was herself guilty of the same kind of forgery which she had laid to the prosecutor's charge, for that she, the said Rebecca Shapley, did always wear a pair of steel bodice and a false rump. The Censor ordered the slippers to be produced in open court, where the heels were adjudged to be of the statutable size. He then ordered the grand jury to search the criminal, who, after some time spent therein, acquitted her of the bodice, but found her guilty of the rump; upon which she received sentence as is usual in such cases.

William Trippet, Esquire, of the Middle Temple, brought his action against the Lady Elizabeth Prudely, for having refused him her hand as he offered to lead her to her coach from the Opera. The plaintiff set forth that he had

entered himself into the list of those volunteers who
officiate every night behind the boxes as gentlemen ushers
of the playhouse; that he had been at a considerable
charge in white gloves, periwigs, and snuff-boxes, in order
to qualify himself for that employment, and in hopes of
making his fortune by it.   The counsel for the defendant
replied that the plaintiff had given out that he was within
a month of wedding their client, and that she had refused
her hand to him in ceremony, lest he should interpret it
as a promise that she would give it him in marriage.   As
soon as their pleadings on both sides were finished, the
Censor ordered the plaintiff to be cashiered from his office
of gentleman-usher to the playhouse, since it was too plain
that he had undertaken it with an ill design; and at the
same time ordered the defendant either to marry the said
plaintiff, or to pay him half a crown for the new pair of
gloves and coach-hire that he was at the expense of in
her service.

The Lady Townly brought an action of debt against
Mrs. Flambeau, for that the said Mrs. Flambeau had not
been to see the Lady Townly, and wish her joy, since her
marriage with Sir Ralph, notwithstanding she, the said
Lady Townly, had paid Mrs. Flambeau a visit upon her
first coming to town.   It was urged in the behalf of the
defendant that the plaintiff had never given her any regular
notice of her being in town; that the visit she alleged had
been made on a Monday, which she knew was a day on
which Mrs. Flambeau was always abroad, having set aside
that only day in the week to mind the affairs of her family;
that the servant who inquired whether she was at home
did not give the visiting knock; that it was not between
the hours of five and eight in the evening; that there were
no candles lighted up; that it was not on Mrs. Flambeau's
day; and, in short, that there was not one of the essential
points observed that constitute a visit.   She further proved
by her porter's book, which was produced in court, that
she had paid the Lady Townly a visit on the twenty-fourth
day of March, just before her leaving the town, in the
year seventeen hundred and ten, for which she was still

creditor to the said Lady Townly. To this the plaintiff only replied that she was now under covert, and not liable to any debts contracted when she was a single woman. Mr. Bickerstaff finding the cause to be very intricate, and that several points of honour were likely to arise in it, he deferred giving judgment upon it until the next session day, at which time he ordered the ladies on his left hand to present to the court a table of all the laws relating to visits.

Winifred Leer brought her action against Richard Sly for having broken a marriage contract and wedded another woman, after he had engaged himself to marry the said Winifred Leer. She alleged that he had ogled her twice at an opera, thrice in Saint James's church, and once at Powell's puppet-show, at which time he promised her marriage by a side-glance, as her friend could testify that sat by her. Mr. Bickerstaff finding that the defendant had made no further overture of love or marriage but by looks and ocular engagement; yet at the same time considering how very apt such impudent seducers are to lead the ladies' hearts astray, ordered the criminal to stand upon the stage in the Haymarket between each act of the next opera, there to be exposed to public view as a false ogler.

Upon the rising of the court, Mr. Bickerstaff having taken one of these counterfeits in the very fact as he was ogling a lady of the grand jury, ordered him to be seized, and prosecuted upon the statute of ogling. He likewise directed the clerk of the court to draw up an edict against these common cheats, that make women believe they are distracted for them by staring them out of countenance, and often blast a lady's reputation, whom they never spoke to, by saucy looks and distant familiarities.

141. Later hours kept nowadays

An old friend of mine being lately come to town, I went to see him on Tuesday last about eight o'clock in the

* K 993

evening, with a design to sit with him an hour or two and talk over old stories; but upon inquiring after him, his servant told me he was just gone to bed. The next morning, as soon as I was up and dressed and had dispatched a little business, I came again to my friend's house about eleven o'clock, with a design to renew my visit; but upon asking for him, his servant told me he was just sat down to dinner. In short, I found that my old-fashioned friend religiously adhered to the example of his forefathers, and observed the same hours that had been kept in the family ever since the Conquest.

It is very plain that the night was much longer formerly in this island than it is at present. By the night, I mean that portion of time which nature has thrown into darkness, and which the wisdom of mankind had formerly dedicated to rest and silence. This used to begin at eight o'clock in the evening, and conclude at six in the morning. The curfew, or eight o'clock bell, was the signal throughout the nation for putting out their candles and going to bed.

Our grandmothers, though they were wont to sit up the last in the family, were all of them fast asleep at the same hours that their daughters are busy at crimp and basset. Modern statesmen are concerting schemes and engaged in the depth of politics, at the time when their forefathers were laid down quietly to rest, and had nothing in their heads but dreams. As we have thus thrown business and pleasure into the hours of rest, and by that means made the natural night but half as long as it should be, we are forced to piece it out with a great part of the morning; so that near two-thirds of the nation lie fast asleep for several hours in broad daylight. This irregularity is grown so very fashionable at present, that there is scarce a lady of quality in Great Britain that ever saw the sun rise. And if the humour increases in proportion to what it has done of late years, it is not impossible but our children may hear the bellman going about the streets at nine o'clock in the morning, and the Watch making their rounds until eleven. This unaccountable disposition in mankind to continue awake in the night and sleep in the sunshine, has made me inquire whether the same change of inclination has happened to any other animals. For this reason, I desired a friend of mine in the country to let me know whether the lark rises as early as he did formerly and whether the cock begins to crow at his usual hour. My friend has answered me that his poultry are as regular as ever, and that all the birds and the beasts of his neighbourhood keep the same hours that they have observed in the memory of man; and the same which, in all probability, they have kept for these five thousand years.

If you would see the innovations that have been made among us in this particular, you may only look into the hours of colleges, where they still dine at eleven and sup at six, which were doubtless the hours of the whole nation at the time when those places were founded. But at present, the courts of justice are scarce opened in Westminster Hall at the time when William Rufus used to go to dinner in it. All business is driven forward. The landmarks of our fathers, if I may so call them, are removed and planted further up into the day; insomuch that I am afraid our clergy will be obliged, if they expect full congregations, not to look any more upon ten o'clock in the morning as a canonical hour. In my own memory the dinner has crept by degrees from twelve o'clock to three, and where it will fix nobody knows.

I have sometimes thought to draw up a memorial in the behalf of supper against dinner, setting forth that the said dinner has made several encroachments upon the said supper, and entered very far upon his frontiers; that he has banished him out of several families, and in all has driven him from his headquarters and forced him to make his retreat into the hours of midnight; and in short, that he is now in danger of being entirely confounded and lost in a breakfast.

142. Last session of the Court of Honour

As soon as the court was sat, the ladies of the bench presented, according to order, a table of all the laws now in force, relating to visits and visiting-days, methodically digested under their respective heads, which the Censor ordered to be laid upon the table, and afterwards proceeded upon the business of the day.

Henry Heedless, Esquire, was indicted by Colonel Touchy of Her Majesty's Trained Bands, upon an action of assault and battery; for that he, the said Mr. Heedless, having espied a feather upon the shoulder of the said Colonel, struck it off gently with the end of a walking-staff, value threepence. It appeared that the prosecutor did not think himself injured until a few days after the aforesaid blow was given him; but that having ruminated with himself for several days, and conferred upon it with other officers of the militia, he concluded that he had in effect been cudgelled by Mr. Heedless, and that he ought to resent it accordingly. The counsel for the prosecutor alleged that the shoulder was the tenderest part in a man of honour; that it had a natural antipathy to a stick; and that every touch of it, with anything made in the fashion of a cane, was to be interpreted as a wound in that part and a violation of the person's honour who received it. Mr. Heedless replied that what he had done was out of kindness to the prosecutor, as not thinking it proper for him to appear at the head of the Trained Bands with a feather upon his shoulder; and further added, that the stick he had made use of on this occasion was so very small that the prosecutor could not have felt it, had he broke it on his shoulders. The Censor hereupon directed the jury to examine into the nature of the staff, for that a great deal would depend upon that particular. Upon which he explained to them the different degrees of offence that might be given by the touch of crab-tree from that of cane, and by the touch of cane from that of a plain hazel stick. The jury, after a short perusal of the staff, declared

their opinion by the mouth of their foreman, that the substance of the staff was British oak. The Censor then
observing that there was some dust on the skirts of the
criminal's coat, ordered the prosecutor to beat it off with the
aforesaid oaken plant; 'and thus,' said the Censor, 'I shall
decide this cause by the law of retaliation: if Mr. Heedless
did the Colonel a good office, the Colonel will by this
means return it in kind; but if Mr. Heedless should at any
time boast that he had cudgelled the Colonel, or laid his
staff over his shoulders, the Colonel might boast in his
turn that he has brushed Mr. Heedless's jacket, or, to use
the phrase of an ingenious author, that he has rubbed
him down with an oaken towel.'

Benjamin Busy of London, merchant, was indicted by
Jasper Tattle, Esquire, for having pulled out his watch
and looked upon it thrice, while the said Esquire Tattle
was giving him an account of the funeral of the said
Esquire Tattle's first wife. The prisoner alleged in his
defence that he was going to buy stocks at the time when
he met the prosecutor; and that during the story of the
prosecutor, the said stocks rose above two per cent to
the great detriment of the prisoner. The prisoner further
brought several witnesses to prove that the said Jasper
Tattle, Esquire, was a most notorious storyteller; that
before he met the prisoner, he had hindered one of the
prisoner's acquaintance from the pursuit of his lawful
business, with the account of his second marriage; and
that he had detained another by the button of his coat,
that very morning, until he had heard several witty sayings
and contrivances of the prosecutor's eldest son, who was
a boy of about five years of age. Upon the whole matter,
Mr. Bickerstaff dismissed the accusation as frivolous, and
sentenced the prosecutor to pay damages to the prisoner,
for what the prisoner had lost by giving him so long and
patient a hearing. He further reprimanded the prosecutor
very severely, and told him that if he proceeded in his
usual manner to interrupt the business of mankind, he
would set a fine upon him for every quarter of an hour's
impertinence, and regulate the said fine according as the

time of the person so injured should appear to be more or less precious.

Sir Paul Swash, Knight, was indicted by Peter Double, gentleman, for not returning the bow which he received of the said Peter Double, on Wednesday the sixth instant at the playhouse in the Haymarket. The prisoner denied the receipt of any such bow, and alleged in his defence that the prosecutor would oftentimes look full in his face, but that when he bowed to the said prosecutor, he would take no notice of it, or bow to somebody else that sat quite on the other side of him. He likewise alleged that several ladies had complained of the prosecutor, who, after ogling them a quarter of an hour, upon their making a curtsy to him, would not return the civility of a bow. The Censor observing several glances of the prosecutor's eye, and perceiving that when he talked to the court he looked upon the jury, found reason to suspect there was a wrong cast in his sight, which upon examination proved true. The Censor therefore ordered the prisoner, that he might not produce any more confusions in public assemblies, never to bow to anybody whom he did not at the same time call to by his name.

Oliver Bluff and Benjamin Browbeat were indicted for going to fight a duel since the erection of the court of honour. It appeared that they were both taken up in the street as they passed by the court, in their way to the fields behind Montagu House. The criminals would answer nothing for themselves, but that they were going to execute a challenge which had been made above a week before the court of honour was erected. The Censor finding some reason to suspect, by the sturdiness of their behaviour, that they were not so very brave as they would have the court believe them, ordered them to be searched by the grand jury, who found a breastplate upon the one, and two quires of paper upon the other. The breastplate was immediately ordered to be hung upon a peg over Mr. Bickerstaff's tribunal, and the paper to be laid upon the table for the use of his clerk. He then ordered the criminals to button up their bosoms, and, if they pleased, proceed to their duel. Upon which they both went very quietly out of the court, and retired to their respective lodgings.

The court then adjourned until after the holidays.

Copia vera,

CHARLES LILLIE.

143. *Clerical plagiarism*

ADVERTISEMENT

Whereas Plagius has been told again and again, both in public and private, that he preaches excellently well, and still goes on to preach as well as ever, and all this to a polite and learned audience: this is to desire that he would not hereafter be so eloquent, except to a country congregation; the proprietors of Tillotson's Works having consulted the learned in the law, whether preaching a sermon they have purchased is not to be construed publishing their copy.

144. *Elizabeth Slender's petition and Penitence Gentle's letter*

To ISAAC BICKERSTAFF, ESQUIRE, Censor of Great Britain.

The humble petition of Elizabeth Slender, spinster, SHOWETH,

That on the twentieth of this instant December, her friend Rebecca Hide and your petitioner walking in the Strand, saw a gentleman before us in a gown, whose periwig was so long, and so much powdered, that your petitioner took notice of it and said she wondered that lawyer would so spoil a new gown with powder. To which it was answered that he was no lawyer but a clergyman. Upon a wager of a pot of coffee we overtook him, and your petitioner was soon convinced she had lost.

Your petitioner therefore desires your worship to cite the clergyman before you, and to settle and adjust the length of canonical periwigs, and the quantity of powder to be made use of in them, and to give such other directions as you shall think fit.

And your petitioner, etc.

Query. Whether this gentleman be not a chaplain to a regiment, and in such case allow powder accordingly.

. . . . .

To the Reverend Mr. Ralph Incense, chaplain to the Countess Dowager of Brumpton.

Sir,

I heard and saw you preach last Sunday. I am an ignorant young woman, and understood not half you said; but ah! your manner when you held up both your hands towards our pew! Did you design to win me to Heaven or yourself?

Your humble servant,
Penitence Gentle.

145.   Mr. Steele takes leave of his readers

The printer having informed me that there are as many of these papers printed as will make four volumes, I am now come to the end of my ambition in this matter, and have nothing further to say to the world under the character of Isaac Bickerstaff. This work has indeed for some time been disagreeable to me, and the purpose of it wholly lost by my being so long understood as the author. I never designed in it to give any man any secret wound by my concealment, but spoke in the character of an old man, a philosopher, a humorist, an astrologer, and a censor, to allure my reader with the variety of my subjects, and insinuate, if I could, the weight of reason with the agreeableness of wit. The general purpose of the whole has been to recommend truth, innocence, honour, and virtue, as the chief ornaments of life; but I considered that severity of manners was absolutely necessary to him who would censure others, and for that reason, and that only, chose to talk in a mask. I shall not carry my humility so far as to call myself a vicious man, but at the same time must confess my life is at best but pardonable. And with no greater character than this, a man would make but an indifferent progress in attacking prevailing and fashionable vices, which Mr. Bickerstaff has done with a freedom of spirit that would have lost both its beauty and efficacy, had it been pretended to by Mr. Steele.[1]

As to the work itself, the acceptance it has met with is the best proof of its value; but I should err against that candour which an honest man should always carry about him if I did not own that the most approved pieces in it were written by others, and those which have been most excepted against, by myself. The hand that has assisted me in those noble discourses upon the immortality of the soul, the glorious prospects of another life, and the most sublime ideas of religion and virtue, is a person who is too fondly my friend ever to own them; but I should little deserve to be his, if I usurped the glory of them. I must acknowledge at the same time that I think the finest strokes of wit and humour in all Mr. Bickerstaff's lucubrations, are those for which he also is beholden to him.[2]

As for the satirical part of these writings, those against the gentlemen who profess gaming are the most licentious; but the main of them I take to come from losing gamesters, as invectives against the fortunate; for in very many of them I was very little else but the transcriber. If any have been more particularly marked at, such persons may impute it to their own behaviour, before they were touched upon, in publicly speaking their resentment against the author, and professing they would support any man who should insult him. . . . But what I find is the least excusable part of all this work is that I have in some places in it touched upon matters which concern both Church and State. All

I shall say for this is, that the points I alluded to are such as concerned every Christian and freeholder in England; and I could not be cold enough to conceal my opinion on subjects which related to either of those characters. But politics apart, I must confess it has been a most exquisite pleasure to me to frame characters of domestic life, and put those parts of it which are least observed into an agreeable view; to inquire into the seeds of vanity and affectation, to lay before the readers the emptiness of ambition; in a word, to trace human life through all its mazes and recesses, and show much shorter methods than men ordinarily practise, to be happy, agreeable, and great.

But to inquire into men's faults and weaknesses has something in it so unwelcome, that I have often seen people in pain to act before me, whose modesty only makes them think themselves liable to censure. This, and a thousand other nameless things, have made it an irksome task to me to personate Mr. Bickerstaff any longer; and I believe it does not often happen that the reader is delighted where the author is displeased. . . .

Thus I have voluntarily done what I think all authors should do when called upon. I have published my name to my writings and given myself up to the mercy of the town, as Shakespeare expresses it, with all my imperfections on my head. The indulgent reader's

>   Most obliged,
>   Most obedient,
>   Humble servant,
>   RICHARD STEELE.

NOTES

1.   [1] The first four numbers were printed for the author and distributed free.
    [2] Plain Spanish snuff, frequently advertised in periodicals.
    [3] Kidney was head waiter at St. James's coffee-house.

2.   [1] Charles Jervas (1675–1739), painter, and translator of *Don Quixote*.

3.   [1] The opera-house, built by Vanbrugh and opened in 1706. It stood on or near the site of the present Her Majesty's Theatre.
    [2] *Pyrrhus and Demetrius:* adapted by Haym from the opera by Alessandro Scarlatti.
    [3] This was Dennis. (See under No. 29.)
    [4] Mrs. Manley, a schoolmistress at Hackney, who wrote *An Essay on the Invention of Samplers*.
    [5] *May-fair:* Towards the end of 1708 the fair was complained of, with good reason, as a public nuisance, and was discontinued for several years in consequence. It was subsequently revived, and finally disappeared in the time of George III. Its attractions included rope-dancing, puppet-shows, rarities of various kinds, and performances by strolling players. (See also No. 14.)
    [6] William Pinkethman (*d.* 1725), familiarly known as 'Pinkey'; actor and showman, and (with Bullock) frequently the object of Steele's wit.

4.   [1] John Morphew, the publisher of the *Tatler*.
    [2] 'Bearskin-jobber' was the term applied to a dealer of the appropriate kind on the Stock Exchange. Steele's fortune and landed property (and, as we are obliged to conclude, his chastity) were imaginary rather than real—like the value of the bear-skin before the animal had been killed.
    [3] *Bentivolio:* Richard Bentley (1662–1742), the celebrated scholar, satirized by Swift in *The Battle of the Books*.
    [4] *Personae:* masks or characters.

⁵ Chemists and projectors (i.e. inventors) are general objects of satire.

⁶ Elizabeth Barry (1658–1713), the actress. She retired in 1710.

⁷ *Sir Harry Wildair:* in Farquhar's *The Constant Couple, or, A Trip to the Jubilee.*

⁸ William Bullock (1657–1740?), the actor.

5. ¹ *The Old Bachelor:* Congreve's comedy, first performed in 1693.

    ² This is Swift, whose verses follow.

6. ¹ *Lindamira:* In *Spectator* No. 41 Steele speaks of her as a coquette, whose 'complexion is so delicate that she ought to be allowed the covering it with paint as a punishment for choosing to be the worst piece of art extant instead of the masterpiece of nature.'

8. ¹ The verses are by Jabez Hughes (1685–1731).

9. ¹ Possibly Sir J. Floyer, who wrote *An Enquiry into the right use and abuses of the hot, cold, and temperate baths in England.* Lady Mary Wortley Montagu consulted Garth as to the efficacy of cold baths for children.

10. ¹ The foreign intelligence is probably Steele's work. The ironical account of the news-writers is Addison's first contribution to the *Tatler.* For his other contributions, see under No. 145.

    ² Charles, Viscount Townshend (1674–1738), Walpole's brother-in-law.

    ³ J. B. Colbert, Marquis de Torcy (1665–1746).

    ⁴ The negotiations broke down, chiefly owing to the unreasonable terms of the Allies.

    ⁵ Very loosely paraphrased from *1 Henry IV*, v. ii.

    ⁶ The *Postman* was Fonvive's paper; the *Postboy*, Abel Roper's.

    ⁷ Abel Boyer (1667–1729), author of *The Political State of Great Britain . . .*, and other works.

    ⁸ Samuel Buckley (*d.* 1741), printer of the *Gazette* and the *Daily Courant.*

    ⁹ *Drawcansir:* in *The Rehearsal*, where he serves as a burlesque of the 'tyrant's vein.'

    ¹⁰ John Dyer. *Dyer's Letter*, upon which Addison more than once exercised his wit.

11 Ichabod Dawks (1661–1730), conductor of *Dawks's News-letter*.

13. 1 Dr. Case was a well-known quack and astrologer. (See under No. 128.)

14. 1 Farquhar's comedy. Richard Estcourt (1668–1712), the actor and dramatist, was chosen by Farquhar for the part of Kite.

2 Drury Lane was closed by the Lord Chamberlain's order.

3 *Queens beating hemp:* i.e. in Bridewell.

15. 1 'The business of Spain' was the question of the Spanish succession, from which the war took its name.

2 *Duke of Anjou:* Philip V of Spain, grandson of Louis XIV. Mr. Bickerstaff, always patriotic, declines to allow him his royal title.

17. 1 'Mrs.' was commonly used of grown-up women, whether married or single. So also in No. 13 and elsewhere.

18. 1 From White's chocolate-house. Steele himself had been obliged to fight a duel with a Captain Kelly.

19. 1 Nicolas Boileau, the poet and critic (1636–1711). The reference is to his *Ode sur la prise de Namur*.

2 This is probably Vanbrugh.

22. 1 The Duke of Berwick defeated the Allies at Almanza in 1707.

23. 1 Anthony Fitzherbert (1470–1538), a judge. *La Graunde Abridgement* (1514) is an early digest of law.

2 Hockley in the Hole, Clerkenwell, was notorious for its bull- and bear-baiting.

3 *Bubbled:* cheated.

4 *Gorman:* a prizefighter.

5 *Claviger:* club-bearer.

6 For the sake of the somewhat questionable jest, it may be remarked that Thalestris was Queen of the Amazons.

7 *Lanistae:* trainers of gladiators.

27. 1 Not the 'Old Artillery-ground,' but its successor, west of Finsbury Square.

29. [1] Rich was manager and patentee of Drury Lane Theatre.
     [2] The less familiar of the plays alluded to are: *Cyrus the Great* and *The Unhappy Favourite, or, The Earl of Essex* (John Banks); *Oedipus* (Dryden and Lee); *Aurengzebe* (Dryden); *The Rival Queens,* (Lee); *The Prophetess, or, The History of Diocletian* (adapted by Betterton from Massinger and Fletcher, with music by Purcell).
     [3] *A pennyworth:* i.e. a bargain.
     [4] Valentini (Valentino Urbano), the Italian singer, came to London in 1707 and appeared in several operas.
     [5] Katherine Tofts, the English *prima donna* (*d.* 1756). See No. 14, where she appears as 'the unfortunate Camilla,' her reason having given way.
     [6] John Dennis, the critic and dramatist (1657–1734), whose 'improved stage-thunder' has become proverbial.
     [7] *Spanish-wool:* A cosmetic made of wool treated with dye.
     [8] *Plots:* i.e. stage properties or devices.

30. [1] A handsome tribute to Addison's poem which did so much for his political fortunes.

31. [1] *The chamade:* A signal by drum-beat to announce a desire to parley.
     [2] Admiral Sir John Leake (1656–1720).
     [3] Philip V of Spain. (See under No. 15.)

33. [1] 'Aspasia' was Lady Elizabeth Hastings, daughter of the 7th Earl of Huntingdon. Congreve had already celebrated her under this name in the 42nd *Tatler.*

35. [1] *Genio:* An obsolete form for 'genius.'

36. [1] *Stentor:* Dr. William Stanley, Dean of St. Paul's.
     [2] *The Bridge:* London Bridge is understood.
     [3] 'The neighbouring lions' were in the Tower.

37. [1] Charles XII was decisively defeated at Pultowa on 27th June 1709.
     [2] The king took refuge in Turkey.

38. [1] The reader will remember that this practice was followed by Sir Roger de Coverley's chaplain.
     [2] Jean de la Bruyère (1645–96). *Les caractères:* 'De la Cour.'

39. [1] Charles XII survived these trials and was eventually killed, in 1718, while besieging the 'petty fortress' of Frederiksten.

41. [1] Rosamond's pond, near Buckingham Gate in St. James's Park—the 'Rosamonda's lake' of *The Rape of the Lock*—was a favourite meeting place for lovers. It was filled in at the end of the eighteenth century.

42. [1] *Artillery-ground:* see under No. 27.

43. [1] *Bone-lace:* lace of linen thread originally made on bone bobbins.

45. [1] The battle was fought on 31st August 1709. See also Nos. 46, 49, and 53.

46. [1] The victory was costly, the Allies losing some 20,000 men—a substantially greater loss than that of the French.
[2] Probably Addison is meant.
[3] John, 2nd Duke of Argyll (1678–1743). He distinguished himself in the battle, leading the attack on the woods of Sart.
[4] General John Webb. He was crippled for the rest of his life as a result of the wounds he received.

47. [1] *The Dean:* Francis Atterbury (1662–1732), Bishop of Rochester. At this time he was Dean of Carlisle. His part in the Jacobite plots after the death of Queen Anne is well known. He was intimate with most of the men of letters of the time—particularly Swift and Pope.
[2] Dr. Daniel Burgess, an Independent minister.

48. [1] *Flux:* a medical term meaning to purge.
[2] *Feat:* neat, trim, smart.
[3] The Ring was the fashionable drive and promenade at the entrance to Hyde Park.

50. [1] The joke against the unfortunate almanac-maker, which Swift began in 1708, is alluded to several times in the *Tatler*.

51. [1] Mr. Bickerstaff represents himself as an old man: according to No. 95 he is sixty-four. Steele at this time was thirty-eight.

52.   ¹ *The Contempt of the Clergy*, by Dr. John Eachard, was published in 1670.

53.   ¹ *Pre-Adamites:* a sect claiming to imitate our first parents in their nakedness.

55.   ¹ *Pacolet:* Mr. Bickerstaff's familiar spirit.
       ² A curly-haired lapdog.
       ³ *False teeth:* here signifies loaded dice.

56.   ¹ There was truth in this: see Steele's remarks in the concluding extract.

58.   ¹ *Favonius:* George Smalridge (1663–1719), Bishop of Bristol.

59.   ¹ James Nayler (1617–60), the celebrated Quaker.

61.   ¹ 'Musty' was a variety of snuff.
       ² *The 'Apollo' at the Old Devil:* a room in the Devil Tavern, Fleet Street.
       ³ *Par. Lost*, iv. 750–70.

62.   ¹ This refers to Mr. Bickerstaff's pretended powers as an adept in astrology and magic.
       ² *Astronomy:* astrology.
       ³ *Odes*, iv. vii. 7–8.

63.   ¹ Mother Bennett, a well-known bawd of Charles II's time.

65.   ¹ *My son Smith:* i.e. son in law.
       ² Monk raised the Coldstream regiment in 1659, at which time Mr. Bickerstaff would have been barely fifteen.

66.   ¹ *Artists:* i.e. adepts with magical powers.
       ² A clay churchwarden pipe is indicated.

68.   ¹ Cornelius Agrippa (1486–1535), the German physician and philosopher.   The work Mr. Bickerstaff was consulting was *De Occulta Philosophia*.

69.   ¹ 'Carte' and 'Tierce,' terms used in fencing.

70.   ¹ *Upholders:* undertakers.   The word is now obsolete in this sense.
       ² *Philomath:* a student of natural philosophy.   It will be observed that the Partridge joke dies hard.

71. [1] As armies then went into winter quarters, the new
          campaign would not open until the spring.

72. [1] A perspective or handglass was an early form of the
          lorgnette.
     [2] Charles Lillie, the perfumer, of Beaufort Buildings in
          the Strand, was Steele's agent for the West End of
          the town and got some free advertisement by being
          mentioned familiarly in the *Tatler*.
     [3] *Clouded:* i.e. mottled. Sir Plume, in *The Rape of the
          Lock*, prides himself on 'the nice conduct of a
          clouded cane.'

74. [1] Giovanni Bononcini (1670–1755), chiefly remembered
          as a rival of Handel. Redriffe is Rotherhithe.
     [2] The reference is to Herod the Great and Mariamne.

76. [1] Thomas Betterton (1635–1710). 'Betterton was an
          actor, as Shakespeare was an author, both without
          competitors.' (Colley Cibber: *Apology for his Life*.)
          See No. 99 for Steele's appreciation of him.

79. [1] *Sheer Lane:* near Temple Bar. It was later known as
          Serle's Place and has since been abolished. The
          'late trial' took place at the Trumpet Inn.
     [2] A silver token coined at Bath.
     [3] *Christianity not Mysterious*, by John Toland (1670–1722),
          was published in 1696.
     [4] Now 'whisky,' but then a cordial drink made of spirit,
          sugar, and spices.

81. [1] The hooped petticoat, or 'farthingale' ('fardingal' in
          No. 83). It had a framework of steel and whalebone.
     [2] Sir William Petty (1623–87), the political economist.

82. [1] October ale.

83. [1] *regrators:* regraters, i.e. retailers.

84. [1] *Plumb:* A plum was £100,000. It here signifies one
          who was worth that amount; in other words, a man
          of wealth.
     [2] Lucius Annaeus Seneca, statesman, moralist, and the
          author of nine tragedies. He acquired great wealth
          under Nero, who forced him, in A.D. 65, to commit
          suicide. *Ad Lucilium Ep. morales*, viii.

86. [1] A set meal served at a tavern or eating-house.

89. [1] Ravens observed on the left hand, an ill omen.
[2] As previously, the hounds signify gamesters.

91. [1] *Joll of salmon:* 'Jowl,' the head and shoulders.

93. [1] The 'Grecian hero' of this story was Themistocles.
[2] *To have a colt's tooth:* to be skittish.

94. [1] Cicero went into exile in March 58 B.C. in consequence
of the activities of Clodius. He returned in the
following year. It is to this period that these letters
belong. Steele's example of wedded happiness is
less happily chosen than his extracts suggest.
Terentia was not an ideal wife and Cicero divorced
her in 46 B.C. and married a young girl. As to the
children here mentioned, the daughter died in child-
bed at the age of thirty-one, and the son was extravagant and not particularly distinguished.
[2] C. Calpurnius Piso was the first of Tullia's three
husbands.

95. [1] *Grand climacteric:* the age of sixty-three, from which it
appears that Mr. Bickerstaff is now sixty-four. See
p. 114.
[2] The bound volumes were published by subscription:
the list of subscribers is long and distinguished.

96. [1] One of the happiest examples of Addison's sustained
ironical wit. It is modelled on *Les Précieuses ridicules,*
Sc. x.
[2] The fourth Earl of Roscommon (1633–85). His translation of Horace's *Art of Poetry,* in blank verse, was
published in 1680.

98. [1] Thomas Clayton (*d.* 1730), an incompetent and un-
inspired composer. He brought out his opera
Arsinoë in 1705, and in 1707 wrote the music for
Addison's *Rosamond,* which, largely in consequence,
failed.

99. [1] *Betterton:* see under No. 76.
[2] *Macbeth,* V. v. 19–26. Steele seems to have quoted
from memory, with unfortunate results.

103. [1] III. iv. 31–2.

² III. iii. 346–58.

³ Robert Wilks (1665–1732) and Colley Cibber (1671–1757).

⁴ Samuel Sandford. He was one of the leading actors at the Theatre Royal when Cibber joined the company in 1690.

106.   ¹ The College of Physicians is meant.

      ² James Salter, who kept a museum at his coffee-house in Cheyne Walk, Chelsea; where he bled patients, shaved customers, and drew teeth.

107.   ¹ *The goldsmith's hand:* The modern equivalent would be the bank.

      ² *Warwick Lane and Bishopsgate Street:* The headquarters of the College of Physicians and the Royal Society respectively.

109.   ¹ See under No. 79.

110.   ¹ The grammar of this paper is occasionally unequal to the good sense of the argument.

112.   ¹ To lead apes in hell was the proverbial fate of old maids.

116.   ¹ At the theatre, as Steele says elsewhere, the fair sex occupied the front boxes, gentlemen of wit and pleasure the side boxes, and substantial citizens the pit.

118.   ¹ Evangelista Torricelli (1608–47), who discovered the principle of the barometer.

      ² *De rebus gestis Alexandri magni,* x.

      ³ Dr. Thomas Fuller (1608–61), best remembered for his *Worthies.*

      ⁴ Unfortunately for Steele and Addison the elections went against the Whigs.

      ⁵ *Ep.* i. 6. 15.

120.   ¹ John Banister, composer, and leader of the orchestra at Drury Lane.

      ² André Dacier (1651–1722), the classical scholar.

      ³ *Tramontane:* Beyond the Alps, i.e. remote from Italy.

      ⁴ *Par. Lost,* iv. 768–70.

121.   ¹ Sir William Read was originally a tailor and afterwards

a quack. In 1705 he was knighted for curing soldiers and sailors of blindness, free of charge; i.e. by 'couching cataracts.' He wrote *A Short but Exact account of all the Diseases incidental to the Eyes.* He advertised in the *Tatler.*

[2] The worm appears in an advertisement in the *Postboy*, 27th April 1710, where it is stated to have been sixteen feet long. The cure was effected, according to this dubious authority, by 'J. More, Apothecary in Abchurch Lane.'

123. [1] This fate befell many Whigs in the autumn of 1710, including Addison and Steele.

124. [1] The correspondent is Swift, who is responsible for the rest of this paper.

[2] *Country put:* bumpkin.

[3] Richard Hooker (1554–1600), the author of *The Laws of Ecclesiastical Polity.*

[4] Robert Parsons (1546–1610), the Jesuit missionary and controversial writer.

[5] Sir Henry Wotton (1568–1639); Sir Robert Naunton (1563–1635), who left an account of the leading courtiers of Queen Elizabeth's reign, which was published in 1641; Francis Osborne (1593–1659), a miscellaneous writer; Samuel Daniel (1562–1619), who wrote a prose history of England but is far better known as a poet.

125. [1] Steele regards this august body as a legitimate object of satire.

126. [1] *Par. Lost*, iv. 797–819.

127. [1] *Aen.* i. 102–23.

[2] *Aen.* iv. 160–72, a delicate allusion to the affair of Dido and Aeneas.

[3] This is Swift, whose verses follow, and make an excellent companion piece to that in No. 5.

[4] *Sink:* cesspool.

[5] *Quean:* hussy.

[6] *Templar:* lawyer.

[7] *Kennel:* drain or gutter.

[8] St. Sepulchre's.

128. [1] Thomas Saffold (*d.* 1691), originally a weaver.
      [2] William Lilly (1602–81). He appears as Sidrophel in
          Butler's *Hudibras*.
      [3] Saffold was succeeded by Dr. John Case at 'the Black
          Bull and Lilly's Head.' See under No. 13.

129. [1] The Act of Union had been passed in 1707.

130. [1] Plato, *Republic*; 'Tully,' *Off.* 3, 19, 78.
      [2] The peace did not 'ensue' until 1713.
      [3] *Secret Memoirs and Manners of several Persons of Quality of
          both Sexes. From the New Atlantis* (1709). The
          author was the notorious Mrs. Mary de la Rivière
          Manley (1663–1724). At one time Steele had been
          on intimate terms with this lady.

131. [1] To avoid an accumulation of note-references the follow-
          ing account is given of the more recondite items in
          the list: *bolstered below the left shoulder:* padded to hide
          a deformity; *pair of hips:* framework for the petticoat;
          posnet: small pot for boiling, with a handle and three
          legs; *tongue-scraper:* instrument for scraping fur from
          the tongue; *forehead-cloth:* ornamental wrapper worn
          round the forehead; *plumpers:* for filling out hollow
          cheeks; *black-lead combs:* for darkening the hair; *box:*
          box-wood; *bugle-work:* bead-work; *filigrane:* filigree;
          crotchet: brooch or clasp; *rump-jewel:* (meaning ob-
          scure); *sparks:* brilliants; *Turkey stone:* turquoise;
          Elizabeth and *Jacobus:* shillings of Elizabeth and
          James I; *angel:* gold coin; *crown-piece with the breeches:*
          crown-piece of Cromwell's coinage, the two shields
          bearing a fanciful resemblance to a pair of breeches;
          langteraloo: lanterloo, a card game—otherwise 'loo';
          etuys: etuis, ornamental cases for small articles; *white-
          pot:* a sweet dish made of cream, sugar, rice, currants,
          and spices; *water of talk:* i.e. of talc.
      [2] Pompey's collar would have been of silver.

133. [1] *Squirred:* Threw away with a rapid gesture.
      [2] As above, an allusion to Cromwell's coinage.
      [3] By John Phillips (1676–1709).

134. [1] One who had been in garrison at Tangiers in Charles II's
          time.

² Card games popular with ladies.   Basset was similar to faro.

136. ¹ *Fab.* III. xvii. 12.

137. ¹ John Wilmot, 2nd Earl of Rochester (1647–80).
     ² John Oldham (1653–83).
     ³ A tray containing the leavings of the meal.

138. ¹ The reader will interpret this without difficulty as 'hopscotch.'
     ² J[onathan] S[wift], M[atthew] P[rior], N[icholas] R[owe].

145. ¹ Steele's avowed reason for bringing the *Tatler* to an end is plausible, but probably not the entire truth. It is more than likely that the political situation had something to do with it. Steele was no longer Gazeteer, but he was still a Commissioner of the Stamp Office, and therefore had an inducement to avoid giving any offence to the new government. Similarly Addison, though he had lost his secretaryship to the Lord Lieutenant, was still Keeper of the Irish Records. Mr. Bickerstaff's political sympathies were well known, but Mr. Spectator remained aloof from politics, and occasionally went out of his way to deplore party strife.
     ² Steele's Preface to the collected edition was printed in Volume 4, and in it he acknowledged generously the help he had received. He gave few details, however, mentioning only four of Addison's contributions by name. The numbers of the *Tatler*—unlike those of the *Spectator*—bore no indication of their authorship, and when, after Addison's death, an edition of his works was prepared by his literary executor, Tickell, this question was reopened. Steele warmly denied that he had intended to deprive Addison of his due credit, but he declared that the *Tatler* was his own property, and told Tonson that he had paid Addison for his contributions. The friendship between Steele and Addison had cooled some time before the latter's death.
     In the present selection Addison's most characteristic work can be seen in Nos. 10 (part), 14, 29, 66, 69, 81, 85, 96, 118, 128, 130, 133, 137. The other numbers assigned, wholly or partly, to him, are: 17, 72, 76, 78, 90, 95, 119, 121, 126, 136, 139, 140, 142.